Rakshasa's Wrath

Wrath

The Clawed Chronicles, Book 1

V. Ajinkya

ISBN: 979-8-88653-436-8

Melange Books, LLC
White Bear Lake, MN 55110
www.melange-books.com

Published in the United States of America.

Cover Design by Ashley Redbird Designs

Dedicated to the readers eloquence.

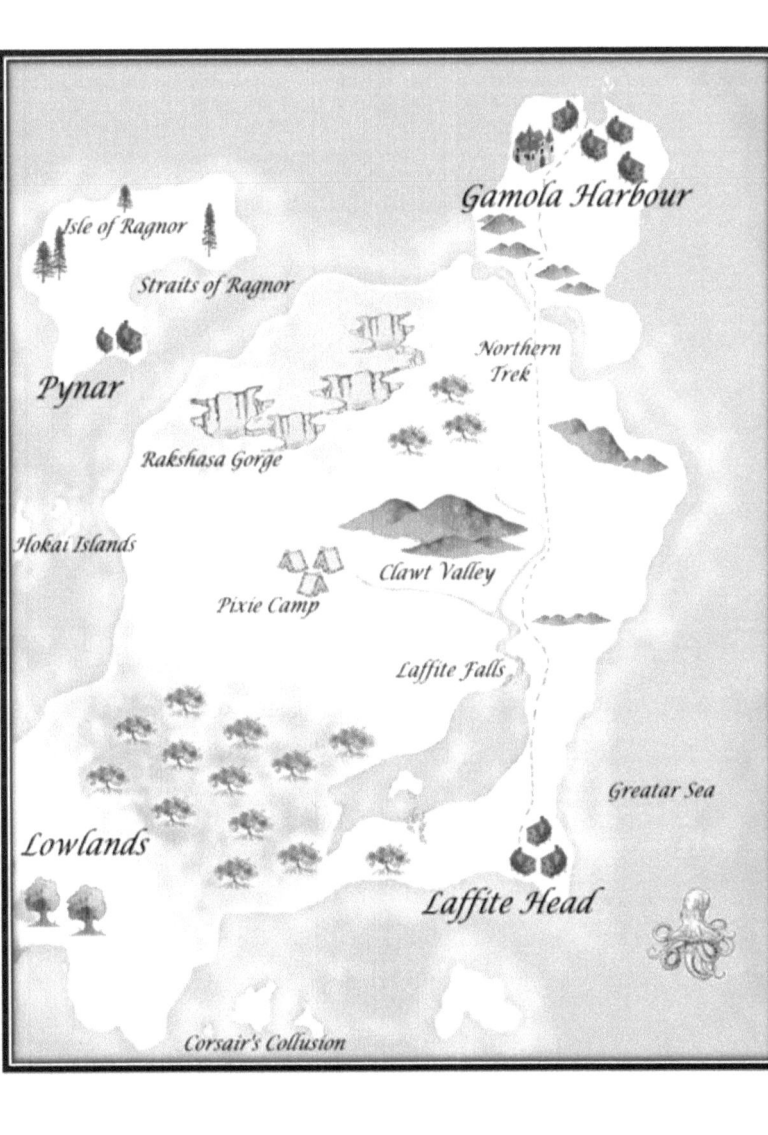

PREFACE

Several species in the Greatar and Lessar Lands of the new world survivors came to call the historic event "The Clash", though most were reluctant to mention it during the early years, so vastly diverse was the loss of life. Humanity reverted to technology of a simpler time. Many believed that magic would take over, while others refused to believe at all.

What caused "The Clash" was never discovered mainly due to the extinction of the giants, but years later, as races began to recover and accept integration with their formerly unknown neighbours such as werecats and pixies, intriguing stories of untold horror emerged. Corrupted fairy magic became the favourite theory as to why much of the population suddenly died, but as the fairies died out with the giants, there was no one left to ask.

"The Awakening" brought forth a renewal of old traditions, such as arranged marriages intended to promote good genetics in the sudden absence of more advanced science. Discontented humans split off to create new factions, further weakening humanity and hobbling development.

As the years passed and the stories were diluted or lost, no one considered who or what might have filled the gaping holes in the world's population. Old, hard-learned lessons were lost to history.

PROLOGUE

Captain Kie gripped the bulwark until his fingers hurt. *Where are they? They must be close.* "Keep a good eye out, men. We don't want to lose her." His loud voice merged with the roaring gale, but his men leaned further ahead in response. Kie nodded briefly, tasting the coming victory. His rich prize had slipped away last time, escaping under the cover of darkness. *Not again.*

White foam, torn from the crashing waves, concealed their quarry. The wind howled in torment, goading the crew as *Savage Heartbreak* pounded against the thrashing water. Her timbers twisted and creaked in the eternal struggle with the sea.

Kie staggered to the ship's violent movements, jamming his heavy gold ring into the flesh of his left hand. He had grown unaccustomed to such seas. In his younger years, this would not have fazed him, but these days, he preferred his office ashore.

Spray bounced over the deck and soaked him. Kie smiled, more a grimace than a grin. *I will find them. They will pay for their escape.*

1

They had first sighted *Comnfe* heading east, making good speed. Even so, she should have been easy prey for *Savage Heartbreak*. With her clean lines and tapered bow, even her large size did not slow her down.

Kie was a hard task master who drilled his crew well, but they were equally familiar with the potential rewards for a prize like the *Comnfe*. *Savage Heartbreak* had swooped down on the unsuspecting merchantman from the cover of the outlying islands and would have caught her easily but for the squall. They had been forced to haul off as the storm descended on them like a rampaging beast bent on revenge. The fates were not in their favour—again.

As night drew in and *Savage Heartbreak's* black sails disappeared into the darkening sky, the chase continued. They lost her as the *Comnfe's* heavy bulk disappeared behind a rolling wave and into the deepening gloom. The last time she had escaped amongst the islets. They were not the first to lose her. Similar yarns were told in taverns in the town; the stories of the riches she carried grew more outlandish with each tale.

Now they searched.

The first mate, known only as Stag, hauled himself up the ladder. "Guns ready, Cap'."

Kie nodded, never taking his eyes from the sea, a strand of hair wisped across his vision and tickled his nose. He ignored the irritation. *I will have her.*

Stag stood beside him and followed his gaze. "We'll find 'em again, boss." He jerked against the railing. "They can't 'ave got far in this." A slash of spray left the mate gasping for breath.

"Get for'rard and keep watch. Make sure you have enough men there. I won't lose this one," Kie snapped, more annoyed with himself than the mate.

2

The mainsail flapped wildly to the gusting wind. Blocks high above the deck rattled in protest. Kie shook his head and clamped his jaw shut.

"Sail ho'," came a sailor's voice through the gale.

"Where away?" Kie leaned forward into the screaming wind, beckoning the miniscule hope that glimmered in his mind. Another failure would destroy the already dwindling confidence he commanded.

The lookout pointed ahead. *Comnfe*.

Savage Heartbreak struggled to starboard to a wave from Kie as though the ship was mirroring her captain's eagerness.

The distance between the ships closed. Time stopped. Closer, closer, until finally...

"Stand to, larboard guns," Kie shouted. The gun captains stood poised over their charges. "Fire as you bear!"

The guns thundered in slow succession. They echoed over the insanity and brought order to the wind's chaos. Kie held his breath as the deck shook with the clashing of the great cannons. *Savage Heartbreak* rolled away from her victim.

Holes appeared like magic in the sails of the *Comnfe*. A sailor fell from the towering mainmast. His body thudded onto the arm of *Comnfe's* main derrick and flopped to the deck.

Kie paused. The echo of the vibrating impact jarred his bones. "Again, hit 'em again," Kie screamed over the final rattle of the last gun being manhandled back into place. "Keep firing, you dogs."

Smoke billowed from the port side, whisked away by the wind. For just a moment, a whiff of gunpowder reached Kie. His memory took over. The acrid stench of smoke was etched in his memory after years as a buccaneer.

He had volunteered to join the pirates. He had not volunteered for the torture and imprisonment that followed. Days of questioning, no food, minimal water, cramped in a hole. That was how he had begun, under the threat of a wizard's wand. Later, as he had risen in importance, he had broken his own principles, killed, received injuries, and stood his ground. *Heartbreak's* previous captain died under his blade, the stench of mutiny choking the air. Kie had gone through so much to get her then to keep her... It did not bear thinking about.

"Keep firing, lads," he yelled.

The *Comnfe* appeared as the smoke cleared, much closer than expected. In physical size, the two ships were the same. Fighting strength was another matter.

They drew closer. Faces grew clearer. The crew of the *Comnfe* rushed about the deck in apparent panic. Kie knew better. Such assumptions could spell disaster for an attacking vessel.

"Keep at 'em, lads. They're on the run now."

Metal balls crashed and threw splinters across the *Comnfe that* seemed to shy away from the onslaught.

"Alter to port!" Kie turned on the startled helmsmen. "To port, to port." He waved in that direction and was rewarded with a nod from the senior steersman who shoved his weight against the wheel.

Savage Heartbreak hesitated for a moment before swinging wildly towards the other vessel. Kie glanced back at the steersmen.

Control was restored.

"Port guns, keep firing. Ready boarding party. Weapons! They might retaliate." He took a breath and scoffed, "No' that there is much chance of that."

The guns banged out. *Savage Heartbreak* staggered and

paused her upward motion as though shocked at the sound. With a tremble, she lowered her bow into the next shuddering wave, continuing her pursuit.

"The *Comnfe's* altering course, Cap'," said the lookout, repeating the message passed from up forward.

"Follow her," Kie instructed the wheel. His memory surged back to their last encounter. He had given this same order, felt the same urgency, and yet the Comnfe had slipped away.

Thick inky air surrounded them. The reek of battle hung in the atmosphere as though unsure what to do next. Another gust cleared the smoke away. Kie took a deep breath for the next order.

"Land ahead, Cap'," the mate panted. He pointed at the dark shadow breaking the waterline. "*Comnfe* still altering t' star'oard Cap'."

Kie nodded and exhaled. He judged the distance. Luckily, the spray had cleared long enough for the shore to become visible. His heart thumped. *What if…*

"We'll have to 'aul off, Cap'ain. We'll be ashore else," said the first mate unnecessarily.

A grinding sound growled across the wind. *Comnfe* shuddered and rolled dangerously towards them. Her turn slowed. They were too slow. *Savage Heartbreak* rocked, her bowsprit threatening to pierce the *Comnfe's* hull. Kie signalled to the helmsman to alter slightly. *Comnfe* buried her bow into the wave as she settled down, dragged lower by the weight of her cargo. Her stern cleared their bow. She was too low in the water.

"Take it easy, or we will collide. Keep her going ahead. Wait for the speed." Kie sharpened his tone. "Set jib on my mark." His eyes traced the track *Comnfe* had taken.

The mate nodded and hurried forward, his hands

reaching automatically for ropes to speed his progress. *Savage Heartbreak* lurched as the helmsmen got her under control and steadied her on a course clear of their prey.

"Raise the jib. Hard to port." *Savage Heartbreak* responded. Stag took over giving orders from the bow.

Kie kept a close eye on the other ship. His people would ensure their own safety. A bitter taste tingled on his tongue. He was going to lose this one. *Not again. Comnfe* disappeared astern, shrouded in darkness. The minutes passed, and he strained his eyes to see the other ship. She was lost. Kie returned his attention to the *Heartbreak*. The helmsmen were struggling to hold her. He leant his weight to their fight against the wheel. Together, they managed to get her round and keep her steady before the waves. Kie heaved a breath, stretching the seams of his tight jacket. The wind stilled, a pause before a renewed effort. They turned, thrashing through the wind.

"Something ahead, Cap'," shouted the lookout.

"Where away?" He turned sharply to find the lookout standing next to him.

"Right ahead, Cap'ain." The sailor stumbled and grabbed his shoulder. "Coming on fast."

She turned complete round! Heat flushed through Kie. *Collision.* "Alter course. To starboard, to starboard. Quick man!" His usual calm was gone, replaced by the urgency of protecting his love. *Savage Heartbreak* was his life. She could not be damaged. Even the sporadic gun shots from *Comnfe* twisted his neck muscles into knots, worse than anything he experienced in the past.

Heartbreak's guns answered *Comnfe's*.

Comnfe descended on them like an avenging spectre framed by angry flames. Her bowsprit nearly touched the *Savage Heartbreak's* main stays. Kie wrenched the wheel hard over. He fought the ship and the stunned immobility of the helmsman. Slowly, slowly the bow turned. *Heartbreak* clawed off to starboard.

Kie held his breath.

"We're gonna hit. Fend off, fend off."

A loud crack and a scream sounded from forward, though from which ship Kie could not tell. A scraping sound vibrated through the hull and tore at Kie's soul. He dug his nails into the wooden railing to transmit his will to *Savage Heartbreak*. He felt the pressure build. He watched, helpless, as the masts and stays ripped past the other vessel.

He stared, transfixed. *Comnfe* was even lower in the water. She was down by the head. *We must get clear.*

"All hands, standby to cut her away," he yelled.

His crew moved, urgency spreading faster than the fire that threatened to engulf *Comnfe*. Axes rose and fell. Ropes were slashed and obstructions cleared away. A handgun banged. An able seaman fell to the deck. The flames on the *Comnfe* lit the desperate faces of his crew as they scurried to contain the blast.

Faster, faster.

Comnfe settled lower into the water. She was sinking. A battle between fire and water. It was only a question of which would claim her.

Stag's voice sounded from the main deck. Cheers rose and stretched along the deck. Kie's hand trembled. His lips parted, and he nodded to the steersmen. They needed no instructions as years of training and survival instinct took over. *Savage Heartbreak* swung away from the billowing inferno.

The *Comnfe* fell away astern. The sound of crackling fire followed them across the growing distance of water, threatening. Bodies, silhouetted against the flames, jumped overboard pursued by explosions from below the *Comnfe's* deck. The water blackened as the distance between *Savage Heartbreak* and the dying *Comnfe* increased. A wave swallowed her bow.

Kie watched, waiting for the *Comnfe* to rise up again. Nothing. Water's triumph over fire. Kie heaved a sigh. "Launch boats to pick up survivors."

His prize was lost, defeated by land, fire, and sea.

CHAPTER 1
ISLE OF RAGNOR

Her stomach churned. Lyliana's arms ached with strain and cold as she clung to the battered wooden plank. Her first glimpse of the land was like a balm from paradise. An image of craggy green cliffs penetrated her blurred vision. She shivered, and her eyes closed. She forced open her heavy eyelids only for a splashing wave to make her snap them shut again.

Lyliana choked back a mouthful of seawater, gasped, and pulled her torso onto a rotten plank. Her arm muscles cramped. Her mind and body drifted over low waves. Charles' bald head was her last conscious image.

As her senses returned, she stretched and rolled over, wincing at the stabbing pain in her muscles. Gritty sand grazed her raw skin leaving red blotches wherever there was contact. She blinked and peered closer at the marks.

As she wrinkled her nose at the cloying scent of the air, a new feeling of steadiness drew her attention. *Sounds like the sea.* Lyliana yawned and stumbled to her feet. Her head swam. *Where am I? What happened to the Comnfe?* She dusted her hands off on her trousers and ran her fingers through her long, blonde hair.

A sheer cliff face disappeared upwards beyond her view, continuing along the beach, huge in height and length. The featureless stone formed a great impassable wall imprisoning her from the rest of the world.

Her feet sunk, disappearing into the fine sand. She wiggled her toes and pulled one foot clear. *How did I get here without shoes?* She searched her memory. Blurry images of fire and noise appeared, in the foreground stood Charles, his arms outstretched to her. His mouth moved in speech, but she heard nothing. She read his lips, *"I love you."*

Lyliana paced down the beach, stepping carefully on her sensitive feet. *I need to find out where I am. Then I can work out how to get back to Charles.* The empty beach mocked her. She walked with the sea on her right shoulder and the water lapping over her toes.

Brightly coloured fishes darted clear of her feet, pink flashes reflecting from their scales. Lyliana leaned closer to the water for a better look at the brave creatures. She got a vague impression of an intricate colour pattern across their backs, not a breed she recognised.

The exercise loosened her stiff muscles. A pain developed in her knee, a dark bruise betraying the source of pain. Lyliana's tongue stuck to the roof of her mouth, and she licked her lips in a futile gesture. Her mind whirled without coherent thought.

I need water, fresh water. None on the beach. A cold flush shot through her system. She took a deep breath and rubbed her arms, wincing as she found more bruises.

"The Clash to me. I should not be here," she said to the empty cliffs.

Silence was her only reply to the historical profanity.

A stabbing glint dazzled her and took her attention away. As she moved, the glinting disappeared. Once more, the shard of light hit her. She crouched and grabbed a handful of sand. Tiny gold flecks sparkled like jewels. Gold mixed with darker red, tinted brown sand that was only clear on close inspection. Lyliana blinked away unwanted tears. *I should have stood my ground and stayed*. She sighed.

Lyliana squinted along the beach and saw a change in the grasses. *There might be a path.*

A chill crossed her scalp. Her fingers twitched against her thigh. She spun on her heel, hoping to catch whoever was watching her. The beach remained deserted, but the tickle at the bottom of her hairline intensified. Lyliana licked her lips.

She eyed the beach and path in turn. *It may be the only one.* She looked again. *Charles would know what to do.* She stared along the beach looking for answers. *Where am I?*

She tied her hair into a knot at the nape of her neck and, taking a deep breath, began to climb. Her feet slipped on the sand and pebbles until she reached tufts of dry grass.

Her breathing came in gasps; her temperature increased with the effort as she gained altitude. Sweat beaded on her forehead, and her back grew damp. Her lungs laboured against the fragrant air drawing in more dryness with each breath. Her limbs grew heavy with exertion.

She brushed the breeze-whipped tendrils of hair from her face, scratched away the resulting tickle on her nose, and stretched her shoulders. The motion jarred her memory. Wind in her hair. At sea. She gazed at the ocean, willing the memory. The tension eased a little. She nibbled at the inside of her cheek and squinted up towards the obscured summit where the winding path disappeared.

Lyliana lifted her feet and checked the condition of

her soles. The reddened blisters were caked with dark muck. She sighed and placed her foot on the largest tuft of grass, savouring the coolness. It wouldn't be long before she couldn't walk. She sucked her tongue at the thought of something to drink. *How long have I been climbing?* Images of a trickling stream came to mind. *If I can just get to the top, I will see for miles.* She looked back at the empty sea. *One foot in front of the other.*

Her knees burned in time with her lungs, but she pushed on. Lyliana tried to regulate her breathing, taking long deep breaths and exhaling slowly. She let out a groan. *The top. The top.* Her thoughts timed with her movements. *The top. The top.*

Each cluster of rocks and clump of dry grass scraped at her fingers and feet. She gave up worrying about the state of her slacks, happy only that she was not wearing a dress. She wiped the sweat from her eyes and rubbed her soaked forehead on her arm every dozen steps.

Her pauses grew more frequent while the brief rests gave her less and less relief. Her nerves tingled. The sensation of being watched itched her mind. She saw no one. Each turn twanged at her nerves. Paranoia spread like a force, driving her on.

The beach grew smaller beneath her. She rocked, unbalanced by the heaviness in her legs. "If I fall now, it'll hurt. Stupid, you'd never survive," She paused, "Great, now I'm talking to myself." She grimaced and wrapped her elbow about a convenient outcrop. Her second break in less than a few minutes.

She rested her head on her wrist and tried to relax her overtaxed muscles. Her stomach lurched. *A deep breath and it'll be okay.* Her eyes fell to her fingers. The nails, once neatly manicured, were now torn, ragged and smeared in dust. Only the nail on her left little finger remained intact.

A cool breeze tickled her elbow, and Lyliana jostled her shoulder. The tickle came again, more persistent. Movement caught her eye. Grasses shifted in the breeze, but only near her right elbow.

A low hissing drew her attention towards a pile of rocks. Was it hissing, or something else? Curiosity beckoned, and against her will, she reached behind the stones. Even at full stretch, there was no bottom.

Something brushed against her forearm and fingers. Pins and needles blossomed. She snatched her hand out, scraping the sides of the hole. Her hair snagged on a bush, lancing pain through her scalp. She jerked away, reaching for her head. Pricks sliced her fingers. Lyliana cradled her hand, rubbing her fingers together. Her eyes itched and watered, blurring her vision, yet she saw there was no sign of the presumed plant that had entangled her.

"Get away-y-y," said a male voice in front.

"Go-o-o-o," another echoed from behind.

"Cry-y-y." A female whisper came from the hole.

Lyliana froze. Her grip on the grass strengthened, her legs locked. The knot in her stomach cramped sickeningly.

"Get away-y-y-y, go-o-o." repeated the voice in front, like an echo of a dream.

Her eyes darted toward something fluttering. She dared not turn her head. The noise was too close to her ear. Her heart drummed.

"S-s-s-s!" The male voice again.

Pixies? It can't be. Lyliana scrambled away. Upwards. Sweat trailed down her cheek and onto her chest. She grasped at the rocks, bringing back the prickles she had mistaken for pins and needles.

A frantic flurry of wings crossed her vision, too close. Her feet slipped on pebbles. Her knees hit the rocks and scrabbled for purchase. Agony stabbed the back of her legs, urging her onwards. She gained a footing. Too low. She pushed herself upwards. Her scalp burned from her hair snagging. *They're pulling my hair*. Her peripheral vision caught a vague image of a small person with wings too big for their body.

Her foot stopped sliding. She wedged it down harder and pushed off without waiting for her hand to reach anything. Her upwards charge gained momentum. Rocks scratched her hands. Bloody footprints marked her progress. Driven by fear, she ascended. Three metres, four. Again, the stabbing at her skull. Shocks in her lower back. Her t-shirt rode up to expose her skin to more pinpricks. She waved her hand behind, and her fingers caught the edge of something.

"Away, run away-y-y." A cackling female voice insisted.

The voice spurred her on. Her only focus was to climb. The urge to escape was familiar, comfortable. Her mind filed away the realisation.

Blood dribbled towards the belt of her trousers, tickling her back. Something pulled her ear. A torment of furious wings. She forced herself to move faster.

The gradient of the path increased, and her speed slowed. The wings fell silent. Adrenaline pushed her upwards, dragging her past her breaking point, past her struggling lungs, parched tongue, and exploding heart. The physical struggle was familiar.

Her hands steadied her exhausted body while the weight of her body forced her momentum. The heaviness in her feet slowed her progress. Her left foot slipped on loose rubble. Lyliana's neck jarred as she slipped. Her jaws clamped shut. She lost balance, arms flailing. She gasped. Her limbs moved wildly for a grip. Her hand slipped from a rock. She fell. Down and down. The nightmare of falling endlessly. Weightless, weakness and finally, unconsciousness.

She woke alone. There was no sign of pixies. Her downwards tumble was marked by scuffs and scrapings in the dust and crushed grasses though all she remembered was falling through space. Fear tingled in her mind as she dusted herself off. Her eyes traced the upwards path. *This time, I'll just keep going. Perhaps they will ignore me.* Her gaze fell on the warm inviting beach. Charles' smile mocked her.

She passed the scene of their attack and continued towards the top of the cliff without further incident, her renewed caution forcing more care.

———

Lyliana lay, resting her tortured feet, and waited for her breathing and heart rate to slow. The sparse landscape was silent. It was merely a sea of a different kind, short grasses, the occasional hillock, and some piles of soil obviously dug up by animals. Nothing that might provide shelter, food, or water. The desolation closed in around her, and she sank back onto the grass. She swallowed back the hollow feeling in her stomach and pictured Charles. He always gave her hope. He was smiling, proud, or perhaps confident, she did not know. *I shouldn't have left. Not for a man I never met.*

Sometime later, as she scanned the horizon for the umpteenth time, a speck appeared in the distance. She narrowed her eyes, trying to bring it into focus, but it blurred into the darker line between sea and sky. *It's different than before. That darkness was not there.* She noted the fluffy white clouds that portended pleasant weather and shade from the sun. Lyliana stared down at her hands to clear her vision, unfocused by the glare. She looked at the speck until she was no longer sure there was anything to see. A grin reached her lips. Her neck tensed, and she rubbed her lower lip with her index finger.

Lyliana leaned towards the edge of the cliff, ignoring her earlier fear, and looked once more towards the tempting speck. Her stomach fluttered. She gripped the short grasses tighter.

How long she sat there on the cliff top staring into the distance she could not tell. As she watched, the blip grew slowly larger, drawing under the horizon line. *It's coming closer, towards me.* She wiped a tear that puddled in the corner of her eye.

The speck expanded and morphed into sails.

A lightness developed in Lyliana's chest, and her pulse raced. She watched closer. *I can't be that lucky. Who are these people? Are they even going to stop? Will they see me?* She looked about her for landmarks that might attract their attention, but the gradual sloping of the cliff top offered nothing. She could not even make a fire; she had nothing to burn and no way to light a fire. Her teeth nibbled the skin of her thumb. Her eyes never left the horizon.

She jumped up and down and waved her arms in the air. Then she danced, her arms flailing wildly. Nothing like the refined dances she learned as a child but a crazy romp. The savage prancing of a desperate person, of the kind that would make early pre-clashmen proud.

The sails drew closer and more defined. The shape gained form. Later, she could make out the goose-wing rig common to vessels entering Hillaway harbour. As the ship merged with the dark water, Lyliana's imagination raced.

Could they be looking for me? She swallowed down her excitement. *If I return to Charles, I will never leave. They will not make me marry a stranger.*

In a last burst of energy, she headed for the path, retracing her track up the hill. Lyliana descended to the beach, hoping against the odds that someone would notice her.

Her minds-eye image of Charles was hopeful and trusting.

CHAPTER 2
HILLAWAY

The dockside had been silent for weeks. The traders grew twitchy and eyed each other suspiciously. One vessel due the week before was no longer expected. Storms were reported across the Deeper Sea. No one hoped for anything before the week's end. No one except Charles Robinson.

Charles paced the docks, retracing the route for the hundredth time since Lyliana's ship sailed from the bay. He awaited news of her safety with growing trepidation as each day passed in a sleep-deprived haze.

On this morning, he walked the stone quayside. He was due to meet with Mikkel, his best friend, who would be waiting on the Seat of the Ogres. It had been their favourite spot since they were boys, and as they had grown into manhood, women had shared their enjoyment.

For Charles, such activities ceased the day he met Lyliana. They were the same age and had lived in the same town all their lives yet never met until then. It could not be said it was love at first sight, but she became tied to his destiny from then on. He never wavered in his loyalty, even as temptation, and his friend, tried hard to influence him.

As he watched the bay, longing for a ship carrying news of his love, a sick certainty that he would never see her again grew into a raging pain.

He stood behind his friend in the spot he first met Lyliana. Mikkel nodded in acknowledgement. Neither man spoke. There was no need. Mikkel removed his floppy hat and turned as the signal flag went up the pole on the hill. After events forced them to realise how vulnerable they were, the town had mandated such precautions, a warning to alert them to approaching vessels. The shape of the bay restricted the view of the sea and prevented the townsfolk from anticipating a pirate attack. Those attacks had grown in frequency over recent months. The long stretching stone of Giant's Causeway protected the north, but the entrance to the bay was vulnerable. So, the flagpole was installed.

Mikkel smiled at Charles. His anticipation unmistakable.

The vessel appeared around the headland. Charles tapped his hand on the side of his leg and watched the ship approach the jetty. *I hope they have news of Lyliana and the Comnfe.*

"Now we shall see, my friend," said Mikkel. "There must be news. This ship has come from Gamola Harbour, I think. That was her destination, was it not?" said Mikkel.

"I believe so." Charles sighed. "It does take an age. How difficult is it to throw out a few ropes?"

"Be patient, my friend. They are making preparations. It will not be long now." Mikkel indicated the busying quay-side where all manner of people waited for the ship.

The skies darkened, and the slight breeze increased, tossing grey-green wavelets across the bay as they watched. Charles moved to shelter against the growing wind and maintained his vigil on the ship. The sudden chill seeped through the thin linen of his shirt.

Footsteps sounded on loose stones. Charles's father approached. He had donned his mayor's attire in honour of the ship's arrival and looked very out of place on the untidy quayside. Most of the local folk wore long shorts and loose-fitting shirts. Some had floppy hats like Mikkel. All lacked the finesse of Mayor Robinson. The image was hampered by his unruly hair, which clashed with his robes. The added grey he had gained since taking his post helped a little.

"Afternoon, son. Mikkel. How are you today? I see our newest visitor is right on time, not like the last few." He stopped. "Yes, yes, this vessel comes from Gamola. Hopefully, Lyliana is safe, and you can get back to your mother. She has been complaining about your absence. She needs help at home. Your brother is of no use at all."

Charles smiled. His father always pretended his mother was incapable and needed help when the opposite was true. "Yes, Father, as soon as I learn of Lyliana, I shall retire to the house. Mikkel can come with me and help. We will be finished right away."

"Might we attend you when you visit the vessel?" Mikkel stood and took a step towards the mayor. He glanced at Charles, Mikkel's youthful features expectant.

"You may but stay out of the way. If you cause any problems, I shall send you both home. There shall be no argument on the matter. Then perhaps we can put this mess behind us, and you can move on with your life, Charles." His father sighed and offered him the same irritated expression he had every time Charles mentioned Lyliana.

"It must be refreshing, being on the ocean, all that space. Time to think," mused Mikkel.

Charles and his father exchanged looks and grinned, both stifling their laughter.

Mikkel gave them an incredulous look. "It could happen. All I would need to do is ask one of the captains. I am certain you would vouch for me, Mayor Robinson. They would listen to you, would they not?"

The mayor smiled and straightened to his full height. "Well, ay, they might, son. But your mother would never forgive me." He ignored Mikkel's irritation at the dismissal of his mother's feelings.

"You are not so young. Captains only take boys so they can train 'em up. So, your only way now is to become a pirate. That might be fun," said Charles.

"Don't speak such nonsense," his father snapped. "They are criminals. Your mother would die of shame." He walked towards the ship, avoiding his son's humour.

Charles looked at Mikkel and shrugged. They had played at pirates when they were boys, but that was before all the troubles. Fifteen years on, it would be frowned on now. He started to follow the mayor but stopped when he realised Mikkel was not coming. Mikkel opened his mouth to speak. Perhaps to reprimand his father? Instead, his mouth closed without a word.

"We should wait for an invitation. That way we don't disrupt their work. Besides, they are not ready yet." He gestured at the ship and her crew who were manhandling the gangplank down onto the quayside and scattering the crowd. Another group was already working the derricks that would discharge the cargo. Mikkel squinted to watch the operation.

"I thought it would be nice to be at sea, not as a pirate though. Think of the sights you'd see exploring firsthand. I am no good at that, but I bet I could learn."

Charles smirked, "Oh, come on, be serious. You have still not walked the Giant's Causeway. How long has it been since you first decided you were going to do that?"

Mikkel's grin only reached one side of his mouth. "I made it to the Seat." His smile widened as they both looked at the crop of land they had just been sitting on.

Charles rubbed a hand across his shaved head and returned the smile. "Every day since she left. You have been with me through all of this. You're a good friend."

"Well, after today you can move on. At least you will know Lyliana is safe. Perhaps one day we can visit in our pirate ship." They laughed together.

The clouds darkened further as they stood and waited for a sign from the mayor who had disappeared onto the vessel while they spoke. Some of the crowd voiced concern over the worsening weather, but the two men paid no attention. There was always someone forecasting storms, even in the height of the calm season.

A party of seamen came down the plank and approached the forward part of the hull. They were armed with paintbrushes to repaint the eye nearest the quayside. Most vessels he had seen enter port had friendly eyes on the front. Mostly they were large blue orbs, their colour matching the water, but this was not the case with this vessel. Instead, the *Medusa* had eyes like a snake. They pierced the soul, more suited to a ship of war than a simple trader. The yellow surroundings and strange eyelashes added to the menace. Charles shivered and turned away from the sailors.

Behind him, the Giants Causeway stretched across the water, separating Lessar Bay from Greatar Bay. The huge rocks that made up the main platform of the structure protruded from the sea like great teeth stained green by

22

marine growth. Dark lines marked the rise and fall of the tides. Charles squinted and tried to make out the far side of the bay. The maps showed that the causeway continued on the other side of the island that marked the bay's east side, but he had never travelled that far.

Mikkel shifted and nudged him. "Get your mind off the causeway. There is time enough for that. The mayor is coming." He pointed.

Charles watched as his father disembarked the vessel and searched the crowd.

The mayor was breathing heavily as he approached. "The captain will come and see you before he goes ashore. He is busy right now but informed me that if you wait in End Tavern, he will see you then."

Charles huffed and looked at his friend. *More waiting for news.*

"Some lunch in the tavern would not go amiss," said Mikkel eagerly.

Charles's father laughed. "Hungry as always." Turning to Charles, he added, "Don't be late. Your mother will have my head. I'll be in the town hall if you need anything."

"I'm a growing lad," Mikkel replied to the mayor's departing back.

"Ay, outwards. Come on, I grow impatient with this waiting," Charles replied. He shuffled forward, scratching the loose stones across the path.

Mikkel donned his floppy old straw hat, more suited for the fields than the dockside, rolled the legs of his trousers down and followed his friend to the tavern. They ordered hops and game pie, which claimed to be bear meat but might be anything, and settled at a battered wooden table to wait for the *Medusa's* skipper.

With their meal eaten and their glasses empty, Charles's

scowl deepened. He shuffled his legs under the table, crossing and re-crossing his ankles, all the while watching the door. Mikkel studied his reflection in the mirrored sign lying on the table. As always, he checked the scar on his neck.

"You still blame me for that?" Charles nodded at his friend's neck.

"Well, it was your fault."

"Come on, how old were we? And you didn't speak to me for months."

Mikkel raised one eyebrow and grinned, "It wasn't that long. Really, I should be thanking you. The ladies love it."

"I'll be sure and tell your wife when I see her. What scars will you get then?" Charlie's attention shifted to the door, "Ah, finally."

The captain pushed his way through the lunchtime crowd. Even his large size would not shift the hungry mob. He nodded to the barmaid for a jar of ale. He pulled the chair clear of the bench with an annoying scrape and dropped his colossal bulk opposite the two friends.

The girl arrived with a jug and tankard, the former the captain took from her immediately and emptied in one huge gulp. He offered it back and indicated she should refill it. Mikkel and Charles watched in awe as he treated the second jug in a similar manner and waited for his third. The next jar of ale actually touched the table. The captain pulled his chair closer and leaned towards Charles.

"Your father, the mayor," he added the last as unnecessary clarification, "tells me you have questions about Gamola?" The captain belched loudly and took another gulp of ale.

Charles nodded.

"Well, lad, ask your question. I don't have all day. Need

to see a woman about a woman." He winked conspiratorially, jerking his long moustache below his pointed chin.

"I wondered if you could tell me about the trading vessel *Comnfe*. She should have arrived in Gamola. My friend was travelling on her. She was due to enter an arranged marriage. I hoped to discover that she arrived safely," Charles rested his head back on the chair and waited.

The captain stared at him with cold grey eyes. "When did the vessel depart?"

"A month and a half ago," replied Mikkel, who had been expecting the question.

"Em." The captain brushed the long cloth of his coat back from his legs and stared thoughtfully out of the paned window behind them. "To my knowledge, we were the first to arrive from here in a while. I did hear rumours of one vessel that was overdue, but I did not catch the name." He paused but continued quickly. "Despite the weather, she should be there by now. If she has not been heard from yet, I fear…"

Charles's next words stuck in his throat. The captain's meaning was plain.

"There is still hope though?" asked Mikkel.

"There is always hope. They could have taken damage and stopped somewhere for repairs. Storm damage might give them no other option. Or they could have been blown off course, and perhaps the wind is against them. She is a well-founded vessel. I expect she has been delayed."

Charles wrinkled his nose and blew out his cheeks.

"Would you let us know if you hear anything more?" asked Mikkel.

"I can, but I shall not return here for at least three months, if not more. Depends on when we sail. The weather will be worsening, and that could delay our next departure from Gamola."

"Thank you, captain. Sorry for taking up so much of your time," Charles said weakly, offering his hand to shake.

Mikkel waited until the captain left and then turned to Charles. "It could mean a delay only. You heard what he said...it might just be the weather. I urge you not to worry. Perhaps they stopped at some other place first."

Charles nodded agreement to his friend's plan, and yet the heaviness in his stomach told him there was more to it than the *Comnfe* just being delayed.

The door banged open, and the governor's thin body blocked the light for a moment. His long gait made short work of the distance that separated them.

"Any news?" The man was breathing heavily. "Did the captain bring a message?"

Mikkel sighed loudly. "Nothing."

Governor MacKenzie leaned on the chair, his chains of rank flapping forward. "I thought there would be something by now. I wonder what happened?" he said almost to himself.

Charles' face burned. "What happened?"

Mikkel put his hand on his arm, but Charles shook him off.

"You sent her away. That is what happened. You and your insane idea that marrying her off would give you some benefit." Charles was nose to nose with the governor. "You, who are supposed to lookout for your people, could not even consider your own daughter's happiness. Now you profess to care what becomes of her!"

The governor shrank back.

"How dare you come here and pretend to be worried.

You were not worried when she told you she did not want to go. You care only for your own advancement."

"It was not like that, you know this." The governor's voice was quiet.

"Bring her back then. Show her that you care." Charles waved his arms, indicating the room in general. "Show *us*."

Mikkel cringed.

Governor MacKenzie straightened. "It is too late. It is done. And *you* have no position to be speaking to me so." His words held power, but his tone was lacking.

"Then leave me, and do not ask me things you know the answer to already." Charles turned away. The room closed in about Charles. He pushed his fingers down onto the top of the table until they turned white. *I should not have let her go.*

It would be another sleepless night.

CHAPTER 3
LOWLANDS

Rustling leaves and the crack of breaking twigs followed Syngh as he ran through the trees. His morning hunt began as the glow kissed the blackness of the horizon. Now he was late. His mother had been adamant that he return home for lunch. As usual, he had lost track of time, so now he was running at almost full speed in the hopes of avoiding Falora's anger.

He reached a clearing scented with a hint of seeds and busy with feasting birds. His mouth watered. Syngh screeched to a halt, his front paws ploughing furrows in the earth and sniffed the air. The sweetness faded.

He slid to the ground and stalked through the long grass, fast and silent. His black shiny fur shimmered as he moved. A purple sheen flashed across his back and merged with the paler fur of youth along his spine. He approached a large rock that marked the centre of the clearing. A panicked rustle betrayed movement.

The sound increased in volume and developed into a hurried flapping of wings. The birds took off five yards ahead, their hollow screeches echoed across the clearing.

He pushed his tongue out between his teeth and tested the air. They were gone. There would be no easy snack before lunch.

He stretched and curled his paws before extending them to full size. At sixteen, his paws were the size of the average dinner plate. In adult cat form, he would be large. He stretched his toned shoulder muscles and stood to continue his journey.

Syngh arrived just as the sun passed its zenith. He reached what passed for the centre of the town and angled towards the newly designated changing area. He disagreed with this latest policy in principle. To him, it was just another way to restrict their activities. No matter his opinion, he complied with the elder's instructions. His time would come. All he had to do was wait. As a feline, he had a well-practised patience.

He trotted under the canopy of trees and into the small hut where his clothes waited. The change was still an exhausting process, even after a few years' practice, and yet he welcomed it each time. *They* said it would get better, but as his muscles contracted and contorted, Syngh felt that his bones would surely split and snap. The pain was momentary but stabbing.

Despite this, it always left him cleansed and refreshed, particularly to change into feline form. He was not a weakling in human form. He did not feel less as a human, but he preferred the freedom of four legs. After changing, he donned his clothes and followed the pebble path to the tree house.

The werecats had not always lived in the trees. Other Prides had different habits. Theirs was a practical decision born of the need to avoid the floods. Since they had moved up the slopes a little, it had become an unnecessary precaution, but the habit remained. The population of the village were more comfortable in the trees. So they had built tree houses. It had the added benefit of being easy to protect in the event of attack, not that there had ever been an occasion to defend their homes.

Syngh entered his house to find his parents waiting. His mother gave him a slightly irritated and resigned look as he sat down at the table but said nothing.

Unusually, they had started lunch, perhaps having finally given up on relying on him. Syngh relaxed into his meal before he realised both his parents were watching him, their food untouched.

He put down his knife and fork and waited. When they said nothing, he broke the silence, "You should just get it over with. Then we can enjoy a meal in peace. I was late. I apologise. I would like to say it will not happen again, but we know that is unlikely." How looked about him. "Where are my sisters?"

"Never mind your sisters. We have news," said Miroslaw, his father.

"So, my sisters can skip lunch, but I'm in trouble for being late?" he said, trying to keep the irritation from his tone.

"Don't be cheeky to your father. You will not be late again. Next week you will leave for the mountains and begin your training. A falcon came from the Coven. It has all been arranged," Falora said, using her sternest 'mother' tone.

"Your sisters and I will escort you into Stormy Range. From there you will easily find your way, and in this manner, they will know where to go when their turn is come." His father returned his attention to his meal.

Syngh's excitement rose, only to be clouded by doubt as he imagined what he would say to Piearsa. "Thank you for arranging this, Mother. I hope I will not disappoint," he hesitated, wondering if he dared change the topic.

"What's the matter, son? Do not tell me you're having doubts now?" said Falora, as always picking up on her son's mood.

"Not at all, Mother, I was just wondering... I mean this is very strange. We never travel, yet now I will go all this distance like so many before me. Some don't ever return. It makes no sense to me why one is okay, and the other is not?"

His father sighed and glanced at his wife who rolled her eyes.

"I suppose we should have expected this question, son," Falora began with obvious reluctance. "We generally do not travel because it's not safe. But we know it is safe to go into the mountains and work with the witches. This is what we've always done."

"I've been out hunting every day for as long as I have been able. Not once have I seen anything that would pose a threat. It is possibly dangerous in this form," he waved his hand across his own body. "As a feline, there seems very little reason to fear. We have no natural enemies. We are at the top of the food chain. What else might there be?"

Miroslaw put down his knife and fork with a loud clatter, "It is exactly that ability to change which protects us. Imagine if that ability were removed. We must remain near the witches. Their magic gives us the ability to change. Without it, we would remain human, so we stay here and keep our options."

Syngh considered his father's words and thumbed his

ear, giving a small start of surprise when he found there was no fur on it. Something gnawed at his mind. He had grown up hearing stories about the witches, and yet no one mentioned they were the source of power needed for the change. Why had no one told him this before?

The family finished lunch, and Syngh helped his mother wash up while his father disappeared for his daily business. Once Falora no longer needed his help, Syngh headed over to Piearsa's home.

As always, he took the route by the small stagnating pond that was the only remaining sign of the last rains. The scent was tolerable to a human nose. Syngh stopped by the water and studied his reflection. His darkening purple eyes matched the changes to his fur. For a while now that depth of colour and his fur when in feline shape had grown more pronounced. He flashed a cheeky grin and a wink to his reflection and continued with a renewed bounce in his step.

Piearsa stood in the canopy when he arrived but jumped down when she saw him. She planted a kiss firmly on his lips and stepped back to look at him. Her piercing blue eyes met his, and Syngh felt the usual up welling of love he experienced in her presence. Even their parents had accepted early on that they were meant to be together although they had pretended doubt until the youngsters grew into adolescence.

He drew her to him and returned her kiss with equal enthusiasm.

Pulling away, Piearsa studied his expression. "What happened?"

Syngh sensed her tension as much as he saw it. "A falcon came from the Coven. My training is arranged. I will leave soon." He allowed his doubts to filter into his voice as he would not do with anyone else.

"Don't worry, it will fly by. Then we can be together. Unless they show themselves true in the meantime." Her sudden harshness took Syngh by surprise.

"What do you mean? It is training that I would not receive elsewhere. This is a good thing. I thought you understood." He almost pleaded.

She inhaled and took his hands in hers, holding him in place. "You misunderstand, my love. I met with a couple of the elders by accident, and we got to talking." She smiled, recognising his shock. "I was surprised also. These things never happen. They must have been desperate for new conversation to even acknowledge my presence—"

"I was thinking just that," he interrupted.

She huffed and continued, "They told me some of the history. Did you know that the witches held us as slaves? For a long time, they used our need of their magic as a way to control us. It is only relatively recently we have gained our freedom. I was shocked. I always thought this is how it had always been. A mutual respect." Piearsa smirked.

"You knew we need their magic?" He frowned. "You never told me."

Piearsa smiled. "I thought you knew. It's common knowledge. But this other bit...about the slavery. I can't believe we still work with them."

Syngh nodded. "We still need their magic. Nothing has changed. You know, even that does not seem right though. I roam all the time. No matter where I go, I have no trouble changing."

"I believe it is a residual connection that must be reinforced. I did not really understand it when my parents told me. It was a long time ago. I never thought about it further."

"Perhaps I will learn more in the mountains." Doubt

clouded his thoughts again. "You will come and see me off, won't you? I shan't be able to leave without seeing you."

Piearsa tossed her long dark hair back from her face suggestively and tugged him towards the trees. "I'll see you off now if you like."

CHAPTER 4
HILLAWAY

"The captain reported in this morning. I met him on the way. The weather slowed their passage from Ragnor after they detoured due to reports of pirate activity along their usual route." Atlas Hemming emphasized his point with a waving of his hand. "He said that while they could not be sure the wrecked vessel was the remains of the *Comnfe*, she was the only ship that usually went near that area."

Charles focused on the missing fingers of the hand that waved repeatedly as each sentence was uttered. He rubbed his palms on his trousers.

"I'm afraid—"

"Charles?" Martha Robinson appeared from nowhere but stopped when she saw the chief banker.

Charles looked between the two. "Tell me. I have to know." He exhaled until his lungs hurt.

"They sighted a pirate vessel half a day out, which they suspected might have been involved in the incident, but my friend's ship is not fast or powerful enough to risk meeting a vessel like that."

It all adds up. Charles gripped the fingers of his left hand with his right, yet the trembling still threatened.

"There is still hope, my dear," said Martha, crossing the room towards her son.

Charles straightened his fingers and shook his head. A thickness rose in his throat. He swallowed hard. Lyliana's blond hair flashed before his eyes, how it bounced across her shoulders when they played as kids. The ribbons that never stayed in no matter how much her parents tried to tie them tight.

He squeezed his eyes shut against the memories.

His grip on his fingers slackened as they mirrored her touch. His lips puckered to the thought of Lyliana's last kiss.

Is she really gone? It can't be.

"No." He stood.

His mother moved towards him.

Charles stepped back. "No." He sniffed and stepped back again as she looked as though she would approach again. "I'm supposed to meet Mikkel." He sat down, the strength gone from his muscles. His shoulder twitched as he tried to raise his hand. Nothing

"There is still hope." Martha cringed as though she knew the words had no meaning.

Charles took a deep breath. "How can you say that? I should never have let her go."

Atlas Hemming plucked his glasses from his mouth and edged back into the shadows of the room and exited silently. Charles stared at the door.

"It was not *your* choice. It was arranged by her father." Martha shrugged off the departure of the banker.

"If she had been promised, that would never have been possible."

"You were both young when that arrangement was made. What could you have done?" She raised both eyebrows.

"Something, anything, but it's too late." He blew out his lips and huffed.

"It is never too late unless you give up, but you did not hear that from me." Martha patted him on the shoulder and sidled from the room.

He nodded gently as he tracked her departure.

Charles rested his hands on his knees and allowed his elbows to take the weight. The door rattled again, beckoning. He grabbed his coat and slammed it behind him.

The Seat of the Ogres was his favourite spot. It had always provided calm and comfort, even when the weather was bad. When the wind churned up the bay and flecked white spray across the sea, he imagined it was blowing his worries away. As the ships left the bay, he dreamed of distant adventures on lands so different as to always be interesting. But not today, the romance of his solitude was lost. His eyes fixed on the gold charm on the end of his chain, a memory of good times, dreams of a future they could never have.

I let her go. This is my fault. I must get her back. If I can just find her, it will all be different.

He glanced back at the town. *I told them this was a bad idea. People should not be used as bargaining chips or to make alliances. I should have fought harder.*

Mikkel sat down next to him without a word. Charles nodded in acknowledgment. He stared out across the water and imagined her drowning, watching the ship sail away without her, with hundreds of pirates on board. Perhaps she would be better off that way. *What could they do with her then?* He shuddered.

The wind dropped a little as they sat and stared into space. Charles rubbed his index finger between the fingers of his other hand, harder and harder until the pain forced him to focus. His exhausted mind struggled to make coherent thoughts, to fix on something, to make a plan. Her name echoed in his mind. Images of her face haunted his thoughts.

"What shall we do?" said Mikkel, sounding like he was discussing their plans for the evening.

Charles gave him a sharp look.

His friend looked startled. "To get her back. What are we going to do? I think it will be up to us."

Charles cocked his head, his thoughts strengthened, the beginnings of a plan. "I know only that she must come back to me. No more of this arranged marriage nonsense." He smiled grimly, "I didn't condone it in the first instance. Next time, I will have none of it. I suppose *he* does not even know anything has happened."

Mikkel raised his eyebrows and let out a breath. "Then it is agreed. We must do something?"

Charles shook his head and took Mikkel's hands as if to shake it. "My friend, whatever must be done will likely be dangerous. I cannot ask you to endanger yourself."

Mikkel gave him a faint smile, "I did not hear you ask. She was my friend too, perhaps not as close as you, but there you have it." He eased his hand back.

"I just need a plan, but—"

Mikkel twitched his hand, forestalling further comment. "Contingency planning was never your thing. Nor planning of any kind come to think of it." He flicked his eyebrows. "Your father is the mayor. Hers was... is the governor. That is the place to start. Surely, one of them has some way to help. Certainly, her father would, even if yours can't. And the governor has money and ships."

All they needed was a fighting ship, and the rest could be worked out. *Seems too simple though.* "How are we to persuade them to act? It's bureaucracy. They will have excuses."

"Excuses to avoid rescuing his daughter?" said Mikkel.

Charles' smile only reached one side of his mouth as he glanced to his friend, but still a flutter overtook his belly. "Come on, we must try." He rose from the Seat and clasped Mikkel's shoulders, pushing him forwards towards the town.

They found the governor outside the town hall, sheltering behind a wall while his voice challenged the wind to address some traders. There were too many of them to take inside. It was clear that Governor MacKenzie was not persuading the crowd of whatever issue he believed they had misunderstood and equally obvious that they were unprepared to accept any compromises.

It was the first time Charles had the chance to witness what Lyliana had described as ineffectual leadership on the part of her father. Seeing it now, the flutter in his belly sank to nothing. Mikkel pushed him forward, ignoring the throng. They skirted the central statue and shoved past the front rows

"We must speak to you most urgently, Governor," Mikkel raised his voice to be heard over the crowd.

Charles nudged his friend, conscious of the angry stares about him.

"Most urgent. *Sir.*"

Governor Mackenzie nodded and shoved through the mob. He raised his hands to calm the traders. "Sorry, my friends. I must leave you for a moment. I shall return when I have finished with this most urgent matter."

Voices rose in protest, but he ignored them and pushed on towards the doors to the town hall. As the great doors clanged shut and cut off the sounds from the outside the governor turned to them. "Your timing is excellent, boys. What can I do for you?"

"We came about Lyliana. You've heard what happened?" Mikkel asked.

Governor Mackenzie looked at the floor. Remorse clouded his pointed face. "I've been having this conversation all day. First with her mother then the mayor. I suppose I should have expected you." He sighed, "It is not so simple. I must coordinate with her fiancée. This all takes time." He avoided eye contact with either of them.

"She does not have time. They could be doing anything to her. What if she is not even with them? Perhaps she is in worse trouble. She never should have gone," Charles shouted the last, unleashing his frustration to explode in its rightful place.

Mikkel put his hand on his friend's shoulder. "What has been discussed thus far? Could we send some ships? Never mind the other guy. We have no way to know if he has heard what happened yet." He stepped forward. "I will go if there is no one else."

Charles nodded, "Ships come in here every week. Surely one of them wants a go at the pirates. It won't be hard to find help."

"There are ships, but these are traders, not ships of war. These pirates are well armed. We cannot just send any vessel after them," said the governor.

"This is your daughter's life we are talking about. You never should have sent her. Now she is in trouble, and you are doing nothing. I will speak to my father." Charles shouted before turning and storming away. His hands shook in rage as tears blurred his vision.

"I have spoken to your father. He is looking into getting something arranged," the governor said to his departing back. His voice held no more conviction than it had during the entire conversation.

Charles stopped and turned back, "I will speak to him myself." He glanced meaningfully at Mikkel and turned towards the door once more. Whispered voices drew his attention and finally the sound of Mikkel's footsteps.

Mikkel caught up with him. "I'm sure everyone is doing everything they can. It must not be easy for them either."

"I'm sure," Charles replied bitterly. His friend's understanding tone did nothing to help his mood. "Whatever they're doing, it is not enough. Like I said before, it's down to us."

Mikkel gave a slight shake of his head but said nothing.

They picked up the pace as they walked back through the town towards Charles's house. They stopped only once, briefly while Mikkel went into a shop per his wife's instructions.

Charles looked at his reflection in the shop window while he waited impatiently. He noted the paleness of his face. Normally he was fastidious about his looks, yet while he noticed these details, he found that he did not care. Until he was satisfied that Lyliana was safe, nothing else mattered. He turned away from the glass.

They reached the house to find Charles's parents arguing. They fell silent as the men entered the front room. His mother left abruptly, and his father followed her with his eyes before turning to the lads and throwing them a questioning glance.

"You've come about Lyliana?" Felipe asked when they remained silent.

"Yes, Father. Something must be done."

"I know. I am trying to arrange something. It would be easier if I could have some peace to make the arrangements instead of explaining my actions every minute." He hesitated, "Sorry, son. I've been having this argument all day. It is not the easiest thing to do. Be assured I am working on it. I know how you feel. I will do my best."

"I know, Father. I knew I could rely on you. I spoke with the governor. He was not so helpful."

His father sighed and indicated that they should sit.

Charles waited until his father and Mikkel had chosen their seats before perching on the edge of the remaining chair. A clattering in the kitchen told him the maid was bringing tea or possibly that his mother was still angry. It was hard to tell which.

"You must realise that this is a difficult situation for the governor. He is under pressure from many sides. Not least of which will be his wife. She is not an easy woman as I am sure you know." Mayor Robinson brushed back his orange hair and rubbed his long nose.

Charles nodded, "It's his daughter, Father. I am ready to move the earth to get her back. I cannot imagine why he delays. I admit I could have handled it better. If Mikkel had not been there…"

"Perhaps you do not remember Lyliana's brother?" his father cut in. Felipe suddenly realised his left hand was exposed and hid it under his right. Even after so many years, he was still self-conscious about those two missing fingers.

Charles had never discovered how his father lost those

fingers. He asked him once not so go ago, but the only response was his father staring in space and walking away.

Charles raised an eyebrow. "He went to work in Gamola Harbour. I remember when he left. She was upset because they were so close." His memories shifted to the day he spent on the Seat of Ogres with Lyliana crying on his shoulder.

"You were younger then, so we did not burden you. It was kept a secret as you will understand. What I am about to tell you is to stay between us. I need your word, both of you?"

Mikkel glanced at Charles and nodded when his friend did.

"He did not go to work. He was taken by pirates, or so we believed at the time." He wiped his forehead.

Charles leaned in. "You believed?"

"We discovered later that he joined them. Rumour has it that he is now a successful captain in the north. The news nearly broke his family." The mayor took a deep breath and looked each of them in the eyes before continuing. "So you see, this is not so simple for her family."

"And she knew about this?" Charles stammered. "Lyliana knew all along?" The air in the room thickened. His cheeks flushed.

"No, I don't think so. They gave her the same story you heard. The governor told me once that he wanted no more shame brought down on his family, and she was better not knowing. I don't think they ever told her the truth." He sat back heavily in his chair and sighed. Both hands were again visible, the deformed one forgotten amidst the importance of the revelation.

Charles mirrored his father's actions as he took in what he had just heard. He saw Mikkel looking at him with concern. It was too much. So much in one day was more than he could bear.

His mother came in, wiping her apron, her pretty face was drawn with worry. She sat on the edge of the chair and hugged Charles.

He pushed her away roughly and rushed from the room.

CHAPTER 5
LYLIANA

A pain in her hip woke Lyliana. As she moved, the ache became sharp and stabbing. Her wrist burned. The other one was dead. Her left arm was dead. She was lying on it. Her twisted legs were numb.

She opened her eyes to complete darkness. The stench of old wet rotting ropes tickled her throat. She tried to move, and her body ached in complaint. She groaned and managed to shift her head a little. Lyliana moved the fingers of her right hand and felt the ropes underneath her. They were hard and unyielding. No wonder her entire body was in pain.

Her shoulder stabbed with pain as she raised her head and quickly laid it back as a knifelike stabbing shot down her spine. A rhythmic creaking sounded above as her ears adjusted. The noises were somehow familiar, and yet she could not quite place them. Lyliana held her breath. *I've heard this before, recently but where?* She took a breath and held it again, stopping her thoughts for concentration. She searched her memory for clues.

I was travelling, on a boat. A ship! Her thoughts came into focus. She had been on a ship. Memories of the storm appeared in the forefront of her mind. *We collided with a pirate ship*. Sounds of the guns and cannons echoed in her mind. They came out of the storm, like demons. There had been no warning, no chance to escape or give quarter. The captain told her to stay below, but curiosity got the better of her, and she popped her head out on deck.

Lyliana recalled dark rivets of thick liquid trailing across the deck. The stench of blood mingled with the acrid stink of gunpowder formed an underlying metallic pungency that clawed at her nostrils. It gave the air a greasy feel as though it might clog her throat.

She had stood mesmerised as each puff of air chewed away at her confidence. Men were dying everywhere. The final crash of the cannon and the great ripping sound that drowned out every other noise as the mast tore itself from the deck. The ship had begun tilting even as she retreated below decks. She remembered the shouts and frantic screaming. A sailor had come for her finally. They had forgotten about her. She could tell by his drawn, frightened look. That fact made her more fearful than any of the rest of it. Most of the crew were jumping into the water. They would have left her to drown.

Then the beach, the top of the cliff, her relief when she realised a ship was coming. The fog of her mind changed to haze. *Was it a rescue or a capture?* She scanned the darkness. *Capture.*

Lyliana drifted into unconsciousness.

Ship's boats approached the beach. The crew had weapons at their shoulders. They shoved her to the ground. Scouts moved about the beach, checking for others.

"*I am the only one left.*"

"*What are you doing here, missy? You should not be here alone.*

It's not safe," said her would-be saviour with a nasty grin. "A tasty snack for the skipper, ay?"

"He'll 'ave a good time for sure," said another.

She struggled as they bound her. She shouted. They gagged her and threw her into the bottom of the dirty boat.

Through her unconsciousness, she smelt the dirt from the boat on her clothes. The pain in her shoulder heightened the memory. She drifted again.

The boat rocked on the water. She shifted herself upright. One of the sailors scowled. Lyliana forced herself up and wrapped her bound arms about the nearest sailor, hoping to crush him. Another grabbed her and shoved her back.

"Can't you handle one little girl. Tie her up properly else I'll shove you over the side. That'll save you a job, won't it, missy?"

They bound her arms behind her and ignored her vicious raging.

She woke sometime later. Her jaw hurt. She searched her teeth with her tongue. There was a tooth missing. She tasted blood in her mouth. That coupled with the smell made her wretch, but she held back her vomit. With no idea how long she had been in the cupboard-sized room or how long she would remain there, adding to the reeking place was the last thing she wanted.

The floor was moving more than earlier, telling her they were in open sea. She tried to visualise the geography, to imagine where she was, but she didn't know exactly where she started from. If I could see outside, see the sun... Such thoughts were useless. She could not move. She was hungry, alone, and had no idea where she was or where she was going. I must survive and deal with the rest later. She tried hard to convince herself of the wisdom of those words she had once heard in a story from a traveller. He advised her to look to the future during times of hardship.

Hours later, it might have been days, the sound of a key in the lock alerted her to the opening of the door. Even with so little change of light she was blinded, dazzled. She clenched her teeth against the pain in her arms and shoulders as someone untied her hands and refastened them in front. A plate skidded across the floor and hit her foot. A glass of water was placed just inside the cell. The door closed.

Lyliana rolled towards the dish, grimacing at the pain lancing through her body, and ate. She wiped her face on the ropes beneath her then forced herself to sip the tepid water when all she wanted was to gulp it down. Every time she moved, she felt another bruise, but it was the first food she could remember, and her stomach grumbled at the thought of it. Her middle ached with hunger and later from the influx of food.

The increasing motion made it difficult to stay in one place. She banged her head against the wooden walls as she struggled to find a more secure position. By the time the movement ceased, all she could do was remain still to avoid the stabbing pains of her massive bruises.

Finally, over the sound of the water washing down the side of the hull, she heard flapping sails and shouting of orders. The floor levelled and became steady.

Later, the door opened again to reveal lamp light and the shadow of a figure in the doorway.

"Come on, time for you to meet the captain." The guy dragged her from the darkness and onto the floor. Her eyes burned, and she closed them tightly. She fell to the floor and struggled as he righted her and dragged her to her feet. Her legs collapsed, her muscles weak from long confinement. Her lips were dry and cracked, and when she tried to speak nothing but a squeak came out.

"W-w- water," she managed finally.

Salty water sloshed over her face. She licked the liquid from her lips. She forced her eyes open and winched in pain as daylight streamed down the steps and stabbed daggers into her eyes.

Spikes of pain shot across her scalp as the pirate dragged her up the stairs. Her legs barely moved, and she earned more bruises with each step. Once outside, she was dumped onto the wet deck.

"Bring her," said an angry voice from somewhere behind. "And get the woman something to drink. You were supposed to be looking after her. I'll have you flogged for this. She's no good to us if she dies."

A door slammed, and a goblet was shoved in her face. "These rascals should know better than to leave you down there all this time. Take your time," the new voice said as she gulped the water, splashing half of it over her face. "Better find you something to wear. That shirt has more holes in it than the cheese below,"

Through the glare, she saw what she thought was a smile, but it might have been a grimace. He left, and she sat on the deck quietly allowing her eyes to adjust, and her legs to stretch out in front of her. Her hands were still tied, but at least she could move about. The man returned. She could still not make out his features through the murk of her eyes, but she felt the shirt he threw to her. She shifted her shoulders to indicate her bound hands. He produced a knife and freed her wrists.

Lyliana gasped as she moved her arms. Her shoulder muscles screamed in pain, and even her elbows ached as she tried to stretch. She held her arms stiffly, angling her elbows behind her back. It would take some time before she regained full movement. She pushed her arms as far forwards as she could stand and winced in pain. *Maybe a little longer*, she smiled despite herself.

Her eyes adjusted enough to see better, and she looked about the deck. Taking a chance, she stood and further stretched her legs. The men around her paid no attention. Clearly, she was no threat.

The small ship had people everywhere, turning the open deck into a marketplace. Brown triangular sails spread out high above and threw shadows across the sailors as they moved haphazardly to and fro. The front rose to a point and dipped to each passing swell. Ropes lay folded down or coiled over pins. An aura of organisation bellied the apparent chaos around her. At the back, by the great wheel, men stood as though stuck in time. Only the occasional movement betrayed them. A cabin boy rushed past her with a frightened expression, his movement hurried by irate complaints. She managed to slip the newer shirt on over the tattered shirt she'd worn aboard the first ship.

A man approached her. He was armed for war, but his weapons had nothing to do with his commanding presence. In the first instance, Lyliana thought she was looking at the captain. His hat was the typical tricorn shape, worn askew to highlight a small gold earring. Tattoos snaked around his neck and down below his collar. As he bent to help her stand, revealing yet more elaborate artwork on his chest. He smiled at her expression, revealing the first full set of teeth Lyliana remembered since coming aboard.

"Come on, let's see what the captain makes of you." He helped her to a door at the far end of the deck and knocked twice. In response to a rumbling from inside, he opened the door and led her inside the darkened room.

Shafts of light pierced the gloom below decks and stabbed at her eyes. She followed the shadowy figure blindly, almost crashing into him when he stopped. The darkness receded to reveal another person sitting in a chair by the window. She peered at the shape and straightened her back.

"Here's the girl, Cap'ain. We tidied her up a bit." He coughed and turned to her. "She ain't told us nowt yet."

"Did you ask her n'thing?" asked the captain in a tone that suggested he was accustomed to such lack of initiative.

"I didn't. Don't know about them others." The guy shuffled his feet.

There was a sound of the chair shifting, and the shape of the captain stood. He waved the guy away, waited till he left, and then sat down with another scraping of the chair. "Si' yourself 'own 'nd have some beer, girl." He leaned over and put a flagon in front of her. "You must be 'ungry." A plate scratched across the table.

The features of the room grew clearer as she ate. It was sparsely decorated, and they were sitting at the only furniture apart from a chest in one corner. The windows behind the desk were dirty and caked in salt. One shattered pane of glass hung from the frame. The candlestick on the end of the desk held no candles, and there were flecks of food all over the floor.

"So, my crew picked 'ou up from Ragn'. What were 'ou 'oing there?" asked the captain in a friendly voice.

She studied him, wondering how much to tell him. There was no chance that they would drop her off, but perhaps she could make him believe that she was worth keeping alive. *He probably knows the movements of other ships. Wouldn't be much good as a pirate if he didn't.* She took a breath. *The truth is safest.* "I was on a ship, the *Comnfe*. It was taking me to Gamola Harbour for my wedding. There was a storm, and we were attacked. A vessel collided with us. I don't know what happened to the others."

He nodded along with her words, his movements growing sharper when she mentioned the ship. "And none of the crew survived?"

"I didn't see anyone on the beach," she replied between bites of an apple.

"Wha' hap'ned to the ship?"

She shook her head and swallowed.

"Migh' they ha' sail't off wi'ou' you?"

"I don't remember what happened after they said all was lost, and we must abandon ship."

The captain frowned, deepening the gouged wrinkles on his face. "We heard nothing about this. How long ago was that?"

"How long have I been here?"

He considered for a few seconds. "A week."

Her breath caught. *A week...it could not have been so long.* She collected herself. "It was not long, perhaps the next day I was picked up. I was unconscious. I don't remember. We came from Hillaway," she added the last, anticipating his next question.

He remained silent for a few moments.

She noticed a regular twitch of his eye. He blinked faster than normal. The tick added to the friendliness of his face, but the hardness behind his eyes made a lie of the impression. The man sat with an unmistakable surety of position that was only achieved after many years of service.

Lyliana fidgeted with her fingers. *A week...I should have been there by now.*

"I mind the storm. We've seen n' other vessels for a while si'ce. Most woul've stay't in port."

"There was no storm when we left."

His face clouded over. "I am ta'ing you back to Laffite."

Lyliana winced and put her finger to her lips. The nail was already bitten to the quick. She chewed at the skin around the nail. *What's at Laffite? I've never been so far east. There were rumours…*

"Yo'll meet Zarono. He'll decide wha' to do with 'ou. In t' meantime, you'll stay in my chart space." His voice hardened, "If you be'ave yoursel'."

She nodded, lost in her own thoughts.

———

It was another four days after they transited through the Northern Pass before they reached their destination. The weather was good, and the captain treated her well. He even allowed her to eat at his table, although there remained no doubt as to her status. She was not allowed to leave the cabin for any reason. There was a guard placed on the door as she discovered when she tried to go on deck for some air one evening. He had shoved her back inside without a word.

They arrived at Laffite Head with a clatter and bang alongside the jetty. Much shouting accompanied the chaos. It was not the tidy, well-organised arrival she remembered in Hillaway but the hurried fiasco of distracted people, those with their minds on women if Lyliana had overheard correctly.

The trek from the ship up through the town made her realise there was no shortage of places for the pirates to satisfy their urges. On the corner of each muddy street numerous 'ladies' showed off their wares, leaving very little to the imagination. Gambling houses and taverns featured prominently on each lane. Drunken hollering and shrieks of pleasure filled the garish streets throughout the town. Those sounds mingled with squawking parrots, monkeys, and other creatures hidden from view.

Lyliana wrinkled her nose against the scent of life's decay and pleasures of the flesh.

Stale hock smoke drifted through trees that lined the edge of the town. Further inland was industry, wood camps, cook houses, and what looked like iron works up in the hills. They skirted past these and continued towards a large plantation villa-type building. Here the air was different. Money and power replaced gambling and debauchery.

They passed the guarded walls of the property and continued up the huge steps into the cooler villa. Lyliana waited while the captain entered a room at the end of the hall. Silence fell, the sounds from the town drowned out by distance and walls.

It was not long before movement caught her attention. The hallway changed from silent and calm to frantic hurrying, verging on panic. Hurried footsteps sounded by her side. She turned to see a smartly dressed man awaiting her attention.

"I am Lester. I must take you somewhere safe. Please come with me."

She was so surprised by his polite manner of speaking that she followed him without question.

"My apologies, but I must put you in here. They will not think to look in the barn. You should be safe."

She wrinkled her nose as the door wafted dampness over her. "What happened? I believe I am under the protection of the captain and this other guy, Zarono?"

"Not now." Lester shoved her inside.

The door slammed behind her, wafting a musty scent into her face. She was alone in the dark with no idea what was going on around her. Panicked noises escalated outside. Then silence.

Lyliana sighed and let out a deep breath. *If ever I get out of this mess, no one will ever lock me in a dark room again.* She sat and waited.

A rustling and scraping preceded the door slamming open to admit two men she had not seen before. Outside all remained quiet.

Lyliana stood as they entered. They dragged a body in behind them.

She gasped and pushed her hand against her face to stop any further noise when they looked up in surprise.

"Who's she? There's not supposed to be anyone here?" one whispered, pulling the body further into the room. "You said no one would see us."

"She's locked in here. She must be the captive we heard about. Don't mind her. They'll no believe out' she 'ays. Let's just hide him and get out of here before someone finds us," said the other, louder but equally impatient.

One man pulled the body one way while the other struggled the other way. One grunted as he heaved at the same moment as the other let the corpse go. Finally, they tossed a canvas over the body.

"We should bury him. They will find him here,"

"It won't matter. It'll be too late. They won't know it's us if *you* hurry."

The other man glanced at Lyliana, and she took another step backwards.

"She will."

"You won't say anything, will you, lovey?" The pirate paced towards her. "I can give you something better to remember me by." He smiled, and her muscles strained.

She stepped back again and tried to ignore the vile look

on his face. His dirty teeth and mucky fingers repulsed her. She backed away, further into the corner. Bile rose in Lyliana's throat. The man looked at her, much as a predator would view its prey. She flinched. Her stomach recoiled, but she kept her face neutral. The barn grew smaller and devoid of air.

"Leave it out, Jambo. We gotta sort this."

The other man hissed at the use of his name but obeyed and resumed hauling the canvas over the body.

Lyliana averted her eyes from the body but could not resist its allure when the dead man's leg slipped from under the canvas. She was transfixed.

The pirate, apparently called Jambo, caught her eye. "I think she likes what she sees," he said to the other. "Wanna 'ave some fun, Bill?"

Bill grunted and heaved the leg back under the canvas. He eyed Lyliana and shrugged.

She smelt her own sweat. She gripped the wooden wall behind her. There was no way out. They were blocking the door. Her breathing came in loud ragged gasps.

Jambo advanced and grabbed her wrists. He used his chest to push her onto the table.

Bill grabbed a fist full of her hair and pulled.

Lyliana shrieked and pushed them away. Pain shot through her scalp. She fell to the table against the power of the hand placed over her mouth. She clenched her jaw shut. Her fingers scratched at the hands over her mouth.

Bill cackled as Jambo pushed himself between her knees.

She struggled. Her legs were weak. Her knees would not close. Her thighs cramped.

Something wafted by her ear. She moved her torso to shake him off. One of her hands came free as Jambo flapped his hand as if swatting a fly. She used her other hand to push herself from the table. Her arm muscles protested. Lyliana ignored the pain; adrenaline pushed her on. She grappled but could not find purchase. The temperature in the barn increased.

"Ouch, what the hell?"

"What?" asked Bill.

"Summat pricked me. Lend a hand 'ere," he hissed as Lyliana broke free of his grip. "Hold 'er down, man.

Lyliana gasped as they shoved her. Her muscles burned with renewed pain as they tensed against the attack. She kicked at them. Her voice cracked, choking off a scream.

Jambo leaned over her, breathing his foulness across her face. Spittle slithered from his lips onto her nose. Lyliana squeezed her eyes shut.

They tugged at her trousers.

She writhed and bucked. Tears burned her eyes. She barred her teeth with the effort. *Don't give in. Never yield.*

"Hurry up, I wanna go," said Bill, from behind her head.

CHAPTER 6
DILLITAY

The barn door clashed shut, waking Dillitay early from his afternoon slumber. He was so worn out from the morning that he drifted asleep on the rafter beams. The direction of the sun suggested a couple of hours had passed.

Rough voices inside the barn brought the pixie to full alertness. He rolled over his sword, which had lain next to him while he slept, and peered over the edge of the wood to the floor below. Two men dragged a body across the floor. Their trousers had dark bloodstains betraying their recent murderous activities that were confirmed by similar marks on the elder man's face.

Dillitay's gaze fell on a woman in the corner. She watched the men with wide eyes but kept her head high. She was somehow different from the women he was accustomed to seeing in Laffite. Mostly, they were servants or whores. She was neither.

She shifted to put as much distance between herself and the men as possible. His brow creased. There would be trouble ahead even if she did not yet know it. The men dragged the body further inside and back into the opposite corner before covering it with a discarded dirty canvas.

Dillitay rolled back into the cover of the rafters. He pulled his sword and checked its edge. He grimaced. *Maybe I'll need you now*. He slung his bow across his shoulder, carefully avoiding his wing arches. His quiver was full, as it had been since he arrived. He forged his own arrows and tipped them with wasp stings. He licked his lip with his dark pointed tongue and loosened the sword in its scabbard again.

Thus prepared, he flitted between the rafters and perched on a beam that provided a better view. From his new position, he saw the face of the dead man. He didn't recognise the pirate. *They risk punishment for this unsanctioned murder.* He looked back at the woman. *They will be desperate. Be careful, girl.*

She could not retreat any further. From the movement of her ample chest, she was beginning to panic.

Dillitay tightened his belt and placed his bow at his feet with the arrow he had already removed from the quiver. He looked about him. There was nothing small enough for a six-inch man to wield. He had preparations all over town. He had worked on them since he arrived from home, so that by now, he was well supplied everywhere he went. It seemed like a sensible precaution, given that he was the only pixie in the town.

He was too young when he left the main stronghold, but the journey matured him and taught him much. Not least of which was how to look after himself. The voyage on the ship had been the worst, and yet before he departed, he had expected the long trek across the desert to give him the most problems. It shocked him to discover that a ship was a harsher environment for a small person than the heat of the desert.

Throughout those unfortunate days, he discovered that his lessons in hunting had not been in vain. He now understood that survival instincts and training were the most valuable asset to any pixie. Most importantly, he had adapted his keen senses to notice trouble before it occurred. There was still much to learn. Today would be another lesson.

This girl was in trouble. He could not risk revealing himself too early. Pixies were generally likened to bugs, a small irritation that could be flapped away and forgotten. People who made that mistake lived to regret it. If they lived at all. But Dillitay was alone. What could he possibly do against two fully-grown humans?

He held his breath as they finished covering up the corpse. Their scuffling feet gave away that they were at least partially drunk and unsteady. More frequently, their eyes strayed to the girl. Their expressions grew hungry and excited. Dillitay tossed his dark hair away from his eyes and flitted to the next beam to get closer to the action.

"I think she likes what she sees," the older pirate said. "Wanna 'ave some fun, Billie?" He rolled up the long sleeves of his dirty shirt. The man advanced on the girl who backed up and tripped on the table leg. He grabbed her wrists. The other one, Billie, took a handful of her blond hair, and they pulled her down onto the table.

She shrieked.

Dillitay was in the air charging towards them almost before he made the decision. With his sword bared, he flew at the elder man. He stabbed at his neck, flitted around, and repeated the action on his other side. He completed the routine again.

The man flicked his head and hollered in pain. The man's hand came up to flap him away. Dillitay thrust again with a short, sharp, jabbing motion. He kept moving, back-and-forth. His training kicked in. It was not enough. He needed help. Dillitay retreated, heading for the gap above the main door.

What can I do? I am but one man, and a small man at that. This is a big person's fight. In a sudden flash, the answer came to him. *I need a human.* He alighted on the rim of the door and folded his delicately tinted translucent wings so he could fit through the gap. A breeze tunnelled through the gap, momentarily putting him off balance.

The younger man's voice reached him as he crawled through the space between the door and frame. "Hurry up, I wan' a go." Dillitay was already forgotten.

He reached the outside and looked around desperately. *Never a human when you need one. Any other time, they would be all over the place, infesting the world like parasites. Now there is not one about for miles. Bloody unreliable as always. Now I have to chase around after another one of these useless blood sacks.*

A man came round the corner, his pale ginger ponytail lay next to the tails of the head scarf. He wore a large hat that shadowed his face There was an unmistakable surety in his expression confirmed in his long, self-assured gait. Dillitay considered Lester to be one of the more honourable of the pirates. A perfect choice despite being one of the scoundrels.

Dillitay flew to him and got in his face. He kicked his nose gently and then flitted backwards to give him space. *Humans do not react well to small irritations.*

Lester stopped, startled, and rubbed his sun-reddened nose, which had been brightened by years of excessive imbibing.

Dillitay bobbed up and down in the air in front of the man. He stopped and waited for the human's eyes to focus on him.

Lester's expression was as Dillitay expected. Shock, but his incredulous expression turned quickly to acceptance. Clearly, this 'Lester' was a man of quick thinking. Dillitay smiled. He had made the right choice.

"Come quickly. The woman needs your help. She is in trouble. You must come," shouted the pixie, in his high-pitched fast tones.

The startled expression returned to Lester's face. He squinted and tilted his head slightly, frowning.

Dillitay repeated himself.

A flash of irritation crossed Lester's face. He took an impatient step forward.

Dillitay bobbed up and down once more. He stopped and pointed his sword, aiming at Lester's nose.

Lester stopped. "I don't un'erstand you, pixie."

Dillitay took a breath and collected his thoughts. Forcing a calm and measured tone, he repeated himself slowly. He registered the understanding on Lester's face and turned sharply, darting towards the doors of the ancient barn.

He slipped back between the door and the frame. Warmth flushed through him when he heard the latch click. Lester had arrived. He might have been slow to understand, but he was not slow to act.

"Wha's going on 'ere?" shouted Lester as he slammed the door open and took in the scene before him.

The sound of gasping and shuffling preceded the table clattering to the ground.

The men and their stunned expressions. He was satisfied. The larger man tripped as he moved, beaten by his fallen trousers, slack about his ankles. He sweated profusely.

The pixie stifled his laughter as Lester marched across the small space and grabbed the man, throwing him to the ground. His head hit the wall, and Lester held him in place with a knife to his throat.

Dillitay moved swiftly, scratching Jambo's face, and forcing him to remain on the ground. He hovered a measured two or three metres away and held him in place as Lester dealt with Bill.

The girl shuffled back across the floor, finding shelter behind the overturned table. Distractedly she pushed away strands of her dirty blond hair. Her eyes glanced between the three men. She did not notice Dillitay.

The pixie returned to the rafters, satisfied that Lester was in control. He was forgotten already. That was the way with humans, and history proved it was much safer for pixies. He would not need to tell the clan of this. They would not approve.

His mission was to watch, report back, and wait for instructions. He was to be the clan's eyes and ears on the other side of the world. They made it very clear that he was not to get involved. He should not expose himself in any way, and yet he had done just that. *They'll never know unless I tell them.*

He watched from the rotting wooden beam as Lester cleared the men from the room. The tell-tale sound of chains outside the barn told him they were being arrested. He wondered if they would face any punishment for their 'almost crime'. It was not the way of pirates to punish such things. That was just what they did.

He looked back at the girl. She was still shaken but appeared to be recovering. She collected herself and stood, rearranging her clothes to turn her dishevelled state back to normal.

He nodded. *She might just survive here. I will keep an eye on her.* He filled his lungs to capacity and rose to his full height. *I'm not so short anymore. She is in my care now. That is what I was sent here to do. You are not alone anymore, human lady. Neither of us is alone even if you don't know it yet.*

CHAPTER 7
LOWLANDS

The entire village turned out to see him off. The only absentees were two or three adolescents who had been left to look after the children having their weekly play date.

Syngh scanned his memory, unable to recall such a turnout at similar gatherings. Youngsters regularly left to go to the Coven for training in preparation to become productive members of society. Yet their departures were mostly less grand.

At the head of the procession, his family waited with Piearsa whose look of longing caused tears to well up. He sniffed and looked to the floor. *This is silly. It's not as though I will be gone so long.*

Piearsa gave him a weak smile and gestured an 'okay' sign with a slight tilt of the head to turn the expression into a question. He returned her reassurance and twisted to accept his mother's hug.

Falora gripped tightly about his waist and pulled his face to hers. "Take care, my son. Learn all you can and come back to us. You will leave a gap in my heart until you return that even your sisters cannot fill."

"Do not fret, Mother. The time will be short. I will return, all grown up, professional, and responsible." His smile contained the joke of the statement. "All the things you have wished for so long."

He turned from his mother to speak with the rest of his family, only to find his sisters, Nassoma and Zendaya, gone. Even Piearsa was disappearing round the corner. He looked to his father who nodded in encouragement towards the departing back of Syngh's mate before following her at a quick pace.

A lump grew in the lad's throat as he misinterpreted their actions. Were they so keen to finish the goodbyes?

In a sudden wave of understanding, he realised they must be going to shape shift into cat form. His father and sisters were to join him for most of the journey, but that did not explain Piearsa. He expected she would stay until the last moment. The lump in his throat became a boulder. He fidgeted, shuffling his feet back and forth.

Falora pulled him into another hug so tight he could not breathe. She was surprisingly strong for such a small woman. "You had better get ready, son. Your gear will be sent with the next trading wagon. That way you can have a clear run, and you will be able to concentrate on the surroundings. Make sure you know how to get home." Her smile ebbed.

"I told you, Mother. I shall find my way home. Even from the edge of the earth. I have always had a good sense of direction. The coven is not so far. I shall be back as soon as I may." He nodded to the rest of the group and followed in his father's wake.

When Syngh returned from the changing area, his father

and sisters had taken cat form. Behind them stood Piearsa, sleek and majestic as a feline. Their eyes met across the heads of his family. Warmth engulfed him. *She never told me she was coming with me*. A great weight lifted from his chest.

"You should make tracks, son," said Falora, nodding confirmation to her husband. She wiped a tear from her cheek and dabbed her eyes, blinking rapidly.

Miroslaw bobbed his head and wiped a paw across his face, flashing a dark blue sheen against jet-black fur as he moved. He looked intently at his son, his almost navy eyes sparkled with pride.

Syngh arched his back in response to his father's gaze and then shook himself.

Piearsa stood by his side and nuzzled him under his chin whilst pushing him very gently in the direction they were to go.

With a last glance at the members of his pride, he turned and trotted away through the trees, dodging the worst mud patches as he went. Behind him, sounds of crunching leaves confirmed his family were following.

Piearsa would wait until they had all set off together before following. Even as a cub, she developed a habit of ensuring the collective was safe. On occasion, it irritated Syngh to distraction, but mostly, he appreciated her need to protect his family. They were not a vulnerable group, but he was much happier knowing his parents had her support.

Over the last few weeks, he began to feel a sense of duty towards his pride as his parents grew older. He would never dare mention age to either of them, not even in his wildest moments. Such a comment would only result in a hard slap around the face and possibly an unsheathed claw.

The group trotted side-by-side through the trees until

the space opened out, and they turned north to skirt the marshland that protected the north side of the settlement.

Syngh placed his paws carefully on the gnarled branches that snaked from the murky water of the marshes. Hard experience taught him not to slide from the mossy bark into the slippery mud. It took a long time for the layers of his thick fur to dry in the moderate temperatures common to the Lowlands.

Once they reached more solid ground, they accelerated to a sedate run. Syngh and his father soon outstripped his smaller sisters and Piearsa so were forced to slow down.

As the sun rose to melt the ice-tipped grass, they finally turned westwards and headed towards the mountain range stretching in front. The mystical silhouettes of the lower mountains showed dark against the white tops of the massive ranges behind.

They ran all day, only stopping to catch the odd snack or sip of water. Even Nassoma, the eldest of Syngh's younger sisters, had developed a strong constitution and kept the pace throughout. Syngh had not realised his sister had grown up so much. He still saw her as a young cub, but then he knew his father still thought of him that way. Yet he was now leaving home to take his place in the world. It would not be long before Zendaya followed her elder siblings to the Coven.

As the sun dropped behind the mountains, they reached the final tree line before rocks claimed the landscape and hurtled skywards. They stopped, and while the women changed into human form and lit a fire, Syngh and his father hunted.

The men ate in feline form, tearing ragged strips of raw meat from the elk they caught on the plains. Once they had eaten their fill, they each chose a tree and jumped into the lower branches to rest.

Syngh settled down near the trunk of his tree with one paw hanging over the edge and his head resting on the other. Before he closed his eyes, he glanced about him to check all was well. Seeing his family safe and happy, he allowed his muscles to relax and the weariness to overtake him. It had been a long day, and he would need his strength for tomorrow.

The morning arrived too quickly. They finished off the elk for breakfast and switched into human form just to wash up.

"This changing back-and-forth is strange," commented Syngh, who had become used to the changing room despite his revulsion for it.

"This is certainly much more relaxed. When I was your age, I never wanted to be human. It always seems so restrictive. Funny what age and experience can do for a person," replied his father, before raising his voice to all of them. "Come on, let's hurry. We must get a move on so we are off the mountain before dark. Syngh, we shall travel with you until lunchtime. By then we should be at the base of the mountains. From there you can find your own way. Just stick to the path. It will take you all the way. Once you reach the lake, you will know where to go."

Nearer the mountains, the temperature plummeted, and they moved faster to keep warm. The sun disappeared, and clouds drifted, heavily burdened with snow. The wind chill seeped through their fur and hurried them on.

Noon came quickly. They stopped on the track for Syngh to say his goodbyes. Nassoma promised to visit him, but he knew even as she said it that this would not happen.

Nobody visited trainees in the coven. It was not dis-allowed, only frowned upon. He would not wish her to travel alone either. He said nothing, content to allow her the illusion.

His father led his sisters slowly back down the slope, leaving Syngh and Piearsa alone. Their eyes met, and Piearsa closed the distance between them. Syngh put his shoulder against her, and she tucked her nose under his chin. He wished they were in human form, that he could hold her and kiss her and never let her go, but having such possibilities waved in front of him would be too much. He pushed his body against hers and applied a resolute pressure to her shoulder before licking her ear and pulling away.

Syngh got a couple of paces away before he felt the urge to turn around. She was still watching him, her head low to the ground, her tail flicking in agitation. He raised his own tail in response and flicked a sad goodbye with tail and ears together. Unable to take any more, he turned and trotted away.

Syngh's path took him steadily up into the mountains. He had never been so far inside the Range before. As his father said, there was only one way he could go. On either side of the track, shear rock faces stretched towards the sky. Even without the ice, he would not have gotten very far up the steep, rocky scree, that mass of loose rock, before skidding back to the bottom. As the incline increased, so his pace slowed. The harsh crags of the mountainside were barren except for the snow. The few puddles were frozen over and so treacherous he nearly lost his footing several times. Few grasses survived the upland's vicious winds, but other plants were visible. Flowers of all kinds swayed in the wind, throwing colour across the desolate vista. Blue flowers of the kind Syngh had never seen before blanketed the ground to one side and continued upwards even on the steep slopes. He surmised that these flowers could only survive on that side because the sun was there most of the day, whereas the other side of the valley would remain in darkness.

As darkness settled over the peaks, Syngh made his bed on the ground in the relative softness of the flowers. His father had been right. There was nothing to eat this far up, but after a large lunch, he could survive one night. He curled up with his tail wrapped about him and puffed up his fur to conserve heat. With one ear flicking nervously, he fell into an unsettled sleep.

By morning, he was chilled through and hungry. Syngh stretched his muscles to breathe life back into them and set off early amidst a cloud of vapour marking his own breath.

When daylight kissed the mountaintops, he was almost at the highest point of the track and beginning to warm up, but his muscles were still stiff. As he reached the peak of the track, a rabbit rushed past him although not fast enough to avoid capture. He devoured it with no more than a couple of crunches of his teeth and licked an icy puddle to supplement his thirst. The meat of the rabbit had been dry and stringy, a sure sign that the creature had lived in the mountains for a long time.

Syngh looked down over the rolling track that wound down the opposite side of the mountain until it reached a lake that stretched across the valley. On the far side, he could just see the top of a great building. *The coven*.

The sight of his destination gave his journey a new lease of life. He set off down the slope at a run with the chance of a decent drink spurring him on. The lake had patches of steam showing the warmer areas. He relished the idea of a soothing dip in the lake and hurried on, slipping and sliding over the loose pebbles of the path until he finally reached the waterside.

Syngh shape shifted before running into the water to wash away the grime. It was not perfect, but it was better than arriving covered in muck. He pulled his clothes from his bag and wiped himself dry with the outside of his jacket before pulling on his trousers, shirt, and jacket. He followed the edge of the lake round and climbed up the track towards the Coven.

His approach drew no attention. Syngh climbed the oversized steps to the great wooden doors and banged hard on the wood. He imagined how thick the planks must be that they made hardly a sound. *Maybe I should use a rock?* The doorframe sported a metal pull cord with an ornate handle decorated with snakes. He raised his hand to pull the bell and grimaced at the dirt under his finger-nails. He would keep his hands out of sight. The bell clanged, and he stepped back a couple of paces to wait for an answer.

The door cracked open revealing a long-faced young boy about five years younger than Syngh.

"Yes?" said the boy impatiently.

"My name is Syngh. I come from the Lowlands to commence training, arranged by my father."

The boy nodded and opened the door, gesturing him inside. He banged the door closed behind Syngh and led the way through under the high ceilings of the corridor past numerous closed doors and into a reception area. He waved Syngh to a seat and left through one of the doors on the opposite side.

The room was dark despite the candles. The high ceilings made it colder than it looked, and the few decorations on the wall revealed the bare stone. The only source of warmth seemed to be the large rug patterned with the red and blue mosaics in the centre of the room.

The boy returned quickly and ushered him further into the darkness. He left him at an open doorway and indicated that Syngh should enter.

"Come in, come in," said a female voice.

Syngh stepped lightly inside and took a seat in front of a large table. The room was intimidating, but not nearly as much as the woman on the other side of the table. Her harsh eyes studied him, boring into his soul.

"You have arrived from the Lowlands? And you expect to join our training programme. Is that so?" The woman tapped her fingers on the table.

Syngh gulped fresh air and tried to swallow down the dryness in his throat. "That is correct. My father, Miroslaw, arranged that I would come here."

The woman in front of him huffed. The tapping fingers accelerated. "And your name would be?"

"Syngh." His name felt inadequate. His mind blanked so he pursed his lips and tightened his fingers hard into the palm of his hand.

The witch pushed her dark hair over her shoulder. "I am Ceri. *You* shall address all witches in the coven as Mistress once you are allowed to speak. You shall not be permitted to speak for the first three days and thereafter only when spoken to. You may go anywhere within the coven walls or grounds except the central high tower. You may only go there if given specific duties or instructions. When you are in the tower, you are not permitted to speak. Do you understand?"

Syngh nodded and tried to contain the disappointment rising from his feet. His stomach grew heavy as the excitement drained from him.

"You shall begin in the kitchens. From there, we will consider what to do with you. During your off time, you may study in the library if you wish." Her tone suggested that it would be a waste of time. "You will be assigned a tutor with whom you may consult while you are working, and from whom you will eventually take lessons. Remember, *we* are watching you. One final thing, all werecats are restricted to human form whilst within the sphere of the coven. Do you understand?"

Syngh nodded again.

"Did you bring any belongings?"

Syngh shook his head. Realising this response was not sufficient, he mumbled, "My gear will be coming on the next wagon."

Ceri nodded and bowed her head to look at some paper-work on the table. Taking a feathered pen, she made various marks on the paper before standing and guiding him from the room.

They passed numerous winding corridors that left Syngh with the impression of a never-ending maze. Eventually, they came upon the kitchens where he was passed off to another witch.

During the course of the day, he was introduced to a few other young werecats, only one of whom he recognised. Syngh was shown the large dormitory where he was to sleep and the place he would take his meals, but that was all. He received no other attention or induction. Nobody explained anything about what was going on nor what was expected of him. And because he was not allowed to speak, he could not ask.

He went to bed that night sad and lonely and more than a little disappointed with his lot in life. His last thought as he went to sleep was how long he would have to spend in this lonely, savage mountain stronghold without Piearsa.

CHAPTER 8
LYLIANA

Lyliana shielded the dirty broken mirror from the rays of early sunshine. A flurry of dust danced in the bright rays, shining like glitter as she moved. She puffed away the errant flecks and leaned closer to the glass. In shadow, her missing tooth, lost during one of her many recent struggles with her captors, was easier to see. Her breath clouded the reflection. Clamping her lips closed and holding her breath, she studied her now blue-yellow bruises. Although they were healing nicely, her limbs ached, and her shoulder was sore from repeated assaults. She sighed and stared down at the grubby table, empty except for one tankard. The reek of stale beer was sure evidence of Lester's late night the previous evening.

Lester had improved her situation following the attack by taking her into his property. He had given her his bed while he spent the last few days on the rough couch in one corner of the living area. She was determined to pay him back by cooking for him, but it was difficult to find enough ingredients to make a decent meal, and Lester seemed more interested in where the next beer was coming from. If he could not find beer, he would drink anything he could get his hands on.

She brushed back her matted hair and rolled it into a loose bun pinning it up as best she could. Her skirts, uncomfortable and unfamiliar but the best she could find, were crumpled and shabby even after she patted them down and brushed off the lint.

Charles would never allow her to be seen in such a way. He would have made her return and change. She turned away from the mirror and the image. Her vision blurred, and she wiped her face with the back of her hand. Her arms hung heavily at her side, her muscles refusing to work. The ache in her chest expanded until her lungs grew sore. The emptiness of the house closed in around her. A tear wound its way towards her jaw and slipped down onto her chest. She sniffed and rubbed her nose. *Charles*.

The creaking door announced Lester's arrival in the passageway. He was making plenty of noise to alert her to his presence. With only one washroom in the property, privacy was a treasured moment. He was careful not to invade her privacy any more than necessary.

She flashed him a grin of appreciation and headed towards the door, coming to a sharp halt when he put his hand out in front of her.

"Ya look better 'oday. Your bruises are almos' gone. Ya'd hardly notice if you di' no' know where to look." He gave a reassuring smile.

"They are obvious to me, but then they would be. I keep looking at the missing tooth."

He smiled. "Believe me, you ge' use' to it. Before very long, ya won't notice."

"I cannot imagine." She paused awkwardly, unsure of how to continue. Their eyes met. She was very aware of him, of his long straight hair tied back loosely away from his face. His dark, striking eyes were suddenly friendly and attractive. Even his scarred and tattooed arms were now somehow safe even while they were hidden behind erotic pictures and savage visions of war. She gave a throaty giggle.

"Since you are feelin' better, you should go ou'. No harm'll come to ya while you are 'ere. I can promise you tha'."

She hung her head and watched her fingers fiddle with the skirt.

"It is known you are 'ere wi' me. They would no' dare. I enjoy the town. I spend as much time there as possible. So many things to do." He gave a doubtful look. "If ya like tha' kind o' thing?"

Lyliana sucked her lower lip. *A nice thought but what would I do with no friends or knowledge of the place?* "Perhaps I may. I should like to see the harbour. I always liked the sea."

A rattle and bang interrupted them. Shouting outside. Lyliana's question froze on her lips when she saw Lester's concerned frown. She retreated towards the washroom.

Lester held his hand out in front sharply, indicating that she should stay where she was. He turned to leave but apparently changed his mind. He held up one finger and nodded towards the back door. His meaning was clear. If there was any trouble, she should leave. With a final nod of confirmation, he paced from the room.

Lyliana listened to his footsteps and slunk into the corner. She slid down the wall into a crouch. It was not much of a hiding place.

The front door opened with a bang, and she heard the voices of at least four men, but the specific words were drowned out by their stamping. Another door banged, presumably the front door closing.

Lyliana let out a slow breath and held it again when she realised the men were still inside. She strained to make out words over the crashing of her heart in her ears.

Heavy footsteps on wood approached on the opposite side of the wall. She flinched. Lyliana drew into herself to become less visible. She rubbed her clammy hands on her legs and felt the tightness of her shoulders. The chair was not large enough to fully conceal her. The footsteps stopped, and the voices rose until she could hear.

"No one knows, but Zarono was not surprised."

"'e would *no'* be surprised. He has made a lot o' enemies over the years. It were only a matter of 'ime." Lyliana recognised Lester's voice.

"He could not have expected the black spot. That is a step too far," said another voice from further away.

"So it's one of the other factions. No one here would dare. Not after last time," said a deeper voice.

"Per'aps that is the point. If it were me, I would've done it that way to cas' 'picion elsewhere. No' one of you would think of it being someone so close, would ya?" Lester's frustration was obvious in his tone.

"And if he dies, what becomes of us? Most of us rely on his protection in some way or another. Disastrous. There will be chaos."

"We should investigate. Find out who is on our side then we know who we're up against."

"If Zarono or any of his people find ou', it would cas' 'picion on us. You're suggesting we just say it were no' us, and we were covering our backs? We must protec' ourselves. Internal conflic' is not what we need. We are poised on the edge o' some'hing. The question is what?" Lester was clearly trying to calm the others down.

She listened as he detailed the potential problems. To her virgin ears, it sounded as though the entire town would come apart. Even without fully understanding everything being said, she understood the danger such a thing could pose to her. The voices increased in volume again as the argument reached a new turning point.

"I will not just sit here and wait. We must act now to save ourselves. You need to speak with the other captains, Lester. Find out what they think. One of them should attempt to discover who did this. It was someone here. It must've been. We've had no contact with anyone outside Laffite for months."

"Shut up. Ships come and go in this place every day. Whatever we do, we must do it quietly. No one must know except us." The man who spoke sounded fiercely angry.

"Okay, we keep to ourselves. What about that girl, Lester. Where is she?" There was a pause, "You know the one. She better no' be here."

A rumbling echoed through the wood as a chair was pushed back. The shuffling seemed to indicate that someone pushed someone.

"She ain't 'ere. I sent her out this morning to ge' food. She is proving quite useful if she cooks it all," said Lester, without much conviction. "Now back to business. The way I see, it we 'ave two choices. We marshal our forces, or we do the dee' ourselves."

Lyliana had heard enough. If they found her, she would be dead. *It is better that I know nothing then I can't lie. I need to get out of here. Quietly, so very quietly.* She stood slowly, trying not to shift her weight. Even the sound of creaking floorboards might give her away. She could get to the door without being seen, but could she do it without being heard?

She eased her feet forward. With her arms out for balance, as though on a tightrope, she walked the seams between the floor planking. The tension ached, and her pulse thumped in her ears. With each small step, she held her breath and listened.

Finally, she reached the door and slid it open. She bent her legs and took one last jump onto the muddy grass outside. Her footing missed, and she fell into a roll on the mud to reduce the sound and the bruising. Lyliana paused to catch her breath, pushed herself to her feet, and ran full tilt towards the town, dodging the sightlines of Lester's windows.

When she was clear of the house, she skirted the path and leaned her weight against a tree. Its spiky bark tickled her hands, and she adjusted their position before leaning on her arms with elbows locked. She relaxed her muscles and filled her lungs. The grass was soft beneath her feet. She realised that she had come out without any shoes or even her accustomed house sandals.

Lyliana rested her forehead on the back of her hand and closed her eyes. *Will I spend the rest of my life running? Will I never feel safe again?*

Sounds of the town drew her attention and pulled her away from the tree. She followed the trodden path down the slope and soon found herself on what she assumed to be the main street. It looked different now that she was at liberty. The colours were brighter and the music less depressing. She took the time to watch the birds flitting overhead. Mostly they were parrots of all colours of the spectrum. Their wild squawking added to the sense of controlled chaos that pervaded the streets.

She came to a crossroads of sorts, a well-trodden thoroughfare. Patches of mud marked areas most used, and the sudden smashing of glass betrayed the reason for the mud. Clearly, this was a place of conflict.

She turned away from the raucous scene and headed left. Her movements were achingly slow. She stopped regularly to get her bearings. It all looked the same. Tavern after brothel, filled with laughing and cackling, left her with *a devil won't care* impression of the inhabitants.

Lyliana stopped by a tavern table and readjusted her hair. The wind had increased since she left the house. She began to wish she had done more to keep her unruly locks clear of her face. The provision of meagre washing facilities in Lester's very masculine home was beginning to show.

"What're you doing 'ere, missy? This ain't your place. This is my place. Get on out of 'ere."

She turned to see an older woman gesturing at her.

"Go on. Get out of 'ere, I told you once. I been 'ere so long everyone knows this is my spot. Nea' 'ther bugger wor's this spot."

The woman's dress hung drably about her and barely contained her more than ample bosom. Her common attitude left no doubt as to her occupation, and yet there was something homely about her.

Lyliana looked into her very painted face and smiled. "Apologies, my lady. I meant no offence. I fear I'm a mite lost. It is my first time in town." Lyliana smiled in what she hoped was a disarming expression.

The woman looked her up and down, perhaps assessing her income potential. Lyliana imagined she did this with every woman she met. It would be easy to be offended, but it was clear the woman was just doing what she always did.

Seemingly satisfied, the woman huffed. "Ya should not 'ang around 'ere. It don't look good. I will lose business with your like about."

Lyliana nodded and smiled. What else could she do? She was clearly not welcome. She turned sharply and headed back towards the crossroads. She turned once and saw the woman was still watching her. Lyliana hurried on. She gained the impression that one warning was all she would get.

Back at the crossroads, she paused again. With no money and no idea where to go, she could do nothing but wander. What she really wanted was to sit and relax. Her feet ached, and her knees were beginning to weaken. The tension was causing her back to twinge, and a headache threatened. She headed towards the harbour in search of a beach or patch of sand where she could relax in peace. She wandered close to the left side of the path and, with a sauntering stride, continued down towards the water.

She was about three buildings from the water when she heard a commotion inside a nearby tavern. The shouting was followed by smashing glasses and a sound very like a chair being hit on someone's head. Her assumptions were confirmed when a huge screaming woman threw a man out of the front door. The guy fell into the street, rolled quickly, and regained his footing. There was fury on his face. It was clear he was working very hard not to say anything to the huge woman who stood in the doorway.

"How many times do I have to tell you you're not welcome here? Now bugger off." The woman shook her head and rolled her eyes in Lyliana's direction. "What can you do with these idiots, I ask ya?"

Lyliana offered the woman an uncertain smile that prompted her to come down the steps towards her. Lyliana stepped backwards involuntarily, but a smile from the woman halted her.

"I am sorry. I didn't mean you." She gave a huge smile that only made Lyliana more nervous. "I'm Betty. Will 'ou come in for a drin'?"

"Betty. I don't have any money, I'm afraid. I just arrived. I am Lyliana."

"No matter, girly. We've all been 'n your position. Come in, drin' is on the house." Betty turned her huge bulk ponderously and thumped up the steps. She tossed her lifeless hair back over her shoulder as she gained the door.

Lyliana followed the woman into the tavern and took the proffered chair. The dark room reeked of stale ale and sweaty bodies. There seemed to be more mud inside than out, and yet Lyliana suddenly relaxed as though the shabby interior of the property compensated for the roughness outside. Betty ambled over with two small glasses and handed one over as she sat down opposite.

"So, you're the woman Lester has living with 'im if rumour is correct?" asked Betty when she had settled into the chair.

"Yes, he was kind enough to give me shelter until they can decide what to do with me. I'm hoping to be able to send word home soon." Lyliana rolled her eyes.

Betty cradled her drink in her hands and nodded sagely.

Worry coursed through Lyliana, "You don't think I'll be able to contact home? Surely, they cannot keep me here indefinitely?"

"They have done in the pas'. That's how most of us ended up here. Eventually ya just learn to make the best of it. Things are no' so bad once you accept them. Look at me.

I started as a whore in one of their parlours, and now I run most o' the town. No'hing happens here I don't know about, and there is more than one captain who comes to me for advice. Not that most o' them listen. They're too stupid for that." She grinned widely at her jest and pulled her drink closer. "I'll see what I can fin' out for you. I'd bet they have no thoughts of sending you 'ome."

"From what I heard this morning, there are more pressing concerns. It seems I have arrived at a bad time." Lyliana came to realise she could glean much information from this woman so she pressed on with questions that had been rumbling around in her head for a couple of days. "You say that most of you arrived here in the same manner as myself. What about the rest? I didn't even know this place existed until a few days ago. I've never been so far east."

Betty nodded again and looked thoughtful. "I don't know exactly. I've never been able to pin them down to a 'ensible answer, but from what I have heard, they came here some years ago following a 'isagreement between Zarono and some 'ther pirate captain. Since that time, our *gallant leader* has been building the town up as a sort of pleasure stop. I opine the original idea was jus' a place to collect all the bounty 'ogether, but as you can see, things developed much further. We now have the town in our own right. Over the past couple o' years much attention has been paid to defences so that by now we could mount a small 'ar if necessary. The ultimate plan eludes me, but I've no doubt a man like Zarono 'ould no' go to so much effort for no goo' reason." Betty took a long swig of her drink doing a passable impression of a parched man.

Lyliana digested what she had heard. The fears of the residents of Hillaway were well founded. From Betty's description, there were many more pirates than they had previously known, presenting certain danger to the ill-prepared. She wondered idly how Gamola Harbour faired being so much closer. It was lucky for Charles he lived so far away from potential disaster. Even if such distance meant she might never see him again, at least *he* was safe.

CHAPTER 9
HILLAWAY

Learning of the disappearance of Lyliana's brother Theodoro only made Charles even more determined to find her. His stomach turned sour when Felipe MacKenzie tried to dissuade him from his search. Charles had spat at the governor's feet and walked away.

At the first opportunity, Charles donned his best outfit and walked into the town. Most of the captains went to End Tavern at some point during their day. So did members of the military. If he was going to get help, that was the logical place to start.

He surveyed the tatty bar. Everyone looked as though they just fell off a ship. He might have bet any money they were all fishermen, but he knew better. In his youth, he had known them all, fishermen and storekeepers alike. The growth of the town changed all that. Now there was a distance that had not existed when he was a kid.

Charles chose the table where he had the initial discussion with the captain when he first suspected there was a problem. The familiarity provided the illusion of comfort.

He swallowed down his hops and pushed himself to his feet.

The door clicked open, and Mikkel stalked straight to him.

Oh, here we go. Is there no peace anywhere? Charles rolled his eyes at his friend. *The babysitting continues.* "Don't say anything. I suppose my mother sent you?"

Mikkel removed his floppy hat and liberated his medium length hair. He scratched at his two-day-old stubble and straightened his trousers, scruffy next to Charles'. "No one sent me. I know you. You know I don't agree with what you are doing, but I am here to help."

"I'm just going to talk to them...see if they have any ideas."

"They will say the same thing as all the others but go ahead. Just don't get into a fight." Mikkel grinned.

Charles smiled back. The tension snapped like a twig, and he waved Mikkel into a chair. "I am sorry about how I have been the last week or so. It was not fair to you."

"No matter. Now, what is your plan here? I should like to know what to expect." He waved at the barmaid for a drink.

"You'll see. Just give me a minute to work up the courage." Charles flicked his eyes at the tankard in front of him.

Mikkel gave him a tired smile, and they sat in silence for a few minutes.

Charles watched his friend. Mikkel had been a pillar through these last days. He had treated Mikkel poorly. *Still, at least I realised in time. It would not do to lose friends over this.* The familiar ache returned. *Oh Lyliana, what have you done to me?*

The scent of poorly cooked meat drifted over to the

table, and his stomach recoiled. Charles downed the rest of his beer and stifled the urge to escape. He stood, feeling Mikkel's eyes on him, and wandered over to the bar. He straightened his shoulders, trying to pretend he belonged in this dive.

At the bar, his world contracted until it just included himself. His empty stomach churned, protesting his last drink. He took a deep breath. "Excuse me," he said quietly to the room at large.

Mikkel made a 'speak up' gesture followed by a thumbs up.

Charles swallowed deeply and, in a louder voice, repeated himself. "May I have a moment of your time, neighbours?"

With a general shuffling, the group turned their attention on Charles. The loud movement of chairs startled him, almost making him lose his nerve.

He looked about the expectant faces and almost choked on his words. That was the moment, he decided, that he was not a public speaker.

Mikkel made a move to join him but sat back when Charles subtly waved him away.

For Lyliana. He took a breath and slowly exhaled. "I am appealing for your help. As you know, my Lyliana has disappeared during her trip to Gamola Harbour. I have no concrete evidence that the pirates have her, but that's my assumption." He paused to allow them to digest the information. "I intend to get her back. Whatever it takes. I need help so I am asking if any of you would be prepared to give me passage."

The silence drifted through the room like a force. Dread seeped through him like an unstoppable energy. He coughed awkwardly and stared at the floor. The room closed in around him. Their attention was like a vice about his neck.

"I would love to give you passage, but I have no space on my vessel. We are not going that far, and besides, we have no weapons." A man from the back spoke up.

"My vessel would stand no chance against pirates. Even if I got you there, we could do nothing once we arrived," said another. Another shuffle and murmurs of agreement around the room.

"Do you have a plan, or do you think they will just hand her over?" asked another.

Charles thought for a moment. "I know it's dangerous. I would not ask any of you to risk your own people. I had thought to land somewhere north of their suspected location and hike from there. The element of surprise would give us the advantage."

Mikkel nodded along with his words.

"You plan to go in alone. That is suicide," said the first guy.

Behind Charles, the barman banged a glass loudly on the counter and sniggered quietly. *They all think I am crazy.* He thrust his hands into his pockets and tucked his elbows into his sides. He did not want to admit to the crowd that he had not thought so far in advance.

"What do you know about pirates, son? They are bloodthirsty brutes. If your girl was taken by them, the best thing you can do is to move on and find another." The man raised his hands against Charles's protests. "I know it's awful to say, but you won't get anyone here to take you within cannon range of them. Their ships are fast and well-armed. We have no military vessels to speak of."

Another man stepped forward, nodding so that the skin under his chin flapped like a turkey. "Even if we did, it would take a concerted effort to dislodge them from their stronghold. Months of planning and multiple vessels. This is not an endeavour you just set off for, son. Be reasonable."

An older man whom Charles vaguely recognised stepped forward from the back of the bar. "I'll ask around for you, but don't hold out much hope. These *gentlemen* are correct. We would all like to see the pirates contained, but they have a strong foothold and contrary to the stories, they are well organised. Especially defensively."

Charles nodded, thanked the crowd, and turned back to the bar. He hunched over the counter and hung his head. It was deadweight in his palm. Mikkel appeared at his shoulder.

"I hope you are not too disappointed. You must have known how this was to go." Mikkel waved over two more drinks. "I am heart sorry for you. I wish there was something I could do."

Charles' heart contracted and shrunk deep into his chest. *Yes, I knew, but I did not want to admit it. I thought I could beat the odds.* "We must think of something else." The counter stunk of stake liquor and alternately disguised odours. He lifted himself above the smell.

"I have been mulling it over ever since we heard about this. The fact is we can do nothing unless we can get there. We must solve one problem at a time. Something will come up. It usually does. We just have to be patient." Mikkel sighed into his beer, avoiding eye contact with Charles.

"I will go there even if it kills me. I won't give up on her. She would move the heavens for me. I know I sound crazy, but surely you can see, I will not abandon her." His jaw ached from the strain, but he looked Mikkel straight in his dull grey eyes.

His friend exhaled and returned his look. "I would do

the same for my wife. Of course, I understand. That's what we do for our loved ones. I am with you all the way, my friend. Even if now is not the time."

"I appreciate the offer." He placed his hand on Mikkel's shoulder. "But you have your responsibilities. You cannot endanger yourself. What would your wife say if you were injured? There must be other options. I just have to think of them. I have not spoken to Trey yet. Perhaps he can help?"

Mikkel nodded, took a sip of his drink and remained silent.

CHAPTER 10
LYLIANA

Lyliana sat at the counter in Betty's bar, a habit developed over a few days. She and Betty talked of all manner of things between serving customers, and Lyliana occasionally lent a hand during the busy hours. In the meantime, she had taken quite a liking to one particular drink with a name she could not pronounce, that tasted something like a very potent ginger ale with a spicier tang. Betty informed her that not many places in the town served it.

Betty and Lyliana had become good friends, considering the short length of their acquaintance, a situation derived from Betty's continuing efforts to steer Lyliana clear of the countless men who chatted her up. For the most part, Lyliana was flattered by their attentions while Betty was concerned, and often very vocal, as to her opinions of the men in question, being from the lower end of the pirate scale. Betty informed Lyliana that they were not worth her consideration.

Though Lyliana secretly believed Betty was rather harsh on the men, she did appreciate her loud and robust method of scaring off her would-be suitors. It was only when she arrived each night back at Lester's home that she became concerned about her apparent newfound enjoyment in the town and what that might mean for her future.

She thought regularly about Charles, and the ache in her heart was solidifying by the day. There was no denying the gaping hole in her life. She used every chance to surreptitiously inquire after the possibilities of sending him a note, but on each occasion, such a thing appeared less likely.

At length, she realised Betty was correct. Even if she could find a way to send him a letter, there was no guarantee he would receive it.

"You are truly out o' sorts today," Betty said, upon her return from cleaning the tables following the lunchtime rush. "Your face is as lon' as a fiddle."

Lyliana nodded absently, her intention to plan her escape that day was failing.

"Still plotting your escape, I thin'?" Betty smiled, forever laughing at her own jokes.

Lyliana offered her a weak smile. "I was pondering what you told me that first day we met...that it was unlikely I would ever get home. If true, I should find something useful to do. I cannot spend my days irritating you. I must find some gainful employment."

Betty nodded and adjusted her customary flamboyant dress. The dappled green and yellow silky fabric shone under the candlelight and the glare from the windows. "You are 'ere so much you may as 'ell be 'orking here." She waved her hand about as if Lyliana needed a reminder of where she was. "And we know the punters 'ave taken a shine to ya."

"It might be worth a try, but I don't think you have enough work for both of us."

Betty laughed. "I imagine we'll get more customers 'ith

you here for a full shift, once 'ord gets around. Tha' won't take long 'ereabouts."

"I think I could enjoy that," she hesitated for a breath. "If you are serious?"

"Let me give it some though'. It's true I don't have s' many customers right no'. Many of the ships are a'ay. Perhaps I could find something for you 'hen they return. I expect them next 'eek sometime. Of late, they've been keepin' fairly regular routines. No' always good for business, but a' least there's some consistency. I'll give it some thought." The latter she repeated with more conviction.

Lyliana nodded and indicated her empty glass, accepting the newly concocted and named Spicy Rose, with a smile when Betty placed a fresh beverage in front of her. Betty still refused to explain the drink's name.

Betty tucked her table rag into the band of her dress and skirted the bar to resume cleaning. The place was messier than usual, evidence of the success of the previous night. It looked as though a pack of wild beasts had been through. Lyliana did not like to consider what they had done after they left. There were still some things about the island she was reluctant to question.

That night as she curled up in Lester's big bed, loneliness crept in again. She wrapped the downy blanket about herself and pulled it up over her shoulders until only her head was free. She curled her knees up to her middle and buried her head down deep into the pillow. The bed was surprisingly soft, not the lumpy mattress she was accustomed to in Hillaway. She allowed her muscles to relax and closed her eyes.

Betty's proposal had been intriguing, but what worried her most was that she was considering it. There would be no quick fix to her imprisonment. *Perhaps Charles will under-*

stand. After all, I was never supposed to see him again. I should've been married by now. I'm still in some way free to decide what I want for my future. I may be stuck here, but I can at least choose what I will do with my days, not just spending them cooking and waiting to get pregnant. It may be that Betty's proposal will give me the freedom I have been looking for.

Her mind drifted back to the state of the bar. Betty could certainly use the help. The woman was alone. She did everything herself. *She must have no time off and, after dealing with all those rowdy men, she could probably use some.* Lyliana turned over and stared at the covered window. Faint shards of brighter darkness crept in around the drapes, throwing shifting tree shadows across the walls.

The wooden floor in the other room creaked. The door to her room edged open and quickly closed again. It was only Lester checking she was safe as he always did. She heard the telltale clink of a glass and the pop of a cork, Lester's routine every night since the argument between him and the three other men.

The next morning, Lyliana was awake with the parrots. She took a morning walk through the trees to allow Lester the chance to have his home to himself for a while. He had appeared not long after her, still dressed, his hair askew. His face showed the signs of too much liquor and a lack of sleep. His drawn expression and sluggish movements dissuaded conversation and encouraged Lyliana to make herself scarce.

She pushed through the many tropical plants skirting the edge of the property. The flowers in the undergrowth were in full bloom, adding speckles of colour to the otherwise green forest. Lyliana clambered uphill and allowed her mind to drift.

As she turned back towards the house, a mist began to

rise amongst the plants. The day was heating up, and even after her short time in Laffite, she could recognise the start of another hot and humid day building to full power.

By the time she returned, Lester was gone, leaving a tangle of discarded clothes as the only sign of his hasty departure. Hurriedly, she got ready and left the house. Instead of heading directly towards Betty's bar, she avoided the town and took the long way round to the harbour.

Out in the bay, a new arrival was at anchor. It had certainly not been there when she walked that way the night before. Lyliana squinted through the glare but could not see enough to recognise the vessel. *Betty was correct. This must be one of the ships she was expecting.* On the horizon were signs of another two vessels, presumably coming towards the harbour although from such a distance Lyliana could not tell.

An image of Charles came to mind, and she imagined boarding one of the ships and heading home. She smiled at the thought of the look on his face during their reunion. *If I get back, I will never leave him. Not again. No matter what.* She resolved to wait until the other vessels came in and search the town for their captains. If she wanted to get a message out to Charles, she would have to arrange it herself. With her mind made up, she headed back towards Betty's.

"More ships arrived in the bay," said Lyliana as she stepped through the bar entrance.

Betty nodded absently and continued rubbing down the tables before swapping her cloth for a brush to sweep the floor.

"Betty, did you hear what I said? There are more ships in the bay. You said that was good for business. It's brilliant. I thought you'd be more excited," Lyliana added when she received no response from the other woman.

"Indeed, it is goo'. But they'll all be 'ere soon, an' the place is a wreck."

"I will be here for a while. I can help you. How about those glasses behind the bar? They need cleaning, no?" She moved behind the counter.

"So you 'ave decided? You'll come and work for me?"

Lyliana harrumphed. She should have expected the question. She stared at the counter and shuffled her feet. *Wasn't she supposed to think about it?*

"There's no hurry. It jus' seems like you're 'orking anyway, you might as 'ell get paid."

"It's not that I don't want to. I appreciate the offer, and I am very interested." She rested both hands flat on the bar and stared at them for a moment. "You may think me a fool, but I still hope for rescue or escape. I know neither is likely or even possible. It is just—"

"You feel as though to accept my offer means you're givin' up. Means that you'll never go 'ome. That you have accepted your fate?" Betty interrupted impatiently.

Lyliana sighed and looked her straight in the eyes. "Some such like," she agreed and watched Betty return to work. The very idea that she had nothing to say in response filled Lyliana with anxiety. *Betty still clings to a glimmer of hope. Perhaps I can work with that...get her to help me.*

A throng of customers came in a few minutes later. Loud raucous laughter filled the previously empty bar with life. Betty and Lyliana switched places, and, while Betty served, Lyliana swept up the dust, shards of glass, grass, mud, and leaves and piled them all by the door.

The crowd dispersed into the far corner, and soon others filled the vacated space. A whole host of new faces, their attire and numerous tattoos marking them as sailors. They were already half drunk and telling competing sea stories in loud obnoxious voices, challenging each other to reach new levels of outlandish telling.

Things were just settling down into the lunchtime rush when the routine was disturbed. The ruckus began outside, but a bang of the front door and the appearance of two pirates brought the chaos inside. The bar fell into silence.

"Zarono is dead," said the shorter man, panting. He paused and looked about the room, waiting for a reaction. "Did you people not hear? Captain Zarono is dead."

The silence prompted the second man to speak. "Do you not understand what this means?"

Lyliana looked at Betty. Her reaction was one of shock mingled with fear. As the news filtered around the customers, her face expression showed signs of panic.

A shiver rippled down Lyliana's spine as her blood turned to ice. *Is this what I heard in Lester's house? Lester.* She threw the broom to the ground and rushed for the door, trying to resist the temptation to run. She knew instinctively that to draw attention to herself would create havoc.

I must find Lester.

In the street, people were shouting. Some pirates cheered but were quickly hushed by the majority. Rocks and other less dangerous items flew, thrown by the rowdiest pirates, rocketed across the path. She pushed through the crowd, desperate to get clear before panic developed into fighting. Her breath came in gasps. She pushed on. Her ankle twisted on a stone, but she ignored the pain and hurried up the street. By the time she was clear of the main walkway, her knees were burning, the pain in her ankle stabbing her with every step. The noise from the town reached a crescendo. The world was going mad.

As she approached the house, shouts and scuffles came from the back. Knowing better than to be caught out in the open by angry pirates, she slid around the wall and hid behind the corner. She tried to flatten her entire body against the stone and held her breath to listen. Lester's voice grew angry. She peered around the corner in time to see him punch one of the other men in the throat. He went down like a falling coconut. Another attacked Lester, keening a battle cry.

Lyliana had seen fighting before but nothing like this. This was a full-on brawl, no thought to honour, just violence. Her heart pounded. If they found her, she was dead. Lester could not help her.

A surprised cry from Lester drew her attention back to the danger. Lyliana ran. Without thinking, she ran away. Round the side of the house towards the trees. She flowed with the breeze northwards, making good progress despite the thick foliage. She stumbled over the bigger plants and broken branches, only just keeping her balance.

Her feet ground to an abrupt stop in a clearing. She held her breath to listen. There were no footsteps or telltale voices. Nothing to indicate she was followed. Lyliana let out a deep breath. She bent down and supported her arms on her knees as she inhaled sharply. Her heart finally slowed to normal rhythm, and she wiped the beaded sweat from her forehead.

The wind ruffled her hair. Irritably, she pushed the loose strands back over her shoulder and twisted her hair into a tight bun before she continued, this time at a more leisurely pace. Her ankle no longer hurt as much, but it would do her no good to test it again. As the heat of the day enveloped the trees, her pace slowed, and she changed direction. *Throw them off the scent if they decide to follow me.* She was starting to think like a fugitive.

As the day drew on, she grew tired, but there was

nowhere to rest. She was well aware of the dangers of being on the ground in the jungle, but she was not a good climber, and the lowermost branches of the trees were too high up. With this in mind, she turned her attention to her plans for the evening, although much of her decision-making would be dictated by finding a water source for she had brought none with her. Her situation could quickly become dire, but to return meant certain death.

CHAPTER 11
THE COVEN

During his week and a half residence at the coven, Syngh's situation had not improved. He was allowed to talk now but could not speak with anyone from who he could learn.

He had made friends with a lad about half his age named Jaden. Orphaned early in his life, the lad had resided in the coven since then. His vast knowledge had proved vital, especially his familiarity with the library, which was all the more surprising considering that he was illiterate. In return for this simple kindness, Syngh promised to teach in his letters. They had been inseparable ever since.

It developed into an effective alliance. The lad was continually bullied by the older boys. Syngh put a stop to that. He used his years of combat training to great effect during one particular incident that elevated him to undisputed leader of the coven pride. Jaden had risen with him. When he was not learning his letters, he was looking at pictures in the great printed books that filled the library.

Syngh was working on an edition written by one Mistress Roxanne. Her notes told of the recent allegiance between the werecats and the witches. He grew increasingly impatient with his findings. Jaden discouraged him from discussing such things with the other werecats. He was adamant about Syngh keeping his theories to himself. It was the strongest reaction he had seen from the lad, and the boy's loyalty touched him.

"*Surely, they would be enthusiastic to learn the truth? Perhaps this state of being has not always been,*" Syngh argued, starting at his own turn of phrase. It had not been the first time he noticed the witches' influence on him.

"*You do not know who you can trust, Syngh. Some of these people have been here since they were younger than me. Loyalty has been ingrained into them. The witches would not be happy that you have information that could be used against them.*"

He remained doubtful.

"*At least be cautious. Find out all you can before you decide to what to do. The witches believe that knowledge is power. It stands to reason that this is true.*" Jaden had returned to his studies as though nothing had been said.

Syngh realised that anyone in the library could have overheard him. His thick thigh muscle twitched. Perhaps Jaden had more potential than was immediately obvious upon first meeting him. His purple eyes fell upon the charcoal etchings on the far wall. They mocked him with the illusion of movement. They were watching him, judging.

Over the next week or so, Syngh read everything detailing the history of the coven from that first book through until the last entry. He found nothing from Mistress Tiniata but was not surprised. She had only just taken over.

Despite Jaden's warning, he questioned the other cats in the coven. They were either uninterested or unwilling to discuss the matter though Syngh could not establish why either scenario should be true. With every failed attempt to gain information, he became more determined, more convinced in a conspiracy theory he could not prove. Finally, in desperation, he began to work backwards from the original book.

He paused briefly to stare at the high arched windows, gaining inspiration from the watery shafts of wintry sun glancing off the dust spreading from the texts. He stretched his long fingers across the table and noticed the developing violet tingle of his cuticles that marked his advancing age. The years were passing faster than he would ever have thought possible when he was a cub.

The soft sounds of the library came into focus and then faded away as he flicked through a volume accredited to Mistress Walhac many moons before his arrival. The coven had been based in the mountains on the other side of Storm Pass. They had moved shortly after her last entry. He looked at Jaden, sitting as always, on the opposite side of the table. The boy looked up and met his glance, sending a glow of warmth through Syngh's chest. He returned to the book, buoyed by a feeling of being part of a trustworthy team, no longer stuck alone in the dark as he had been since his first day in the coven.

Syngh skimmed through the usual entries and lists. The coven had been much bigger at the time but seemed on the verge of collapse judging by the lists. The last few entries sucked in his attention like a starving leech.

'...We suffered great losses. I confess I am at a loss to know what to do. My ideas would likely not be well received, and yet I am forced to conclude this is the only recourse. Times are set to be difficult. If deceit is the only way then I must swallow my principles. Proximity is the key. We are too far from the Lowlands...'

As Syngh read on, he began to understand that the entry

referred to his ancestors. He had no idea how long werecats had inhabited the Lowlands, yet he knew instinctively she was referring to them. His mind blurred into a swirl of questions. What did it all mean? Memories of another passage drew him back to the first book. He rushed to the shelf and dragged the volume from the rack. Back at the table, he flicked to the last few entries made by Roxanne.

'...*Past mistakes cannot be repeated. It is no longer sufficient to dabble in potions. With the werecat nation once more behind the coven, much can be achieved with that stability. Without it, we may all be lost...*'

Syngh let out a deep breath that he had not realised he was holding. Silently, he pulled some paper close and copied the passages out, joining them together into one. The text coalesced in his mind. He swept the back of a hand over his forehead and put both hands over his mouth. Was he reading this right? He read it again, crossing his legs under the table. The room shrunk.

Without thinking, he stood, scraping the chair back noisily across the wooden planks. He shoved the paper into his pocket, scooped up the books, and thrust them back into shelf, disordered.

Down the corridor, he turned a corner and crashed to a halt. Mistress Ceri stood in the middle, blocking his way.

"Pardon, Mistress, I must pass," Syngh panted.

"And where might you be going in such a hurry? Do you not have jobs to complete?"

The dark stone of the corridor shut him in and seemed to suck all the air from the place. "I... This is my study time." The words seemed lame, like an excuse, even to him.

Ceri put one long fingernail on her lip and smiled a grimacing, nasty expression that did nothing to calm to Syngh's growing panic. "I see you spend much time in the library, doing research. Study is good, provided you limit the number of subjects you choose." She paused and stared until Syngh looked away. "Take care on the subject. Too much study, like too much talk, is bad for your health."

Syngh backed off one step, with him realising she had closed the gap between them. Ceri gripped his elbows tight and pulled him nearer.

"You have been warned now. There will not be a second warning." Any hint of her previous smile was now gone. Her eyes burned into him. The power seemed to transmit through her fingers and up his arm to keep the power of the gaze.

Syngh jerked and bucked, struggling to get free. His breath came in gasps as panic overtook him. He broke away and dodged past her.

He maintained his pace until he was outside and on the other side of the rear orchard. Footsteps behind alerted him to Jaden's proxity.

"Wait. What's the matter?" The boy was out of breath.

Syngh closed his eyes, slowed his breathing, and tried to calm his racing mind. "I wish I knew." He held out the copied paper to the boy. *Did she see me take it? No, she would have removed it.*

Jaden took it, looked at it, and turned back to Syngh with a look of disappointment.

"Sorry, I forgot," said Syngh, remembering the lad's limited reading ability that was further hampered by his own hurried script. He pushed Mistress Ceri from his mind. He read out the sheet to the lad, following the words with his finger so the boy could follow the text. "I wish I knew what it meant."

"Where did you see this?"

"The last part was some of the last entries made by the late mistress. Mistress Walhac entered the rest."

"I never heard of Mistress Walhac. Was she before Mistress Roxanne? I do not understand." Jaden looked distressed.

"No matter. I'm not sure I do. If I am right, this would throw all our assumptions to the wall." *How could it be wrong after what just happened?* "I grew up being told that we need witches. That we cannot survive without them. I have thought a lot about this over the last few years. It *never* made sense to me. These texts show our history to be flawed. We always believed our symbiotic relationship was necessary. If this is right… then all those who secretly hate the witches and think we have been enslaved are right. I do not know what to make of it." He took a deep breath. *And Mistress Ceri might have just confirmed it.*

"Perhaps… I am sorry, Syngh." Jaden hesitated but continued at an impatient gesture from Syngh. "Maybe you are only seeing what you want to see. Is that possible?"

Syngh stared at the lad, not for the first time surprised by his quiet intelligence and quick thinking. It was easy to underestimate him. He was suddenly very pleased that he would never be in a situation where there would be a battle of minds with Jaden. Syngh would be at a disadvantage. *I doubt it… but maybe.* "That is what I am afraid of. What if I am right though? I am more worried about that. If it ever got out…"

They lapsed into silence as they considered the possibilities.

CHAPTER 12
LYLIANA

Lyliana reached the water's edge and gasped. They were behind her, following close by, stalking her like prey. She thought she had lost them. *I stopped too long in the woods. I should've kept going. I knew it. I knew it. There's no time. They're going to find me. Oh God, which way now?*

She was panting as she looked across the water and then to her left and right as though she expected to see a sign saying, 'this way to safety'. She glanced behind her. Still no sign of them. *Whichever way you go, you must go now.* She chose right. Neither direction appeared particularly promising.

She staggered as she followed the rough path, keeping the water on her left. If only she could find some hiding place, a hole in the ground, space under a bridge. If there was a tree, she could climb. *I can't climb anyway so it makes no difference.*

After a few minutes, she heard a whistling in the distance behind her. Lyliana glanced back again. *Nothing yet.* She picked up the pace, her lungs and muscles burning with effort. Sweat dribbled down her face and followed the contours of her neck. It was just too hot. She wiped her cheeks across either shoulder, but it was not long before her face was dripping again.

She forced herself onwards. New sounds filtered through the background. As she continued, the noise grew louder and became recognisable as gushing water. Ripples broke the smooth surface of the lake. She pushed herself to a faster pace. All the time she had been gradually moving up the slope. The path grew slippery with mud, and she had difficulty walking on it as she drew closer to the sheer cliff from which the waterfall ran.

Following the path upwards, she avoided the wettest areas until she was in a position to peer down into the water and see the boiling froth churned up from the falling cascade. Lyliana brushed her matted hair back away from her forehead, tucked her lower lip over her upper and blew upwards, trying to cool her face. It didn't work. She pushed her head back and looked to the top of the deceivingly high cliff. The path seemed to go deeper and deeper into the waterfall.

She had to go somewhere; she could not climb up. There was no other option. They would find her long before she reached the top. She had watched them have dagger tossing competitions; some of the pirates could throw a fair distance. A lucky shot would be all that was needed to send her falling to her death.

A furtive glance behind confirmed her fears. *They are coming. I must get out of sight.* She picked up the pace, ignoring the fine mist from the falls. Closer to the water, she shielded her eyes from the damp onslaught and savoured the moisture on her dry lips.

Lyliana ducked behind some hedges that led to the top of the falls. With her progress hidden, she took more time to tread carefully and obscure her footprints. She climbed higher. The loud roar of the water became deafening. The fog thickened as she drew closer to the raging torrent. Closer inspection revealed a faint track leading behind the waterfall. With one last glance down the slope, she pushed through the lower bushes.

She skidded on wet stone. Green slime seemed to cover everything behind the waterfall. With one hand on the cliff wall, she turned carefully, placing each foot before moving the next. It was slow going but with less risk of falling to her death. Cautiously she peered around from behind the water curtain and searched for her pursuers. She saw no one, hoping the hedges and tall grasses would cover the obviousness of the entrance behind the waterfall. Her muscles went weak with relief. Her head spun as the adrenaline hit her senses without warning.

Satisfied that she could not be easily found, she moved further back into the cliff. Her arduous pace remained, as did the ever-present fear of slipping, this time into some hole she could not escape from rather than down the rock face. Further inside, the ground levelled out and stabilised as she moved away from the water. What she thought to be a small cave was actually a tunnel. She felt her way through the darkness with one hand on the wall and the other in front to prevent crashing into the side. The ground beneath her feet turned into a slight incline as she delved deeper inside the cliff.

If she could not see, then they could not see her. The logic of the thought gave her comfort, and she pushed on. After a while her movements became commonplace, a habit born of practise. Although she could not see, her instinct told her the tunnel was long.

Through the endless blackness of the tunnel, she

glimpsed a faint light. Lyliana kept moving but squinted into the darkness to better see the light. As she drew closer, the glimmer developed a bluish tinge and flickered on the stone as though it was reflecting off the water. As if to confirm her assumptions, a soft tinkling sound reached her and echoed against the walls. She focused on the sound and picked up the pace. The area around her began to smell like a stagnant pond. She breathed through her mouth as the scent grew overpowering.

The tunnel opened out into a brightly lit cave. It seemed to Lyliana's dazzled eyes that the water illuminated the cave. A small stream trickled down through the rocks on the far side of the cave and weaved past another group of boulders laid out in a table and chairs formation. The stream ended at a pool.

Lyliana raised her eyes. *Strange coincidence.* She moved closer to the water and peered down into its depths. There was no obvious light source; the water was too deep. Closer inspection revealed a magnitude of coloured lights or so it appeared from the changing tones. She studied the ceiling above the pond and saw the same flashing colours reflected across the roof of the cave.

She edged around the cave towards the rocks on the other side. On impulse, she sat on one of the chair-like stones and leaned against the larger one. The set up was at exactly the perfect height for a table and chairs, yet she was sure this was not the intent of the arrangement.

The harrowing experience of her initial escape had left her mind numb, and her muscles weakened. She sat down for a few moments, allowing the regular pulsing of her heartbeat to calm her. Fear of the pirates made her stop and listen for movement in the tunnels, but she heard nothing beyond the trickling of water.

Her eyes fell on the pool, and a sudden thirst struck. *Is it clean enough?* She cradled her chin in her palms and noted the dirt caked all over her hands and under her fingernails. Her greasy blond hair fell in front of her face. She brushed it back and looked longingly at the pool.

Thirst finally won the battle, and she left her rock to kneel by the stream. She noted the tiredness in her green eyes; their usual glint faded beyond recognition. Gingerly, she cupped some water in her hands and dipped her tongue into it. It tasted like gold, but even with the metal tang, it was certainly better than the ship's supply had been. She filled her hands and drank her fill. *If I can drink it, I can bathe in it.* Forgetting the pirates in that moment, she threw her clothes off and tossed them on the ground to stand naked in the cave above the pool. She glanced back at her forlorn clothing, and in an inexplicable change of mind, she collected them together and dumped them on the rock where they were less untidy.

Clutching the edges of the pool for stability, she stretched out a long leg and dipped her toe in to test the water. Finding it cool but not too cold, she stepped in and lowered herself down until only her shoulders and head were exposed. The water seemed somehow softer than she expected, and it warmed quickly, allowing her to slip down further and rest her head on the stony edge. She closed her eyes and tried to relax her muscles.

A slight echoing drone reached her. She had not noticed it while her eyes were open, but with the loss of sight, the sounds of the cave gained clarity. She listened for a few seconds. *What is that?* She ducked her head under the water and tossed the hair back across her shoulders. The droning was still there, yet she could determine no source for the continuous noise. She wiped the water off and repeated the motion a few times, feeling instantly better. She looked about for a rock to scrape off the worst of the muck but found nothing and gave up quickly.

The water helped to ease her tension, somehow giving her a sense of safety she had not felt upon first discovering the cave. She splashed her hands about in the water and wiggled her toes before turning her attention to the lights in the middle of the pool. With no idea as to the depth of water in the centre, her movements were cautious as she approached the middle. It was only a couple of paces before she was swimming and just one or two strokes before she was directly above the light. Once again, she looked at the ceiling of the cave and saw her own shape casting a dabbled and distorted shadow. She moved her arms and legs, spreading and shifting the dimness into wild shapes. She smiled, amused by the random patterns. The colours were more intense from her new angle as though the water depth enhanced them. The vivid colours made her movements all the more surreal.

She dived again and again. On each occasion, she failed to reach the bottom before she needed to come up for air. *It cannot be so deep. I am not well practised with diving, but I could usually hold my own at home. Perhaps the water is different here, but it cannot be harder than the sea.*

After her third attempt, she returned to the edge of the pool and searched the cave for loose rocks. There were many around the edges, but mostly they were too large. Finally, seeing a suitably heavy piece of stone, she clutched it in both hands and returned to the water. This time she swam at an angle, holding the stone in front of her, and heading directly towards the lights. With some effort, she touched the bottom while remembering to keep a hold of the rock. She saw the lights for one brief second, and at that distance, they appeared to be gemstones, six of them all different colours. She used her feet to shove off from the bottom of the pond again and headed back to the surface for air.

Those gems might be worth something. Perhaps I could buy passage back home. At least I might have some leverage to escape from the pirates. Her gasping increased as she realised the possibilities of her sudden pending fortune. Stealing herself against the renewed effort, she dived once more down into the depths of the pool.

The need to use the stone to get deep enough restricted her movements, but finally she collected all the gems and spread them out on the makeshift table. They were indeed precious stones of some kind, and their colours were even more magnificent than they first appeared. They lit up the cave like a thousand shining candles. She studied each one in turn, inspecting the mystical colours that danced from every angle. Each stone had a different base colour, and yet they all seem to glow in a similar fashion.

She got the impression they were a set. As she studied them, she rearranged them into patterns on the table First blue then red and silver but always the darker one in the middle. Even the middle stone shone with colour, although it appeared to have no light like the others.

The sound of movement filtered through the tunnel. She froze, looking from the gems to the entrance. The sounds grew louder, more intense.

It must be the pirates. What do I do? They found me. Hurriedly she pulled on her clothes and shoved the stones deep in her pockets, hoping the lights would not shine through the cloth. Darkness fell over the cave.

CHAPTER 13
DILLITAY

Dillitay jerked at the sound of swearing voices approaching. They closed in on his position, and he could hear what they were saying. Their irritation with Lyliana was obvious. They were making no bones about what they were going to do when they found her. He moved closer and watched them approach with their weapons barred in front.

They were a more cutthroat bunch than most, from their foul language to the reek of stale sweat. Dillitay glanced behind, listening for sounds of the girl. She was quiet. He flitted higher to estimate how long before they reached her. Not long at all. The leader was hurrying them on as though on a timetable. No doubt, they had drinking plans or some other nefarious activity in mind. Lyliana would suffer from the inconvenience of her presence. The leader slipped and slid over the rocks, causing raucous laughter as he fell and brown goo covered him. The language he used upon finally recovering himself was colourful, even by Dillitay's standards.

I must warn her. She needs to hide. There is no point in her coming all this way just to be caught again. But even as Dillitay thought it, he knew it was not so simple. She *would* be caught. The only question was how much she would suffer. He pushed his hand under his hat and scratched his head.

He flitted back inside the cave, utilising the wind currents to guide him. The small light from his dust helped but only a little as it was mostly behind him. Halfway in, he stopped and checked his position. Cocking one ear, he heard nothing. The pirates had not entered the cave yet, and he wondered briefly how long such luck would last. *Maybe they won't find the cave. Maybe we came to the right place after all.* He continued down the dark tunnel listening for sounds all around him. Rising voices told of the pirates' approach. They had found the cave.

She is hiding. He smiled. *Sensible girl. I knew I wasn't wasting my time with that one.* After a sudden thought, the darkness worried him. *Did she find the gems? I should see some signs of them. I brought her to find the gems. It is all for nothing if she loses them.*

A scuffling up ahead drew his interest and, dampening his dust, he flew to the heights of the cave and surveyed the area. He could not see Lyliana.

The voices behind him grew clearer.

How to find out if she has the gems? Perhaps we can come back later? I just have to wait and see what happens. His heart rate climbed. He found a rock and hid behind it, waiting. Dillitay had hoped to avoid this, wished for her not to be found, and prayed that she and her new charges would be safe...assuming she had them. *I've done my best. I can do no more.*

The pirates entered the cave one by one, noisily and uncaring of the disturbance they created. They yelled idle threats at each other, Lyliana, and anyone else who might be listening.

Lyliana remained hidden.

"Come out. We know where you are. The longer it takes to find you, the worse it will be," said one pirate, slurring under the influence of too much drink. Where he got the liquor so far from camp Dillitay knew not.

"Come on. We only want to have some fun," said another who lit a torch as they advanced through the cave.

Dillitay watched and held his breath. "Stay still. Do not come out," he whispered to the cave wall. No one would hear him; his voice was too faint.

Lyliana remained silent. Dillitay watched and waited, willing her to keep calm. Metal reflected the firelight, showing they were getting closer. They were going to find her. There was nothing he could do. Perhaps he could help her later.

They dragged her from her hiding place. Dillitay watched, helpless.

"Knew we'd find ya. There ain't nowhere you can hide from us. Stupid girl," one of them said, binding her hands.

Dillitay flitted to a better hiding place.

Lyliana staggered, regained her footing, and meekly followed them.

"Good, that's better. Perhaps we can tell the boss that you were a good little girl, and he'll go easier on you?"

"What about you guys? There won't be much of me left by the time I get there. I know how this goes," said Lyliana.

Stupid girl, don't taunt them.

"Thanks for the offer, love," said the one who had done most of the talking. "But we are under orders. Can't annoy the boss."

They passed from the cave and out into the open. Dillitay could see clearly the relief on Lyliana's face that the pirate's revelation caused. She held her head proudly, knowing they could not touch her.

Dillitay shook his head. *Don't get cocky.*

"So, what you are saying is that if I run, you can't do anything?" She smiled as she spoke.

They laughed and stopped to glare at her. "You tried that already, and we can do what we want if we don't leave a mark."

Dillitay let out a deep breath as he watched her cockiness deflate.

He followed them, flitting between the trees and bushes, keeping out of sight. They travelled for miles that day, not even stopping when night fell, and the route became dangerous underfoot. They paid no mind to her difficulties as she struggled to keep her balance with her hands tied.

At one point, Dillitay managed to travel on Lyliana's shoulder undetected, the darkness covering the pirate's view of him. Periodically, he ducked into her pocket where he had found the gems earlier. They were still safe.

The pirates taunted her, calling her names, and painting a vivid picture of her fate once she returned to captivity. Their descriptions left no room for imagination. Lyliana remained silent. Dillitay watched as they took turns trying to get a reaction from her, and each time they tried, the one holding her rope would jerk it hard until she fell. The scrapes on her hands began to bleed, yet she remained quiet.

Dillitay was helpless. He could not even dust her without being seen. He managed to pix the one holding the rope. Great welts appeared on his hands until he could no longer hold the rope. He left another pirate to continue and disappeared between the trees. It was a long time before he returned. As fun as it was for Dillitay to watch the pirate suffer, he could not risk the same thing twice for fear of bringing unwanted attention to Lyliana. Finally, around the middle of the night, they stopped by a stream, tied Lyliana to a tree, and made camp for the night.

The clinking of tippling bottles finally stopped, replaced by snoring. Dillitay settled in his tree above Lyliana and hoped that she would get some sleep. He woke her sometime later when one of the pirates approached her menacingly. She scrambled as far as her bonds allowed. He put his finger to his lips to tell her to be quiet.

Dillitay flashed through the darkness and stabbed the pirate under one eye with his sword.

"What the f...?" He flapped his hand in front of his face but continued advancing.

"I'll scream," threatened Lyliana.

"No, you won't," he said and shoved his hand across her mouth.

The pirate snatched his hand away from her face. *Good girl. She bit him.* Dillitay laughed as the pirate swore and let out a stream of obscenities that would have startled his colleagues.

Lyliana's squeal startled even Dillitay. There was a general scuffling, and the camp awoke. The men rushed over, rubbing the sleep from their eyes, and surrounded the pair. Dillitay flew higher into the tree for fear of being seen.

"That one," she motioned awkwardly in her bonds. "He attacked me. He tried to attack me."

All eyes landed on the pirate. Footsteps heralded the arrival of a man Dillitay assumed to be the leader of the group as he pushed his way to the front.

"What was he going to do? Tell me what?" All eyes went to the leader.

Dillitay could not see his expression in the darkness, but he could sense the swelling rage.

The pixie smiled, satisfied. *She will be safe until we reach camp.*

CHAPTER 14
HILLAWAY

Charles watched the mayor shove his twitching left hand behind his back. The flush of irritation was familiar to him. It hid the worry his father had never been able to hide. His neck flushed, and he breathed deeply, forcing air into his tightened lungs.

"What can we do about this? The lad probably just ran away. Kids do that occasionally. How long did you say he'd been missing?" asked the governor.

"The family will *expect* us to do something. We must be seen to make every effort. The boy is the son of the most prominent banker in town. It does not do to aggravate the man in control of the money," replied the mayor. He shifted his weight from one foot to the other.

Governor Mackenzie hung his head, visibly collecting his thoughts, and reining in his temper. "Do not lecture me, *sir*, on the needs of this town. I know Mr Hemming much better than you. He is fully conversant with our situation. He put forward the money for the defence posts. Honestly, I'm surprised he's not here himself. That is why I wonder as to the veracity of his claim."

The tension crackled like static. Charles took a pace backwards.

"My apologies, *sir*. I spoke out of turn. He would have come himself, but he had pressing business at work. I imagine he is collecting together the expected ransom," said the mayor in full retreat.

The governor huffed. "Has there been a ransom demand? That would certainly suggest pirates are responsible."

Charles nodded. *If the pirates are involved perhaps that is a clue as to what happened to Lyliana. It is worth getting involved just for that.*

"None so far, but it is expected," replied his father.

"If I may?" Saliva pooled in Charles' mouth. "I should like to take part in the investigation. It may lead to information about Lyliana *if* the pirates are involved."

"Son, I understand your frustration with Lyliana's situation, but this is hardly the time. We need to be focused, and your loyalties are divided. I am afraid I must insist on you allowing someone else to do this." The mayor walked over to his son and put a reassuring hand on his shoulder.

They are not divided in the least. Charles stood rigid.

George Mackenzie sighed. "We cannot make any rash decisions. First, we must discover if it was the pirates. There have been no vessels sighted by the lookout towers up and down the coast." The governor waved his arms to highlight his point.

"Perhaps they attacked overland? The element of surprise?" suggested the mayor tentatively.

Charles rolled his eyes. Sometimes his father was in a world of his own. He never thought before he spoke.

"When did you ever hear of pirates attacking overland? They need the ships to achieve anything significant. We will wait for more information." Governor Mackenzie sat behind his desk and busied himself with some papers, pointedly ignoring them both.

The meeting was over.

Charles followed his father outside and across the empty square, dodging puddles from the night's rain. There was much to discuss, and yet he said nothing. His father must be feeling bad enough as it was without him rubbing salt in the wound.

"Thank you for your input, son. I am not sure what the governor thinks waiting will achieve. I must go see Mr Hemming. If you hear anything, you will let me know, yes?"

Charles nodded and headed in the opposite direction. In his mind, his father's last words transferred responsibility to him. *So be it.*

————

As expected, his friend was at the docks, tending a ship. Trey was busy, but never too busy to speak to Charles. As Charles approached, Trey sat on a crate and patted himself down. His knees were dusty, and his sandals featured more grey than brown. The dirt on his face left him looking older than his thirty-five years and highlighted the spreading wrinkles about his eyes. His usually dark hair appeared grey and tired.

"You heard about the missing kid?" asked Charles, coming to a stop before the crate.

"I would be surprised if he was the first. I heard about Lyliana also. I am sorry, my friend," replied Trey.

Charles exhaled. Everywhere he went people asked him of her. It left him so helpless he could almost go to bed and never get up again. "I've heard nothing. It occurs to me perhaps this is connected. My father believes pirates took the lad. He is only concerned about keeping the boy's father happy, but if it was pirates, I cannot imagine how."

"How could it be the pirates?" Trey shook his head. He put his hands down on the crates on either side of him and leaned back. "We've seen no pirates for months. I hear of them in the north but none here. Of course, the seas are still dangerous, but less so than in the north."

"I was hoping you might have heard something on your travels." He swallowed and chewed the inside of his cheek. "Perhaps something you are reluctant to say in open company?" The inflection in his voice turned the statement into a question.

Trey looked at the ground and shook his head. He scratched his nose and wiped one index finger down the right side of his lip. "I don't know. We hear all kinds of things. I heard that the Coven has taken to kidnapping people and doing tests. They are trying to make some kind of super witch," he scoffed. "It is mad what people will say. Witches have not been major players for years. Most people don't believe in them. My parents believe that if the witches do *exist*, they're just a group of humans playing with chemistry. Besides, if they were kidnapping people, some would need to escape to tell these stories. What poppycock."

Charles smirked at the odd word and cast his mind back. He remembered seeing some strange-looking people in town of late and noted them as oddities. *Could they have been witches?*

Trey eyed him. "You know something?"

"I did see some strange people around a while back." He shrugged. "As you say, they are reputed to stay hidden. I still believe this is related to what happened to Lyliana. Perhaps the pirates are expanding, and this is all part of the plan. *I* would go to Gamola Harbour and investigate." He rolled his eyes and scrunched one side of his mouth. "My father will not authorise it." He shifted and sat next to his friend.

"Not everyone needs your father's approval." He cocked an eyebrow. "If you must go, it is better you go with friends and weapons. I would do it for you and Lyliana, but..." He paused and raised his hand to stall Charles's response. "I have a full schedule."

Charles exhaled sharply and held his breath. He shook his head slightly. "No, no, I know you are busy... I was not expecting..." *He understands. There's no need to explain.* He closed his eyes for a moment and then looked straight at Trey. "It is hard, not knowing, not being able to do anything. I did not mean to imply—"

"I know." Trey hesitated. "I mean, I can imagine... I can check the charters again, but I think there is nothing for a few weeks at least. It is a long voyage. Not something I could cover with a believable excuse. And the crew..."

"Yes, they could not keep that a secret. A few jars of hock and the story would reach the ends of the Giant's Lair." Charles nodded and smiled weakly at his friend. There was no way.

Trey frowned and held up one finger before pacing away towards the gangway. Charles watched him disappear and kept his eyes on the gangway until his friend returned a few minutes later.

"I am not sure," Trey shunted some sheets through his fingers. "Ah, yes. There it is. Not this month, but the one following. I would need to do some planning. It will not be easy." He pursed his lips, but his eyes brightened suddenly. "I make no promises, but next month I might be able to help you. The less I say now, the better, but there is a chance. You will need to let me know if you are interested, and I may need some help to pull it off."

Charles shoved his hands in his pockets and clasped the fabric tightly. "Anything, I—"

"Remember, no promises," Trey whispered.

"I understand." Charles stopped himself from asking if there was some way they could leave earlier. If this were to happen, even he understood the danger Trey was putting himself in, and not just from the voyage.

"We shall talk again the weekend after next. In any case, I shall listen out for news of the boy."

"Thank you, my friend. I would have you know how much I appreciate all your help. Until the next weekend then?" He stood, shaking hands with his friend in a tight grip. "You never did tell me where you come from?"

Trey smiled and clamped his second hand over the first. He nodded once and let go.

Charles sighed as he left the quayside. *Why do I keep asking? Perhaps one day?* He had not gotten what he came for, but the consolation prize was worth more. For a chance to find out what happened to Lyliana he would have done almost anything, and yet, in the end, nothing had been required. He headed home with a spring in his step, his mind clearer than it had been in weeks.

CHAPTER 15
LYLIANA

Lyliana lay on the soft grass of their favourite spot. It was far enough from the house to be private. The clearing had just the right proportion of shade and sunshine to make it warm and comfortable. The nearby stream trickled a calm watery tingle and added to the private ambience. Lyliana's suggestion that it would be a nice, secluded camping spot was met with amusement, and yet Lester showed no reluctance to spend many an afternoon there.

On this occasion she was alone, leaving Lester to his piles of worked created by Zarono's death. His increased status had resulted in a corresponding expansion of his duties, contradicting the assumption of nepotism in a choice of lieutenant, given the recent history of betrayal. But the new guy, whose name Lyliana did not yet know, had no interest in such things. By Lester's account, he had very little interest in anything, particularly administrative duties. They had discussed this lapse in leadership more than once with growing concern.

Lyliana rolled and propped herself up on one elbow

where she lay for some time watching the forest hopefully for signs of Lester. She missed him. Not for the first time she realised that his absence made her ache. It was also not the first time such thoughts drew her attention to the fact that she was beginning to adapt to her new environment.

A pain in her arm interrupted her thoughts. Ignoring the tingling of her elbow, she rose from the soft grass and headed into the nearby bushes, following her secret markings along the path until she came upon her goal: a small mound of recently dug earth sitting under a gay cluster of flowers. She laid her hand flat on the dirt and softly rubbed the soil between her fingers. Her wry smile faded as she considered the implications of burying treasure while surrounded by pirates. The comparison with children's bedtime stories drew too close a connection to be ignored. Ancient tales from books left behind centuries before by early humans who had lived before the arrival of the new species. Her knowledge of history was limited, arrested by a long family tradition not to believe in the old ways before The Clash. So little was known of that era that it was barely mentioned in the school rooms back home.

She dropped to the ground and rested her arm on the mound of treasure. No one else knew about this place, not even Lester. He had been within a few metres of the hoard but never close enough to suspect.

Her decision to hide the gems had been instinctive, inexplicable, and out of character, not to mention lucky in that the pirates had not searched her when they returned after her attempted escape. *They may be a way to get home. They are obviously valuable. Maybe I could sell them?* She thought at first that they were made up of swirling colours and had mistakenly interpreted that to mean there will be worth a lot of money. Upon closer inspection, the swelling patterns were not colours. There was something inside, an artefact of unknown origin. So, at the first opportunity when Lester started to let his guard down again, she buried them and carefully made sure no attention was drawn when she inspected the stash.

Warmth radiated through the soil, at odds with the cooler ground round about. She moved clear and put the back of her hand on top of the pile. The temperature was higher than it should be in the shade of the trees.

A lightness in her chest hurried her digging. She shoved away the loose dirt, taking care not to scatter it too far so that she could replace it when she had finished her investigation. She bent low into the hole and removed the final particles of soil before gently lifting the leaf-bound bundle clear.

She placed them carefully on the grass beside her. The leaves smouldered in the scolding heat, and she flicked them free. A blinding light emanated from the gems, brighter than she had ever seen them before. As she sat back and stared, the heat spread outwards to reach her across the clearing from the orbs.

The twisting movements inside each bright shade of light expanded. The dark swirls intensified as though the shell of the gems was thinning. She drew closer and studied the blue jewel. Lyliana glanced about her and listened. Looking for any sign of intrusion.

The red gem flashed brighter, turning from deep crimson to pink. Redness mingled with the blue light of the other jewel and combined into a purple glow that turned the nearby foliage a sickly mud colour.

She sat back as one by one the stones floated into the air. Each hovered at varying heights above the ground. They twisted, turned, and intermingled amongst themselves as though dancing their own intricate rhythm. The glare intensified, and all colours of the rainbow spread. Lyliana shifted further backwards to give them more room. The stones flickered and vibrated, leaving echoes battling through her brain. Not so much a noise as a sensation. The surrounding foliage shook and quivered as if in fear of a powerful spell.

Lyliana thrust her hands over her ears and closed her eyes and mouth. She gritted her teeth against the grating mental screeches. She rolled backwards, fighting her unfocused mind. Was she shaking, or was it the ground? She forced her eyelids open and squinted through the glare. There was nothing but bright rainbow lights, rotating, swirling, and merging. She squeezed her eyes closed tightly and curled up in a ball. As the reverberations grew unbearable, they ceased suddenly, leaving only the light. When Lyliana finally opened her eyes, only a slight glare remained, yet the memory of the onslaught burned her corneas.

It was an amazing sight. Despite all the brilliance and power and burning intensity of the lights, the grass about the gems was untouched. The plants round about bore no evidence of the apparent burning. Even the birds in the trees continued to chirp.

With some effort, she pushed hands out in front of her and stared as though she had never seen her fingers. Her skin was normal, her nails untouched. The temperature in the clearing was normal, like nothing happened. Lyliana rose and looked about, reassuring herself that all was well. She frowned as her mind wrestled with the confusion.

A second glance confirmed her thoughts. The gems were no longer. Only the light remained. Six creatures now sat where the stones had been.

The animals curled together as if protecting each other. Their heads snapped up at her approach. One sat up above the others and hissed. Its golden colouring flashed in the residual glare that dappled through the surrounding plant life. Startled, she paused. The creature hissed angrily then retreated back to the safety of the group.

From a cautious distance, she studied the animals. They were reptilian with glossy scales and very sharp teeth. Ridges followed the line of their back from a point on their forehead. A small blunt horn adorned the top of their nose. From her point of observation, she could see a long skinny tail that tapered into two prongs in a V shape.

She edged closer and lowered herself to the ground, instinctively knowing that making herself small would appear less aggressive. Finally, after some careful manoeu- vring, she got closer. Every now and again, one of them gave her a wary glance, but after a while, they became used to her. They seem to accept her. She lay in wonderment for some time studying them.

When a red leg stretched out from the huddle, she saw powerful hindquarters and small feet with toes tipped with sharp brown claws. Orange flashes shimmered over the scaly leg, mesmerising Lyliana with the beauty of the various rippling shades.

"Astounding," she murmured.

Steeling her courage, she shuffled closer and held one hand out across the grass, palm upwards. Six pairs of eyes followed her movements. Once she was sure they were accepting her, she reached her arm out further. Closer and closer still until she was just inches away. She watched, her body frozen in caution. She waited, frozen in nervous awe, just a slight twitching of her index finger to mark her intent.

When there was no reaction to her finger movement, she gently tapped the ground. "Come on, come to me," she whispered, in a soothing tone. She hissed slightly to get their attention and patted the ground again.

The golden lizard raised itself and opened its mouth in a silent hiss. It just watched with reptilian eyes. It appeared to be studying her, sizing her up. A pale pointed tongue emerged and licked the top lip furtively.

They watched each other for some minutes. It rotated its head through almost one hundred and eighty degrees as it eyed her from different angles. The twists in its neck threw shards of light in every direction but allowed her to see more clearly the ridges along its back. The protrusions gave the impression of solid armour plating, yet they were flexible and very shiny. She slapped the ground.

The creature tossed its head irritably and bounded upwards, stretching its wings in an impressive spectacle of power.

They have wings. They look so big with their wings spread. It can't be possible. They're so small. How did I not see? She estimated the animal to be about twenty centimetres, allowing for wingspan. The wings folded again as the creature landed before her. It raised the leathery, almost transparent extremities and gave her a perfunctory sniff. Apparently satisfied, it jumped forward again and landed on her hand. It sniffed her palm. It looked up, keeping its head below its body and arched its wings. The creature hissed once showing a double line of sharp jagged teeth.

Lyliana smiled, "Hello, little one. You're very light." She kept her hand still as the animal settled into her palm. She drew her hand closer. It watched but made no effort to move away. Finally, she was holding out one finger in front of the creature's face. It tilted its head, one eye wide, and then leaned forward for another sniff. It jerked its head back and jumped into the air to land once more, this time on her outstretched finger.

With her attention on the golden creature, she had ignored the others. Their protective huddle had loosened, and they were sitting nearby almost in straight line watching her. The forward most one squeaked, attracting the attention of 'Goldy'. The other creatures bounded in her direction. They encompassed her in a semicircle and sat watching. Lyliana returned their attention, keeping one eye on her newest friend.

What are you? I never saw such animals. I never even read about anything so small and cute. And so friendly. It's like they want to play.

A resounding bang interrupted Lyliana's thoughts. The result was immediate. The golden creature leapt into the air and landed on her head. The others, still on the ground, turned sharply, stretched out their wings, and lowered their heads. They hissed furiously. The one on her head gave a sort of bark and launched itself into the air where it hovered, hissing and spitting. The others remained on the ground but watched intently.

Lyliana watched awestruck. *They are protective. They are protecting me.* The realisation was startling. She raised her eyebrows. *They are protecting me.*

A fluttering behind made her turn. A pixie hovered above her. The little man was dressed like her imagination of Peter Pan, the character from the ancient stories. He had a savage face, softened by long dark hair, and yet the sight of his weapons contrasted sharply with her first impression. At any other time, she might have been surprised, but the arrival of the animals desensitised her.

"Hello, my name is Dillitay. You are going to need my help." He bobbed in the air and looked warily at the lizards.

CHAPTER 16
NEEM

The pixie, Neem, pushed back the leaves that sheltered his small residence from the ravages of wind and weather. Sunlight etched against twitching leaves, ruffled by a light breeze. A perfect setting for his morning nectar fix. He pulled a small bench forward a little so that he could lean back comfortably against the wall. He perched with his legs stretched out in front of him and looked out over the surrounding land.

He had purposely chosen this location for his home. With a clear view of the bridge across the river, it seemed like a good place to keep an eye on the comings and goings of the enclave. Primarily, his motive was to distance himself from the clan. Close proximity resulted in an expectation to partake of despised enclave rituals. He had enough of those in the past, but now the situation had changed. Of late, he was getting the distinct impression that it was time to reassert himself.

He sipped his nectar, savouring the sweet tangy aromas that tingled on his tongue and the smooth subtlety of the sensations in his throat. His morning routine had been the same for years. That was set to change. The time for his revenge fast approached. It had been three or four years since 'the incident'. His resentment still burned as fiercely as it had back then. They had no right to bypass him that way. They had ignored him as though he was nothing and after he had given so much. Neem had been instrumental in forming the enclave. He had worked tirelessly to build the town and protect its citizens.

What had he received for his trouble? Nothing. He had not needed recognition, yet it would have been nice to be acknowledged. To know that all his hard work was not in vain. To be appreciated. At the time, he had meekly put forward the point that without him, they would not have been so successful. His complaints fell on deaf ears. Neem was determined to set right those wrongs.

The pixie clans had been on the verge of civil war. The former Emperor's dictatorship spanned the generations and brought them to the edge of disaster. Even now, no one knew how he endured so long. Some blamed dark magic. Others claimed he was a freak of nature. Most were just pleased he was gone.

Since that time, there had been no emperor. The position had been demolished, as though to erase the title they would erase the shame and history of what had gone before. The king was the second reigning monarch in the new order. The first had been just and fair. Some called him weak, but they were unheeded. Many were unsure of the new king, but one thing was certain, he had a vision, and he would go to great lengths to realise it. First and foremost, had been the defence of the clans, and to that end, he created the Enclave. His most trusted advisers had guided the building of the stronghold. Chief amongst them was Neem. But he had fallen into disgrace due to his liaisons with females of the court. Not wanting to be tarred by this reputation, the king demoted him.

At first, Neem had not blamed the king. He deserved punishment, and he would take it with his head held high. But as the months ran on, his resentment grew. So began his plans to exact revenge on the very nation he had fought so hard to protect. These thoughts coloured his vision. They filled his every moment. He grew bitter. He moved away from the main town and isolated himself. No one saw it coming. Neem had no family, no one to turn to. No one who would pick up on the subtle hints.

Every morning he sat in his seat, staring out over the bridge, planning and plotting. In honour of the occasion, Neem donned his best outfit, not the uniform he had once been accustomed to wearing but one with little differences that no laymen would see. He took great care over every detail before finally straightening his jacket and regarding the results in the mirror. He polished the shining ebony bow and refilled his quiver. He checked that his dagger was neatly ensconced in the scabbard and finally donned his pointy scarlet hat that he cocked a little bit to the left, just to set him apart from those he would be going against.

Neem checked one more time in the shiny paper he used as a mirror and exited silently, pulling the door closed behind him and replacing the leaves that hid his small abode.

No one noticed him enter the palace. The guards were mostly new recruits. Those that had been there when he was in place had been promoted. The rest were gone. There was no one to challenge his presence.

He went into the great entrance and walked the hall adorned with all kinds of decorations and trophies of battles and hunting. Every item was familiar. Every passageway and every hiding place was his design. It was too easy. Neem hid himself in the dark corner of the main hall that led down to the caverns.

It was not long before he heard voices approaching. At that distance, it seemed likely from the general tones that it was some of the royal family. He strained his ears and heard the princess. Her high-pitched voice was distinctive as was her excitement. He concentrated his attention towards her.

Neem peered down from his position on the doorway ledge and confirmed it was the princess, and her mother, the queen. Queen Termurica looked as lovely as ever, her flowing golden hair secured tidily in an elaborate braid of the kind that only well-trained maids could fashion. Her bright eyes shone from behind luscious lashes. Her delicate make-up was perfectly donned to show off every gorgeous feature of her smooth face.

For all the queen's beauty, her daughter outmatched her in every way. The girl had taken to dying her hair with red rose petals. The effect was to give her long dark locks a reddish tinge that flashed in the light. Such reflections were not in view from his position. He could only visualise them from memory. Where her mother had pale features brightened by her makeup, the daughter was dark in every way. Her rouge was brownish rather than pale and her lip colouring a dark maroon that highlighted the red specs in her eyes. The habit of wearing dark dresses was softened by the adornment of paler decorations, usually red.

On this day, the princess was wearing maroon slippers and a matching sash draped round the skirt of her dresses. Her hair was piled high above her head and secured with red gems that flashed as she moved. For a moment, Neem forgot the purpose of his visit. Enchanted, he watched the ladies glide down the corridor towards the cavern. As they drew closer, he overheard their conversation.

"I saw the glow when I went to break my fast. I never saw such a sight. The only thing down here is the box. I thought I had better bring it to Father's attention. I could not find him, so I came to you," she spoke rapidly with hardly a breath.

Termurica, by contrast, spoke slowly, calmly, and with the measured tones of command. "We shall have a look, my dear, but I am sure it is nothing. No one comes down here. Even your father and I very rarely venture into the caverns. There is just no reason. They are so well guarded. I am sure everything is as it should be."

Neem watched the pair disappear into the lower chamber of the cavern and listened intently. There was no sound and no sign of the light Frankine reported seeing. Footsteps signalled the arrival of the king. He appeared in the small opening just as they exited the lower cavern.

"What occurs here?"

"She thought she saw a glow from the cave, so we went down to have a look. Everything seems okay. There is no sign of tampering, however unlikely. I thought it best to check it out. You know our daughter is more observant than most."

The king put his arm around his daughter and pulled her close. He kissed her on the forehead. "My dear, it is good that you are so vigilant. You know I have always appreciated your support." He kissed her again and then turned at the sound of more footsteps clattering on stone.

Neem pushed himself further onto the ledge and out of view. He could not afford to be caught. The king would recognise him.

The footsteps stopped, and the Neem heard the clear tones of the clan chief Galen.

"Majesty, we have received a letter from the east. I know not how long it has been in transit. It was just delivered. It bears the seal of the Roamers."

"Did you open it? What does it say?" asked the king impatiently.

Neem heard the rustling of paper and the clear sound of a scroll unrolling.

"It says, Majesty, that there has been a great event. It is written by one… Dillitay," he hesitated over the name. "If I recall, he is the young man we sent east to keep eyes on the pirates of Laffite." There was an extended silence before he continued, "It tells of one woman who has found some gems. The lad is not certain, but he believes them to be wyvern eggs. Additionally, he reports that she appears to think they are jewels of monetary value. The girl is being held captive by the pirates. He writes that if he is correct about the eggs we should be informed immediately. He includes at the bottom of the letter a description of the items in question."

There was another rustling of paper, and Neem looked down just in time to see the king snatch the scroll from his chief hands.

"This description seems consistent with what I know of wyvern eggs. I must consult the histories."

"It is not possible, my love. These creatures have been gone for so long. Where would the girl find such a thing?" asked his wife, the disbelieve clear through her tone.

There was a jostling sound, and Frankine spoke, "I wish I could see them. I read all the stories. They are supposed to be very exciting beasts. And full of magic that nobody could understand. I thought this was just a fairy tale."

A coughing from the corridor sounded like the king.

"Myself, I cannot imagine the lad is correct, but I must make sure. Galen, you will reply to the boy and find all the information you can. Perhaps he will have learned more by the time the letter reaches him. In the meantime, I have some research to complete."

Neem relaxed as the footsteps echoed into the long corridor. He sighed deep breaths and considered what he had heard. The information could not be right. It was not possible. Neem had done much studying in his early days, and he had never heard of any such thing. He dismissed the idea as phoney or mistaken and shook his mind clear of the question.

He spent the rest of the day in various hiding places in the main palace of the Enclave. As the sun kissed the horizon, he grew dissatisfied with his progress. He learned nothing new. There was nothing significant going on and no weaknesses he could exploit. His mind returned to the conversation he witnessed earlier, analysing every word.

Nothing was forthcoming. In desperation, he moved position to a discreet place off one of the many tunnels leading to the meeting place of the Enclave. It was a large space, a hole bored in the rocks years before. Despite being partially underground, it was light and airy, exactly as he had designed it. He squeezed himself deeper into the hole and settled down to listen to what was going on. The rumours of a forthcoming important meeting were confirmed in short order as the hall began to fill with people.

When they were finally gathered, the king called the meeting to order, and silence washed through the palace. Neem could imagine him standing at the front, towering above all the others as he floated in the air, as was his want on these occasions. He did not need to be in the room to know where people were sitting. They were creatures of habit, their seats denoted seniority within the Enclave though not necessarily rank seniority.

"I have called this meeting to disseminate some disturbing news I received this morning. A letter came from the east. It stated that a female human has found something that the writer described as wyvern eggs. Despite my doubts, I could not completely dismiss this information. I spent the afternoon doing research based on his description. Apparently, the girl thought they were jewels, so she is keeping them to trade for her freedom from the pirates holding her hostage. There may be some merit to the lad's disclosure. I have sent for more details, but it will be some time before he can reply," said the king in a loud echoing baritone.

Another voice piped up, "This is an odd development. Is it not true that these creatures died out before the Awakening?"

A general mumbling from the crowd was the only reply.

Another voice, this time female, "It is easy to believe what we're told. It is less easy to think that our understanding has been flawed for so long. I advise we pay close attention to what the lad has to say. Who was the message from, my king?"

"A youngster named Dillitay," said the king.

The female voice spoke up again. "And he was new to the calling?"

"It is his first assignment. I am encouraged to believe that he was well versed during his studies. I am reluctant to disregard the lad's comments merely because he is young. I agree that we must pay close attention to the development of the situation. My fear is that the lad is right, and this development will portend some greater problem. The stories tell us that wyvern have power beyond that of any other creature. We must remain vigilant, at least until we know more." He raised his voice, and Neem could visualise his change in demeanour as he addressed the crowd. He could even imagine him sticking his chest out as he usually did during these meetings.

"If these wyvern creatures really played a part in The Clash, there is a need to ensure we are ready for all eventualities. Their sudden return might herald another such event. To those ends, I am ordering additional guards around the town and in the palace. I shall also be detailing guards to our *most important charge*. It is my true belief we have not seen an end to this issue. For reasons I cannot explain, I feel we must be cautious. Expect the unexpected. We shall convene again when I have more information. In the meantime, please consult whatever books you deem pertinent."

A chair scraped across the floor. As though the end of the meeting was a signal, an idea formed in Neem's mind. He knew what he must do.

Revenge drew closer.

Realising how limited his time was, he squeezed out of the hole and ran quietly down the passageway back towards the caverns. He must act before additional guards were detailed. He retraced his steps then turned and followed the passage down into the caves.

Neem reached the great room, the most protected spot in the palace, and was relieved to see a torch still burned. He went straight for the box, stopping only a moment to take in the vision of such power. He threw down his dagger, and his bow and quiver, and wrapped his hands around the chest. He placed his feet on either side and strained to straighten his legs. The pressure burned on his face. The box did not even shift a little. He stepped back and considered his predicament. He was reluctant to open the thing. It was one thing to hide it away and hold it hostage, quite another to peek inside. Who knew what it would unleash? The stories were well told within the pixie clan, and the theories as to the results of such blunders were boundless. Still, he had made his decision. It was too late to turn back. If he were caught, he would suffer the severest punishment. Now was not the time to hesitate.

He took a final pace forward and laid his hands on the box. Its metal edges transferred the cold to his hands. He shivered as though the box itself was chastising him for his thoughts. He took a breath then lifted the lid. Rays of purple light sprung from inside. The light intensified as the chest swung open. The infamous stones shone like glittering stars. They appeared to be locked together in a three-dimensional jigsaw, yet each piece was clearly identifiable as separate.

He moved one hand cautiously towards the glowing shapes. There was no heat. A stale, musty scent wafted over him, followed a dry sweet aroma. Silence surrounded him. He moved his hand closer and watched the glow reflect off his skin. Somehow, he had expected the box to be bigger, more akin to human size than pixie.

His hand moved within inches of the puzzle. With one final hesitation, he snatched at the top piece. Its purple light shimmered with streaks of red reflecting on his skin in time with a low humming that might or might not be his imagination. Neem held the stone away from his body and studied it critically. Etchings on the lower dark side of it left shadows on the remaining translucent sides.

Ex nihilo nihil mali deitatis.

Neem stared at the words. The letters seemed to float into his numbed brain. They glowed red and flashed intermittently darker. The words returned his stare. His vision blurred against the growing intensity of the lights. The strange words burned, etching into his brain. His scalp tightened, magnifying the throbbing pulse banging inside his skull. His pulse banged inside his skull.

He put the stone down and sighed heavily at the release of pressure. Curious, he retrieved it from the ground and cradled the stone gingerly in one hand. Nothing happened. He stared at the words, and revulsion surfaced like a mud slick. He had never liked the old languages. For the first time in his life, he wished he had paid greater attention to his studies. One word stood out as though typed in bold font. *Deitatis. God.* His mind churned. *Yet the details of the ending could change the meaning.* He sighed. He struggled to piece together his reluctant schoolroom learning.

He placed the stone inside his pocket and tied up the opening. On impulse, he turned back to the box. Next on top were two irregular shaped stones, much like the first. He stared, noting the shadow left by the missing stone. The light glowed at him, tempting him. Daring him to draw closer. To touch the other stones.

He considered the options. He could take them all but not without drawing unwanted attention. *No one actually opens the box, so how could they know?* Taking only one was risky. *But more is more*, he reasoned. *But if I get caught? They have been stuck in this box for as long as time itself.* He grinned. *The all-powerful box. Hockum.*

Throwing caution to the wind, he reached inside the box and savoured the warmth. His fingers curled over the next two stones and plucked them away. The second hand followed the first and took the next row of glistening rocks.

He shoved them into his pockets and rearranged them to hide the growing bulge. Once satisfied, he closed the lid, flattened out the sand to cover his footprints and slunk through the shadows as unnoticed as he had arrived.

The hard part was done now. All he had to do was walk out of the palace as if he belonged. His heart raced in time with his footsteps, and before he knew it, he was flying clear of the palace.

CHAPTER 17
LYLIANA

I t was the first day for a good while that Lyliana could remember clouds in the sky. The irony of that being the day she decided to swim was not lost on her. First, she swam hard and fast, increasing the heart rate and warming her body. Later she trod water and looked back at the land. It was like any other stretch of beach, and yet behind those golden sands were pirates. Granted, she had adapted to their ways. She had even fallen in line with some of them, but still they were pirates. *Never forget what they are.*

Finally, she grew tired, stretched out, and headed back to the beach at a leisurely pace until the surf took control and threw her onto the sand. She lay gasping. Her heart thumped against the side of her chest.

She washed the sand from her flesh, rubbed herself down, and donned her clothes before heading back towards the harbour. Her casual stroll was interrupted as she drew closer. Loud voices filtered between the buildings. Shouting and arguing drew her attention.

A crowd had gathered at the harbour. Lyliana increased her pace, tying her blond hair in a knotted bun at the nape of her neck. She tucked her shirt in her trousers, pleased she had abandoned her skirts that seemed inappropriate in her new environment. The whores wore dresses, low-cut to reveal their bosoms, barmaids dressed like old motherly types, and the shop girls dressed in shirts and simple skirts. Lyliana was none of those things. Why should she dress like them?

She reached the top of the small slope that stretched down towards the harbour. The crowd was focused on someone at the front who stood on a crate. The rowdiness increased as she approached and pushed her way through the bodies. She had already seen Lester's head poking up above the men around him. The edge of the crowd was easy to push through, but closer in, the townsfolk and pirates were more insistent that they should not be simply shoved away. After a couple of aggressive shoves, she wound her way to Lester and put her arm through his by way of silent greeting. He glanced down and smiled, offering her a grimace and a quick glance towards the crate.

Lyliana followed his eyes and saw their new leader. She could not remember his name. He had planted his huge bulk, which massively outweighed his height, on top of the crate. It seemed as though his feet were stuck to the wood as he ineffectually attempted to calm the crowd. His voice was barely audible even at her range.

"The town needs money."

"Our businesses are dying."

"What about trade?"

The crowd warmed to their theme and began to chant. Any subject was fair game: piracy, food, money, slaves.

Lester looked about him and squeezed Lyliana before raising his voice, "We need to send the ships out. All the ships. They have not been raiding for weeks."

The leader did not seem to hear him. He was so swamped by complaints from the crowd he could do nothing. No one was listening. They were just complaining, protesting, shouting.

After what seemed like an age, the lieutenants arrived and pushed their way through the throng. They used horse-whips with practised skill to bring the crowd to order. Squeals and squeaks sounded through the crowd until finally, reluctantly, they fell silent. The atmosphere crackled like fire poppers in the distance.

"People, people," shouted their leader. "I see you are worried. Things are not so simple, but I promise you I am dealing with it. I shall not let you down. Please disperse. Go back to your homes. Give me time to deal with this. Trust me." He nearly pleaded the last.

The crowd shuffled and murmured as if collectively deciding what to do. For a moment, it looked as though his pleas would go unheard, but under the not so gentle urging of the lieutenants, the crowd reluctantly subsided.

Lyliana felt Lester's hand clasp hers as he led her away. She reached over and gripped his upper arm, holding him close as they walked the streets towards Betty's bar.

"Well, that was exciting. I never saw such a thing," said Lester as they wandered up the street.

"It was certainly different. That guy seems unsuited to his role. I had always imagined pirate kings to be vicious and decisive. Kill first, ask questions later...that sort of thing. But he has not had the position long. Perhaps he will improve."

"I canno' see tha' 'appening," said Lester seriously. "'e was no' picked. 'E was jus' the only one there. After what 'appened to Zarono, nobody wan's to be next." He smiled and raised his eyebrows. "We're stuck wi' 'im."

"We're not stuck with him. There's always something that can be done. We just have to find out what." She squeezed his arm.

Lester looked at her in amazement and smiled.

"What?" Lyliana noted his expression.

"You said 'we'. It's the first 'ime you've included yoursel' as a pirate."

"Yes, it would seem I'm beginning to accept my fate. That does bring me to one item of discussion. What about Charles? We need to talk about him." Lyliana tightened her grip of Lester's arm and leaned her head briefly against his shoulder.

He stiffened and turned to face her. His expression melted into her core. "Please don't talk abou' Charles. It has not been so long, but I don't know 'ow I'd react if you said you wan'o return to 'im."

Lyliana gave him a gentle smile, "No, that's not it at all. I was only going to say that we must think about what we will do when he comes for me."

Lester's grin widened. "Don' concern yoursel' with that. 'E would no' come here. How would he even nah where to look?" He pulled her closer, "We are not alone here. Not in the least bit vulnerable, except perhaps for..." He looked back towards the harbour.

"I am telling you he will come. His family has resources and money. He was not happy at the arranged marriage in the first place. I promised I would write and let him know I am safe. When he does not receive a letter, he will come. Assuming he has not already heard what happened to the *Comnfe*."

Lester wrapped his arm about her shoulders. "I shall look after you. Don't worry. Nothing bad will happen." He pulled her round and guided her towards the centre of town with his arm protectively over her shoulder.

Lyliana sighed. *Men. No matter who they are, they don't listen.* "It is not me I am concerned about. He will forgive me anything. But the more he needs to forgive, the worse it will be for those around me. He will see that I am distressed, and he will act without regard for anything else."

"I 'ardly think you are in distress." Lester gave a huge grin and hugged her tightly as they walked.

"Not now perhaps... Only... I do not want anything bad to happen to you. Charles has never needed to take action such as this before, but he learns quickly, *and* I suspect, knows more than he ever let on."

They were almost at the crossroads of Betty's bar. Lester glanced at the building before replying. "Let's just 'ake it as it comes. We'll receive notice of any strange vessels comin' this way. There is time enough to think of these things."

Warmth spread through Lyliana's body, smothering the nagging doubt that remained in the back of her mind. Despite the clouds, she was suddenly hot. Taking Lester firmly by the arm, she led him into Betty's.

As always, Betty was busy cleaning, refilling bottles, and wiping tables, but she stopped when they entered and offered them a table. "You two 'on't be 'anting to sit at the bar, I thin'?" she said as she wiped down the table she was offering.

"Thanks, Betty. Two of the usual, please, and one for yourself. You should join us," said Lyliana as she sat astride one of the chairs.

Lester nodded his agreement and pulled a chair closer before sitting and resting back as though he belonged in the place. "It's bee' a long 'ime Bets."

'Bets' flashed him a grimace and glanced in Lyliana's

direction. "Not long enough if you're still calling me that. How've ya bin?"

"Not a fan of change, you know?" Lester replied suggestively, catching Lyliana's full attention.

Betty nodded sagely.

"Wha' do ya think of the situation? Thanks." His last was in response to the drink Betty placed in front of them.

The chubby woman tucked her cloth into her apron and froze, considering his question. "It's no secre' the *Parrot* wasn't supposed to 'ave the position. I imagine there is no one left who doubts that he's no' suited to the role."

Lyliana glanced at Lester who was nodding. The relief on his face told her he finally knew their leader's name.

Lester took a deep breath before replying, "There were no one else."

There was you. Lyliana searched his face for signs of modesty and found none. *Does he not want the power? Surely, he would dream of having such control? Perhaps he never considered it.*

"I told 'ou to ma'e your move 'hen the problems first star'ed," Betty commented and offered Lester a wide smile. "I blame you f'r this."

So he did think about it. Or at least, Betty did. So why did he do nothing?

"And I told you I don't wan' it. Pirate kings 'ave a very short lifespan. I'd need the suppor', which I don't 'ave."

Betty huffed, "You've plenty o' support, and you know it. You just needed to ma'e the move."

Lester took a drink before flashing an irritated look at Betty. "Wha' about you? You could 'ave taken control. You effectively run the entire town. None of the captains would've dared argue."

Betty laughed, a great sound that came straight from her

belly. "I'm no' cut out for that. Besides, I am a 'oman, and these men require a firm 'and. Having said that, from what we're seeing 'ere, I could do no worse."

Lyliana leaned into the table and tried to think of something to say. Her mind remained void.

Lester smiled, "So there we 'ave it. We both could have, but neither o' us did." He put his drink down. "Perhaps we'll get a second chance."

They fell silent as new customers entered. Betty stood and went back to the bar while Lester avoided eye contact with Lyliana.

The increasing wind whistled through the closed door and forced Lyliana to move round the table.

Lester watched her and leaned across to take her hand. He held it tightly for a moment before letting go and leaning back.

Lyliana watched his changing expressions. He was worried, as well he might be with this new commander. *Perhaps now is the time. It might cheer him up.* "I have something to show you later. Let's say, it might give you some ideas."

Lester sighed and pushed his chair away from the table. He picked up his tankard and took a long swig. "I'm no' thinking of taking o'er from Percy. Don't even mention it. The man needs time to adap' to his new position."

You don't believe that any more than I do, and what do I know? "That was not what I was going to say," she lied. She would never say it, but she was beginning to think Betty might be right.

"Change the subject?" he snapped.

"I was doing that. It's you who keeps returning," she sighed. "Now, are you interested in what I want to show you? You must promise not to be angry that I kept something from you." She reached her arm across the table and felt the release of tension when he took her hand and gave her a weak smile.

"I am sure ya 'ad your reasons." There was no conviction in his tone.

They finished their drinks in silence and left the bar. Lyliana left Lester to his own thoughts, knowing he was working out his issues in his own way. Her sixth sense was screaming for her to remain silent. They had only been together a couple of weeks, and yet she could sense his mood as easily as her own.

She would introduce him to the dragons. That would give him something else to think about. She had been keeping them a secret from everyone since they emerged. They were so small. Dillitay had been there watching her. She would have been annoyed that he was spying, but as it turned out, he had been very helpful. She knew nothing about the creatures, not even what they were. *I hope he is there to meet Lester. He is always there. What am I thinking?*

Lester followed her without question when they returned to his house. She led him to the outhouse and lit the candle she had taken from the kitchen. He looked about as though he had never seen the inside of the place then turned a questioning eye on Lyliana.

"So, what did you wan'o show me?" He had one hand in his pocket that only added to the tension.

"This," she lifted the cover of a box.

Lester peered over the edge. His hand went to his mouth. He gasped. He reached out and pulled his hand back quickly in response to an angry hiss from one corner of the box.

"That's Grygon. Careful, she's a bit touchy." She wiped her hand on her trousers and held it out slowly. The dragon hopped onto her palm.

Grygon twisted her head and studied Lester. Her slatted eyes blinked. She lowered her head and reached towards him. She gave a small hiss as Lester offered his hand again. Grygon pulled her head back sharply but kept her position.

"I think she likes you." Lyliana smiled. She moved her hand slowly towards Lester's.

Grygon jumped onto Lester and stretched her wings as she continued to study him.

Lester returned the dragon's gaze moment for moment. He glanced briefly at Lyliana but turned his attention back quickly. "Wha' is it?"

"A dragon," she said matter-of-factly as though they were so common it wasn't worth mentioning. "Don't worry. They are friendly."

"They?" Lester asked in a voice pitched just a little too high.

Lyliana reached down into the box. "Yes. That is Grygon," she repeated, indicating the shiny golden lizard on his hand. "And this is Roylei, and Svation," she added as two more creatures bounced onto her arm.

Roylei clambered up her arm and perched on her shoulder while Svation climbed jaw over claw, using her hair as a climbing rope and finally stood on her head. Roylei flashed his dark red wings in time with Svation as Lyliana bent down once more.

Svation hissed and hopped quickly from Lyliana to Lester. He ducked his bright silver head down to nuzzle Grygon who returned the gesture.

Lester's mouth dropped open as another three creatures emerged from the box. Lyliana introduced them all in turn. Briscay, a glossy black shadow, jumped from the box straight onto the floor, to become almost invisible against the dark ground. Yastat, bright yellow except for his face that merged into a light brown, perched on the side of the box and studied Lester, much as Grygon had done, and finally Tisray whose blue-green sheen rainbowed with every movement.

Lester gaped, eyes wide as saucers, unable to move his gaze from Grygon who was working her way up to his shoulder.

"What do you think? Beautiful, aren't they?" Lyliana giggled.

Grygon, now on his shoulder, prodded Lester with her nose horn as if demanding a reply.

Lester opened his mouth to speak, but no words came.

"Don't worry. It took me a few minutes to get my thoughts together when they hatched. Whatever I was expecting, it was not that."

"'atched?" Lester managed finally.

Lyliana gave him a look as if he was stupid.

"You *found* their eggs?" Lester asked, finally rallying.

"Yes. I hid them, thinking they were gems. That I might be able to sell them to get home."

"Sell dragons?"

"No, the gems. When I thought they were just jewels. I would not sell dragons. They are mine...they are my friends."

A sudden movement of air and the flapping of wings signalled Dillitay's arrival. "I've told you before. They are not dragons. Wyverns, W-Y-V-E-R-N." He spelled the word slowly in a loud voice as if he was talking to stupid people. Dillitay landed on the bench in the opposite corner of the room and folded his wings.

Briscay snorted and launched himself from the floor. He landed clumsily on the table. Dillitay staggered clear.

"And did I mention they are a nuisance," said the small

man once he recovered his balance. He reached out and tickled Briscay under his chin.

"Dillitay, this is—"

"Yes. We've met. Lester?" The pixie turned the statement into a question as he turned his attention to Lester.

The pirate startled as he was drawn away from his shock. "Yes, to great effec' as I recall. It's good to see ya well, pixie." He moved to shake hands and thought better of it. "And thank you."

Dillitay bowed almost imperceptibly in acknowledgment and turned a questioning glance on Lyliana.

"I thought it was time. We can trust Lester."

Roylei shook himself and half jumped, half flew to the table. He inspected Dillitay who returned his scrutiny warily.

"They're fascinatin'. It is almost as though they understand wha' is going on," said Lester, without taking his eyes from the table.

Grygon lifted her wings and hissed. With one flap of her wings, she joined the others on the table.

Dillitay moved slowly away, visibly nervous.

"You mus' tell me everything. They're amazing creatures. I read about 'em, but never thought they're real, much less that I would see one."

Dillitay flew upwards until he was eye level with Lester. "They seem to be a group. They don't like to be separated. They eat rats and mice, and they clearly have an intelligence that we don't understand. That is all we've worked out yet. We only just confirmed that they can fly, although the wings did provide a good clue." He rolled his eyes.

"We must learn more. They can't stay here. Bring 'em into the house. And you, Mr. Dillitay. If you can find a sui'able place inside to call 'ome, you are welcome. You shall 'ave all the privacy of your own property."

"Much appreciated. It would give me a good place to keep an eye on these seven." He smiled and nodded towards Lyliana.

"I don't need a keeper," Lyliana replied sharply.

As soon as she raised her voice, Grygon and Briscay flew to her and landed, one on each shoulder. Yastat hissed from his position on the edge of the box. The other three contented themselves with watching closely.

"Fascinating," exclaimed Lester, "and yes, *you* do." He glanced meaningfully at Dillitay who confirmed with a nod.

How have I suddenly got two bodyguards? This was not the plan. Lyliana might have complained, but the warm feeling of being cared for took over, and she remained silent.

CHAPTER 18
ENCLAVE

Light showed under the great wooden door. It reflected off the raised stone slab floor of the chamber. Light scintillated, a mere phosphorescence, as though a candle had been left burning, shining brightly, burnishing the room in a rippling purple glimmer that pulsed and whined. Glittering shards bounced within the confined space. There was no one about to see, but if there had been, they would have noticed the dappled effect multiplying. They might have wondered if there was a living being inside the box as the light brought with it an impatience, an air of anticipation that permeated the very walls. The box shone through the night, unnoticed despite the luminescence that finally escaped through the tunnels.

The Princess Frankine was the first to notice. She had completed her morning toilette and was on her way to break her fast. She walked past the entrance to the caverns as she did every morning. At first, she thought it was candlelight, yet it was too early for the morning box check. Even so, she thought nothing more of it and continued on her way.

It was not until she had almost finished eating that she rethought through the logic. Excusing herself from the table, she went directly to the caverns, her footsteps quick and measured. She thought she had seen it glowing a few days previous. This time she must make certain. She could not go to her mother and father again with a false premise. She would be marked as a liar, not a good reputation for anyone, especially a princess. Her slippers echoed on the stone as she stepped carefully down the steps that wound down towards the cavern. She had no need of a torch. The clear purple glow lit the path well enough.

This time it is really a light. It must be coming from the box. There can be no doubt. I have never seen such a thing. She increased her pace and pressed her hand against the wall for balance. It would not do to twist an ankle.

Frankine need not go further into the cavern. There was no doubt in her mind what was going on. Her pulse raced, and the sound of her breath grew loud in her ears as she realised she had confirmed that the box was glowing. *I need to tell someone, but who? Who is going to believe this when no one else noticed? Even Mother will doubt me after last time.*

They said she had imagined it, that she had a fever remaining from her illness. She knew better. It had been a few days now since they confirmed she was well. This time they must believe her.

She turned sharply at the sound of footsteps descending from the top of the walkway. She slunk back against the stone walls as she saw the shadow of one of the roaming guards. She froze in place like a robber caught in the act.

"Hey, down there. Who is down there?" The guard's voice echoed off the stone.

Frankine stayed put. Not a muscle moving, only a slight heave of her chest betrayed her breathing. Her left wing scraped against the stone; small pebbles fell from the concrete.

"I know you're down there. You are not supposed to be here. Whoever you are, appear, and make yourself known." The guard was getting agitated.

Gingerly, Frankine pushed herself away from the wall and stalked up the centre of the path to give the guard a clear view.

"Hurry up now. I don't have all day." The guard moved forward as if to drag Frankine clear of the darkness.

She scuttled sideways to avoid his hand and slinked past him into the main corridor.

He turned sharply to follow her then stopped dead in his tracks. "My lady, I apologise. I had not known it was you. What do you do down there? You can have no business in the caverns. Does the queen know you are here?" The man was babbling.

It was not so long since Frankine would have quailed under such questioning. She would have answered dutifully and done as she was told. Her illness and near death had put a different slant on things. Now she understood the power she held.

"I shall go where I wish. You are not to be questioning me. I am the princess. There is no part of this palace off-limits to *me*." She lifted her chin slightly and surreptitiously straightened her clothes. She flicked the dust clear of her wings and eyed the guard up and down.

"Your uniform is a mess. Call yourself a palace guard indeed." She used her best superior voice though it sounded weak to her ears. "You shall be lucky if I do not report you to my father, *the king*. I go to him now. If you wish to discuss something with your liege, you may escort me." She spat the last.

The soldier stepped back and flattened himself against the wall. Frankine took that as a negative response and rushed past him. She turned the corner before she realised she was alone. At least he had enough sense not to accept her offer.

She found her parents in the consultation chamber surrounded by advisers. There had been a number of changes since she had been ill, and she was not familiar with all the people in the room. She paused in the doorway, unsure of how to proceed. It had been a habit to stay away from the clan's politics and internal affairs, but since her illness, she felt that she should become more involved. The only question was how to proceed.

"We have discussed this before, my dear. This must involve the dragons. It is the only thing that has changed of late. How could we possibly think otherwise?"

"You are my husband, and I respect your opinion, but it is not possible. The dragons are a long way away. Now we have this situation, and it is not the first thing that has gone wrong."

Frankine remembered her tutor telling her that everything before the word 'but' should be disregarded. She gained a new respect for her mother's deft handling of the king.

"It has always been generally understood that the downfall of the dragons was the catalyst to the current state of being. I confess I doubted this Dillitay. He is so young. How could he know anything about this? Yet we cannot ignore the facts."

Perhaps 'yet' is the same as 'but'? mused Frankine.

"Sire, those who know him say he is a smart kid. I think we can trust what he says."

Frankine approached the group slowly, trying not to

interrupt their conversation. Her breath caught in her throat at the idea of speaking in front of so many strangers. She swallowed hard and pushed on.

"Father, the news gets worse. The box is glowing. This time I went down to confirm it. I knew I had seen it before." She looked to her mother, pleading with her expression. "I am not imagining this. You must come and see for yourself." She headed for the door, but no one followed.

"This is another sign if the girl is correct. What is going on here?" The security adviser gave her a perplexed look. "Increase security. If I may be so bold, perhaps the army is the wise choice here. Also, we must consolidate our training regime."

Frankine's mother looked at him and then to her husband. "I think he is right. We must assume there is more going on here. We cannot rely on humans. You know how slow they are to act, so we must take the initiative. We are more vulnerable than them."

The king glanced at his daughter as if to get a final confirmation on what she was saying. "Okay, does anyone have anything else to say? Such preparations can be misinterpreted as acts of war even while we hope to avoid such events. We must tread lightly. Until we are certain of our facts, we must do nothing to provoke a confrontation. Especially before we are ready."

The group nodded. Frankine eyed each of them in turn but could not tell what they were thinking. She did not know them well enough. At first glance, they all seemed to agree with her father. The knot in her stomach untangled as she realised she was the only one who doubted these actions. Things were not so simple. She kept her own council.

"To get back to this box. We must find out for certain what is going on," said Termurica.

"How are we to do that?" The king sighed. "All we know of it has been passed down through generations. Even I have no idea what might be setting it off." He blinked tiredly.

Another advisor stepped forward and coughed lightly. His wings flickered for attention, and all eyes turned on him.

"I have a suggestion, my lord. If I may?"

"Of course, Bael." The king waved everyone else to silence.

"I think we need to open the box. Perhaps it will reveal something we are missing."

There was a stunned gasp. Even Frankine held her breath. She had heard the stories, the same as everyone else.

Bael held his hands up in submission. "I know this is not a popular idea. Some may call it rash at best. But for the want of any other information, surely it is worth the risk?"

"What a suggestion. Have you even considered what could happen? We have no idea what tampering with it will achieve. It is too dangerous."

Frankine sensed a general feeling of agreement with the king, but no one said anything either way.

"Sire, with respect. That is the point. We do not know. It may be that the very act of *not* acting could be the thing that finally brings us down. If we do not touch anything, merely open it, I cannot see there would be a problem."

The king moved around the group until he was standing directly behind them. "What do you think as our resident scholar?" He addressed the pixie in front of him.

All eyes turned to the man. He was tall for a pixie and

quite old so that his thinning figure made him look even taller, while his slight stoop shortened him ever so slightly. He turned to the king and paused before replying.

"I would like to say one way or another, my king. Unfortunately, I just do not have the information to give you an educated opinion. In theory, Bael is correct. There might be no harm in just opening it, providing that nothing is touched—"

"My dear—" Termurica stepped forward urgently.

Myrrhta held up his hand to forestall her interruption.

The scholar gave her an irritated, withering look before continuing. "I would err on the side of caution. This box is clearly magic. We have no idea what safeguards are in place to prevent tampering. It might be the case that we are being overly cautious, and that nothing will happen, yet I am forced to consider that we would not have been given such a historical charge without reason. If the box *were* harmless, there would be no reason to protect it as we have been doing for generations. I am forced to advise caution until we know more."

The king nodded.

"My Lord, I believe we should still make preparations for attack. The box itself may not be dangerous, but it is clear that something is happening beyond our understanding. I am nervous to do nothing and simply wait," said Bael.

Myrrhta took his wife's hand and signalled for Frankine to come to him. "I agree with you all. We shall proceed on all fronts. Now I think we must also at least look at this box." He led the procession towards to the great doorway.

CHAPTER 19
LYLIANA

Lyliana wrung her hands and flicked drops of water into the bowl. With the breakfast washing-up done, she turned and surveyed the house. *It could do with cleaning.* Dust particles danced between shafts of light shining through the windows. She wandered in a circle and studied the various surfaces. *It's definitely worth my while.* She retraced her steps, heading back towards the sink. Svation alighted on the edge and flicked his wings to correct a stumble. Lyliana smiled. A pervading warmth settled over her as the comfort of the dragon's presence relaxed her.

She and the dragons had settled comfortably into Lester's house as had Dillitay who joined them with a marked reluctance. He commandeered one of the cupboards and, from the little Lyliana saw, had made a good job of turning it into a home. Lester claimed he enjoyed the noise and liveliness of their company, and yet over the last few evenings he had been out more than he had been with them.

Lyliana shook and stopped herself from thinking about it again. She had tried to conceal the worry, tried to convince herself there was nothing wrong. He was just busy. His problems had become stellar since it became evident their new leader was incapable of rising to his position. The deterioration of organisation had been mirrored by corresponding erosion in morale so that even Lyliana, who barely knew the place, recognised the difference.

Svation squeaked and settled himself on the edge of the copper sink. He inspected the water, his long tail acting as a counterweight as he nosed down into the bowl. As he studied, he raised his tail a little and flicked the whiplash end with a sharp crack upwards. Without warning, he arched and raised his wings menacingly over his head. His nose shot up, and he hissed.

Lyliana increased her pace. What was wrong with the water that Svation should react so violently? She reached the sink just as a rattling reached her ears. She gazed into the bowl to find a spoon in the bottom. It had been empty before. She frowned and glanced at the dragon. Svation jumped up and down and squeaked. He flapped his wings and bounced onto her shoulder. He nuzzled her ear. Absently, she picked up a small sliver of meat she kept stocked for the dragons, put it on her finger, and offered it to him. She stretched out her other hand with the fingers splayed wide and rested it on the water. The sting of cold water numbed her fingers. She snatched her arm back and twisted her neck round to look at Svation.

The water was ice.

"Did you do this?"

Svation bobbed his head and shoved out his wings for balance as he moved

"I needed that water." Lyliana stared. *He made ice.* She shook her head in admirations and smiled. *That will make drinks more interesting in the future.* She gave the creature a curious look. *Perhaps you could make something nice for Betty. Could be a steady income.* She dismissed the idea. She could not use the dragons for labour. They would do anything for her, but she would not take advantage.

She banged a hole in the ice that was thankfully thin and dipped her hand into the now freezing water to retrieve the spoon. Svation remained on her shoulder, flicking his wings every now and again to keep his balance as she moved.

News arrived just as she finished dusting.

"Lyliana, come quic'," shouted Lester as he hurried into the house. "You mus' see this. They're really goin' at it in the town. There might be a riot." He saw the look on her face and hesitated, "Maybe 'ot. They are good people. It's no' the kind of thing they'd do. Anyway, *ya* must come."

She tossed her cloth back to the sink and followed him. "Svation made ice. He can freeze things. Washing up was interesting." She smiled when Lester stared. "I have a dragon that can make ice."

"I'm no' sure what to make o' that."

"I guess we make ice." Lyliana laughed and pulled a shawl over her shoulders.

A light flutter of wings announced Dillitay was joining them. The tension in her stomach lifted as he alighted on her shoulder, taking the place that Svation vacated.

She stepped outside behind Lester and a clatter of bat wings greeted her as the dragons arrived. "No, no, you all stay here." She shooed them off.

There was a general scramble, and all but Roylei and Yastat disappeared into the trees. Lyliana stopped and held out an arm for them to land. They folded their wings, and she tickled each under the chin. "You must stay. I cannot risk you. You are too young yet." She tickled them again and stroked the top of their heads, making them stretch upwards in pleasure. "When you are bigger," she promised and tossed them into the air so that they flew to join the others.

They reached the town to find the situation much as Lester described. The huge crowd was centred around Betty's crossroads. The shops and most buildings round-about were shuttered. Lester stopped dead at the spectacle. Lyliana came up short, nearly crashing into his back. He exchanged a worried glance with Lyliana and pushed heavily through the crowd. The voices were loud and angry. People pushed back aggressively as Lester shoved his way towards the front. As before, Percy stood on the top of a crate and tried to calm the crowd. His attempts were futile. Even his lieutenants were keeping at a safe distance or so Lyliana supposed because she could not see them anywhere.

She pushed through the crowd with Lester. The two of them worked their way around until they were level with the crates. From that position, they could just hear what Percy was saying.

"My friends," Percy said in a soothing tone. "I have taken steps to improve the situation. Please be patient, good people. All will come good in the end. I am sending envoys to Gamola and Hillaway. With any luck this will increase our trade, and perhaps we can make some kind of alliance to fix our current situation until we can find a more permanent solution."

Lyliana looked about her. Doubt etched the faces of the crowd. She glanced back at Percy. He was losing his audience, if he had ever had it in the first place. He was either unaware of the fact or did not care.

Most of them had not even heard him, and the rest seemed not to be listening. Instead of paying attention to him, they were busy picking fights amongst themselves.

Lyliana instinctively sensed that the crowd was going to erupt. She looked at Lester and saw the verging panic on his face. *So it's not just me then.*

Percy was rambling. She chewed her lip. Through the voices a murmur rose. The murmur grew to a purr and then a low growl. It rumbled between the buildings and bounced around the crossroads. A scraping of unsheathing weapons joined the chaos.

A woman waved her cleaning rag angrily.

Lyliana's mouth went dry. She cleared her throat. The dryness was choking. She pushed past Lester.

He grabbed her and tried to pull her back.

She pulled away and pushed forward. A fluttering signalled Dillitay's proximity. "What are you going to do?" he asked, worry tinged his voice.

"Nothing. I just want to see what is going on." She took another few paces forward.

Dillitay was suddenly in her face. "Don't do anything stupid. This lot are going to erupt." He brandished his sword.

"Someone has to do something before it's too late."

"My friends," Percy tried again. "You have nothing to worry about." He stretched out his hands in a calming gesture.

Heat flushed her face. Lyliana fisted both hands. She elbowed through the last of the crowd between her and Percy. A couple shoved back. She ignored them and clambered onto the first crate. She skirted past Percy and onto a higher crate.

"What are you doing? I told you not to do anything stupid." Dillitay was shedding bright red dust. He bared his sword and flicked it casually in her direction. He waved it in her face when she ignored him.

"Shut up," she said. It was unclear whether she was talking to Dillitay or the crowd.

Dillitay gave her one last look of disparagement and dropped back into fighting stance. He faced the crowd.

"Shut up." Lyliana shouted. She surprised herself with the volume of her own voice. She waited, poised.

The noise from the crowd lessened ever so slightly.

"I said *shut up!*" Lyliana stiffened as all eyes turned to her. The sudden silence was more frightening than the sound of the angry mob. Her hands clenched harder, and the dryness in her mouth threatened to silence her. A pressure in her skull made her light-headed. Her muscles tensed as the final few people fell into silence.

She waited until she was sure she had their attention. "My name is Lyliana. I have not been here long, but some of you know me. Some of you captured me, and some have never met me. Clearly, this situation is not working. Something must be done. Tell me what you need and—"

"This is not your place," raged Percy from below her.

She gave Percy a disinterested look. "It appears that it is not yours either." Lyliana smiled nastily and turned back to the crowd. "—and I will do what I can for you. If you let me." She held her hands out in an appeasing gesture and waited.

The crowd adjusted themselves in a non-descript shuffling manner. Some yelled across the heads of others. A very few began to name things that they needed. Money, trade, luxury goods, and cloth were but a few.

Lyliana let the tension ease and adjusted her stance. She nodded, being careful to show the crowd that she was listening and, more importantly, understanding. She glanced at Lester. He was still tensed and standing just below her, waiting. He had not relaxed even a little. He never took his eyes off the crowd.

When the shouting died down, Lyliana coughed and waved the voices down again. "I will make no promises, but I will do my best to get you what you need. If you will have me, I will be a *just* commander."

The talk of being in command got Percy's attention. "You have no place here. You cannot take over. You do not have the experience."

"Experience," said Lyliana, turning her attention on him. "You talk about experience, and yet you have none of your own. Had you any effective knowledge, you would have done a better job. These good people would not be standing here complaining of your inaction. You would not need to be here listening to them...if you ever did. You would already be serving them. And yet, you have not. You are in no position to tell me where my place is." She took a breath. *Too much. Too far.* Her temperature rose. "If experience is all I lack then I can learn so I have one up on you."

The crowd murmured, and there was a general shuffling of bodies.

"He may have a point," piped up a man in the back.

Lyliana could not see who spoke and could not think of a response. She slouched in acquiesce.

"You have not been here long enough to tell us what to do," yelled a woman.

"I have not told you what to do. I asked you what you needed *me* to do. I asked you if you will accept my leadership." Lyliana raised her voice for all to hear. "I am asking if *I* can help you."

"We don't need your help."

"We can manage just fine on our own."

Lester shifted his stance, and Dillitay lowered a little and shook his sword in silent threat.

"We have done just fine up till now. Why don't you people just leave us alone?"

"I was not going to force you to do anything." Lyliana growled. It was all going wrong, and yet she was determined that she would take over. It was no longer a matter of what they wanted. In her mind, she needed to do this.

"How can you possibly do anything he cannot? You have not been here long enough to know the politics around this town. I do not accept your leadership." The crowd nodded in agreement and clapped each other on the back. When they returned their attention to her, there was a new menace in the air. A couple of them looked at her fiercely and pushed forward.

Lyliana took an involuntary step backwards. Dillitay was in front of her poised, so was Lester. But the two of them could not take on the whole crowd alone.

"Remove yourself," insisted one of the closer people.

"Go back where you came from. Leave us in peace." The crowd's mood was escalating. They were feeling each other's rage and unreasonably directing it towards her.

I was only trying to help. Now what? We are trapped.

Bile rose in her mouth. Her leg muscles quivered. Her hearing echoed. Sounds dimmed becoming distant. She took another pace backwards.

The crowd growled. She froze.

There was an audible twang, and something snapped in her mind. Suddenly she was not alone. A presence. Something new, something alien, invaded her thoughts. Her mind echoed a ricochet. The fear evaporated.

Wings buffeted, and suddenly, she was surrounded. Dillitay skittered clear in a torrent of wings. Grygon hissed menacingly. Svation closed on Lyliana from the side.

Roylei hissed a jet of fire from his mouth.

The crowd hesitated as one. The silence was deafening. Those at the back pushed forward. People at the front scattered. Svation and Grygon growled and flapped ferociously above Lyliana. Roylei hovered with his mouth ajar. The threat was clear. Three or four of the braver members of the crowd pushed forward and shouted incoherent words. They were defiant, challenging.

Roylei hissed in concert with Svation. Grygon charged the crowd, a small golden streak of snapping savagery. The crowd growled. Roylei hovered lower with Svation above him and let out a hiss of flame. Svation hissed, and a cloud sped from his mouth. Suddenly Roylei's flame was a massive jet of fire, raging over the crowd, reflecting their anger back to them.

Lyliana ducked, the heat transmitting itself to her despite being well behind the dragons. She spared a glance to Lester who was pinned up against the crate below her, frozen in awe.

Lyliana could not move. Stunned by such a display of violence from the beasts. They were so small and yet clearly not as defenceless as she thought. The flame from Roylei was now seven or eight metres long. He had been joined by Grygon who hissed menacingly above her mates.

The crowd cowered, silent. Some threw themselves to the ground and hid their faces. A few of the men covered their women protectively.

The point was well made.

Lyliana stepped forward. She took a deep breath and centred herself. "Now. Are you ready to listen, or shall we continue this battle of wills?"

The flame stopped abruptly. Grygon landed on her right shoulder. Svation flew backwards and hovered above Grygon, flanked by Roylei. They hung over her, waiting. One man, the instigator, stood first. He pulled a woman to her feet and turned to face Lyliana. The defiance on his face was still there, but when he spoke, his attitude was one of capitulation.

"I never saw such a thing. We have no choice but to listen," he said.

Lyliana's lip twitched. She let the silence drag on. "You have every choice. It is not my intention to force you into anything. My dragons are a little overprotective, it would seem. I apologise." She shrugged. "They are young, but so decisive. I am proud. I can only hope to emulate their proactive behaviour." She spoke solemnly and professionally, yet an emptiness remained after the dragons' displays of ferocity.

A woman over to the left stood, drawing attention. "I admire her audacity." She smiled at the crowd. "First, she threatens us then she claims she has not, and she only wishes to help. I believe her. She could not have planned such a display." She turned, "Tommy, did you not see her shock at the dragon's behaviour? She might be just the person we need. Who would defy such power? If we would not, then surely no one else will?"

Tommy nodded reluctantly.

Lyliana sensed a change of atmosphere and relaxed just a little. Things were coming together in her favour. "I ask that you consider my proposal. If we cannot work together, I will step down, graciously and willingly. I promise you only that for the time being."

There was a general sense of acquiesce, and the crowd

began to disperse. Lester stayed firm where he stood. He kept his eyes averted.

Lyliana sat heavily down on the box and cradled her head in her hands. *That was close. Thank you, my friends. My family. My dragons. My wyvern.*

Dillitay alighted on the box next to her. "You are a demon," he whispered.

Lyliana glared at him, the residual fear making her more abrupt than she intended.

"I mean, you have the luck of the devil. They could have killed you."

She smiled and glanced at Lester who remained silent and resolute.

"I don't think we 'ave to worry abou' that anymore," Lester said then glanced at the dragons.

"It would seem that baby dragons are not as defenceless as you thought, Dillitay," said Lyliana, half in jest.

"I confess, I never heard of such a thing. In all the stories, it was never mentioned that they were so protective or unwontedly savage. How did you tell them you were in trouble?"

How indeed? "I did no such thing." She rubbed her head and stared at the dispersing crowd. The crossroads were almost clear except for a few who remained, entranced. Lyliana's eyes met with a man on the other side of the road. It was Tommy. He started towards her as their eyes met. Lyliana's innards recoiled. *I am not in the mood for another row. Can't this idiot wait at least a few hours?* She adjusted her position on the crate and made herself as unapproachable as she could manage from a sitting position.

"Be careful. This is not over," Lester whispered as he rose to his full height.

"May I speak with you, Lyliana?" Tommy bowed his head a little.

She nodded and waited.

"I would apologise. We've had to put up with much over the last month or so. It has strained our metal."

"Accepted," she said in a clipped tone.

"On behalf of the town, we accept your help."

Lester shifted position and exchanged looks with Dillitay.

And who is he to speak for the town? Lyliana kept her thoughts to herself. "Accepted. There are conditions." It was now or never.

Tommy indicated for her to continue with a brief nod.

"I will engage lieutenants in due course. They will not necessarily be the same people as previously. That was not working. That much is clear," she paused.

Tommy nodded.

"I will be making changes, some small, others more far reaching. My instructions *will* be followed. If the people don't like it, they can speak to their representative. I will not tolerate another show like today. If they are fair with me, I will do my best. But things will not always go to plan. They must understand that." She paused and looked hard at him. "Okay so far?"

Tommy scrunched his lips together and nodded.

"You will remain as the representative of the people. You will be held responsible for their wellbeing. I want to know everything that concerns them. Any sign of treachery and you will be replaced. I am going to work hard, but I need your help. I cannot do this alone. Finally, I need a favour, but first I must prepare. Is this acceptable?"

"Yes, missy."

"Lyliana is fine. Thank you for your co-operation. I shall contact you later."

Tommy left quickly and headed for a crowd that had been trying to pretend they were not watching the conversation. Lyliana watched as he recounted their discussion and appeared to receive a positive response. Lester and Dillitay were paying equal attention to her and the group that were now leaving.

"What just happened?" stammered Lester.

"The coup is completed. Lyliana is our new leader." Dillitay lowered his voice, "Now the real work begins."

CHAPTER 20
NEEM

Neem had chosen daylight to encroach the palace boundaries. A principle of reverse psychology designed to draw the least attention. A bold manoeuvre of subterfuge. The scorpion's nocturnal instinct gave him an added advantage though he would still have the dragonflies to contend with.

The success of his infiltration was measured by his solitude. No one interrupted him leaving so the option to act as though he belonged during his departure still existed. He would be long gone before anyone realised he was an impostor

He reached the outside safely and checked the sky before heading away from the palace. The dragonflies were still busy with their food. His escape remained covert. He rushed to the tree line where he watched anxiously for signs of pursuit while he caught his breath. His arm brushed his pocket, feeling the solid gems inside. A smile grew on his lips. *Stage one completed.*

When he arrived home, the others were waiting for him. Tyame, Parcelus, and Avienna were playing Twiggy on his front porch. They had removed the protective leaves that hid his house from prying eyes and were getting rowdy. Leaves twitched, betraying prying eyes.

"I told you to wait until I returned," said Neem, irritation sharpening his tone.

They laughed, obviously drunk, although how they achieved that state so quickly was beyond him.

"Keep it down or go home. I cannot afford the attention right now."

"We were waiting for you. That's what you told us to do. Come play," droned Avienna, staggering to her feet and snagging her blond curls on an arrow tip hanging on the wall.

Neem slithered from her reach and skirted the room. His friends followed his movements with glazed eyes. "Come inside. I have something to show you."

Tyame and Parcelus headed straight for the door while Avienna waited for Neem.

"You're very pretty," she drooled as he passed, doing his best to ignore her despite her pretty green dress.

He put on a pot of tea, his efforts hindered by Avienna's sloppy attempts to assist. He turned and took her firmly by both shoulders, holding her steady until she calmed down.

With the tea brewed and the group settled comfortably, if not quietly, he briefed them on the morning's events. Any irritation he felt at their interruptions was masked by the pleasure of their shock.

"You're telling us you invaded the palace *and* made it all the way into the caverns without *anybody* noticing?" asked Parcelus. His frown deepened the dark lines that marked his face.

Neem closed his eyes in resignation, "This was what we planned."

Avienna stood sharply and leaned protectively over Neem. "That is a little harsh," she said, jumping to his defence. "Entirely unjustified," she slurred. Her perfume wafted over Neem, adding to the sickening tang of intoxicating liquor.

Neem set back in the chair and sighed.

The silence lengthened. There was nothing left to say.

Tyame rubbed his hands and leaned forward. "Neem, tell us what you found. This time we will listen. I still can't believe you actually went back. You were against the idea."

Neem took a deep breath and told them what happened in the cavern. He recounted his encounter with the dragonflies, laughing when he described arriving in the cavern unseen. He described the box and its contents and tried to describe the lights, but his words were desperately inadequate. Their tea remained untouched. He had their attention.

"I brought a couple with me. Thought they might be worth something." He stood and went over to his discarded jacket. He fumbled through his pockets and pulled out the stones, laying them one by one on the table.

They crowded forward and peered at the rocks. The tension ratcheted until it was almost palatable. Neem smiled. Each of them was struggling to resist the temptation to reach out and touch the gems. With their concentration now cemented, he presented the problem.

"Each stone has some kind of inscription. I read the top one, but it makes no sense. The language is ancient, from before The Change, but other than that, I can determine nothing. This one has something to do with God's door spirits—I think?" He pointed at a stone.

Avienna looked at him for confirmation and reached forward to pick up a shiny rock.

"No, not that one, the other one," said Neem, pointing at the first stone.

"It looks like the top of the pyramid. Was it a pyramid, Neem?" Avienna pushed back her blonde hair and tossed it over her shoulders. She crossed her legs in a feminine display and held the apex close to her face. She turned it over and studied the inscription with an air of understanding. After a few moments, she looked about the room before locking eyes with Neem. "I agree with you. It seems to refer to some greater power, but I am not sure. I know someone who could read this. He is a scholar of sorts. It does not come without risk."

Tyame leaned forward, his face pinched and angry. "Why are we discussing this? We cannot bring anyone else into this. Neem, do you realise what you have done? You have stolen from the palace."

The tension pinged round the room like a bouncing ball. The three pixies sat on the edge of the long chair while Neem turned and busied himself unnecessarily with the teapot.

Parcelus coughed, shaking his grey locks, "It is too late for such concerns. The thing is done. Now we must take steps to cover our tracks. No one must learn of this. There is no time for petty bickering." His stomach bounced to another rasping cough.

Neem turned back to the group in time to see Parcelus give Tyame a nasty look and twist his head to one side in challenge.

He sighed. *Perhaps this is not going to be as easy as we first thought.* "Well, what about you two? Do either of you have any ideas? It may be useful if you look at the inscriptions instead of just sitting and criticising."

Tyame plucked up another stone with his long fingers

and glanced at it disinterestedly. "If *she* cannot understand this how do you expect me to be able to? When we said we were going to get revenge, I did not think we were going this far." He sat back, distancing himself.

"*We* have done nothing. Calm down," said Parcelus. He tugged his hands into the folds of his winter boots that he wore all year round.

"Nothing! Let us have a look at this nothing, shall we? First, he broke into the palace then he opened a sacred box and stole the jewels from inside." Tyame waved his hands in the air, "Lastly, and by no means least, we have no idea what effect removing the jewels will have. We might now find out if the rumours are true in ways we hoped to avoid. If so, we are in big trouble. This has gone too far. I want nothing to do with it." Tyame stood and marched for the door, scooping up his bottle on the way out.

A glass clinked. Parcelus moved with startling speed gained in a lifetime of training. The old pixie seemed to double in size as he barred the exit. He took up the entire doorway. His angry red dust reflected about the doorway.

Tyame stopped short and glowered at Parcelus. "Get out of my way. I am leaving. You people are crazy. I want no part of it." He shoved the old man hard.

"You are going nowhere." Parcelus snatched the bottle from Tyame and brandished it over him.

Avienna rushed forward, her arms outstretched. "Stop it. Stop the choo-choo at once," she said as she moved to stand between the two pixies.

Neem frowned at the strange expression.

Tyame shoved her clear. She froze, pinned against the wall.

"Get out of my way, old man," Tyame shouted. "I shall

tell no one. You have my word, but I will not partake of this anymore." He shoved Parcelus back.

There was a crashing of glass. A blur of red pixie wings. Suddenly Tyame was on the floor. Neem watched helpless as Parcelus jammed the now broken bottle into Tyame's throat. Avienna gasped. She crept along the wall towards the door.

"You are going nowhere. We are in this together," said Parcelus. "Now, here are your instructions. Neem, go find a place where we can bury Tyame. Avienna, clean up this mess, and help me wrap the body. We shall need to do something about his wings."

Neem did as he was bid. He moved as though in a trance. *What happened? How did it come to this? What is he going to do next?*

CHAPTER 21
LYLIANA

Zarono's office was a mess. Lyliana had been stuck alone behind the desk, sifting through papers for three long days. Lester and Betty had helped where they could, but their findings just brought up more questions. The most recent being: where was the data on the ships? Either Percy or Zarono had been ultra-paranoid to keep such information so well hidden.

Lyliana stood and rolled her head on her neck and stretched her arms. She glanced at the sun's position. Nearly lunchtime. Flinging herself heavily on the chair behind the desk, she closed her eyes. It was not comfortable but good enough for a few minutes rest. She leaned her elbow on the chair's arm and put her head on her palm. Every time she looked about the office, the workload multiplied. If only her predecessors had been conscious of the need for record keeping like her father was.

Briscay entered through the open window. Tisray and Yastat sniffed his air trail and returned to scavenging about the floor. Lyliana smiled briefly. At least they had finished terrorising the townsfolk. By now, the people in the street were warily watching the skies for mock attack. At one point, the street had grown crowded with people watching them, but they dispersed quickly, harassed by a flood of menacing hisses.

Lester opened the door and stalked into the room. "Don't tell me you've given up already. I don't think this town could survive another change of leadership so soon." He smiled and put a plate of sandwiches on the desk in front of her.

"Thanks. I hadn't even thought of food," she sighed.

"I guessed ya would na' be interested, but I thought I would bring 'hem. There's more chance of you eating with the stuff already here than me taking ya for lunch."

Lyliana smiled. He was getting to know her so well. "I suppose you're right. I'm sorry. I have not been much fun since I accidentally took over this job."

"Ya still using that line then," he laughed and gave her a suspicious look.

"I'm not using any line. What do you mean?"

"That ya took over accidentally. I saw the look in ya eye when ya saw that crowd. Ya planned this."

"Really I did not. It just sort of happened," she said with as much conviction as she could muster. She was not so certain any longer. She considered the possibility that she could do a better job than Percy, but that would not have been difficult. Had she really thought about taking over before it happened? It was possible, and yet she had not even known it. In either case, it no longer mattered. Planned or otherwise, she was in charge, and it was much more work than she first thought.

"Ya' need a break. Ya've been locked up in here now for days. Ya canno' change everything at once. 'Alf these papers are useless to ya now. Zarono was secretive almost to the point of stupidity, but I can tell you this, he did no paper-work in the last four months. Anything you have here is now so far out of date ya' may as well throw it away," he picked up a sheet of paper and balled it into his palm as he spoke. He aimed the now tightly crushed sheet at the open window and launched it.

Briscay dashed outside in a flurry of black wings. He caught up with it and bounced it off his nose, tossing it in the air once more before catching it in his teeth. He flew back into the window and hovered in front of Lester.

Lyliana watched fascinated as Lester reached out with his hand, and Briscay dropped the paper into his palm.

Lester smirked at the dragon and exchanged an amused look with Lyliana. "I never knew they did that."

"Nor did I. It's so cute. Do it again."

Lester complied, and Briscay played with him for the next few minutes. It was not long before Yastat flitted through the window and landed on a stack of papers that threatened to overturn under his unbalanced weight. He observed the game for a few minutes and then chased after Briscay. Yastat was faster than Briscay, and the game developed into a competition between the two dragons.

Lyliana slid a paper from the pile balled up her own piece of paper and threw that out of the window at the same time as Lester. Both dragons chased both balls. They both came back with a ball each. Lyliana smiled. She was not likely to get any more work done. The four of them played on until they were later joined by Svation and Roylei.

They ate lunch while they continued to play with the dragons. Grygon, Roylei, and Briscay worked together to catch and return the paper balls whilst Svation, Tisray and Yastat perched on the edge of the table where Lester and Lyliana were eating. The dragons had a large bowl of water and some scraps but seemed more interested in the food that was tossed to them. Lyliana took scraps from the plate and threw it in the air for them between throwing paper balls for the others.

As they finished lunch, the dragons became distracted until finally three of them charged out of the window after a ball of paper and began to fight over it. It was tossed into the air where it seemed to pause longer than it should have done. Briscay stared at it as Grygon and Roylei let out a wash of flame and burnt the paper to ashes.

Lyliana watched fascinated. Did they do something to that paper? *Was it my imagination, or did it hover a little before they burnt it. I wonder.* She looked at Lester. The expression on his face suggested he was suspicious also. He opened his mouth to speak as someone knocked, and one of the lieutenants entered.

"One of the townspeople is here to see Lyliana. She says her name is Sheilah."

Lester banged his hand on the table, "Never a moment's peace. I 'ave been dealing with these people all da'. Wha' does she wan'?"

"She did not say. Should I bring her in?" asked the lieutenant, not at all fazed by Lester's sudden show of temper. He left the room, following a nod from Lester.

"Take it easy, my dear. The man is only doing his job. Besides, you have not been dealing with this all day. It's only just after lunch." She laughed and turned her attention to the door as footsteps announced the arrival of her visitor.

The woman took the seat that was offered and the drink Lester put in front of her. He retreated to the back of the room and disappeared into obscurity.

"How may I help you?"

"Well, you see it's like this, miss. We have been using

the well for water for a good long time. It supplies the whole town."

Lyliana nodded, familiar with the service. "Go on,"

"The well is dried up. No water anymore. They collect water in the tank at the harbour, but it's a good long way to carry water up the hill."

"I see. This just happened this morning?" Lyliana leaned forward slightly.

Sheilah nodded.

"So, we need a new water source or to unblock the well, however unlikely that might be," Lyliana said into a sigh. "Be assured I will make this my first priority. Thank you for bringing this to my attention." Lyliana shook the woman's hand and walked her to the door.

Once more alone, Lester perched on the corner of the table and grasped her hand in support.

Lyliana's brain suddenly snapped into focus. An idea blossomed. "Get her back quickly."

Lester shoved off the table and hurried after the woman. Noises at the end of the corridor confirmed that he had caught up to her.

"Tell me something. How did the well dry up?" Lyliana tensed for the answer she was expecting.

"The water was fouled during the riots. Some of the townsfolk emptied it to fix the problem. It just never filled up again."

And you did not mention this before? "I may have an idea, but I've never tried it before so you will have to bear with me. What I need, Sheilah, is for you to collect some of your friends together, and I will meet you at the front door in one hour. Do you understand?"

The woman nodded and fled. Lyliana exchanged glances

with Lester and shrugged, "What can I do? I must try. But this is a long shot."

"If a long shot is all you 'ave, it is all you 'ave." Lester eyed her. "Where'd this mysterious idea come from?"

Lyliana tossed her hair back. "Back home. Father's friend had a load of books stashed upstairs. We used to play up there. Mostly they were boring journals. We used to read them when it rained. One day we found these story books."

Lester's eyed went wide. "Ya gonna try something from a story book?"

Lyliana grinned. "No, I found another book much later that described the technique in some detail. Until then, I thought it was fiction."

"Do you 'ave a backup plan?" asked Lester, clearly not believing what he was hearing.

Lyliana nodded, "Of course, but it is not pretty." She sat back in the chair. "What I need now are a couple of buckets of water. Two should do it. Just leave them out front, and we shall see what the close of the hour brings."

An hour later, the tapping of her fingers on the desk matched the rhythm of Lyliana's heart, and the hollow sound echoed in her ears. *This one small action could be the cornerstone for my entire future.* The door remained stubbornly shut. Leaving the table, she paced back and forth. A scent of baked bread reached her. *It'll be easier for them...if it works.* She paused mid step and cocked her ear. Nothing. Lyliana heaved a deep breath and forced herself to go back to the chair. A few moments later, she was pacing again. *For sure, it's a gamble.*

Someone knocked at the door, and she rushed to sit back down. "Come." She listened to the woman's message and followed her outside where a crowd waited.

"I only needed a few of you. You had no cause to bring so many." She offered a contorted smile.

"I know, miss, but they wanted to come. Water is a concern to us all, especially with the distance we must go to get it. My back ached this morning so I could hardly get out of bed."

Lester appeared and placed three buckets of water at Lyliana's feet. She indicated that he should put them in the centre of the square, and Lester indicated the same to his second standing close behind him. He put down the twigs he was carrying and moved the buckets to the centre as directed. He spread the water carriers in a triangular pattern then retrieved the sticks and presented them to Lyliana.

She looked down to see that he had indeed followed her exact instructions. The sticks were about three foot long, consisting of a forked branch with a short section of single stick. She handled one of the items. The smoothness of the wood transmitted a softness through her fingers as she rested it in her hands and felt the weight. They were not perfect as per her studies, but they would do.

"Now then, before we begin, I have to get you to test this theory. This has never been tried before, but I have read about it. The method is water divining or dowsing. These sticks here," she waved one hand towards the stick in her other hand. "Should be elm or some such, but I believe it does not matter. Each of us will try this with an actual water source so we can tell instantly whether someone can do it or not. This is not an exact science. Some of us will not have the skills. Now, if you have this talent, the stick should dip a little when it senses water. Watch how it is done."

Lyliana proceeded to demonstrate how to hold the sticks. According to her research, they were to be held palm upwards with each branch between a thumb and forefinger. The other end of the branch was held half a foot above the ground while a methodical search pattern is walked. Seeing that the audience understood, she handed over the sticks all except one and encouraged the crowd to try it out for themselves. With the crowd distracted, she hovered the stick over her own bucket of water.

She rolled her head back and stretched her neck muscles. *It cannot work if you don't try.* When no one was looking, she directed the stick towards the water. The weight of the wood pressed hard against her thumbs, but it was only normal weight. She adjusted her grip as the stick dipped.

No movement, not even a twitch.

It has to work. Her grip tightened.

The stick did nothing. She shot a glance at the crowd. No one else had any success either. She shoved the stick at Lester.

Laughing drew her attention away from Lester's attempts. Even if they were not successful, some good was coming from the project. The townsfolk seemed pleased by her efforts even if they were doubtful as to the results. That was to be expected, and yet for all the doubts, they were at least trying. *A positive sign if ever I saw one,* she nodded slightly to herself.

An abrupt yell attracted their attention from across the square. One of the townsfolk was jumping up and down and waving, beckoning them over.

"He's done it. Look, look at it. The thin's moving on its own," shouted a young boy who could not have been more than ten years old.

"Do it again. Show us all," instructed Lyliana. She

jumped as Tisray landed on her shoulder. A low purring growl told her that Grygon was nearby.

Roger backed up until he was on the other side of the bucket, and then holding the stick as before, he moved slowly forward towards the water. Lyliana was so transfixed that the surrounding area blurred into nothing.

Was that a movement? Did it dip?

Imperceptibly at first and then with more determination, the stick dipped and strained in the man's hands. He frowned.

Lyliana studied his face and saw only concentration, the kind of deep concentration that comes from a desire to do well or a disbelief in one's success. *This is the real thing. He can actually do it.* She stepped forward to get a better look. The crowd had fallen silent. The stick dipped again, straining against the man's hands.

The motion of the stick grew violent as he moved over the bucket. With one last tug, it broke free of his hands and fell. The stick lay lifeless on the ground, not a quiver of motion visible.

He looked up straight into Lyliana's eyes. "I can't believe it." He rubbed his hands together with enough pressure to reveal his work hardened muscles. "That really hurts."

Lyliana laughed as the tension slipped from her. The gathering had grown, and the laughter spread throughout. They had done it. They had someone who could find water.

The yelling and laughing grew form and became cheering. "Cascada. Cascada." *Water Water*.

Tisray flicked his wings, and Lyliana snapped her head away as the dragon bounded from her shoulder to the bucket of water. His nostrils flared as he bent to sniff the liquid. He shook his head and sniffed again. His wings and tail flicked to keep him balanced on the unstable container.

He leaned too far forward, and the bucket tittered on the edge of overturning itself.

Lyliana squinted at the water. The bucket had been almost full. She leaned forward. *Is there less water?* She took a pace forward and bent to get a closer look.

The bucket tipped, and Tisray flapped his wings. His claws gripped the edge of the bucket, pulling it upwards.

She moved forward again. The bucket was now half-empty. Leathery wings pounded the air near her. Tisray was now flying. She looked again. He seemed bigger. His chest was puffed up, and his wingspan had definitely increased.

Lester approaching, frowning. He looked from Lyliana to the dragon, and his frown deepened.

So, it's not my imagination. The bucket was now empty. She shoved it with her foot and tipped it over. The water was gone. She stood it back up and cocked her head at the dragon.

Lester stepped back, and the crowd mirrored his movements. A shocked hush fell over them.

Tisray flapped higher. His wingspan had doubled in length, and the air moved violently when he rose. Lyliana stepped back to be clear of the wings and watched in awe.

The dragon landed on the end of the bucket that was now too small to support his weight. It tipped over again, and Tisray landed on the ground in a heap of flailing wings and thrashing tail. He rolled upright and shook his body as if he was clearing away his own stupidity. He stretched his neck to full length, his head high towards the sky.

A jet of water spat from his mouth and rose upwards above the crowd. As the water rushed skywards, Tisray shrunk. In a few moments, he was back to normal size.

A rustle of movement behind her told Lyliana that the crowd was watching. She smiled. *He can manipulate water.* She stepped towards the dragon. *It no longer surprises me what these animals can do.* Lyliana reached towards Tisray to pick him up.

Footsteps sounded behind. Lyliana stumbled as a body pushed past her. A man rushed at Tisray. The man grasped at the dragon that jumped high into the air. Wings flashed past her.

Lyliana froze. The man's hands missed the dragon that was now higher than his reach. Grygon appeared in a flurry of angry teeth, snapping wings and waving tail. She hovered just below Tisray.

A cloying force gripped the air. The grass around the bucket wilted. Dead grass spread outwards towards the crowd.

As one, the gathering stepped back. Tisray was growing again. He was double his size once more. The man beneath him stood frozen mid-step, his arms held outwards towards the dragons.

Tisray was now triple his original wingspan. The breeze from his wings lifted strands of Lyliana's hair.

The man below him seemed to realise he was in danger and turned to run away.

Tisray roared. The crowd threw themselves down. A huge jet of water gushed from Tisray. The man was thrown to the ground, pinned down by the sheer weight of water. Spray covered the crowd who raised their hands against the onslaught.

As the water petered off, Tisray shrunk to his normal size and landed in the puddle of water where the bucket had been. Lyliana cocked one eyebrow as a slow smile crossed her face.

The man, realising the danger had passed, pushed

himself to his feet and turned to Lyliana. "That beast attacked me."

Lester, now directly behind Lyliana, coughed.

She frowned. Her pulse pounded in her ears. She pointed at the man. "Tie him up." *He will die for what he has done.* Her eyes met Lester's calm expression. Her frown deepened. *How can he be so calm?*

The man shrunk away as two of Lester's men moved to obey her command. Tisray hissed at them but made no other move. Grygon stayed where she was. A winged guardian over her mate.

The man struggled as the pirates grabbed him. "It attacked me. It attacked me-e-e." His shouts became wails as they carried him away.

Behind her, Lester said, "He'll join the punishmen' detail. His fate'll be decided later."

She turned and met Lester's gaze.

"They are scared. And no wonder. We mu' expect such reactions." He took a deep breath. "Don't be too 'ard on 'em."

"An attack on the dragons is an attack on me." She waved the issue away.

Lyliana waited until the roaring in her ears dulled to a low thudding and then ordered the buckets taken away before sitting down with the town's new dowser, named Roger, to develop a plan for how they would locate water for the town. Assisted by input from the others, they decided on the best area to search and three other places in order of convenience. Thus instructed, Roger took the stick away with him and promised to return once there as something to report. The other members of the group hung around for a while as though they expected to see water sprout from the earth.

It was late in the evening by the time she had finished questioning the man who had threatened Tisray. He was tired, drained from the guards' treatment. Lyliana did not care. She had continued until she was satisfied that he had told her what she wanted to know. She was about the return home when she heard of Roger's success.

He discovered water in their second option location. From the behaviour of the stick, he surmised it was a large body of water. He had marked the spot with stones to show where to dig.

"The problem is, miss, it is right in the middle of the street. If we dig it up, and it turns out to be nothing then what? I should continue looking. There must be a better place for a well."

"We designated these locations as priority for a reason. If that is where the water is then so be it. We must just follow the chips where they fall. Tomorrow I will detail a digging party. Don't be alarmed if we find nothing. It only means we shall have to look again," said Lyliana in the most reassuring voice.

"I think it will work." He offered her a fearful glance. "I'm sure of it. You need not worry." He relaxed slightly when she smiled. "My sons can do the digging. They are all strong lads. The five of them should make easy work of it."

"Thank you, Roger. That shall not be necessary. This will be a punishment detail. It seems fitting that those who cause disruption in this town should be the ones to provide a convenience."

CHAPTER 22
ENCLAVE

Termurica alighted on the outskirts of the Enclave, having completed her ritual morning exercise before the sun rose. With a slight adjustment, it included a short walk. From where she landed. she would walk home to the palace.

Dewdrops soaked her bare feet as she rearranged her wings and settled them in a comfortable position. She pulled her skirts down over her legging-covered knees and resettled her weapons across her back.

She moved carefully, well aware of the early morning dangers to people of her size. Insects, in particular, seemed to have severe morning tempers, disproportionate to their size. Ever vigilant, she walked quietly with one ear open for the sounds of danger. Her eyes darted left and right looking for anything that might signal an attack.

As a pixie, she spent very little time on the ground, but sometimes she threw caution to the wind and, as with this morning, took her life into her hands to see things from a different perspective. Her husband would not be happy if he found out that she had been so cavalier with her safety.

By the time she neared the complex, she was beginning to relax, and her guard was down, otherwise she should have noticed the silence. The ominous lack of noise that preceded an attack. Most notably the birds, usually so vocal in the morning, were muted and furtive. Their few chirps were cut short as though silencing each other's fear.

It was the morning crickets that got Termurica's attention first. She stopped between the stems of two flowers and listened, hearing only a slight hushing made by the wind as it travelled through the blades of grass. She flicked her wings once, checking the air currents. It was then she noticed the silence of the birds. Termurica looked up. Her scalp tingled.

Abandoning her stroll, she took to the sky for an aerial tour of the Enclave. There was no point to go back and tell her husband she had a feeling. He would laugh like he always did. Usually, these feelings proved to be nothing. They always joked that one day she would be right. She hoped fervently that today would not be the day.

She circled the treetop buildings, surveying the Enclave's interior. The town was very much still sleep. An old woman shuffled about outside her house, and one or two plumes of smoke rose from early cooking fires. From the air, she could observe the entire town. The last of the night watch scorpions headed towards the den where they spent the days. Security was as tight as ever.

Her scalp tightened like a drying pelt.

Where are the dragonflies? How did I not see before? Where are the lookouts? Termurica's skin tingled with sudden cold. She flitted frantically round the settlement again.

There were no dragonflies.

Her stomach quivered as she took to the air at full speed

in the direction of the dragonfly pen. There was not a moment to lose. Her bare feet twitched in the cool air.

Termurica landed hard on the decking outside the pen. Her heart raced. She peered into the darkness of the enclosure, listening. Nothing. She held her breath. Leaves rustled behind her.

Nothing.

Her mouth dried to sand at a slight movement inside. The queen dragonfly, noted by her distinctive red back stripes, staggered towards Termurica. She was unsteady, as though drunk, and yet apart from her shaky gait, appeared healthy. She closed on the pixie, canted sideways, and fell to the ground. Her legs splayed wide, and her wings twitched fitfully. There was a slight murmur and a last sign of movement before the queen sagged and fell still.

Termurica fell to her knees. Her dry mouth developed a scratchiness at the back of her throat. She sniffed. She reached out and placed one hand gently on the fine translucent wings of the beast. There was no movement. The usual bright veins in her wings grew dull even as Termurica watched. She lowered her head until it was level with the dragonfly's. One tear dropped from her wet eyes.

Her vision grew accustomed to the dark, revealing the rigid corpses of the dragonflies. All of them. Her lip trembled, and she wiped the dampness from her cheek with the back of one hand. As she leaned forward, the queen's necklace fell forward clinking on the floor. She fingered the platinum decoration.

They were all dead. No sign of violence. No struggle. No forced entry.

She took a few deep breaths, and her stomach lurched. She rushed from the pen. Without breaking stride, she stepped off the platform and took to the air, arrowing towards the palace entrance. She moved so fast Termurica took the guards by surprise, speeding past them to find her husband.

"Myrrhta, Myrrhta! Where are you, my husband?" Termurica shrieked as she ran through the corridors.

Her husband rushed to the door of their chambers as she reached the room. "What is it, my love?"

"They're all dead. Every one of them dead. Even the queen," she said between gasping breaths.

"Explain yourself, woman," said her husband impatiently. He took in the expression on her face and took her hands in his. "I am sorry, my dear. Please explain."

Termurica hung her head and collected herself. "They are all dead. As is the queen. She died while I was there. All the dragonflies have been killed. I know not how. I noticed they were not out when I returned from my exercise. They're all dead, my husband."

Myrrhta's expression flashed from confusion, to disbelief, to anger all in the space of a few seconds. He snapped his fingers. "Come here. You at the side. Come here now." The guard at the end of the corridor rushed to the doorway. "Go and check on the dragonflies. Something has happened to them. Call out the guard, and someone to check on the scorpions also. Hurry, man." This last he added as the lad gave him a confused look. Myrrhta turned back to his wife. "Come in, my dear, and sit down. You are quite pale."

Termurica did as her husband bid. She sat heavily on the large bed the two of them shared and rested her weight on her elbows. Her wings drooped, her bow stuck into the back of her left knee.

Myrrhta removed the bow from her shoulder carefully as though she might shatter from his touch and laid it down on the bed. He followed this with the quiver and then removed his wife's belt.

"What are we to do? What is going on? I do not understand. Somebody *attacked* us?" asked Termurica in a low voice.

"We shall discover the truth soon enough. The guard will be back, or he will send his captain. Do not worry, my love. We will find out what has occurred. You should lie down and take some rest. Truly, you do not look well." Myrrhta got a damp cloth and applied it gently to his wife's face before cradling her in his arms and whispering consoling words in her ear.

As they waited, Termurica developed a headache. It began as a slight discomfort and quickly became a pounding, unforgiving agony that stabbed behind her eyes. Finally succumbing, she lay on the bed with her head on Myrrhta's knee. His heat erased her pain a little. She closed her eyes against the growing light.

The guard returned, carrying his helmet and quiver in one hand. He knocked lightly on the open door and entered without waiting for permission. His steps were short and fast. Termurica registered his demeanour and sat up. Her head pounded in response to the rapid movement, but she ignored it.

"It is confirmed, my lord. They're all dead. There's no sign of a struggle, but there *were* bits of food all over the floor. I would hazard they were poisoned. I have men out. I took the liberty of looking myself, and I could find no tracks. The culprit must be a pixie. Without the dragonflies, they could have flown out without detection." said the guard in short, clipped sentences.

"And the scorpions?" asked the king.

"The scorpions are untouched, my lord. They are resting

in their den. I put extra guards on them. I sent out a party to retrieve more dragonflies, and I will set to training them as soon as they arrive. It won't be easy. It is not their time of year." It was not clear whether he meant for catching or training them.

Myrrhta nodded and signalled for the guard to leave. He turned to his wife, rubbing his beard thoughtfully. "Who would do such a thing? There is no reason for this. The guard reported no damage. Nothing stolen. So why?"

Termurica stood sharply. "Did anyone check the caverns?"

The king mirrored her movements and marched towards the door. "I shall see to it at once." He nodded to his queen and stalked from the room.

Termurica took a deep breath and turned to her dressing table. Before she reached it, her attention was drawn by the sounds of running footsteps drew her attention. Frankine appeared in the doorway, followed closely by her father.

"Mother, Father, the cavern. You must come quickly. She turned and rushed for the door with her parents in quick-step behind her.

They were not even in the cavern before they realised there was a problem. There was an obvious glow emanating from the darkness. They rushed in, almost tripping over each other in their hurry. The entire area glowed purple with ripples and pulses. The cavern stank of distress.

Frankine stopped dead. Her parents crashed in behind her.

Termurica stared, unable to believe what she was seeing. It was open. Someone had opened the box. Dread filled her. What could this mean?

"What happened?" Myrrhta whispered in a panicked

tone. "Why? What is going on here? The box is open. I never saw the box open."

"It's awful," said Frankine who had recovered quicker than her parents and was now kneeling down over the box. "Some stones are missing. Come, and look, Father. Come, and look. It is quite obvious." She beckoned her father over.

Termurica kept pace with her husband and stared into the box. Her daughter was correct. Darker patches marked the area as though the missing stones had left a shadow. The atmosphere rippled with discontent just below the surface, noticeable only to those who knew the cavern well.

Termurica shivered and stared into the dark empty spaces, sensing the deep loss of the space. The question remained: how many were missing. She exchanged a worried glance with her husband and clapped an arm protectively around her daughter.

CHAPTER 23
SYNGH

The letter arrived around noon during Syngh's lunch break in the library. It was the first few minutes he had to himself recently, and he was trying to make up for lost time. He had just started Mistress Roxanne's 'History of the Modern Coven' when Jaden brought the note to him.

The lad was beginning to act like his own personal manservant, and Syngh's appreciation was marred with embarrassment. He was little more than a servant himself in this place.

Jaden placed the sealed note on the table in front of him just within arm's reach. Syngh looked at him and pushed the book to one side. "What's this? I was not expecting anything for another week."

"It came with today's stores wagon. The man said to bring it directly to you. He was quite insistent. He said the falcon could not bring it," said Jaden, smiling.

"Most likely the weather up here." Syngh reached for the letter, nodding his thanks to Jaden. He ripped open the seal in one smooth movement as though he had been doing it all his life. In fact, it was only the second time. The paper crackled as he unfolded it to reveal Piearsa's very distinctive hand.

He skim-read through the usual pleasantries, inquiries after his health, and details of various activities since he left. The tone of the letter changed all of a sudden, marked by a decline in the tidiness of the handwriting. His pace slowed as he stopped skimming and concentrated.

Syngh tugged at his hair as he read. A sharp intake of breath drew Jaden's attention, pulling him close. It was not so much Piearsa's words that created the reaction but more the tone of her writing. Syngh's pulse increased, and he rubbed his eyes as he continued to read. She left the worst until last. He read the words twice before they sank in.

'You must come home immediately. Your family would never ask it of you, but they desperately need your help.'

He rose sharply, knocking the chair, exchanged a brief glance with Jaden, and stormed from the room. Footsteps behind confirmed that the lad followed him.

He reached the dormitory and marched over to his bed, dropping to his knees to dig his bag out from underneath. He opened the leather satchel, shoved in a change of clothes, his firelighters, and his favourite book from the library. He gave no mind to the fact that he was stealing.

Jaden watched wide-eyed as Syngh latched the straps on his bag. "Syngh, what are you doing? Where are you going?" Jaden whined.

"I am a slave, lad. My family needs me." He stuffed the last few items into the front pockets of the bag and tossed it across his shoulders.

He got a few paces before he realised Jaden was following him. Syngh turned and put his hands on his shoulders. "Don't worry, Jaden, you will be okay here. It is a good future, and you will always be cared for. But *I* must leave. Someday, I will return to visit you, but I cannot say when. Thank you for your help. It was a pleasure knowing you." He offered the lad a weak smile and ruffled the top of his head.

He was out of the door and halfway down the path before he realised the lad was still there. He *was* there, but there was hesitation in his step. *He will go back soon.* Syngh continued until he was out of sight of the coven building before turning once more to face the Jaden.

"You never told me where you are going. Why are you leaving like this? I should go with you. I owe you so much. You have looked after me since you come here. You are the only reason I got this far."

Syngh smiled. "Never mind that, lad. I have enjoyed your company. You are a good friend, and you have helped me study and learn. You owe me nothing. My family needs me. You know of the bad feeling spreading throughout the werecats here. It seems, from what my girlfriend tells me, that this is spreading elsewhere also. I must be there to face whatever is coming."

"In that case, I must come with you, Syngh. Whatever you say, I owe you everything, so I owe your family. It would be wrong to speak otherwise. I shall spend this day until my last repaying your kindness to me." The lad smiled widely, showing his every thought across his small face. "If you will have me, that is?"

His reciprocal smile held more feeling than he thought possible. Jaden was a good lad after all and the one reason he had been happy to stay in the Coven. His father had said such loyalty was hard to come by, though it seemed almost natural between them. Finally, he nodded and put his arm around Jaden's shoulders as they continued down the track.

When they reached the bottom of the slope, he threw his bag on the ground and turned to Jaden. "Now we must change. It is a long journey, and we must be over the ridge by nightfall. It will be much easier on four legs."

The boy nodded reluctantly.

As they changed into feline form, the bells in the coven building sounded. Syngh had not realised there were alarms. It was against coven policy for werecats to be in any form other than human. It never occurred to him that there was a method of alerting them to such things. He exchanged looks with Jaden, scooped up his bag in his mouth, and accelerated to a full speed run. He heard Jaden follow, and they set pace for the run around the lake. There was no time to spare.

Syngh slowed a little as his longer legs out paced the smaller cat. He had to admit the lad was fast for his age. When he grew, he would be much faster than Syngh.

The pair circled the lake without looking back. If someone were following, they would have heard. They kept going until they reached the bridge and finally descended out of view of the Coven. It was not until the sun had already disappeared that Syngh decided they were safe enough to stop for the night. They turned off the track and climbed higher to a secluded ledge behind some rocks. From that position, they could see the track below and both approaches.

After a restless night, they started off again early before the sun rose. Their feline vision helped them through the predawn gloom, but the ground was still treacherous under-foot. Jaden found it especially difficult as he slipped over the unstable terrain. A life inside the grounds of the Coven had not prepared him for such rigorous exercise. He never explored the mountains that surrounded the witch's gentle pathways.

Halfway through the next morning, they reached the lower slopes. Feeling more secure now he knew no one was following them, Syngh slowed his pace. Jaden had never complained but was clearly relieved.

Sometime later, they reached the place where Syngh had stopped with his family weeks before. Knowing the area, he decided that would be a good place to stop for something to eat, and without warning, he changed back into human form. The pain in his muscles was more than he remembered, but he put that down to the infrequency of changes caused by the Coven's restrictions.

Jaden's eyes burned into him, but the boy said nothing. Syngh tried and failed to ignore him, so instead he sent him foraging. Syngh knew the lad had no idea how to start a fire so it would be a waste of time for him to change into human form just now. His time would be better spent hunting.

The lad nodded in response, flicked an ear in a goodbye gesture, and set off between the few trees, the most likely source of food.

When Jaden returned, Syngh had already started the fire and was boiling some leaves he had stored away at the Coven. He poured the thick warm pulp into a cup while Jaden changed. Having drunk his fill, Syngh refilled the cup and passed it to Jaden who was once more in human form. They exchanged a smile. They were both stark naked in the freezing lowlands of the mountains, and yet neither of them was cold, one advantage of were-blood running through their veins. Still, it would not do to burn the extra energy it took to stay warm very long.

Syngh threw a couple of birds into the pot and added a

few herbs he had found en route to turn it into a stew and give them a quick meal before they continued. He stirred the pot and surreptitiously watched Jaden as he moved about their makeshift camp. "How are you doing, Jaden? I told you it would be rough, but we are more than halfway now." He avoided the lad's eyes as he spoke.

"I am not tired at all," replied the Jaden with forced enthusiasm. "I could go like this for days."

"Depending on what actually happened, you might need to. Piearsa was not specific in the details."

Jaden stared at the ground. His fingers fidgeted by his side. Without making eye contact, he asked, "What do you know? You never told me anything more than your family needed you. If it is okay to ask?"

"Piearsa wrote to tell me that the pride was in trouble. I assume there is some strife with another pride though I cannot imagine what. We have little contact with others." Syngh shook out his cup onto the ground. "Not clean, but it will do," he murmured.

"So really, it might not be serious at all?" asked Jaden as he wiped his mouth with the back of his hand.

"Piearsa would not have written were it not serious. I know only this. I must go home and as soon as possible. We must hurry." With quick movements, Syngh finished his own stew and piled the various items back into the bag. Very soon, they were on the move again.

———

Dusk was drawing in when they completed their journey and arrived at the edge of the tree line that led to the pride's village. Sounds of frantic, hurried motions came from the between the trees so Syngh and Jaden approached cautiously.

A chill spilled over Syngh. Something was watching him. A rustling drew his attention to a dark patch of trees. A shape landed in front of him with a heavy slump.

Jaden started, shocked by the sudden movement. Syngh froze where he stood. A slow smile broke through his tension. Piearsa tilted her head in a questioning movement, but her expression brightened as she rushed to him and pressed her head under his chin in greeting.

Piearsa and Syngh changed on their way back to village, ignoring the rule about changing in one place. No one saw them. Jaden made an excuse and left them in privacy for a while after ensuring he knew how to get to the village.

"What happened that I don't already know?" asked Syngh after they had finished the usual pleasantries and more personal greetings.

"We were attacked by another pride. We don't even know who they were. Janneson followed the few who escaped, but he lost them after nightfall. We heard reports of similar things occurring all over. No one knows why." Piearsa paused and turned to look into his eyes. "There's something else..."

Syngh's stomach twisted, he nodded for her to continue.

"I couldn't tell you in a letter. It's Falora...she was hurt."

"My mother...is she okay?" Syngh took a pace towards the village. The twist in his middle grew to vice-like intensity.

"For now, but they are not sure. I'm sorry, my love. It does not look good. We tried, but we did not get there in time."

"Father?"

"He has not left her side. I believe he blames himself. It

was not his fault. I'm sorry, Syngh. I was closer. I didn't get there fast enough." She took a step towards him.

Without another word, Syngh turned and stalked towards the village. He ignored the greetings from his friends and headed straight for his parents' tree house. Piearsa followed a few paces behind.

Syngh climbed the ladder, skipping numerous rungs, calling his father before he entered the door.

"Syngh, is that you, son?" asked his father and then in a quieter voice, "Syngh has returned. Falora, your son is here to see you. I told you he was coming."

His father's words cut a track through Syngh's heart. He forced a smile as he entered the room, hoping it was enough to hide his fear. He rushed to her bedside and clasped her hands in his. They were cold and clammy. Falora's face was drawn with strain and obvious pain. Syngh swallowed hard as his eyes told him what his girlfriend had not.

Behind him, Piearsa hovered in the doorway.

"Tell me everything, Father."

Syngh listened with hardly a breath as Miroslaw described the early morning attack, the confusion, and the noise. He recounted what he had been told of the chase. The attackers had run eastwards into the marshlands. They could not be tracked further, according to the younger lads who had given chase. Miroslaw recounted his dismay upon his return to the house to find his wife in Piearsa's arms with the medic on the way.

"Since then, we have tried to find out who was responsible so we can decide how to respond, but other prides have suffered the same, and no one can give any explanation. We know there will be retaliations, but we decided not to act until we have more information. Things will only

escalate, but personally, I believe we must do something."
His tone hardened. "If only because of this." He indicated
his dying wife.

"I will deal with this," Syngh said, his tone dissuading
any argument. "I will start tonight to prepare. This will not
go unanswered."

"Your mother would not want that," replied Miroslaw,
but his voice held no conviction.

Piearsa's hand rested firmly on Syngh's shoulder, and
they exchanged glances.

She was all the support he needed.

CHAPTER 24
LYLIANA

"Your wa'er divinin' idea was brilliant. Come, and 'ake a walk with me, and ya will see. They are all so happy they think ya'r the second light." Lester pulled Lyliana from her office and down onto the street.

"I could do with a break. They might be happy, but for me, I did not realise that there was so much paperwork. Pirates don't do admin. Shouldn't it be all raping and pillaging?"

Lester raised his eyebrows and led the way down the street.

The morning sun spread its rays relentlessly down onto the empty town. The townsfolk were few and far between until the pair reached the harbour. Market day crowds turned the docks into a hive of activity.

Lyliana surveyed the scene and smiled. There were stalls of all variety, fish, meat, and sugar products spread down one side of the corridor between the stalls while on the other side, there were all manner of other wares. Lyliana stopped at a liquor stall and was amazed by the sheer variety of products. Until that moment, she had no idea there were so many different ways to make the vile potions Lester enjoyed.

"Hello, miss. Welcome," said the stall keeper as soon as he saw her. Not so long ago, they would not have been able to pick her out of the crowd, and yet now, this man who she had never meant before recognised her on sight.

"Hello. I wish you luck with your sales, sir," she replied dutifully.

"Can I get you something? A sweet rum perhaps?" He shuffled round the table and stood beside her.

Lyliana resisted the temptation to step away from the man's foul breath and turned her head instead, under the pretence of studying the bottles. "I confess I am not familiar with rum. I am sorry," she said meekly, making sure that her face was suitably remorseful.

"No matter, miss. You can try some of mine. Perhaps you will find something suitable, and I can make sure that I always have a stock in for you," he simpered. "The name is Tracker, miss. Old nickname from my sea days," he added this last in response to her confusion.

Lyliana nodded and exchanged a glance with Lester who was looking distinctly amused. She took the small sample cup from the man and put a few drops on her tongue before handing it to Lester. "He knows more of the flavour than I." She smiled at Tracker. "He is my consultant," she explained when Tracker shoved his hands into the pockets of his flea-invested pants.

Tracker nodded enthusiastically and handed over another small pot of the bronze liquid. After numerous tasters, Lyliana felt obligated to buy something and choose his favourite. She would not be drinking it, but the man did not need to know that.

Lyliana found a similar welcome at every stall, even those she passed in which she had no interest. Stall owners frequently hurried over to encourage her to inspect their wears after just a glance from her, and the infectiously friendly atmosphere spurred her on. She came away from the market with a couple of items, neither of which she actually needed, but the boost in her self-confidence was well worth the money she paid for the items.

"I told ya. They all love ya." Lester pulled her into an embrace once they were around the corner and out of the way of the general view. "That was a hell of a thing ya pulled off, and to think, if I 'ad time to think about it, I would ha' recommended it no be attempted in case it failed and your standing in the communi'y were damaged." He smiled affectionately with just a hint of regret.

"Risk nought, gain nought, or something like that." She returned his smile and led him out of the back street and round the outskirts of the town. It was her favourite route, mostly because there were not many people. The cooling air from the water was refreshing. Lyliana had grown uncomfortably warm under all the unwanted attention and proximity to the crowds.

She hooked her arm into his, and they continued along the front at a leisurely pace until it was time to turn the corner back up towards the town.

"We should spend the afternoon in our spot behind the 'ouse. It has been a while, what with all the excitemen'," said Lester as they approached the first couple of buildings.

"I would love to, but I really have so much work to do. Once I'm caught up then I can relax a little." She grinned widely to soften her refusal.

Lester stopped and turned her towards him. "You know, there is no one to check up on you. They will not scold you if you don't do something or have the afternoon off without permission…unless you scold yourself, of course." He grinned and tucked her hair behind her ear.

"I might just do that actually." She knuckled his arm playfully. "I know all this, but I have this awful dread that it will all go wrong if I relax before everything is done. Besides, a little effort now will hopefully make it easy later."

Lester nodded slowly, obviously not fully convinced. "Will you at least have a drink with me before I walk you back?"

"Betty's?" She cocked her head.

"Where else?" He offered his arm to her and led her back into the town.

Lester held the door open for Lyliana, and they entered Betty's bar together. The sudden gloom blinded Lyliana. She headed for the bar, using her memory to guess the positions of the tables. A scuffling and clinking of glasses signalled that Betty had seen her and was heading in their direction.

"All 'ail the conquering hero. Drin's on the 'ouse," she declared.

Lyliana heard her friend's steps as she went back behind the bar. "Just the usual please, Bets. Thank you very much."

"Don't be silly. This is a celebration. I'm going to ma'e something very nice for you," she giggled. More glasses clinked.

Lyliana tried not to grimace, knowing Betty could see her even though she was still blind. Her eyes slowly adjusted, and she was able to watch as Betty mixed the concoction for them. She was pleased to see that the ingredients were not quite as wild as normal. Not that she would have any choice but to try it.

Betty placed a great jug in front of them with three

glasses into which she poured generous measures of pink liquid. Lyliana studied the contents of the glass. The drink was almost the same colour as the psychedelic dress Betty was wearing. Whether that was through intention or spillage was hard to determine.

Betty and Lester clinked their glasses onto hers in salute, and all three drank deeply, finishing in a time even the hardiest pirate would approve of. Lyliana was surprised to find that she quite enjoyed it and was eager for a second glass. After the third refill, Betty thanked Lyliana again for the well and politely excused herself, returning to the back of the bar to continue with her work.

Lester carried their drinks over and sank down into a chair at their usual table. His shoulders drooped, and he took another big swig of his drink.

Lyliana watched him but said nothing. She realised suddenly what a strain it must be to worry about her being in front of the crowd when he could not predict their reactions. She smiled inwardly and put her hand on his. "Thank you," she kissed him on the cheek.

He frowned slightly, "What's tha' for?"

"Your support and for keeping me safe. It cannot be an easy job *some* of the time."

Lester giggled and squeezed her hand. "*Some* of the time, it ain't."

"I promise you. No more surprises."

He nodded but looked less than convinced.

Clever boy. She shook off her musings.

"So, now that you have your audience, what is next?"

"What makes you think I have a plan? None of this was planned."

"So you keep sayin', but I know you 'ave something

going on in that 'ead of yours I am getting to know ya quite well by now." He took another drink and settled himself back into the chair.

"We need to do some rearranging. I don't believe all our staff are entirely trustworthy. Then there is the matter of Bill and Jambo. They are still locked up, I assume?"

"Per your instructions. I'm no' in a hurry to let 'em go anytime soon."

She downed the rest of her drink. "I shall deal with them this evening," she said with authority.

Break time was over.

———

Lester marched around the corner. Two of his men were guiding the shackled prisoners to their punishment. He had not even flinched at Lyliana's suggestion of their punishment. She got the impression he thought she was too lenient, but he had the sense not to say so.

Lyliana watched them approach and noted the grins of anticipation from the crowd. They might have been very nice to her all morning and showered her with praise and apparent love, but underneath they were still the savage nomads that petrified the people of Hillaway. Lyliana sensed their enthusiasm as though it was a physical thing. Her disgust deepened at their bloodthirsty attitude. It was a punishment parade, not in-house entertainment.

She scanned the crowd once more, noting the children, equally enthralled. *What chance do they have? They should be in school or at home learning. Not out here with this barbaric lot.* She shook herself. Just as she began to think she was fitting in, something occurred to remind her of her roots. *What would*

Charles think of all this? He would most likely want to kill these two, but he would not approve of the audience.

Lester caught her eye, and she nodded that he should bring the prisoners forward. The crowd silenced and became very still as Lester and his men made their way through the gap in the people and reached the front just before her. His men threw the chains down at her feet as though they were offering the two men up as a sacrifice. They nodded to her and backed away to a respectful distance. Lester moved forward and stood next to her.

Bill and Jambo look her straight in the eyes, not a drop of fear in sight. It was obvious the pair expected someone to come to their rescue. They would be disappointed.

The crowd stared at them with malevolence.

Lyliana scanned the throng before turning her full attention on the men. "You two men are charged with attempted rape. Do you have anything to say?"

Bill averted his eyes when she said the word *rape*. Jambo looked at her indignantly. "You can't prove that we did anything. I deny the charges." He stared at her defiantly.

"I don't have to prove it. I was the intended victim," she replied in a calm voice that was loud enough for everyone to hear.

"You still have to prove it, bitch."

The crowd gave a guttural growl and appeared to shift forward though there was no obvious move. The sound of scraping metal brought him to a halt. The guards stood with their swords brandished.

Bill gave a quick upwards glance then returned his eyes to the ground.

"Okay, that's fair enough. I was also going to charge you with murder, but I actually cannot prove that you did it.

Only that you hid the body in the same barn where you attacked me, so attempted rape will have to do. It won't matter much anyway. If you are prepared to admit your crime, your punishment will be lessened."

Lester stared at her in shock and concern as the crowd grumbled more decisively. She held up one hand to forestall his complaint.

She looked back at Jambo and glanced at Bill. "What about you? Are you going to let him give you a greater punishment, or will you admit your guilt?"

"'old your ongue, shi'ate," Jambo hissed at the other man.

Bill never looked up but shook his head.

Jambo glared at her triumphantly. "He knows you can't prove it, see? Busted. He turned sharply towards the crowd. "'re 'ou useless lumps goin' to let this con'inue? This is not a trial."

"Some of the audience shook their heads disapprovingly, but no one made any comment. Nor any move to come to his defence."

Lyliana smiled, "Lester can confirm everything I am saying if you really need me to prove my accusations. I would not want these good people to think that I hand out unfair punishments." *Not bad for a first time manipulating a crowd*. She did her best to keep a straight face and not show her satisfaction when the crowd, as one, looked to Lester.

"I arrived just in 'ime to prevent harm coming to 'er," he said to the crowd in general.

Lyliana spread her hands out in front of her in an appeasing gesture. She could feel the support of the crowd like a soft cushion.

"He would 'ay that. He would protect 'is woman. His

opinion does no' count. This is an 'nfair judgemen'," Jambo pleaded, wriggling in his bonds.

"So would we all," shouted someone in the crowd.

"I demand a retrial," shouted Jambo. Bill glanced up hopefully but looked quickly back at the ground when one of the guards moved towards him.

"I should double your punishment just for your lies," Lyliana hissed.

Lester looked at her and gave an almost imperceptible shake of his head.

Jambo jerked back and yelled, pulling his hands to his face. A streak of blood appeared on his cheek. Dillitay flew above him and landed on Lyliana's shoulder. He grabbed a strand of her hair to steady himself as she turned too quickly to try and look at him.

"Steady on, you almost had me off there." He raised his voice and himself above her. "I witnessed the entire event. They were both complicit in the crime. Had Lester not turned up when he did, I have no doubt what they would have done. They already had her pinned to the table."

The crowd growled, louder this time, and shifted menacingly towards the prisoners. "Hang 'em," shouted various women. The men were silent but clearly agreed with their women.

Lyliana shook her head slightly. *They are rapists and murderers and probably a whole host of other crimes I don't even know about. Hanging is too humane.* She looked at Lester. "Strip them." She nodded in response to his unspoken request for confirmation. She turned to the crowd, "From this day forward, the punishment will fit the crime. Tie them to that stake. They shall stay there naked until I am sick of seeing them."

"There won't be much to see." A snigger from somewhere in the crowd was greeted by raucous laughter.

Lester directed his guards to follow her instructions and then disappeared back round the corner before returning after a few minutes. He caught Lyliana's eye and held up two small bags that bulged as though they were full of oranges. He nodded his head towards the prisoners and looked down at his crotch.

Lyliana allowed herself a slight smile and waved her hand in acquiesce. Lester grinned and tossed the bags over to the guards. It was obviously not the first time they had seen this punishment. They bent before the prisoners, and when they rose again Lyliana could not help but look. She glanced at the crowd who wore mixed expressions of shock, surprise, and amusement. Not one of them seemed upset by the development.

She followed their gaze and collected herself to look at the spectacle in front of her. Each man had a bag tied to his genitals. The look of horror on their faces was surpassed only by the stunned silence of the crowd. As she watched, a young child ran over to the men. A yell from the group signalled the panicked attempt of the mother to chase the kid who closed on Bill and flicked the bag. The kid shrieked wildly in delight as the bag swung and hit Bill in the stomach. He howled in pain and rage. The kid froze, took one look at Bill, then ran back to his mother who had only made it halfway across the plaza. The crowd erupted into laughter and cheered the child who buried his head in his mother's skirts.

Lyliana smiled weakly. *My people*. Her smile faded as her eyes fell on Percy. He was on the edge of the crowd, glaring at her. The air cooled measurably. Lyliana looked over to Lester, but he had not seen the exchange. Her eyes met

Percy's, and he drew one finger across his neck in an unmistakable gesture. She shook her head slightly. *What can he really do to me unless he wants to tangle with Grygon?*

She turned her back and walk away from the group. Lester and his guards followed behind her and stayed in close formation until she reached the main building and headed for her office. She still had much work to complete before the end of the day.

CHAPTER 25
ENCLAVE

A new mist drifted in from the east. It twisted and curled through the grasses. It meandered across the forest floor just above the earth, creeping towards the Enclave. A breath of air snaked in, twirling delicate patterns through the grey darkness. Grasses shivered, though nothing moved them. The fog circled the Enclave. It slipped and slithered, blanketing the ground beneath, leaving darkness in its tracks.

The picket guards shivered under their ponchos. Their wings hummed a fast rhythm in an effort to stay warm. The tallest guard pulled his scarf tighter about him and shoved his hands into the pockets of his tightly fitting trousers. He wiggled his toes inside his heavy boots to ward away the dampness.

He did not notice it at first. The hour grew late, his watch was almost over, and the blurriness in his eyes was not uncommon. Yet this time it was not his eyes at fault.

His watch mate tutted and moved the tiny chess piece in mock attack. The game had lasted four-night watches already and showed no sign of concluding.

The thin cloud edged closer, sliding upwards a little as though studying them before it moved on.

The lanky guard shoved himself back against the bark of the tree, using the thick trunk as a shield against the searching cold. He stared into the darkness and squinted. The hairs on the back of his hand stood on end. He sucked at the inside of his mouth. It was dry like a desert. He leaned forward, ripped the end of a leaf free, and shoved the chewy frond between his teeth. He chewed hard and sucked at the flesh of the greenery. Even so, his mouth grew dry again quickly.

He turned and looked towards the palace and surrounding buildings. In the distance, the scorpion guards were moving about. He could see their ghostly shadows amongst the leaves on the ground. He imagined he could see their eyes glowing in the dim moonlight. He could have sworn one looked at him and shook its lethal tail. He shuddered although whether from the cold or the creature's eyes, he was not sure.

The scorpions disappeared into the fog, leaving only their tails poking above to mark their movements. As he watched, the guard could have sworn he felt a presence. Something malevolent. Something you could not pin down or explain and yet knew, without a doubt, was a threat.

With a sudden rush, more scorpions appeared. They grouped together and stood facing outwards, their tails poised aggressively. They skated sideways back-and-forth, as if expecting some kind of attack. They froze, rigid. Not even a twitch to show they were breathing. They bristled and turned towards each other. Another appeared out of the darkness and charged. The guard flew. Lethal tails stabbed savagely. Another pair circled each other, feigning stabbing motions to throw the other off-balance.

Never taking his eyes from the scorpions, the first guard untangled his hands from the folds in his poncho and hit his mate on the shoulder. "You seeing this?"

"You're just avoiding your move, so you do not loose... again," said the other man, simultaneously chewing the end of a grass shoot.

"Stop messing and stand to. Something's up with the scorpions, Newton."

Newton stood and stared at the scene unfolding before them.

Beyond the mist were more scorpions. They were going crazy, running at each other, clashing headfirst into anything in their path. Their tails slashed madly but did little damage. One dashed into the path of another's tail and was killed instantly as the sharp spike crashed through the armoured head of the running creature.

"Should we tell someone?" asked Newton.

The taller guard readied his bow tipped with wasp stings. With his spare hand, he brandished his knife. *Can they climb trees?* He would not be caught unaware. One damaged wing and he was dead. He hovered above the scorpions, hearing the hissing and swooshing of their tails and the loose rumblings of stones scattered about the floor.

"We should tell someone." *And leave this place quickly.* There was clearly some force acting on the scorpions. He had been a palace guard for many years and never seen such a thing. He looked below, staring through his grey dust tinged with pink. They were dying. Killing each other. Without mercy or thought. *Why?*

A silence descended over the ground as the pixie guard flew low. He hovered just above the murk. The cold clutched at his feet. It soaked through his thick boots. He shivered.

A force pulled him. It dragged at him, clawing him towards the mist. He panicked and flapped madly. He gained altitude slowly, every slight gain sapping his energy. The force weakened. He pushed himself higher and higher. He looked down through the gaps in the fog. The scorpions were dead. Every one of them dead.

Not a movement or hint at life. Just dead.

CHAPTER 26
RAKSHASA GORGE

Warm winds play across the sands as always. The occasional movement of dead leaves and grasses break the silent stillness. Far above the scorched landscape, a single Sasko vulture circles, dark wings cast shifting shadows across the plains. Finally, it descends towards its prey. The shadows stretch as it spirals towards the ground.

A casual observer, had there been such a person nearby, would have noted nothing out of the ordinary in this desolate place. An area long since abandoned by any living creature except those who call the desert home.

But the scorpion notices. A creature whose species stood the test of time even whilst all others ran to hide underground or died under the forces at work against them. In their hurry to escape, they had forgotten the lessons the scorpion learned well.

Acrid warmth accompanies the increasing breeze to smother the oppressive air. Rocks shift in ominous patterns towards the end of the gorge. They tumble and bounce as though trying to escape from the wind. The sand shifts, constructing small dunes to obstruct the scorpion hurrying into hiding. He narrowly misses being thrown into the deep chasm of the canyon.

Other creatures run for cover. They hide deep in the sand to escape the cloying heat and dust. The sand burns. It scalds the feet of the slower insects. Some are not fast enough. The stench of burning flesh reaches the scorpion deep in his lair.

A force emerges. Something ancient. Power permeates the ground. The desert is no longer the most inhospitable entity in this savage landscape. Its panoramic vista is dwarfed by the raging energy arriving with the wind.

A cacti, erect for decades, bows to the force and then crumples, its store of moisture depleted. It dies as quietly as it grew, unnoticed.

The effects of the new arrival creep onwards. Brittle skeletons lie in its wake. Not a drop of liquid remains.

It is searching. Lost, confused, frustrated. It knows this place but barely. The memory has not stood the test of time. It will return. This it knows.

The force recoils and regroups. It has been many years since it traversed these shores. It must get its bearings. It is weak, barely conscious, and yet the sand trembles before it.

It knows power. It can feel it, sense it, almost taste it. And yet it lacks essence, meaning, and focus.

It must get lower. Below ground level. Somewhere close, deep. It must have space to grow and develop. It bides its time. It does not want to wait. It is awakened as before. It is vengeful, impatient.

Rage fills the energy at such a slight and the forgetfulness that created it. It has not been a long time, not so long to regenerate.

It is ready…almost.

Not long now.

They will pay. Whoever is to blame, their identity means nothing. They are already finished. They are the scourge of existence.

CHAPTER 27
LOWLANDS

Miroslaw and Syngh stayed by Falora's bedside all night. They watched, helpless as she faded, as her body gradually succumbed to the darkness. Their cries joined with her coughing and broke the night silence. Syngh buried his head in his mother's bedclothes and sobbed, all pretence at being strong lost during the hours of torment. His father remained quiet. He shed no tears. Syngh suspected he had long come to terms with the fate of his wife. Syngh was left to wish he had been there in her hour of need, to protect his family when they needed it.

Piearsa had left them alone despite Miroslaw's assurances that she was as much a part of the family as anyone. As Falora's life force diminished, so did the nighttime darkness. She finally, fitfully slipped away as the sun rose. Syngh prayed for his mother's soul. For the chance to ensure his father would not be lonely. Most of all, he prayed for revenge.

Later that day, the village gathered once more in the forest. This time to say goodbye to another of their dead. Many friends had kind words for the family. There were speeches and toasts drunk in Falora's honour. Later that night, they danced and sang as was the custom of the pride. First, they mourned their fellow's passing. Later, they celebrated the life.

Obscured under the veil of celebration, Piearsa made plans of another kind. Her rage almost matched that of the family.

Despite Syngh's initial reaction that he would move the waters of the earth to find the culprit, the fire in his heart burned out quickly. He still wished for revenge yet he was no longer sure he was capable of such things himself.

Piearsa was of a different mind. She thought not of Syngh's mother, but of the village and all they had lost. Syngh observed the darkened stain on his girlfriend's heart. It had not been there when he left for the Coven. Now it radiated power. It offered strength and a remarkable power that he admired even while he worried.

As he watched Piearsa addressing the group, he marvelled at the strength of the woman he loved. He had always known she had suppressed inner strength yet, as she stood and led the fight against those who would harm them, his chest swelled. A tightness in his stomach contracted as he stood to offer support to her words. He swallowed his doubts and showed the united front they had come to expect from each other. It was this, more than the proceedings, which gave him the strength to continue. Yet how would he tell his father he was leaving once more?

Miroslaw would not be entirely alone. Syngh had already discussed with Jaden the need for someone to watch out for his family while he was away. Jaden, as Syngh had known he would, readily agreed to help in any way he could, and openly admitted he was not much of a fighter. He would be happy to keep Syngh's father company as Syngh had done for him in the mountains.

"Whatever happens, Jaden, you have given me a gift. You brought my love back to me, and you are continuing to support us. Syngh has told me of your history. You are alone no longer. You are part of our family, and you shall always have a place here with us. For as long as you desire," said Piearsa. Her words broke through Syngh's thought as if they were his own.

The lad's eyes grew watery, and he hung his head. "How long will you be away?"

"As long as it takes. We must find the other pride. I suspect they broke camp as soon as they left here," replied Syngh, thinking aloud to himself. "I have a few contacts round about. We shall go there first and find out if they have heard anything."

"You should not go alone. It is not safe. What if they follow you?" asked Jaden.

"Worry not, my young friend, we shall be well. We have a few days yet. There are many preparations to make before we depart." Syngh slapped the lad on the shoulder and let him back to the party.

Sometime later, Syngh and Piearsa sat on a log by one of the many party fires. Jaden sat at their feet, drawing his letters in the dirt, and glancing up occasionally to receive reassuring looks from Syngh that his symbols were correct. Piearsa's head rested on Syngh's shoulder, and her hand was on his knee in support. The night's festivities had worn out both him and his father. The latter had retired to bed, but Syngh did not want to be alone. The many discussions about his mother had brought tears to his eyes on more than one occasion, so Piearsa had taken him off to one side to give him some time. They said nothing, each knowing what the other would have said without the words being spoken.

Mesmerised by the fire light, Piearsa and Syngh sat arm in arm staring at nothing. At first, it was hardly noticeable. A gradual brightening of the flames. The corresponding increase in temperature dismissed as comfort, a result of their extended time in one place. Jaden was the first to react. He gradually moved away from the fire, retreating into the darkness.

They did not notice as they began to squint against the light or that the surrounding area was growing comparatively darker. The pale orange flames became more intense, deepening, until the orange was dark and thick. Small flakes of ash rose quickly and kept their embers longer until there was a steady stream of burning ash drifting from the fire.

Syngh stared deep into the flames, memories of his mother's face flickered in the bouncing flames. The stones about the camp started to glow, in the beginning just as a reflection, but later as the stones grew hot, a slight tinge of green developed.

It was not until the flames developed a bluish tinge that either werecat realised something was amiss. That neither of them had ever seen such a display of colour in a campfire before.

"I don't think I ever saw something so pretty," said Piearsa, indicating a dark purple lick of flame that seemed to be trying to escape the fire.

"It is nice although not the natural way of things. I wonder what causes it. Look at the stones. They are like rainbows."

"We sat here many times before using this camp ring and never did we see such a thing. I wonder if they are new stones?" Piearsa turned the statement into a question with the inflection in her voice.

"Stones are not damaged by fire. Why change them?" asked Syngh.

Jaden moved round the back of them and stared into the darkness. "Someone is coming," he said, sounding unduly worried.

Syngh's muscles and chest tightened simultaneously. The tension had been there all night, but it occurred to him that it might not have been anything to do with his mother's passing. The air seemed somehow thicker as though it was the wind that brought the strain, not some internal feeling of his own. He looked at Piearsa. She gave no outward sign that she sensed anything strange. Normally they were very aware of each other, and yet on this occasion, it seemed that the feeling was his alone. He clasped his hands tightly and released them slowly.

Footsteps approached. Syngh glared into the darkness. Two figures meandered towards them, their voices not quite reaching the fireplace. They had not come to see him. They were just moving about the camp. Syngh's knuckles cracked against the flexing of his fingers.

Piearsa looked at him curiously but said nothing. She moved her arm off his shoulder and leaned forward to poke at the fire with a stick. There was a whoosh as it went up in flames, and she jumped back to avoid the sudden flare.

Jaden moved behind them but remained standing as the two approaching shapes materialised into people. Two young men stopped when they saw who was sitting on the log. Their eyes glowed green in the firelight.

Syngh sighed at the intrusion and pointedly ignored the two. They were the last people he wanted to see. As cubs, they had been his enemies; nothing had changed as they grew into adults. This was the closest Oswald and Kalito had been to him in many months. Piearsa nodded to them. Her fingers gripped his arm tighter as the only sign of her feelings.

"Sorry about Falora. She was a good woman. I did not know her well, but my parents spoke well of her," said Oswald.

"You must be disappointed that you weren't here to help," added Kalito.

"Yeah, you could have finally been of some use at last," Oswald sneered.

Syngh gave a snarl of warning but swallowed his irritation. They were just trying to get at him. Years before, he would have reacted. That would have given them the excuse they needed to continue needling him. He no longer allowed himself to be baited.

"Leave it out, lads. This isn't the time." Piearsa's grip tightened, the pressure of her fingers kept him calm.

"Ah, another woman who can't rely on his protection," said Kalito, ignoring Piearsa.

Jaden shifted closer behind Syngh, moving his feet loudly.

Piearsa stood and took a step towards the men. She towered over them and moved menacingly closer, leaving them in no doubt as to her opinion.

Kalito stepped back from the threat, taken aback by her aggression, but Oswald seemed to take strength from the threat of conflict.

"Ah, coming to the defence of your boy. How sweet. Shame really. I hate to be right. I said he would never become a man," Oswald sneered.

Syngh's pressure rose at the allusion to his past torment. He swallowed hard. That was all in the past. They could not get to him now. "Look, you know I am game for anything most of the time, but today is not the time," he said, looking Oswald straight in the eyes. He clasped his hands together and gripped tightly.

"Now is exactly the right time. You should be ashamed that you were not here to look after your family. Funny how you turned up after the trouble had passed," Oswald spat.

"That's enough. It was not his fault," shouted Jaden.

"Easy, lad." Syngh raised his hand to forestall the boy. "They are just trying to get at me. They don't know what they are talking about. They have always been idiots."

Jaden retreated but stood poised.

"Idiots ay, that's new. Grown a spine while you were away, have you?" asked Kalito. He moved next to Oswald and gave Piearsa a defiant look.

"Seems he's not the only one. Now look *you two*, we can happily discuss this away from camp, but not here. Surely neither of you can be so disrespectful that you would wish to make a scene at a passing ceremony?" Piearsa took another pace forward.

Syngh glanced at her. Her tone sent a chill down his spine. He stood and smiled at his childhood bullies. Now he was bigger than they were. His grin widened. *Now might be the time.*

Neither of them moved as Syngh passed them. Piearsa put out her hand as he passed her. He squeezed her hand as he walked. Jaden followed and hissed as he passed the men.

Oswald moved in a quick jerky motion towards Jaden. The lad skipped away, stumbled, and skittered clear.

"Hey, don't walk away from us." Kalito yelled to Syngh's departing back.

"He's leaving you, girly. Ain't you gonna go after him?" drawled Oswald. When he got no answer, he grinned widely. "Fine. I will then. It's time the boy learnt his lesson."

"Yeah, who is he to walk away from us? We'll show him."

Syngh spun, hearing the trouble behind him. He need not have bothered.

Oswald got five paces before his path was blocked. The huge black cat in front of him hissed and arched its back.

Syngh had seen it only in a flash. He had never believed it was possible to Were so fast. Piearsa was huge, savage, and spitting anger. She blocked the path between Oswald and Syngh.

Oswald dismissed Piearsa with a wave of his hand. "What's she going to do?" He marched forwards.

Kalito hung back.

Piearsa pounced before Syngh could reach her. Her blue sheen rippled over her flexing muscles. The distant fire light shone off her shiny fur. The white of her teeth showed against the darkness. Oswald was down and gasping. A great gash opened in his cheek. Piearsa's saliva dripped to mix with the pooling blood on the ground.

"Get off him," yelled Kalito. "Stop."

"Piearsa. It is okay. Stop," coaxed Syngh under his breath, knowing that her feline hearing would catch his words. "You'll get in trouble."

A rumbling growl was the only response.

Oswald lay spread-eagled on the floor. His breath came in short bursts. He stayed deadly still. Only his breathing betrayed him. "O-kay... get... off. So-rry," he managed between intakes of air.

Piearsa flicked her tail in the air and relented a little. The weight came off Oswald's chest, and he visibly inhaled.

Syngh moved to her side, partly in support, but mostly

to try and calm down the situation. He breathed deeply, forcing himself to remain calm in the face of what could turn into murder. He had always known she had a temper but nothing like this. She had acted without thinking. The fallout from such behaviour might finish them. There were very strict rules in the town, purposely, to avoid such situations.

"Come on. He is not worth getting in trouble. You know how serious this can get. If he makes a complaint…"

"I…won't…I promise," said Oswald.

"*I* will. This is out of order. We were only having some fun," said Kalito, forgetting himself.

Piearsa growled and shifted her weight back.

Oswald gasped. "Idiot. Leave it be," he hissed at Kalito. "I'm sorry." Oswald shifted as best he could and looked Syngh straight in the eyes.

Syngh placed his hand on Piearsa's back and stroked her fur. Her back flexed, and he sensed a calm seeping through her. She relented.

"What is going on here?" asked a deep voice.

They looked up, dazzled by the light of the fire. A figure stalked across the clearing. The person was silhouetted against the orange light, but Syngh could see it was a man. A much older man.

"Get off him at once. What is the meaning of this outrage?" bellowed the elder, stopping two metres away from the scene and taking it all in.

"Just a misunderstanding, sir," replied Syngh, attempting to gain control of the story.

Piearsa retreated and moved to crouch beside Syngh. Her growl became a shallow purr that rumbled across his feet.

"*Indeed,* and what of you? What do you say about this? I

suppose you were the misunderstood?" He looked at Oswald who was picking himself up off the floor.

"Y-yes sir, entirely my fault," he stammered with a furtive glance at Syngh.

The elder gave a slight nod and raised an eyebrow. "No matter. The rules are clear. You," He pointed at Piearsa, "Wered without permission inside the town boundaries, outside the changing area. The rules are clear to all as is the punishment."

"There were circumstances—" offered Syngh.

"You will be heard as is procedure. Until then, you will come with me." He snapped his fingers at Piearsa as though she were a dog being brought to heal and turned back the way he came.

Syngh followed without even a glance at the other two. "It will be okay, my love. Don't worry. Once they know what happened, I am sure they will understand. I will stay with you."

Her large blue eyes turned to him, and such a look of love passed between them that his heart almost broke.

"She will be held until the hearing. You should think yourself lucky you are not implicated," said the elder over his shoulder.

Syngh suddenly realised the elder was leading them towards the jail. "This was all my fault. I should have dealt with those two...bullies...years ago."

"I shall convene a tribunal. The truth will be told." The elder hardly sounded like he cared.

A tribunal...they always end well. What then? Some sentence, hard labour, banishment? Death? We just broke a lousy rule. Happens all the time. But then... Once she is in their hands, they can do anything to her. Oh, Piearsa, what have I done?

CHAPTER 28
ENCLAVE

"This is unprecedented. I wish I knew what to do. I read much of the history of the clan when I was a child. No one has ever dared breach the box before," said the king in a frustrated tone.

"We will work it out, my dear. We must just take the time to do the work. Do not worry," replied his wife in a patient voice.

The couple continued on their walk. It had been necessary to remove the king from the palace, lest his temper cause them even more problems. Under normal circumstances, he was generally accepted as a kind king. Recent events proved that kindness overshadowed a massive rage that he had unleashed upon discovering the stones had been taken. Even his daughter was subjected to his wrath. She had run away crying. Her mother had not seen her since.

A while later, Frankine emerged from her hiding place and settled the matter. "I have been searching the Enclave's records. There was mention of some other source of information, but it remains hidden."

Termurica gave her daughter the usual look of disbelief. "All the reports have been scoured for information on the stones. We found nothing."

"I do not remember which text it was now, but I am certain it was there," replied Frankine in a frustrated tone. "The text referenced the source of the Shah de Ville River. It is but one day's journey." Frankine was almost pleading with her parents.

Myrrhta sighed and looked to his wife. "It is worth the time if she is right." He moved towards Termurica and took her hand.

"I could go with you, Father, and help you look."

Myrrhta felt his wife tense. That was a step to far. "Neither of you will go. I will take six of my best fighters. It will be a quick mission. No stopping for sightseeing." He looked pointedly at his daughter who looked to the floor in submission.

———

The expedition left at first light the next morning. There was no fanfare, no one to see them on the way, just a stealthy departure. The mission was to remain secret, just in case there was a spy in their midst. Termurica laughed at this idea. Her mirth evaporated when the king reminded her that someone, who could only be from the Enclave, had already breached security without any regard for the dangers to the rest of the world.

So many security breaches, the theft, the inexplicable deaths of the scorpions and dragonflies. The serious threat caused by that brief lack of security made her all the more uneasy in the face of the planned outing.

The king and his escorts completed their journey

without incident, arriving just before dawn on the following day. As soon as there was light enough to see, Myrrhta removed the parchment from its case and gently unrolled it. On it, there was as much description as Frankine could find as to the location of the ancient scrolls. She surmised they would be buried in a place that was easily accessible and obvious once found. They would be guided by the land but still not easy to find. The king looked at his daughter's description and rolled his eyes. So many contradictions. How could such a thing be reconciled?

They found the stream's source in a wooded glade about halfway up a slope. The small trickle of water appeared from underneath a tiny tunnel that led into the side of the hill. Above the entrance was a large stone slab that looked as though it was purposely placed. There were rocky areas all over the ground so that some of the trees looked as though they grew straight from the outcrops. Myrrhta instructed his guards to separate and search the immediate area while he inspected the ground closest to the water.

The sun was well past the zenith before they took a break for lunch. Even a meal of roasted insects and petals for lunch could not alleviate the king's disappointment at their collective failure. At his suggestion, they used the trickling water from the river's source to wash away the excess crumbs and wiped the small plates down with their hands.

One of the guards, making more mess than the others, stuck his hands into the trickle and splashed them up and down the direction of the flow. "Sire, I think I found something here," he said, pulling his hand away quickly.

Myrrhta rushed to the guard and began to copy his motions. His hand found a squared off corner not common to natural rock formations. He manoeuvred his hand for better reach and clasped the box-like item. His arm ached so he held his elbow with his other hand and rested a moment. He exchanged looks with the guard and smiled.

"What did you find, my king," asked another guard whose name Myrrhta did not know.

In response, King Myrrhta let go of his elbow and the weight of the box pulled his hand down to the water. He snatched it clear, scraping his fingernails on the rocks. He lifted the box into the air and showed the guards. The bottom of the container was rectangular as was obvious from his watery examination. The upper part of the box curved into a shiny dome. Ancient patterns the like of which Myrrhta had never seen before etched the top. He turned the box around and found what looked like a round keyhole about twice the size of his fingernail. He searched the hole with his little finger.

Nothing.

He handed the box to a guard and placed his hands on either side of the dome, trying to lift the lid.

No movement.

His hands traced the etched patterns along the top of the box. The markings scratched his fingers. *It's writing, perhaps instructions on how to open the box. Damn. What does it say?* He had no idea even where to begin looking for the origins of such a text. Frustrated, he stripped off his jacket and flapped his purple-tinged wings in the air. A blue dust marked his passage as he flew upwards and landed on a branch. He placed the box in front of him and began to study it closer.

The guards flew up around him, abandoning the washing up. They watched intently as the king went through a list of everything he could think of that might provide some clue as to how to open the box.

"Maybe we should leave this until we return, my king. Perhaps there is some book at the Enclave that will help us," one of them suggested.

"My daughter Frankine has been through all the books. That is how we know of this place. In none of her studies did she find any instructions on how to open it or even what it looks like." The king huffed and slammed his hand down on the trunk of the tree. "Why are these things never easy?"

He lifted one side of the box and leaned forward to inspect the bottom. He had little hope it would reveal something. His fingers traced the bottom at the same time as his eyes. As he leaned forward, the chain round his neck fell clear of his undershirt and dangled precariously close to the box.

One of the guards gasped and flew forwards, reaching for the necklace. He stopped in mid-air and snatched his hand back. "Sorry, my king. Your necklace. Have you noticed the size?" He dropped back again.

Myrrhta cradled the trinket in his hand and studied it. He had worn it for so long he barely looked at it now. "My father gave this to me just before he passed. I have no idea where it comes from."

The guard moved closer. "May I?" He reached out for the necklace.

The king lifted it over his head and handed it over. He eyed the man curiously.

Lifting the chain into the sunlight, the guard peered at the object from many angles. "Do these markings look the same as those on the top of the box? I am not much of a reader, but they may be connected." He handed the golden chain back.

Myrrhta took it and held it next to the box. He clenched

his jaw, and with pinched lips, he lowered it until it was level with the hole. The gap was nowhere near deep enough for the sphere.

"Perhaps if you fold it together, sire? It is an Armillary Sphere. I saw something similar at the Stronghold when I was there years ago. It turns into a simple ring."

Myrrhta gave the guard a quizzical look and followed his suggestion. He fiddled with the rings until they became one and placed it once more near the keyhole. Gingerly he pushed it inside.

With a click, the lid snapped open.

Myrrhta glanced at the guard who nodded his satisfaction. With care, he opened the stiff lid and peered inside. Lying alone on the bottom of the box was an old scroll. The king reached in and picked up the brittle paper. Using only two fingers, he unrolled it and laid it gently on the branch of the tree. Water dripped from the seams. Most of the text was smudged and unreadable. On the top was a diagram of the stones. Below it, in ornate handwriting, was a list. From what he could decipher, it appeared to be a detailing of the stones on the box. The diagram showed how they should fit together.

The entire bottom of the sheet was soaked and useless, but the top he could read easily. *Lacertae ut libet parva praevaricati.* His mind spun. Foreign words flashed in front of his eyes. Hazy memories glanced across his mind.

As a young prince, he had been forced to read the ancient languages and learn their meanings. Relentless hours studying a subject he viewed as pointless. His tutors insisted that if he was to be king, he must learn it in case it was needed in his later life. Right in that moment, he began to wish, for the first time in his life, that he had paid closer attention to those studies.

His memory clasped onto the words he could piece together, "Lizards like small betrayals."

"Sire?" asked the guard who had been watching his thought process.

"The meaning, I think it is something like that. The ancient languages were never my strongest subject."

"Lizards like small betrayals?" the guard frowned and cocked his head. "Forgive me, sire, but that does not sound right even to my untutored ear." He moved backwards out of range.

"Nor to mine. We must get back. I wish we could read the rest. This is some kind of prophecy, I think. We must find those missing stones. Break camp immediately. There is work to do. I must arrange an expedition." He was moving even before the sentence was completed.

"At once, sire." The guard hurried away.

CHAPTER 29
LYLIANA

Yastat's wings scraped over the wooden floor as he approached Lyliana. He stopped and gave her a furtive glance before launching himself off the ground to pounce on a scrap dropped by Tisray. He bit into it once, shook his head, paused, and then tossed the crumb in the air, snatching and swallowing it in one movement. Grygon snapped her head and hissed at Yastat.

Lyliana watched the dragons from the chaise lounge, occasionally tossing them a titbit from her early lunch. Briscay flapped over to her and settled himself on the back of the sofa. He balanced his weight with flicks of his tail as he took food from her hand. She would finish her meal still hungry.

Lyliana giggled. "You're always hungry, aren't you, boy?" she asked the dragon who flapped his wings once as if in response.

Svation watched Lyliana. His gaze occasionally moved to Grygon and Roylei who alternated their attention between playing and the great slab of meat that lay prone on the floor. Svation preened himself almost like a bird and then settled on his haunches with his wings folded over his back.

As always, the light shining off Svation's silvery scales fascinated Lyliana. They made an even more impressive show than Grygon's splendour. She tried to call him over, but the dragon just looked at her through his slatted eyes. There was no recognition in his expression. She raised her eyes at the creature and pushed herself off the chair. She picked up the feather she found in the yard that morning and walked over to Svation. She waved the bright red rectrix feather at Svation and watched as his eyes followed the fronds. She moved it towards his nose until it tickled him. Svation sneezed.

A flapping flurry signalled the attention of the others. Svation's gaze switched from the feather to a place behind her. She turned to see Roylei now behind her head. Grygon was just above him, her head darting forward to get a better look. Briscay approached silently, her only warning was a twinge of her scalp. He snatched the feather from her grasp and shot upwards before turning sharply. He shot for the open window.

"Hey, that's not fair. I can't fly." Lyliana laughed as the others darted out after him.

They returned with the feather that they fought over for a few minutes before including Lyliana in the game. This time, they were the ones taunting her with the feather.

Through the sounds of the wind buffeting against the window, another noise filtered in. The chanting voices had increased to the point where they drew attention. The words were not clear, but the meaning was plain. Lyliana cocked one ear and listened, realising that she had been hearing the voices for some time, but not enough to pay attention. Her kneecaps tingled.

Lester entered the office, flanked by three guards. He searched the room, confused. His gaze passed through her.

The window shuddered. Lyliana shivered.

Lester checked behind her desk and scanned the rest of the room again.

What on earth is he doing? Clearly, he is in a hurry. Why doesn't he just get on with whatever he has to say? Lyliana pulled at her sleeves as Lester completed his checks and headed for the door.

"I don' know where she is. Send someone to fin'er. Check Betty's." Lester shouted as he reached the threshold of the office.

Lyliana frowned and studied his expression. "What's happened now, Lester? Out with it." He stumbled to a stop just outside the room.

He peered round the corner, looked about the room, and frowned. His irritation was tainted with the hint of something else. Was that fear? Lyliana noted his white knuckles gripping the doorframe. His eyes drifted past her, searching. They passed again, not a hint of recognition.

She waved. *He can't see me. Oh God, I am invisible. How?* She looked at the dragons. The idea drifted into sync with her mind. *Unbelievable. They made me invisible.* Her body weaved with indecision. *I wish there was time to enjoy this.* She gave a great sigh. "I am here, right in front of you."

Lester started. "Lyliana, where are you? Stop playing games." There was a new edge to his voice.

"I'm here. They made me invisible...I think. How is that possible?" she whispered.

"Tha's a neat trick. Could come in usefu'. Now, if you could undo it, or wha'ever the term is, I need to *see* ya," he said with a forced patience. His right hand clenched at his side.

A tingling in her knees and she was visible again.

"There's some'hing of a problem brewing out'si'e." He said, greeting her visibility.

"I heard. What is the matter with them now?"

"Three ships arrived. They're na 'appy about the changes 'ere. I've tried to talk 'em down, but as you 'eard, I 'ad no luck."

Lyliana sat back heavily in the chair. "So, they have never met me. Have not been here to witness my actions. They have not been ashore long enough to have heard anything," She tickled off the points on her fingers. "*But* they don't want to work with me?"

"That's abou' the sum of it, ay." He gave a casual wave.

"They are ship's crew?"

Lester nodded. His upper arm muscles twitched and flexed under his inked skin. "Yes. Better to deal with 'em now and no' wait until they are fully inebriated. There might be problems. I told ya it would na be all smooth sailing. There're bound to be hol'outs."

"Any suggestions?" Lyliana cradled her chin in her hands and closed her eyes against the growing ache edging across her forehead.

"They were Percy supporters. No' easily persuadable." He gave a quick shrug. "Cap'ains should have been involved in the decision or some such. Now they believe they are being ignored." Lester heaved a resigned breath.

"*I* was left out of the decision. It just happened," she winced at the pain in her head.

"I explained, but they are simple men." He gave her a look as though it should not require more explanation, but he continued when she eyed him. "They respond to power or threat o' violence. I know the cap'ains. They are reasonable, but their lives are risked if they ignore the crew." His tone suggested he did not believe they were truly reasonable, any more than Lyliana was inclined to believe it.

"The captains only lead while the crew allows it or are powerless to prevent it?"

"Exactly." Lester tilted his head slightly and watched her mind working. He poured a drink from the decanter on the side and waited.

"So there is no point to appeal to each of the captains in this matter? I must convince all or none?" Her inflection turned the statement into a question. When he nodded, she added, "In that case, I shall face the problem head on and a Clash to any who oppose me."

Lester's mouth dropped open at her use of the old saying but made no comment. He held the door open as she exited the office and headed down into the square filled with waiting pirates.

The street was packed. Without counting, there was upwards of two hundred pirates milling about. They had arranged themselves into three groups, though some individuals moved between the groups. Without asking, she knew these numbers only represented about half the compliments of the three newly arrived vessels. There were obviously representatives from all ships, not including the captains, whose relatively tidy appearances marked them apart from the crew.

The latter were a strange mix of all colours and creeds, some entirely alien to her. A couple in the group had much darker skin than the rest, presumably from further away than most people here. Their startling green eyes shone like the navigation lights of the vessels they worked on while simultaneously enhancing the depth of their skin tone.

From what she could see, they were quiet men who stood apart from the rest of the group, literally as well as in respect of their different colourings. She caught the eye of one of them and smiled. The huge man grinned back, and Lyliana got a vague sense of his reluctant presence.

With the exception of the three captains, the crews were dressed very much in the same style. Many of them wore the baggy shorts she was accustomed to seeing on the sailors back in Hillaway. Most had open shirts, or no shirts at all, and every one of them was deeply tanned from long stints of working in the bright sunlight. Many carried the remnants of deep scars, some on their back, more in other places that spoke of fights rather than punishment.

Lyliana stood apart from the crowd, waiting. She scratched her right ear unnecessarily and rubbed the back of her neck. Her shoulders were tense. She resisted the urge to loosen them. About her, the air was charged though she sensed that she was the only person who noticed. She glanced at Lester who gave an almost imperceptible shrug.

Determined not to be the first one to speak, she leaned back against the building behind her and tried to give the impression of nonchalance. She rested one foot behind her at knee height and concentrated her attention on the distant rooftops. Lester moved closer, his stance charged like the air.

At length someone noticed her, and there was a general shuffling as one pirate nudged the other and so on until one of the captains caught the vibe. Lester stood straighter as the command trio approached. Lyliana forced herself to remain still although it took all her willpower.

"About time. You're the *bitch* who outed Percy," said a short rotund man with most of his teeth missing and a savage scar just visible under his shirt.

Lyliana eyed him but said nothing. She stared him straight in the eyes

"I thought you'd 'ave more to say. From what I heard you never sh'up." The other two closed up behind the first captain when it became clear that she had no intention of arguing. Lester took a step forward. His hand was on his sword.

The captain's gaze switched from Lyliana to Lester. "You! You traitorous hound. 'Old your position. I shan't 'ave nothing to do with you." He turned back to Lyliana, "You should 'ave 'ung this dog before you find knives in your back."

Lyliana forced herself not to react although her blood was simmering.

"Don't you wan'o know why we be here? Me shipmates and I 'ave some things to work out with you."

She raised one eyebrow.

"Maybe she's a mute," piped up one of the sailors behind them, clearly emboldened by her silence.

"Stow it," growled the tallest captain. By his movements, he seemed to have one leg shorter than the other and moved with a kind of sideways tilt.

Lyliana smirked but remained silent.

"You 'an 'ear us 'en?" The first captain's voice was getting progressively louder, either through increased confidence or anger. It was hard to tell. "She came out to talk, yet she says nothing. Meb'be you should speak for 'er so she knows her place." This last comment was to Lester.

"She—" Lester began.

Lyliana coughed subtlety, and Lester stepped back a pace.

"Seems we wasted our 'ime, lads. She is not in charge. We'll just go 'bout our business. Wha' you say, lads? No need to worry about 'er." The crowd grumbled. He turned and took a step away from Lyliana.

"That would be a mistake," she said quietly. She felt Lester tense as the captain stopped in his tracks.

"Eh?" he asked, turning back. "Wha' you saying?"

She pushed herself away from the wall and raised her voice for them all to hear. "I said *that* would be a mistake. You have some grievance so speak. So far it is you who have been wasting my time with pointless comments and insults." Her skin was almost shaking, and she was convinced it was obvious to anyone who was watching.

"I...we," he paused and searched the group behind him. "Don't recognise your authority 'ere. We'll no' accept it." His voice was more forceful, following a general murmur of agreement from behind him.

"Tell her if she does 'no relinquish this position that is not hers, we shall leave," said the third captain, who had barely moved since the start of the meeting.

The first captain growled something but otherwise ignored the other captain. He kept his eyes on Lyliana, "We'll no' leave. We'll take our righ'ful place in this town."

"Okay," said Lyliana, giving the impression she was acquiescing. "I have not the pleasure of your name?" she glanced at Lester who gave her a pained look.

The captain closed his eyes a little and scowled. "Sasha, captain of the *Platypus*."

She gave a slight nod and indicated the other two with a raised eyebrow.

"Caesar of the *Giants Tooth* and Rob of the *Clashes Bane*." He waved in the general direction of each of the other captains.

"I will not debate the past with you, Sasha of the *Platypus*. It is done. Who is your second?"

A black man with a crooked grin and more gold rings

than she had ever seen before stepped to the front. "Ed, miss," he said by way of introduction.

She gave Ed a quick nod and turned back to Sasha. "Are you certain of your decision?"

"I will not yield," Sasha said forcefully.

"I understand. Neither will I." She turned back to Ed. "Congratulations on your promotion. I hope you are ready."

The air about her stilled, and without a sound, Svation, Tisray, and Grygon flapped through the upstairs window of the building behind her.

"There is no option then." She glanced at the dragons and then looked Sasha in the eyes.

Tisray flew over Sasha, and he was suddenly covered in mist. Svation roared, and Grygon flapped menacingly above her.

The two other captains scrambled backwards and looked to their colleague.

Sasha did not move. Not a muscle. His mouth was open in a gasp, but no sound came out. His hand was raised to warn off the attack.

Lyliana smiled.

Grygon flapped higher and screamed.

The watching pirates took a few paces back. They never took their eyes off the dragons. Svation and Tisray flew back to Lyliana and perched, one on each shoulder.

Still Sasha did not move.

Ed stepped forward and poked his captain with one finger. "What did you do? He is solid."

"He is dead," replied Lyliana in a matter-of-fact tone. "You have his job. Unless you will not follow me either?"

He shook his head and opened his mouth, paused then shut his mouth.

"It is settled then," she glanced at Lester. "Unless there

is anything else you want to discuss, *I think* we are done here," she said to the rest of the crowd.

Briscay gave a great squawk from the window ledge above her, and the crowd began to move away, most not bothering to pretend not to be scared. Caesar and Ed looked up for a long time and then at Lyliana. Neither said a word before they followed their crews away from the scene of their friend's death.

"Was there na other way?" asked Lester in a weak voice when the crowd had dispersed.

"They are hard men. They respond only to over-whelming force or power. There was no other way. *You* taught me that." She tipped her head to one side and looked at him.

Lester gave her a queer look but said nothing. Instead, he led her back to her office.

CHAPTER 30
NEEM

Neem skirted around the ropes laid ready for mooring and dived over the bulwarks. He was followed closely by Avienna and Parcelus. They dodged and danced around the waves, hardly noticeable to an average person but mountainous to a pixie. They left the ship before docking to avoid the port and any pixies living there. It was imperative they were not seen. King Myrrhta had sent numerous parties to search for the missing stones. Neem was disappointed to find other teams on the ship but not surprised. Gamola Harbour was the obvious starting place.

The passage had been rough, exacerbating the usual dangers of a ship. The human crew was unaware of their presence and so took no precautions against harming them, not that they would, had they known. Loose equipment on board posed as much of a threat as the passengers and the weather reduced their hiding places. Once or twice, they had seen other pixies who were part of the search team, and this had made their attempts to hide even more perilous.

With half a mile of choppy ocean to traverse, their flight

was no safer than the passage had been. On a couple of occasions, waves kissed Neem's feet, and he escaped drowning by a fraction of a second. They came upon a rocky islet that looked a little out of place somehow. Waves crashed around the base of the rocks and climbed high up the straight sides. At first, Neem thought the island was actually a castle. The top of one end was much lower than the other that appeared to be slightly separated from the rest of the cliff. The angle sloped downwards towards the left of the cliff with small turret-like shapes along the top. The group skirted down the higher south side and headed for the small cliffs of the mainland coast.

The pixies made landfall just south of the town. They found a tree and rested on the branches to catch their breath. Neem studied his surroundings. His face dropped as he saw the bleak emptiness of the desert. His first re-emergence to the outside world was a shocking disappointment.

"There is nothing here," he said to no one in particular.

Avienna sidled up to him. "It is quite desolate. I wish we could explore the town. I heard it is very different to Hillaway."

Neem shuffled slightly away from her and stared across the plains. "We might get a chance once the mission is completed, but for now we must get going." He shrugged and put an extra half step between himself and Avienna.

Parcelus took to the air, an irritated red dust trailing behind him.

Avienna waited for Neem and fell in line behind him. "Where are we going first?" she asked as they flew from the shadow of the lonely tree.

Neither of the men answered her. They had discussed the plan before leaving the ship. They would head south and hide the stones randomly. The only boats scheduled to go back to the Lessar Lands sailed from Gamola, but the return journey would be easier without the weight of the stones.

They flew fast over the land, rising over the air currents. They made their camp that night in a small coppice of trees and barely finished their meal before they were asleep. The darkness found them unconscious.

Neem woke early, shocked by the sound of birds. Instinctively he froze and held his breath. Their panicked squawking left no room for doubt they were under attack. The telltale sounds of swooping reached Neem through the trees. He held his breath. A final squawk confirmed the presence of a falcon. He peered over the branch just in time to see the raptor take off with its catch in its talons. He heaved a deep sigh and laid back to wait for his heart to return to its normal rhythm.

He checked the position of the sun and looked over to where he had left Parcelus and Avienna. He had moved away from them during the night, trying to put more distance between him and Avienna who crept closer throughout the night. He smiled. At least he would have a few minutes of peace before running the Avienna gauntlet again.

Their journey continued while the sun stretched towards the zenith. Neem left one of the stones under a thick hedge in a grove and decided they would not leave another until they had crossed the Clashing River. Parcelus grew ever more impatient and irritable as the day lengthened, and the river remained elusive. As the evening drew in, they found themselves on the edge of a group of trees that grew out from what looked like a manmade flowerbed, an island in the middle of a vast wasteland. A good find, considering their dwindling food stores.

They lit a small fire and roasted their petals over it, much like a human would make toasted bread on the end of a stick. Avienna laid back against the brush and let the men work on the food while she studied the remaining stones. Her silence told of her inability to understand them. Neem was pleased to see her distracted for a time, his patience being delicate and frayed after spending the day trying to avoid her attention.

Neem flicked his eyes in her direction and looked pointedly at Parcelus. He offered a knowing grin and returned his attention to the collection of flower buds.

"We have to get rid of these things as fast as possible. Every delay increases the chances of being caught," said Neem, almost to himself.

Avienna sat up and looked at him from under her long lashes. Her wings flicked. "We are doing it. We just got rid of another one. They will never think to look this far away in any case."

Parcelus huffed and dropped red-purple dust as he flew over to them. "Stupid woman. They are already here. They were on the same boat as us. We are maybe…" he paused to consider. "Perhaps one day ahead of them. Maybe less."

"But surely they will search the town first. That would make the most sense?" asked Neem quietly.

"No doubt, but what then? It is not a big place, and there are plenty of them. The only place they can go then is south, and their next stop will be the camp."

Neem nodded slowly. "Then that is where we must avoid, at least until we get rid of these things."

"I don't even know why you took them. I know it was our idea, but I don't think any of us really thought it through." Avienna dropped level with the others.

Parcelus tossed the pair of them a flower petal each and

munched on his, swallowing hard to empty his mouth. "It is too late now. They will never find us, and even if they do, they cannot prove anything."

Unless they find Tyame's body, of course. Then they will know it is us. "Still, we must be careful. They will not spare the noose if they put everything together."

Avienna collected the water carrier and went searching for water, nodding to Neem as she left.

"What could they find out that they don't already know?" said Parcelus impatiently.

Stupid old man. "Well, if they know *I* am involved, they know I have reason to want revenge. I have motive. They know it even if they won't say so. I could not survive a wing burning. I've seen too many." Neem plucked another couple of petals from the flower and handed one to Parcelus.

"You would not have to worry about banishment." He smirked. "I cannot imagine not being able to fly...to walk everywhere." He shook his head. "I remember when I was a young lad. A boy in my class was banished not long after maturity. We never heard from him again." Parcelus offered Neem a distant look.

"Such things should be enough to discourage us from doing stupid things like this, don't you think? Not that you have much to worry about where theft is concerned." Neem allowed the sarcasm to drip from his words.

"I am not sure I understand your meaning," Parcelus growled.

"What I mean," began Neem, rising a little higher and putting his hands on his hips. "Is that theft is nothing compared to murder." His red dust turned distinctly orange as he ascended.

Parcelus flew upwards sharply. "Say that again."

"I believe you heard me." Neem's heart raced. It

occurred to him that annoying a murderer might not be the wisest thing he had ever done, but he was now committed.

"I did what had to be done," said Parcelus, notably calmer as he dropped back slightly.

Neem shrugged.

"What would you have done, sharp wings?"

The strange expression made Neem pause for a second. "I don't know. Not that. There must have been another way."

"He was going to tell someone what we did. I saved our lives."

Neem flew backwards once more away from him and turned himself so that the sun was behind him. "He said he was not going to tell anyone."

Parcelus scoffed, "And you believed him?" he spat sarcastically. "Young bud. He would not have been able to keep quiet. They never can. It was the only way to ensure our safety."

"What's going on with you two? I can hear you all the way over there," Avienna asked as she flew over the grasses and joined them.

"Nothing. I am going to get some sleep. It will be a long day tomorrow." Parcelus left them in a rush.

Avienna gave Neem a quizzical look and shrugged in response while indicating that he would also like to get some rest.

———

Early the next afternoon they reached the Clashing River and hovered over the side of the cliff looking down at the tumultuous water rushing through the narrow pass. Neem and Avienna had never seen it before and stood transfixed as though it hypnotised them. Parcelus, who had taken the route a couple of times in his life, took one of the stones and buried it in a crag about half a metre down from the ledge. The sheer cliff side would prevent anyone from finding it too soon and protect it from scavengers until it was time to retrieve the stone. Whenever that might be.

When Neem came out of his trance, he took careful note of where the stone was hidden and waited until the others were not looking before he noted it on the secret map he was keeping of each location.

They ate lunch and had their afternoon nap before, with renewed energy, they crossed the river. Air flows were unpredictable over the gorge, so they flew higher than normal in an effort to avoid them. When they reached the other side, all three were out of breath. The air was too thin for pixies so high up, even though to a human they would have hardly noticed the difference. Once they had recovered, they continued south.

CHAPTER 31
LESTER

The dinghy rocked mercilessly to the tiny swell running through the docks. Every now and again, it rolled, and water would lap over the gunwales and soak Lester's feet. As the day wore on, he became less interested in bailing the water from the bottom so that as dusk came over the port, his feet were constantly wet.

He hardly noticed. An empty bottle rattled, unimpeded, back and forth across the bottom boards. The ambient sounds of the port had long since turned to white noise, and his nostrils had become used to the stink of the dirty boat. Lester drained another bottle and tossed it carelessly over the side. Watching the bobbing bottle made him queasy. He leaned over the side and emptied the contents of his stomach into the water. Feeling better, he cracked open another bottle and took a long swing.

The world swam, his eyes would not focus on anything outside of the boat, and even those details grew blurry. He leaned back against nothing and fell backwards off the thwart. Lester lay for some amount of time staring up at the occasional, pink-tinged clouds that rushed across the sky.

Finally, and with no little effort, he pulled himself upright and stood unsteadily. The boat pitched and threatened to throw him to the water. His stomach heaved, and his last drink hit the gunwales, half in the water, the rest splattering the bottom of the boat. He staggered back and fell onto the ropes behind him. His newly opened bottle tipped and rolled backwards. He scooped it up on the second attempt to catch it and smiled at his success.

"Thanks 'ock," he said to the bottle. He took another swig, pushed it around the inside of his mouth, and spat it over the side before filling his mouth again and swallowing the second mouthful. "You're a nice bottle. You'll un'er-stand. I can talk to ya."

He watched the bottle and waited.

When there was no reply, he continued, "There was no'ing I could do. She only listens when she feels like it. I've warned 'er," He stroked the smooth neck of the brown glass. "I 'old 'er they would na like it, and when they returned, there'd be problems. Now she thin's it's over." The bottle remained silent.

"You know better. You should tell her 'ow it is really. That they tell 'er what to do, not the other way around."

His attention returned to the bottle. "She'll wan' proof. She'll na believe the've just agreed to give 'emselves time. She thinks they're just stupid pirates. She forgets 'ow they became so successful."

"She will learn. She must."

Lester nodded sagely at the bottle, "You're wise beyond ya years."

"I am older than you know and nearing the end o' my life. When I am gone, you mus' know what to do. If you don't know by then I've friends who might 'elp you."

"I know. I see 'em." He looked at the fast-dwindling

crate of hock. "And people say there's no sense to be 'ad from 'rrinkin." He smiled lovingly at the bottle in his hand.

"You must act. There's na good to be 'ad hiding out 'ere."

He nodded again and held the bottle close. "Thank you, wise 'ock." He closed his eyes.

"You really think he can help us, 'Oatswain?" asked a gruff voice.

Lester had not even heard anyone approaching.

"Skipper thinks so," said another voice.

Lester opened his eyes, shifted, and slid lower down the ropes. His legs splayed out in front of him.

"He's talking to a bottle. Seems like a lost cause," replied the first voice.

"Orders is orders, Tee."

There was a shuffling sound, and the boat rocked dangerously. Lester squinted at the men on the jetty. They were just blurry shapes to his unfocused vision, but he recognised their voices as trouble.

"Toss a bucket over him. He stinks."

"'Swain."

The sound of splashing brought Lester into full awareness. "Hey, 'ey, there's no cause 'or that." He waved away the oncoming water that never came.

"Better," said the boatswain, "Now we can talk. Skipper wants to see you, Lester. Matter most urgent."

"I'm busy." Lester waved him off and leaned forward to search for his missing bottle. The boat rocked, and he fell forward onto the boards that were now swimming with water, hock, and vomit.

"Cap'ain wants to see you about your bitch. Come on, snap 'o it. He don't like to be kept wai'ing."

"I've naught to say. Naught to do with me. Go awa'. I'm busy." He dismissed them again, but in the back of his addled mind somewhere, Lester knew it was not his best move.

Somewhere in the distance, a woman screamed. The sound cut off abruptly and was followed by another scream. The high-pitched squeal broke the silence of the night like a cannon shot crashing home. The men looked down the jetty towards the shore. Even Lester stuck his head up above the gunwales and searched the beach with watery eyes. Squawking birds added to the noise. A pistol fired then all was quiet.

The boatswain seemed to be convinced by the scream and nodded to the other men. "Tee, Zee, get him up. He's coming with us."

Lester giggled at the names of the men and watched them as they moved towards the boat. For the first time, he noticed they were twins. Identical in every way. Both men were thickset, burly, and dark-skinned with faces like chiseled stone. Simultaneously, they stepped into the boat that nearly overturned under their combined weight.

"Take it easy," Lester giggled.

Vomit-riddled water washed over the feet of the men, and the scent of reeking water hit them. They looked at the boatswain and grimaced, "Ah, boss, really?"

"Get on with it. We ain't got all night," said the boatswain turning away from the stench.

They grasped at Lester. He struggled, fighting them off. The aim of his hands was off. They dodged his wild motions easily, but the crazy rocking of the boat hampered them. More than once, they nearly fell over the side. Lester kicked and punched. One of them got hold of his neck, and he bit. The hand was snatched away. A foot kicked him from the opposite side.

"We sure this is worth the trouble, Boats'? He's not

gonna remember a thing in the morning anyhow," said either Tee or Zee. Lester was not sure which.

Somehow, in all the confusion, he was growing increasingly sober. Realizing that his very drunken state might be the thing that would give him time to regroup, he decided to play the part. "No-o morning, morning no goo'," he drooled, purposely not focusing on the other men. He picked up a fallen bottle, "Pretty-y," he coughed, spluttered, and grinned foolishly.

Tee and Zee gave the boatswain a pleading look and opened their palms in a big shrug.

The boatswain huffed visibly, "Alright, leave him. We'll get no sense from 'im tonight. Cap'ain won't be happy, but we can't take him there stinking like that." He gave Lester a sideways look. "We could dunk him in the dock. That would sober him up."

"Gotta catch him first, 'swain."

"Ay, there's that. Now listen, you," he pointed at Lester. "Cap'ain wants you to control that bitch. What happened to Sasha was no good. I didn't like the fella, but there were no course fir that. Skipper ain't gonna hang about and wait to be castrated so sort her out. I'd sugges' you go see the skipper in the morning. Get this straightened out. I ain't gonna do this again. Next time you'll know about it. As it is, I'm gonna 'ave to face the skipper for leaving you 'eer." He waved the twins out of the boat.

The boat's motion helped Lester sit up as the two stepped out. His heart didn't feel like it was racing. It was more like a constant beat. He eyed the boatswain defiantly.

"You hear me? I need to know you understand. I'm gonna take flack for this. I'll do it 'cause I know you're a good guy. Or you were before she corrup'ed you, but you must take this seriously. It ain't just our skipper who's angry."

"I go' it," Lester replied, forgetting that he was supposed to be drunk. Thankfully, none of the men noticed his sudden sobriety.

After what seemed like an age, but was only a few minutes, all three men left. They paced quickly down the wooden jetty, their feet echoing and fading into the darkness.

Lester sat heavily back on the thwart. He did not even remember standing. His heart rate slowed, and the alcohol began to take effect again. *What the hell do I do now? They're going to kill me if I can't talk Lyliana down. She won't stop now. She has the taste of power. I can't tell Caesar that though, can I?* He picked up another bottle but paused before it reached his lips. He had not realized until that moment that he had recognised the boatswain as one of Captain Caesar's men. *I'm a dead man. No doubt at all.*

CHAPTER 32
HILLAWAY

Martha Robinson removed her ever-present apron as her youngest son clambered into bed. It was past his bedtime, but then it always was these days. The family routine had been uprooted since Charles discovered what happened to Lyliana, and despite her best efforts, she could not shield Roger from the upheaval.

She settled herself into the rocking chair at the side of the bed. Roger snuggled down under the blankets and buried his tousled blonde head into the deep pillows. He smiled at her. Candlelight distorted his expression, conjuring memories of Charles at that age.

A clink of glass and the accompanying whiff of spirits confirmed her husband was having his after-dinner tipple. She had time to spare.

"Mama, I'm not tired," said the six-year-old.

It was the same every night. "Of course not, my dear." She leaned forward to pull her hair free from the tight bun she kept it in during the day. Long brown strands fell down her back and across the chair.

"Mama, perhaps I could stay up a little longer. With you and Father?" The child pushed the covers down hopefully.

"No, my dear. You need your rest so you can grow big and strong." She used the same excuse almost every night.

"Mama?"

"Yes, dear." She exhaled.

"Why is Charles sad?" The quiet voice was reluctant.

Martha sighed, a deep echoing sound filled with the worry. Her brow furrowed. It had been that way for a few days. "He lost his Lyliana, and he is worried about her."

Roger looked thoughtful. "Does he know where he last had her?"

Martha frowned at her son and cocked one eye in question.

"When you and Papa lose something, you always ask where you last had it."

She nodded. A brief smile broke her frown. "He did not lose her like that. She is missing. When she left, she got lost during a storm. No one knows where she is."

"Is that why Charles is going away?" Roger's voice was quiet.

Martha stared. Her shoulder twitched. They had been discussing how to break the news to the lad. He and his brother were close. The darkness of the room was almost suffocating. Her mind scrambled to find a reply. She pressed her lips tight.

"He is going on an important quest," Roger explained when she said nothing.

She suppressed her irritation at her older son for revealing these problems to Roger. "Yes, dear, it is something he feels he must do." She did not add that she had disagreed with his decision. There was no need to burden Roger with such things.

"He is very brave, Mama." Roger beamed with a pride that even the darkness of the room could not hide.

"Yes, he is, dear. Your brother is an honourable man. Just like your father."

"What does hon-r-ble mean?"

"Honourable," she repeated slowly. "It means someone who takes care of people who are not strong enough to look after themselves.

Roger nodded slowly. "I am honourable. I will be honourable."

"I am sure you will, dear. Your brother and father are good role models." She raised her hand to forestall any questions about what a role model was. "Now then, time for bed."

"Tell me a story please, Mama." He snuggled down further, his small hands clutching the covers and rolled over to face her.

"You've heard all the stories, my dear."

"Tell me a new story. Something scary. Please, Mama?" His begging eyes worked their way through her resolve.

She rubbed her aching eyes and tried to think of something that would satisfy her son's ever-growing thirst for stories. "How about the legend of the Sandstone Army?"

"Oh, yes, I heard that one." He sat up.

Candlelight flickered across the window and shone in her eyes for a moment. A silent warning from beyond perhaps? She coughed to clear her throat of the sudden dryness.

"The story goes that many years before the Clash and well before the Awakening, the world lived peaceably. Humans going about their day-to-day farming and fishing as normal. They continued in this way for many years until the day everything changed.

"It is told that it was the chaos that brought it. Nobody really knows." She sucked her left cheek. "Modern scholars agree on only one thing, the arrival of the Sandstone Army spells disaster. The controlling mechanism that keeps them in check relies on magic, so *they* say. If awake, they seek retribution against those who wronged them. The Sandstone Army claim the ultimate penalty as their revenge. Nobody knows when they will come or why. They only know that at some point they will return to seek vengeance upon those who wronged them.

"As a child I was told they were great monsters made of sand as big as a tree, maybe even a mountain. It is said that they float above the ground and that they suck their energy from the very earth.

"The book my mother read me had pictures of barren landscapes devoid of life. Not even a blade of grass remained."

Martha added her own touches to the story. As she spoke, she wondered whether her mother had done the same...if this was how the story of the Sandstone Army came about. She shivered. Her feet ached. Her fingers twirled with her earlobes absently. It was a ludicrous idea to think that monsters made of sand towered well above the mountains and devoured the very life from the earth. After all, if there was no life then how could the land recover after such an attack? Whatever the case, Roger was enthralled.

She swallowed a hard lump from her throat. "From the pictures I saw and my mother's description, these creatures have eyes so hollow that they can suck the soul from a living being. It is rumoured they search for the Orchestrator of Chaos and use their hollow eyes to exact their wrath on the perpetrator. My mother always told me that they never rest. They never stop, never have a conscience, and never pause to question what they're doing. I once asked her what they do when they have completed their mission, and she told me they never complete their mission. But I know this cannot be true for they disappeared without any explanation. They were not seen again, and it is my fervent hope that you shall never see them, my son. And, yes, always be aware they could come at any time for whatever reason. This is why all people are encouraged to be true and honourable. Because no one really knows the reason they come or where they come from, or how long they will stay." She rubbed the side of her neck and swallowed again.

Rather than falling asleep, Roger was now more awake than at the start. She smiled at his wide eyes and fascinated stare. His tousled hair now stood on end as though she had electrocuted him with her words.

He sat up in bed, suddenly dead straight. "Is that true, Mama. Will they really come?"

Martha smiled warmly at her son. She drew closer to him and settled Roger back in bed, checking the bedclothes and tucking him in tightly. "No, son, of course not. These are just stories. Legends of old that have been told throughout generations even before the Clash and the Awakening. There is no need to fear, my son. Think about it. If the story *were* true, I would not be here to tell it. And you would not be here to hear it."

Martha began another story, a common one that Roger had already heard, and before she was a few lines in, he was snoring soundly. She flopped back in the rocking chair and let her muscles relax. She purposely never told the story of the Sandstone Army because it made her tense. As a child, she had believed every word she heard, though as an adult, she could offer no explanation for such ridiculous tales. A sensation in her gut that she could not pin down and yet knew something was there hovered in the background like a Spectra, waiting for the right moment. Until she, and the world, had forgotten and were relaxed. Waiting until they would be taken by surprise.

She left the sleeping child, closed the door quietly behind her, and returned to the sitting room. She skirted around the lounge chair and looked down at her husband sleeping soundly. His glass balanced precariously in one hand with his other clutching his knee. She had managed to put her entire family to sleep with one story. *It is a shame I will not sleep so well. It is funny that I have not told Roger the story before for fear of keeping him awake, and yet now it'll be I who is bereft of sleep for the night.*

She grimaced in the direction of the sleeping room. Reluctantly, she wandered over to the window and pulled back one of the drapes. She put her face close to the glass and stared into the darkness. There were no movements in the shadows. No sound of stealthy approach. No telltale rustle of leaves or breaking of sticks. Everything was as it should be—for now.

CHAPTER 33
THE COVEN

Tiniata stood and bowed to the room, the rustle of her skirts broke the static silence. She surveyed her new charge sadly. Coven leadership was not an honour she had requested, and yet it was bestowed. She sighed. For years now, she had formed ideas and made plans without ever a notion of putting them to use. *And so, it all begins here.*

The abnormal silence chipped away at Tiniata's confidence. Usually, the coven members would talk amongst themselves until the last moment. On this day, most sat, subdued, expectant. As though fearing the worst. She swallowed hard.

"Thank you all for the honour of your trust. We are all joined in sadness over the loss of Mistress Roxanne whose benevolent leadership carried us thus far. Now we begin a new era and look to the future. We are all mindful of the portents of evil that throw darkness upon our lives. I myself have seen the signs, the bubbles in the lake. Many amongst you have noticed the furtive looks of the werecats. Some of you recognise the distance our feline friends put between us." She looked about the room, gratified to see nods of agreement. "Many years ago, we left the Walhachin Mountains to guard the Storm Pass in quiet reflection. Those times are gone.

"I pledge now, in this most hallowed space," she raised her arms to indicate the room. "That I will lead you faithfully through these dark hours and I know I can rely on the support of my comrades." She placed both hands firmly down on the table and made eye contact with those in the front before casting her gaze around the room. "The time for innocuous potions, medicines, and remedies has passed. We must turn our attention to more powerful concerns. We must prepare. Meanwhile, we must continue to foster relations with our more powerful neighbours and support as many friendships as may be. We are weaker than the coming challenges."

She straightened her back. "But we will grow strong. I propose those amongst us who retain the most skill at creating medicines and healing potions will continue to do so. Those remaining will turn their attention to study, crafting, and forging. Then we shall have the tools we need to rekindle our power and take control of our future." She took a deep breath and looked up to gauge reactions.

Her stomach muscles relaxed a little at the general murmurings of agreement. The only question remaining was how to enact her plan. It would not be easy in such an isolated location.

Patience. She raised her hands to subdue the filtered mutterings. "Any questions?"

A voice rose from the back of the room. "I watch the signs. The weather is always a good tell as an omen, and yet, still I am unsure. I opine caution. As for the werecats, they have been unhappy for some time. They will not suddenly decide to do anything rash. What do you propose?"

A hushed assent washed through the hall. A hundred eyes burned into her. The weight of so many minds hard at work to pick fault, to disagree, or perhaps, if she was very lucky, support her. The stillness mocked her as though waiting for a mistake.

It would be disappointed.

When in doubt, focus on the task in hand. Tiniata scratched at the base of her neck and cleared her throat. There was no response to such a theoretical enquiry. Her skin tingled, and a headache hovered just inside her awareness. "I cannot say for certain that anything *will* happen. If we are to face our foes effectively, we must ensure that we are not taken by surprise." She raised her voice to reach the entire room. "I charge you all to be vigilant. Anything more?"

Silence fell. Wind buffeted the drapes, bringing the occasional snowflake in through the high windows. Candles flickered and cast mysterious shimmers across the tables. The only movement in the room were the werecat orderlies, restricted to their human forms, who moved silently between tables, filling glasses, clearing plates, and replacing candles.

"I will need to form a chain of command, adjusted to include department heads. I have some ideas for smooth adaptation. Those of you wishing to hold such positions may petition personally. I caution you, my decisions will be based on ability to fulfil the role. I shall also review all current positions. In time of war, there are different demands on our resources, so all placements will be subject to change until the final decisions are made. To those ends, I will pick a second. If my ideas do not work, I shall change them.

"We must work together. You will muster all your books to search for anything that might be relevant to our magical development, disguises, mind control, or black arts. All prior restrictions are now removed. You will not be penalised for owning such books and accoutrements that appertain to the black arts. Our very survival may depend on them. If there is a fight coming, I intend to win. We cannot prevail with one hand tied behind our backs."

At an unheard signal, the werecats left the room as silently as they had entered. The general muttering rose in volume and more than a couple of witches also departed. Tiniata waited for them to settle and stared down a couple of the more vocal members of the audience.

Without looking, she could have pictured the worst offenders, easily picked out by their more elaborate adornments. Their faces painted brighter colours than the others, their clothes darker, and yet with more jewels than the usual fair. Tiniata admired their ability to stand out from the crowd. That was before she had risen in rank. Now she was poised to assert her authority if challenged.

"I would like volunteers for an expedition. This is out of the normal way but necessary and immediate. We must play to win. Numbers are against us. Knowledge will be our greatest weapon. We will send out an expedition to assess the capabilities and intentions of our foes. Most notably to confirm the rumours from Laffite Head." The crowd shifted at her mention of the infamous town and its strange creatures.

She paused and heaved a great sigh at the interruption. "We have all heard the same rumours and have equal reluctance to accept them at face value. If they are true, we must be sure how this impacts us. If the Seers are correct, I fear a time will come when we need to pick sides." Tiniata paused for a heartbeat. "Take time to consider my words. We shall reconvene a few days from now. Please feel free to visit me in my chambers should you have any concerns or questions. Once our structure has been fixed, you will coordinate through the coven seniors. For now, we shall make the best. Now get to work."

Tiniata sagged as the room emptied. She rocked. Her brain seemed light and wispy. She closed her eyes and allowed herself a moment to regain control. She had expected more resistance to her suggestions. Tiniata sat down heavily on the chair behind her and rested her head in the palm of her hand.

CHAPTER 34
LOWLANDS

Syngh came to the edge of the forest and stopped. The view took him by surprise. He never explored this far; now he knew why. He could not imagine anything so torturous as imprisonment in such a place. Where the trees ended, so did the joy. The only redeeming feature was its downward slope. That at least allowed the drainage of water that would otherwise turn the area into a sticky marshland. Even so, wide puddles interrupted the landscape. The trampled grass turned the land into a soggy mess.

Piearsa sat hunched on a flat stone in the middle of a cage. Her prison was made of thick metal bars rising from the thick mud, much higher than necessary, well beyond the height someone could climb. The enclosure appeared to have no supports holding it up. Syngh had a feeling that this was an intended illusion. Surely, Piearsa would have tried to escape. She would not be the first. No doorway was evident as though the bars had been erected around her. At one end of the small enclosure, there were brackets with planks of wood laid atop to provide a meagre shelter from the regular rains. Syngh noticed, with some consternation, that the enclosure was designed purposely to be uncomfortable. The stone seat was placed at the opposite end from the shelter. Not that the rough covering would provide much protection from the recent chilly, torrential downpours.

He traced careful steps towards the bars, dodging the worst of the mud. His sloshing footsteps betrayed his presence before he got close. Piearsa turned, and her face brightened when she saw him. He returned the smile and rushed to the bars. They pressed their faces against the metal and kissed.

Syngh studied Piearsa. Her bruises took him by surprise as did her general appearance. Her normally tidy presence was now bedraggled, and her legs were caked in mud. Her soaking wet hair did nothing to help the impression of her depression. He gave a weak smile and then gathered himself. He needed to remain positive. He must appear happy and upbeat to give the impression that all was well. He must do this for her no matter how much he doubted it.

He took her hand and pulled her closer. "How are you?" he cringed at the question.

She smiled in recognition of the pointless query and shrugged. "I'm having a great day. Later, I am going out to a party, and I will invite them back for late drinks." She flashed her eyes at him. "I am sorry about all this. It was not supposed to go this far."

He gripped her hand tightly and looked into her dark eyes. "You're sorry? This is all my fault. I should have dealt with them years ago. It is me that got you into this. I should be sorry, not you."

"We might go back and forth like this forever. Let's just wait and see what happens. It is *their* fault, not ours. We must not dwell upon it." Piearsa sighed. "I did go a little over the top. What happened to your mother affected me more than I wanted to admit... No, I am not going to use that as an excuse for poor behaviour. I will take whatever punishment they give me, and then we can forget about this."

"It should only be some manual labour about town. It might drag on for a bit, but it depends on which elder leads. All will be well," he agreed although he was not sure which of them was trying to convince the other. "We should discuss something else to take our minds off this. Any ideas?"

She shook her head, lost in her own thoughts.

"All will be right again. You will see." He pulled her closer and held her, wrapping his arms about her just a little too tightly. They pressed hard against the cold metal.

After a few moments, she refocused on him. "It might have been the people of the mountain pride that attacked us," said Piearsa in a thoughtful tone.

Syngh started at her change of subject. "How would you know that? Did you remember something more from the attack?"

"I heard some of the guards talking. They said they were going to volunteer for the reconnaissance expedition. That there was evidence they came down from the mountains."

Syngh leaned both hands on the bars and allowed his arms to take his weight. *It is unprecedented for the southern prides to travel north. They are even more indoctrinated than ours. They would not leave the mountains.* He frowned.

"I know what you are thinking, they never come north and certainly not to such low latitudes. The guard said he heard they were migrating," she said, her expression telegraphing her doubt.

"And attacking for no reason? That does not sound right. We are no threat to them. I read about the history of all the prides working together but never attacking each other."

Piearsa moved backwards to sit on her stone. Syngh followed her around the edge of the cage. She sat leaning forward with her weight on her knees. "Something must have changed. Look at the evidence. Years of peace and now, all of a sudden, violence in our town. Prides migrating and rumours of other strange occurrences. And where are the witches? They never came after you. No letter of complaint. No emissary. We should have incurred their displeasure by now. At the very least they should have informed your father of your departure." She cocked her head.

"Nothing," he replied to her unspoken query. "I had not considered…"

Piearsa stood and drew closer to him. She reached her hand through the bars and took his, "What, my love?"

"Everything is connected."

She raised one eyebrow and smiled, "Even my arrest?" her grin widened.

"Perhaps…"

"I was joking," she scoffed. "This was my own fault. I should have known better."

"Everything that has happened is connected somehow," he insisted with more conviction. "The more I consider it, the more I become convinced. The rumours, the attack, I bet even the migration. If I am correct then what changed recently, after so long in peaceful coexistence?"

Piearsa eyed him. Her expression was unreadable, but there appeared less doubt than expected. Her long nail traced the corner of her mouth in a manner all too familiar to him.

Syngh grinned, "What are you thinking, or do I really need to ask?"

She fixed her gaze on him intently and flicked her eyes upwards in silent promise. Her expression blanked. "The effects seem to be too widespread for them to be connected. Walhachin, Laffite, and who knows what is going on in the Lessar Lands?"

"We need to find out and quickly before things get worse."

"Why do you think they would get worse?" She looked about her as though afraid of being overheard.

"How could they not? I fear this is just the beginning. We need to find the mountain prides," he said then lapsed into silence.

It was clear that Piearsa was not following his reckoning, but she was willing to go along with it. "It is up to you then. I can do nothing from my cage. I may be here for a while." She pulled away from him.

Syngh looked at her. He opened his mouth to speak but could think of nothing to say. It was not so much her words as the expression on her face. She bore the gaunt features of one condemned. How did he not notice it before? Had it been there all the while they had been talking? Was he so wrapped up in his thoughts that he had failed to understand there was more going on? He studied her face and decided now was not the time to allow himself to be distracted. He must make sure he was there for her.

CHAPTER 35
LESTER

Lester found the street in the bad part of town, an area that resisted attempts at improvements. The proverbial back street was hardly distinguishable from the rest of the town. Buildings had gone up randomly with the later more organized plan forced to incorporate the scattered older structures. This street, unflatteringly named by the locals, Shaggy Row, was a perfect example of the old ways. The haphazard buildings created a twisting street of differing widths. In the heat, the squalor seemed to steam off the permanent puddles and permeate the surroundings.

He dodged a particularly questionable puddle and continued down the hill. His usual confidence had abandoned him, along with his balance, so that between the path and his lack of sleep, his journey was precarious.

Lester had woken before the sun rose. He still ached all over from sleeping on the dinghy. If his unconscious state could be described as sleep. Lyliana had remained asleep through his arrival and while he changed his clothes and washed. He almost woke her when a couple of bottles clinked as he ploughed through the seating area. He had watched her for a few minutes, contemplating his actions and chances of survival over the next few hours. Lester debated waking her to say goodbye, but she did not need the worry. So, he left the house as the sun's glow kissed the horizon and headed for town.

Exerting more effort than was wise in his condition, he reached the establishment he was searching for. Never had he ventured so far from his comfort zone. By necessity from his previous position, Lester had not been one to frequent such places as Sandrine's Shag. As second in command under Zarono and Percy, he felt it dubious to be seen in the area even now. Lester's preference was more mainstream, less unconventional.

The faded sign above the door was unreadable and hung precariously by one nail. The barred shutters matched the worn wooden flowerpots and the weeds they contained.

He pushed on the door to open it, but upon finding it would not move, he banged his fist on the wood. A man cracked the door ajar and grunted.

"I'm 'ere to see Cap'ain Caesar."

"He ain't here. Go away," the man said.

Lester steadied himself on the wall, "He's expec'ing me...Cap'ain Lester." The use of his full title had the desired effect. The door swung open, emitting a whiff of putrid humanity. Lester gagged and huffed air through his mouth.

He followed the man down the dark corridor and into a gloomy sitting room. It took a moment for his eyes to adjust. Two figures sat in the corner of the room. Lester approached cautiously and stood in front of the circular table. His stomach lurched. Bile rose in his throat. He held himself rigid, afraid that at any moment his belly might betray him although whether from his developing hangover or the stench of body odour and smoke he would never know. Sweat spread across his forehead and twitched at his neck. He did not move, focused on keeping his breathing steady.

"Well, shake my sheets! I figured you'd forge' last nigh'. My men said you were three shee's gone. Get lost." Caesar directed his last comment to the woman sitting on his lap, and she left reluctantly.

"You wan'ed to see me. 'Ere I am. Next time ya can just come ya'sel'. No need to send the thugs." Lester was determined that he would not show weakness though his compliance with Caesar's demand was a weak start.

"Do you know wha' this is about?" Captain Caesar moved over to another table and snatched two glasses and a decanter. He threw himself back in his seat and indicated that Lester should sit.

Once he was settled, a glass scraped over to him, and he shifted it to the edge of the table. He did not want to offend this vicious man, but the scent of the liquid conjured a heaving inside him. "You still 'ave a problem with our new management." He sat back in the chair with an air of disinterestedness. Lester massaged his temples, trying to ward off the emerging headache. "I don't know why ya're talking to me. Go see 'er."

"Normally I wouldn't expect much sense from a woman. In this case, I already know I will not get any. Her defiance is clear. Why waste my time when I know *you'll listen* to my concerns?"

Lester swallowed back his initial retort and coughed. "She is na different to anyone else. She does na respond well to undue force. You should have approached with the respec' of her position."

"I don't accept 'er position. She weakens us. The question is, what are we goin' to do about it?" Caesar's glass clicked against the wood of the table, and the decanter made a bang as he refilled his glass. Caesar ignored Lester's untouched drink.

"You've only just returned. If you had been here, you migh' think differently. There have been many changes...to the benefit of all. Ya worry that she might lose sight of the threat we face every day. Yet I see 'er building up to such concerns. Assuming her as weak's a mistake. In the space of a very short time, she gained many supporters. Perhaps you should assess the situation. See her progress for ya'self," Lester suggested tentatively.

Caesar huffed and took a huge gulp of his drink. He glanced at Lester's glass and frowned.

Lester took a small sip and tried to swallow it bit by bit so as not to upset his stomach. When the drink settled, he continued. "We're both men of the sea so we rebel agains' change. I promise ya. This a good thing. Try to work with 'er. We all start the same."

"She did not." He pointed one finger in the air. "She might have the town convinced, but they are no' the people who pour money into this dive."

"Fair enough, but 'ow much did either of 'er predecessors listen to ya?" Lester waved his glass in the air to punctuate his point.

Caesar mulled the idea over before nodding. "Fair enough. I'll consider your words. But if you are wrong, you are gambling your life. Keep 'er on track. Now—"

The door opened, and the girl came back in with a fresh decanter that she placed carefully on the table. She hovered over the table, her breasts thrust towards Caesar, clearly intending to stay.

Caesar gave her a look that would have sliced their

drinking glasses into two shards. She smiled widely and shifted closer to Lester. A movement at the door drew his attention, and he saw two men standing in the doorway. He could not be sure, but they could have been Tee and Zee. His memory would not come into focus.

"I told you to get los'. This is a business meeting," Caesar snapped at the girl when he noticed she was still there.

She slunk from the room. The man closed it behind her but stayed in the room.

Caesar turned back to Lester and raised his eyes. "So, that's settled. I will see her myself, and we shall come to some arrangement. I suggest you keep this conversation to yourself."

Not much choice. What would she do if she heard about this? Not worth the trouble. Lester nodded but filed the threats into his memory. He opened his mouth to speak.

"Now, t'ther matters—" Caesar sneered and rocked the chair onto its back legs.

Lester raised his one eyebrow. *What now?* He fixed his gaze on Caesar and used his sharpest tone. "Before we ge' to that," Lester sat straight up in the chair. "You need to do something for me."

Caesar looked as though he was going to argue but lapsed into a resigned silence at a look from Lester.

Lester took a breath, forgetting the smell, gagged, and collected his thoughts. "I know ya have sway with the other cap'ains. I need ya no' to voice your displeasure to'em. Ideally, it would be useful if ya'd take some steps to ensure they support Lyliana." He swallowed back his sarcasm. "I cannot 'ope to convince her to follow your...our agenda without a show of support from the cap'ains. She would have no reason to help."

Caesar nodded slowly, taking in Lester's words. "So, she does have an agenda of 'er own?"

"All this 'appened so quickly. Percy was starting a riot, and she jumped in and calmed the crowd. It was quite some'hing to see."

The other captain's eyes narrowed at the mention of Percy.

"If you'd all give her a chance, she'll surprise you."

"I've no doubt she will. The question is, will we like the surprise?"

Lester deflated. He had thought that he was making progress, "You won't be disappointed. I'd stake my life on it."

"*That* you're doing already. You ne'er struck me as a gambler." He huffed loudly and sat forward. "I'll go see 'er, and we'll plan wha' we're going to do about Mack's Seadogs." He smirked at his invention of the name. "There's one other matter. Sasha's death canno' go unanswered."

Two hands gripped his shoulders and pulled Lester to his feet. He was stunned. He had forgotten about the others. Strong hands shoved him into the middle of the room.

"Sasha was my friend," Caesar growled and nodded to the twins before leaving the room.

The first punch felt like a stone. Lester staggered. He jerked sideways. A fist crashed into the side of the head. Lester raised his hand to fight back. Another blow jarred his chin. He tripped over a foot and onto his face. His arm was yanked, and he fell. He was on his feet. A blow to the stomach and he doubled over to receive a knee in the face. Lester's jaw cracked. His hand protected his bleeding face. His finger was pulled back, and another punch took him in the eye. Pain shot through his hand and up his arm. He tried to make a fist, but the finger was broken. He covered his face. Blow followed blow until he was on the floor. He couldn't open his eyes.

The creaking door announced Caesar's return. "Enough. I think he understands. Ge'im out of here."

Lester was dragged upright and thrust out of the door.

"Remember this well. I'll 'ave a meeting wi' your bitch, but if she doesn't satisfy me, you will pay with your life. One way or the 'ther, I will have revenge for the Seadogs." The sound of smashing glass was the last thing Lester heard before he was tossed outside and into a puddle on the ground. The smell blanketed him. He retched over and over again, vomit mixing with the blood.

Revenge. I will have revenge. He lost consciousness.

CHAPTER 36
LYLIANA

The image sharpened, blurred, and then came into focus. The red glow shifted into a detailed picture, the Seat of Ogres. Charles's face, at first superimposed on her mind, strengthened into prominence. His happy impatience shone below his bald head. A vague memory surfaced, when he first had his head shaved, not a popular look amongst the men in Hillaway, and yet he could pull it off. *Charles wore the same smile that made her fall in love with him. His face faded. Mikkel appeared in the background, mirroring* Charles's *expression. Charles came back into focus, his lips moved, uttering silent words.*

Lyliana squinted, searching her memory. She strained to grasp the vision. She relaxed her mind, trying to focus through less effort. The image repeated the words she could not hear. *I love you.* She smiled. No matter if that was not what it was saying, he loved her.

She moved her fingers, and the sand scraped along her skin. Lapping waves invaded her thoughts. She was on the beach. For the first time since she had washed up on the shore, she was remembering why she used to enjoy the coast. A few minutes to herself, secure in her private sanctuary, her first moments of peace in the last few days. Lyliana relaxed her eyelids and allowed the merciless red glow to brighten into her thoughts while the sun's warmth caressed her skin.

"Miss Lyliana," the voice barrelled through her. "Miss Lyliana."

She opened her eyes, pushed herself onto her elbows, and stared through the glare towards the voice.

"You must come," said the guard as he drew closer. "The captain requires ya presence in your office."

Lyliana sighed as she pushed herself from the sand and stood to face the guard. *Who is this one? They all look the same. I must learn their names.*

Apparently satisfied, the guard turned back and headed towards the town. She caught up with him and kept pace until they reached the road where she replaced her sandals.

"What is the problem?" *What is so urgent? Events move slowly here.*

The guard turned and pointed to the horizon. "Ships coming this way, miss. We expec'ed none."

She followed the line of his arm stretching towards the stark blue line of the horizon. She saw nothing.

"They were seen from the headland. Warships, miss. Too far awa' to see their colours," said the guard by way of explanation.

She nodded. "Lead the way then. Did Lester...? The captain...did he say anything else?"

The guard shook his head. "No, miss. Just for me to fetch you and send the lieutenant to him."

She held out her hand for him to lead on. They remained silent for the rest of the walk to the office.

Roylei flapped from the window as she approached and, after a brief hesitation, landed. Lyliana entered her office with him on her shoulder. He hissed at the soldiers talking to Lester. She tickled the creature under his chin. From behind her desk, Lyliana studied Lester's bruises and his black eye, careful not to let him see her scrutiny.

He finished with the others and turned to her with hardly a breath. "The lookout sighted the ships jus' before I sent for you. Sorry to disturb ya."

She bobbed her head once. "What preparations have you made thus far?"

Lester took a resigned breath and enumerated his instructions to his lieutenants. He made a couple of extra suggestions on arming the town guard, which she agreed with, and then he added, "I did mention to ya tha' this might 'appen."

"What do you mean?" she asked.

"I said when the other pirates learn o' the coup they'll assume we're weak and attack."

A shiver speckled over her arms in response to his word choice. *Yet you could not predict them exacting revenge on you?* "You did, yes, but surely if they heard I took over, they also heard I am not weak. How would I commit a coup d'etat if I was?"

Lester approached the opposite side of the table and leaned towards her. "Normally, I'd agree, but they are unlikely to believe stories o' dragons. I might no'. If I hadn't seen it for mysel'. And taking over is no' running the town. A sneak attack might give you control, but not command. There is also... Well, there're some who might..." He stared at the paper on the table in front of him, his hand going absently to his damaged eye.

"Go on," she prompted, feeling the frustration that comes with knowing someone is holding back.

He looked her square in the eyes. "You're a woman." He looked down and rubbed the back of his neck.

Lyliana took a quick intake of breath. Her heat rose with her temper. She shoved it inside. *He is only doing his job*. Her shoulders drooped. She shifted round the side of the table to take his hand. "That should not matter," she replied in a low voice.

"I'm sorry, but it does. It matters to 'em. Women are weak—in their world."

"*You* believe I am weak?" A muscle in her neck tightened.

He looked into her eyes and gave her a smile. "No one 'ere thinks *you* are weak."

Lyliana smiled with one side of her mouth. "When others think it, we have the advantage." She tilted her head to one side and allowed her grin to spread as he nodded. "So, what is the plan?"

He led her back round the table and pulled out a chart of the harbour. Lines and numbers, looking like something a drunken spider might weave, covered a sizable sheet of colourless paper. Lyliana leaned closer and focused on the apparent confusion. Lines blurred before her eyes.

Lester pointed, tracing the line of the bay, such as it was. "This is us. The fleet is coming roun' the headland here."

She nodded her understanding and pointed to some small islands on the edge of the paper. "What is this?"

"Collusion Islands," he replied, frowning. He pointed to the largest island. "That is Corsair's Collusion."

"How far?"

"Three days sail. Why?

"No matter. I had a thought we might hide our fleet there,"

"Too far and too late."

"For the future, I meant," she huffed.

He shook his head and a moment later gave a sudden intake of breath. "What about 'ere, only half a day away and plenty o' shelter for most o' the time?" His finger shifted to Corsairs Collusion.

"It could work. How far away?"

"Half a day thereabouts. The island was a place to exile pirates when the group first arrived here."

"Sounds perfect. It will have been forgotten after so long." She blinked. An idea formed.

"There's a good view from the top o' the hill,"

"So it can be seen, but only the captains know of it." She nodded in understanding.

"Right, so we need a plan for hiding our vessels. This cannot be an attack. There's no reason for one, but it is prudent to have one for the future. When will this flotilla arrive?"

"A couple o' hours. What're ya planning?" he asked doubtfully.

"I will talk to them. We are not ready for a confrontation."

"This might be a mistake." She knew it was as close as he dared to disagree. He relented, "Let's see wha' occurs. I'll 'ave the launch prepared and my vessel. You must keep ya guards close." He thought for a moment, "It might be better to 'ave 'em come ashore. We'll have more control then?"

She frowned before realising he was talking of the fleet, not her guards. "So, they can see how weak we are? No. I shall go to them. If anything happens, you can take over here. That is the plan." This last was in response to his obvious intention to argue with her.

Reluctantly, he nodded and went to the door to issue instructions to the lieutenant outside.

Lyliana leaned on the table and allowed herself to rock gently back and forth. She stared at the chart. Her lips parted as she controlled her heavy breathing. *Why is it that every time I try to make a change, I meet with resistance? Shouldn't he just do as I ask? Advice is one thing, but the constant disagreements...*

Voices rose outside, and Lester disappeared out of sight with the lieutenant.

Lyliana did not see Lester again before the arrival of the ships. The chart distracted her as she tried to develop countermeasures against an attack. The only information she had on the subject was what she had gleaned from Lester's discussions, much of which was useless without context. Lester saw everything from a pirate's perspective, not considering a military standpoint. Some preparations were obvious. A good lookout and alarm system she had learned about in Hillaway by watching the town's preparations. Maintaining the fleet in a state of preparedness was too obvious, and she was pleased with the idea to hide them even if Lester was sceptical. Ideally, she would like to increase the number of fighters and form a proper infantry. Lester assured her it was in hand. Reorganisation of the crews had been completed though certain captains remained unhappy at the changes. There were just not enough ashore. She considered a recruiting drive but how to achieve such a thing? Everyone was already engaged. Even the slaves were accounted for.

An idea sprang from the map as though the ink spread to her mind. *A land irrigation system,* it would reduce the number of slaves needed and potentially increase the number of pirates to be designated to posts on the vessels.

Fewer slaves required fewer guards, and if they were assigned to the ships... Her mind expanded, stretching the idea. Less control. Less money. Better containment. More fighters. She made mental notes of the benefits.

———

The small group clattered along the wooden jetty behind Lyliana and Lester as they headed towards the launch waiting to take them out into the bay. Lyliana chewed her lip as she took a sailor's hand to help her down into the boat. The lead vessel had hoisted a white flag over her purple sails as soon as ships got within range. Purple was the colour assigned to Hillaway harbour ships. The other three in the convoy carried dark green canvas, confirming to them as Gamola-based.

The launch was twenty metres long with a small cabin in the back. She found a seat under the canopy, grateful to sit on a steady surface. The waves were deceptively large against the side of the small vessel.

With the wind was at odds with their motion, the crew pulled on their oars, their faces red with strain as the boat crawled towards the waiting ships. The stroke oarsman grinned at her watching him but looked quickly away when she caught his eye. As they passed, Lester pointed out his own ship, commenting with disappointment on how little time he spent aboard since the regime change.

Lyliana looked from the ships and back to their small boat. Another idea formed in a rush. Something else to discuss with Lester. Oars had potential as a weapon of surprise.

The air chilled as they pushed out into the bay. Lyliana pulled the hood of her shawl over her head and half turned her body against the wind. There was plenty of activity on the deck of the vessel they were approaching. She guessed that most of it was preparation for her arrival.

A splash to her left revealed Tisray emerging from the water. He shot straight upwards, spinning in the air before coming to land unsteadily on the side of the boat. Lyliana smiled. The dragons were never far away. He flapped once and took off again to dive back into the water. *They swim well, another discovery to add to the list. Who knew?* She watched with rapt attention.

He emerged a minute or two later and landed on the gunwale. His body was puffed up, like a bird drying its feathers out. He shook himself, showering the crew. Tisray opened his mouth and flicked his snake-like tongue. His wings raised in a threatening gesture. As Lyliana reached out to pet him, he stretched his head up to reveal the full length of his neck. His tail extended, and he opened his mouth. A great jet of water shot straight up more than a few metres. The second jet was accompanied by clattering oars and screams. One oarsman fell back as his oar blade got stuck under another and then came clear unexpectedly. The boat's forward motion faltered. The deluge ceased, leaving puddles of water in the boat and the damp grinning crew.

Tisray lowered his head and folded his glistening blue green wings along his back. Lyliana smiled at his apparent look of joy. He was not bloated anymore. His tail bobbed to maintain balance. Lyliana held out her hands for him, and with one flap of his wings, he landed on her palms. She felt his weightlessness and cuddled him to her chest. Tisray sniffed her neck and pulled back. Her perfume made him sneeze, a quiet contained sound, very weak after his impressive display of strength.

"Eyes in the boat," ordered Lester in response to the boat's idleness. He turned back to Lyliana, "Those dragons are a constan' source o' surprise." He looked appreciatively at Tisray but made no move to touch him.

A squawk from above drew Lyliana's attention up to the top of the bare mast. Almost invisible against the sun, Yastat perched on the very top of the mast, his wings and tail splayed out for balance. "Where there is Tisray, be sure there is Yastat," she said to Lester as she indicated the top of the mast.

"He's sneaky f' sure," said Lester, never taking his eyes off Yastat.

"He is faster than the others. His speed increases daily. He likely arrived first. Yastat follows him more often than not." She gave Lester a relaxed smile.

By the time they reached the visiting vessel, both dragons had gone. The only sign of their continuing presence was a silence within the boat. As they approached, they were hailed from the ship and instructed to come alongside. Against her better judgement and the advice of Lester, she decided it would be a show of good faith to board the ship.

Lester made one final attempt to dissuade her from boarding before he finally gave up and stood to help her climb the tumblehome.

"You were wrong about this being an attack." She smiled to soften her comment. "I am trusting you to be wrong about their reason for coming here also." Lyliana kissed Lester lightly on the lips, "Trust me. Everything will be okay."

"If it ain't, I'm coming after you. If you don't return 'ere, I'll rain dragons an' wrath down on 'em." He hissed so that only she could hear him.

A warmth rushed over her. She felt safe. Lyliana squeezed his hand tightly and allowed his power to wash over her. She never felt this way around Charles.

She arrived on the deck surrounded by the sound of flapping canvas and creaking blocks. The captain met her as she stepped lightly onto the deck and caught her breath. "I am Trey," said the dark-haired man. His eyes pierced through her skull as he stepped forward and offered his hand. "You remember me?"

She looked him up and down, from his damp brown sandals to his muscly arms toned from years working at sea, to the growing wrinkles about his face. She guessed he was in his early thirties, quite young for a captain of any type of vessel. His face was vaguely familiar.

"Perhaps. I am not sure. Sorry." She took his hand.

"I am Charles' friend. We traced you here by a process of elimination." The wrinkles around his eyes deepened as he smiled.

Her breath hitched, and she staggered slightly. Her eyes grew wide. "Charles is here? Where? I must see him."

Trey held out his hand to stop her. "He is below decks. He decided to stay there is case you should not wish to see him."

She opened her mouth to reply, but he stopped her again.

Trey dragged his index finger along the right side of his mouth and exhaled visibly. "I should tell you, while we have been on this voyage, he has become increasingly convinced you did not return on purpose. You should be careful what you say. Seeing you come on board in apparent freedom might be too much for him."

Her face tingled with heat that burned her cheeks. "I

must see him right now. Please take me to him. I do not mean to be rude—"

"I understand." He moved to lead her back towards the cabin but stopped short. "Please do not be long. These waters are not safe for us."

She rushed to Charles as soon as she saw him. Lyliana wrapped her arms around him and clung on tightly as though she would never let go. After a slight hesitation, he pulled her close and put his arms on her shoulders. He kissed her on the forehead and then pulled away slightly. She stepped back and looked at him. His usually lively dark eyes had lost their glimmer. His hair was starting to grow out, and he looked more tired than usual.

"It is so good to see you. I can't believe you came all this way," she rubbed the back of her neck.

He looked at her with a hint of sympathy. "Of course, I came. You were in trouble," He looked her up and down, pointedly. "Although not as much trouble as I thought."

"Did Father send you?"

"No."

She frowned at his short reply but said nothing.

"He is an old hat at loosing children to pirates. He thought all was lost," said Charles without a hint of humour.

Lyliana stared at the wooden deck beneath her feet and shuffled uncomfortably. "I am sorry I never told you. There just never seemed to be the time." The darkness of the cabin seemed to close in on her as if it was an omen for what was to come. *To claim lack of time is lame. I should have come up with something better. The truth perhaps?*

"It is no matter. We shall have plenty of time to talk on the way home. I am so pleased I found you. When we set out from Gamola Harbour, *I thought* all was lost. It took a lot of persuading to get these other vessels to come with us. Even with Trey's help to persuade them, they were reluctant. I really thought you would have made it to Gamola." He paused and looked at her. "Why do you look like that?"

The air about her thickened, and her throat closed up.

"Lyliana, what is going on? Don't worry. There will be no problem with you leaving. I will not let anything happen to you."

She took a deep breath and took both his hands in hers. "I am not ready to come back with you yet—"

"Lyli—"

Lyliana held up her hands to stop him. "No, wait. If I leave this place, I must marry him. I cannot, not now. Not after everything. There is so much to be done here. If there is no way I can be with you then I should stay here and try to change things from the inside."

"They took you and held you captive. Why would you want to be with them?"

"I am in charge now. The dragons... They changed things for me. I cannot explain it, but...they are the reason I am here. Something important is going to happen. I could not say this to any but you. People would think I am crazy. This is where I need to be. You should stay here with me then we could be together." Even she heard the doubt in her voice.

"That would not work out. What would my parents say? I cannot lose you again. Please come with me. You will be safe at home. I will speak with your intended. I am sure we can work something out."

"Please speak with him. Tell him I am sorry, but I cannot go through with the marriage. Whatever happens here, I will not be with him." She pleaded with her eyes for an understanding she knew would not be forthcoming. "Wait for me. When I am finished here, I will come to you. We can be together."

He moved away from her. "When will that be? What will I say to your parents? Your father will be mad that I even came. To go back without you will finish him off."

"I will come back when my work here is done, whenever that is. I cannot leave this place while there is so much to do. I do not expect you to understand, but please try. I am not leaving you. This is just something I must do for myself. Tell my parents you did not find me. Or tell them you did, that I am well, and I love them. Tell them I will return home as soon as I can. It is up to you."

"I cannot do that. You know your family history. Do you think they could handle the news of another child running away to be with pirates," he spat. His face lit in understanding, "Are you pregnant. Is that it? That would explain all this."

Lyliana blanched at his flash of anger. She shook her head, choking back her astonishment. "Of course not. I cannot adequately explain. This is all too much right now. I have no words."

"No words are needed. I shall speak with actions. Be assured of that. Best you leave now." Charles went to the door and held it open for her, his stance rigid and determined.

As she passed him, he looked away without even a good-bye. As she stepped off the deck onto the ladder, Trey looked at her with pity and offered a slight nod.

CHAPTER 37
LOWLANDS

T he crowd at Tiger's Eye Ellipse grew steadily. It looked like the entire town might eventually arrive. Syngh sat on the edge of the saucer-shaped gouge in the ground and eyed the arena. It had originated as an amphitheatre, but time and lack of interest had taken a toll. The sides sloped down to a flat area in the middle with a vast stone table on one side. In the absence of any other practical use for the space, it had become the de facto town court.

Trees lined the clearing around the arena, leaving just enough space for a path around the outside that met the walkway from town. It could have been a picnic area were it not for the hovering doom in the atmosphere. Two modest stones stood in the centre, traditionally used by the accused and anyone who spoke for them. Syngh was reluctant to venture towards the centre, his skin tightened about his forehead at the realisation that he must go, even though the elders had refused him access. It would be worse if he gave them notice of his presence.

His mind reverted to the last time they used the Ellipse.

What was the outcome of that hearing? His thoughts edged towards a guilty verdict, but doubt tickled his mind. He recalled one adult saying that there was never an innocent verdict when a person appeared in the Ellipse. *Old wives' tales.* He pursed his lips and swallowed back a sour taste from the back of his throat.

Piearsa had remained positive, even calm, until that morning. Her incarceration eroded her outlook, and Syngh worried about the lasting effect on her. He replayed their earlier conversation.

"You must be strong for me, Syngh."

"I am always here for you, my love. Everything will be fine. They will see the history. They will forgive all."

"Perhaps for the slash on his face but not for changing. They already said I broke my vow. They will not accept such treachery."

Syngh had laughed uncontrollably at the idea that such a lapse in temper was defined as treachery. He had been gasping for air before he realised she was serious.

"The elders are old men, out of touch with the events of the current day. Better sense will prevail. You will see. Someone will speak up for you. This is your first offence."

Her silence had unnerved him, but despite his best efforts, she would speak no more about anything that might have happened prior to the incident at the funeral.

"You must take care of my family. Whatever happens to me, I must know they are cared for," she pleaded.

"That goes without saying, but it will be unnecessary. You might face punishment. Nothing more. Believe me, everything will be fine."

"I wish I could. I am not so lucky as others. Perhaps it will be quick. I could not bear to suffer."

Syngh was startled by her willingness to give up and the lack of optimism she displayed. It left him lost for meaningful words at the wrong moment. He chewed his lip as the crowd came back into focus.

Piearsa's parents entered the clearing and nodded to him. Syngh offered them a bitter smile but kept his seat. He could not bear to listen to them lament over their daughter's misfortune.

Jaden followed behind them and walked straight over to him. "How is Piearsa? You saw her this morning, didn't you?" he asked before coming to a halt.

"About how you would expect. She seems to have given up. Honestly, Jaden, I'm worried for her."

His expression fell, and he moved to sit by his friend. "You will get through it. She did not do anything so bad."

Syngh smiled. "That's not what the elders are saying."

"Well, there's no reason to stay here. You can move somewhere else. Perhaps go back to the coven." He grinned at the suggestion.

"Yeah, I bet they will be delighted to see us. It is not a terrible suggestion though. We should have gone that night."

"You'd have had to fight the elder. That would have made things worse. At least she has a fair chance today. It is no fun not having a home or ties to your origins."

Syngh looked at the lad, and his heart ached. He choked back a growing thickness in his throat. "Come on, let's watch her arrival. Show our support, aye?"

Jaden nodded, and they stood together, skirted round the Tiger's Eye and headed for the path. They arrived just in time. Jaden nudged Syngh in the ribs as he caught a glance of Piearsa.

Syngh gripped the lad's shoulder, and his eyes met Piearsa's. He smiled, hoping to offer reassurance, but her stony expression remained. She looked tired, but she held her head high. He maintained eye contact with her as she followed the jailer to the Ellipse and took her place on the centre stone.

The crowd took their seats, and silence fell over the clearing. Syngh skirted the throng and stood as far forward as he was able, staying in Piearsa's line of sight. She kept her eyes forward, never glancing in his direction.

Syngh choked down the offence caused by her lack of attention. She had more important things to worry about than his feelings. He exchanged a look with Jaden who flashed a glance in her direction. Syngh gave a little shrug and stared at the ground. A rustle circled the crowd, signalling the arrival of the Pride Master. The throng hushed as he took his place in the ellipse.

The elders, led by the master and flanked by two guards in feline form, entered the arena and took their places. Their official black cloth with gold facings gave them a commanding presence as they surveyed the crowd. The hostility in their eyes spoke of resentment or intolerance.

A chill flushed over Syngh as the elders held a conference amongst themselves in low whispers. Their eyes turned to him. The cold stare of the Pride Master would have chilled the fires of a volcano. Syngh shuddered and forced a stoic expression onto his face.

The opening declarations were completed, and the proceeding handed over to the challenging elder who thanked the Pride Master and moved swiftly to the matter at hand.

"Piearsa, you are charged on three counts. Wilful disobedience against our laws, wanton disregard for the sensibilities of the society, and premeditated violence."

The elder sitting one over from the challenger coughed pointedly, and the first elder leaned over to conduct an inaudible discussion ending in reluctant agreement. He turned to address the crowd. "A fourth charge has been levelled, attempted felocide." A great murmur passed over the crowd. "How do you answer these charges?"

Syngh's breath caught in his throat. He squeezed his eyes shut and forced air into his lungs. His hand went to his mouth, but he snatched it away and glanced at Piearsa. *Felocid? Who came up with such a thing? There was none of that. At most, it was self-defence.* His arms shook in rage and disbelief. *Oh, how did it come to this? There is nothing I can do.* He stared at the Pride Master, his jaw clenched. *I will make this right, one way or the other.* He looked at Piearsa, afraid of what he might see. There was nothing.

He frowned. *Did she know about this? It would explain a lot.* His mind numbed. *Why did she not tell me?* He coughed loudly. Piearsa did not even flinch.

Piearsa stood staring at the members of the tribunal. Her chin held high, her eyes distant, her expression frozen like a glacier. She said nothing, not even an acknowledgement that they had spoken.

"Piearsa of the Fang, how do you plead?" repeated the elder.

Syngh stepped forward without realising. The tribunal members eyed him.

"May I be heard?" Syngh said in a loud voice.

Piearsa did not move.

"Syngh of the Claw," the elder studied him. "The Claw will remain silent. This does not concern you." He turned back to Piearsa, "You must enter a plea."

"On all counts excepting one, not guilty," she replied in a neutral tone.

Syngh caught his breath. Which one was she copping to?

Why does she not deny them all? What is she doing? Does she realise how much trouble even one of those can cause?

The Pride Master sighed and looked at his peers. The one leading the proceedings shook his head like a long-suffering parent. He waited, expecting as everyone else was, that she would continue.

Piearsa remained silent, yet a smile twitched her lips.

The elder rested his hands on the table in front of him, and, with more forced patience, he said, "Elaborate."

Piearsa drew herself up to her full height, and Syngh saw the moment her fight returned. He mirrored her movements and focused his attention. He did not want to miss a word.

"I acted in self-defence. Those bullies had this coming for a long while. There was no premeditation. Only action. Had prior preventative measures been taken, this would not have been necessary. Without intent, your last two charges are void. I did not disobey any instruction from an elder. I was given none. As to wanton disregard, this suggests I have no respect for the rules of this pride. On the contrary, I follow all the rules, all of the time. In this case, the situation demanded action. I had no time to consider the ramifications of my actions. For *that,* I apologise. I acknowledge I completed my transformation to my feline persuasion outside a designated area and can only promise that it will not happen again."

Syngh dragged his attention from Piearsa and back to the tribunal. Two of them were nodding and appeared satisfied. The other three wore irritated frowns. Syngh could not observe any change in the Pride Master. They just exchanged glances.

"A fine speech," said the Pride Master. "I believe we all understand—"

"Priedor, if I may?" The elder did not wait for a response but addressed Piearsa. "Yes, it was a fine speech. Yet we did not ask for a speech. Only an answer to the charges. I was present on the night in question. Even if I accepted your claim of self-defence, which I do not, it was still excessive force. The rules about shape shifting are for the protection of everyone, including the changeling. Our laws must not be ignored at will." He took a breath to continue, but another member of the committee held up his hand.

"We have not come together only to have the rules recited. The issue is not whether our people know the rules. It is whether they were broken," the elder said in a harsh tone.

"Quite so," agreed another.

A flutter tickled through Syngh. *They do not even agree with each other. This could be good.* His mind floated above his body as though he were seeing the proceedings through different eyes. *Or it could be terrible.* He glanced at Piearsa. She was not reacting, but he thought he could see the anticipation emanating from her.

The seniors behind the table were moving about restlessly. He squinted at them, looking for subtle tells. *Is something more going on here?*

The elder at the far end of the table spoke up for the first time. "There might come a time when such initiative may be necessary. We were attacked once. We must take steps to prevent it from happening again."

"Again, that is not the question we are here to respond to," the first elder replied. "I would like to hear from the victim of this unprovoked attack," He waved in the direction of Oswald and his family who were standing with Kalito.

"I object," shouted Syngh, rushing forward.

The elder, and self-proclaimed leader of the tribunal, turned his glare on Syngh. "*You* cannot object. Keep your place, or you will be removed." He pointed at Oswald. "Come forward, young man."

Oswald approached the gathering and stood off to one side of the Ellipse. He stared at the ground and shuffled his feet in the dirt.

"Tell us what happened, son. In your own words now, and tell it true," the elder instructed with a merest hint of threat.

"Well, it was just a bit of fun at the start. We have played these games for years. Syngh knows the routine." Oswald looked pointedly in his direction.

The elder followed Oswald's gaze and gave Syngh a daring look.

"I admit it might have been bad timing. Considering what happened to his mother and all. Still, that was no excuse for him setting *her* on us," he nodded at Piearsa who scowled in reply. "We were saying how lucky it was that Syngh returned in time for his father and for the time when families should be together. We went over to say how sorry we were. She flipped out. She was possessed." He wiped his cheek as though he had been crying and continued in a lower voice. "I never saw anything so demonic." He stared at the floor for a minute before meeting the stares of the tribunal.

"Easy, son. We can see that you have been through an ordeal. Just take your time," the elder coaxed.

"That's the whole story. Next thing I know, I am on the ground fighting for my life."

"You feared for your life?" questioned the elder who seemed to be warming to the topic.

Syngh knew the reply before it came. He began to

suspect Oswald had been coached.

"No, not at first. When she stood on me, I thought she was going to crack my ribs. I am not proud of it, but I confess I panicked." Oswald's tone suggested anything but panic, but no one else seemed to notice.

The members of the tribunal murmured amongst themselves before one of them leaned forward and asked, "Were there any witnesses?"

Syngh stepped forward. "I witnessed the entire event."

All eyes turned on him, and the tribunal whispered between themselves again.

"You were involved in the incident, were you not?" asked the Pride Master, taking the question himself.

"In the beginning, yes," Syngh replied.

"In fact, they were arguing about you, were they not?" asked the elder.

The Pride Master shook his head without waiting for a reply. "Were there any *other* witnesses?"

Oswald turned to look at Kalito. The man stared at the floor. Syngh watched them both and then turned his eyes on Piearsa. She looked at neither of them. Kalito could have told the truth, but instead he said nothing. *Piearsa already knew. Has she really given up? If only they would listen to me.* He turned back to the members.

"Honoured members, may I have permission to speak?" asked Syngh.

"I have told you to remain silent, boy. Anymore disruption and you'll be removed from these proceedings," hissed the elder.

The Pride Master looked around the tribunal and shook his head. "Perhaps I would like to hear what he has to say. He was a witness after all. If that is okay with you?" He looked pointedly at the elder, but his tone brooked no argument.

The elder waved his hand in reluctant acquiesce.

"Go ahead, Syngh of the Claw." The Pride Master sat back.

Syngh stepped forward, just short of the Ellipse. He would not step inside. There was no point. He must state his case in a couple of sentences or risk being silenced again. "Oswald of the Plain speaks a falsehood. They have bullied me since I was a cub, and I have taken it this far without complaint. I would not be knocked down by such childish games. On this occasion, they went too far. Considering the events of the day, it was an ill-timed attack on me. Piearsa of the Fang came to my aid at a time when I had no strength to do so. This was an act of self-defence, not an unwarranted attack. His life was not in danger, merely his perceived honour. As he has demonstrated today, his fears were unfounded. He has none to be threatened—"

"That will be enough. We are not here to sully the names of witnesses to the proceedings, only to discover the facts," said the elder with a wary glance at the Pride Master.

Heat rose in Syngh. Piearsa was looking at the floor. His temper snapped. "With respect, the truth is not what you seek but vindication."

"Enough," the Pride Master glared at Syngh. "Thank you for your statement. It shall be taken into consideration." He turned to the proceeding at large. "Would anyone else like to speak?"

Silence closed in around Syngh, leaving only a tight tunnel of connection between him and Piearsa. She stood stoically, as though her mind was elsewhere and she was not part of proceedings to determine her fate.

The elder glanced at his colleagues and banged his fist

on the table, "In that case, we shall retire to consider evidence and render our verdict. Once a result has been decided along with any necessary punishment, we shall reconvene for final arguments and mitigation. A sentence shall be rendered at that time. Thank you to all those who took part. We are—"

One of the elders at the end of the table whispered something to the one sat by him who nodded and stood. "Excuse me. We..." he looked back at the other for a second. "We are ready with our decision."

They looked at each other and even from his distance, Syngh saw their agreement.

This is bad.

The elder beside the Pride Master leaned in and spoke in his ear. The leader nodded and lowered his hand.

"By unanimous agreement, guilty on all counts!"

The crowd gave a murmur of delight.

"We will hear arguments in mitigation tomorrow. Adjourned."

Thank you to those that lied and gave him the excuses he needs to make an example of an innocent girl. Syngh watched as the guards hustled Piearsa through the crowd. He felt Jaden next to him, the reassuring presence that he had come to need without even knowing it. He exchanged glances with the boy and nodded. They followed Piearsa and the procession.

Time to make plans.

CHAPTER 38
LYLIANA

"I cannot imagine how I believed this for such a long time. All my life I grew up on stories of the Awakening and the Clash. The more I see of the world, the more I realise that no one knows anything," said Lyliana, as she spooned dregs of soup into her mouth.

Lester smiled, more of a smirk than a grin, as she looked closer. He covered her hand with his and squeezed it. "What do ya mean?"

Lyliana pulled her hand away and rose to clear the table, "Mother used to tell me stories when I was a child. They were just tales, children's stories. After the last months, it is hard to deny some truth there. I am curious about the other details. What else mislead me?" She clattered the plates together and tossed them into the sink.

Lester refilled their glasses and shoved the candlestick across the table, careful to ensure he didn't catch Dillitay's outstretched wings. The pixie had joined them when they poured the wine. Now his drunken snores rattled gently across the wooden surface.

Lyliana returned to the table with a napkin that she

placed under the pixie's head and resettled herself in the chair.

"Such as what? In this modern age, na' one allows 'emselves to credit such fantasies." Lester leaned back in the chair and wiped his hands on his own napkin. "This's why so many revel in the ope' lifestyle we enjoy. No rules, na' too many anyhow, and the chance to do and say any'ting wi'out judgement"

"You are just using this conversation to justify your money-orientated habits." She raised one eyebrow at the jest. "The problem is only a lack of understanding. Take the pixies for example." She glanced at Dillitay and lowered her voice. "And witches. Do they exist or not?"

"Ya, of this we're sure. They are rumoured to live in the south'n mountains."

"What I mean is, are they really witches? Do they have abilities, or is that just what they call themselves? If they do, what can they do? There are no tales about that. Pirates," she raised her hand and indicated her surroundings. "They are not so terrible. Things started out rough, granted, but a lot has changed since then."

Lester sighed. "You have support and dragons. The dissen'ers don't know what they can do. The dragons proved 'emselves to be dangerous. Remember many of the tales ya 'eard are from the victims of pirates. Gentle sailors roaming the seas don't make for exciting stories t' keep young's in line.

"They 'ave their own agendas, wi' reasons na obvious to those telling the stories. We're just trying to survive. I suppose witches 're looking for answers. Per'aps a way to be peaceful and safe. Pixies are devoted to their own sacred callin'. Even ya own tribes must have goals."

Lyliana spluttered. "We are not tribes. Just normal

towns. You sound as though you think us savages." The room closed in around her. The thick curtains that framed the windows twitched in the breeze.

"O' course not," he had the grace to look a little chastised. "It's well known the opinion of the pixies is that 'umans are a scourge, a necessary evil, whose demise they await." He glanced once more at Dillitay, his face relaxed in slumber.

Lyliana followed his gaze and watched the light rise and fall of his chest. "That explains their reaction to me on that cliff top. Before I met Dillitay, I thought they were nasty savage creatures. I could never imagine knowing one I could trust my life to." She looked away as the pixie shifted.

Lester shrugged. "They're all you describe, but also, loyal, trus'worthy, 'onourable, and slow to trust. It's a matter o' survival, in their world. Their sacred callin' is no mean feat for such small beings. I a'mire their dedication as much as I fear their savagery."

Lyliana turned to look at Dillitay. He had not moved, but he was wide awake, listening to everything. His expression shone with pride. Lyliana gave him a flash of a smile and a very slight nod. Tuning back to Lester, she said, "You mentioned their calling. Tell me about it."

"I'm not sure of the truth o' it. You need to ask 'im." He indicated Dillitay who rose to a sitting position.

Lyliana kept her gaze firmly on Lester. "Tell me anyway."

"It's one of those unconfirmed 'egends. The tale was 'anded down throughout 'istory." He took a deep breath. "It is rumoured tha' the stones are kept in a box, guarded by the pixie emperor. Over the years, guardianship was transferred from each pixie comman'er in succession, charged with its safety. It was said to be a clan secret. Tha' the stones were designed as the clan chair or throne. The only person allowed to rest 'on it were the Emperor, so he could keep a close eye on his charge.

"The box contains numerous stones, etched with secre's known to none. The story tells us that while the stones are in place, the world shall remain neutral. The most renowned scholars o' the time studied the phenomena. They thought tha' if one stone is 'moved from the box, chaos will reign throughou' the land.

"The stories 'old of the stones being the source o' all the bad things in the world. As a child, I was told that the pixies have only opened the box once. The resulting disaster cured their curiosity. Most likely it is hockum, and the stones do na exist."

"Oh, but they do. I saw the box," interrupted Dillitay, breaking his silence.

Lyliana eyed the pixie with curiosity. "Have you seen inside it?"

He smiled slightly and shook his head. "We do not open it. The Chief does on occasion, just to check, but no one else is allowed. Everything Lester said is true. The box is never tampered with. We do not want to know what will happen. We have no idea what a missing stone would unleash."

"It *really* needs protecting in that case?" Lyliana mused.

"It *is*. That's what we have been doing for years," replied Dillitay, obviously offended.

"They protected it so well it remained unknown fo' years. Even now, knowledge of its existence is so restricted there is na way to confirm it. I'd say it's well enough cared for," said Lester.

Lyliana considered Lester's words for a moment. "You

are talking of a time when no one except the pixies knew. I am right, yes?" she looked at Dillitay.

The pixie bristled and relaxed almost immediately. "I suppose you are correct. More people mean more danger. I am sure the Chief has considered this." He did not sound certain.

"Wha're ya getting at?" asked Lester, moving closer to Lyliana.

She ignored the question and returned her attention to Dillitay. "My friend, I would trust you with my life. I am in no doubt that the clan is just as honourable. But are you sure they can provide the protection the box needs if a large force attacked with the purpose of obtaining it? I mean no offence, but what is the size of the box? Can it be easily moved or stolen? How about the stones?"

Dillitay considered her question, his attention divided between the twitching of the kitchen door and the conversation.

"You're suggesting there migh' be more danger than they think. Do you mean to say they have na considered such things?" asked Lester in an offended tone.

"Lyliana is correct. She is suggesting we are complacent and blind to a growing threat." He turned back to Lyliana. "The box is too big for us to move except with many of us. In an emergency, it would be impossible to hide." Dillitay hesitated as though deciding whether to add something but finally lapsed into silence.

"Lyliana, wha're ya planning? I know ya well enou' by now. Don't do anything rash." Lester closed the remaining distance between them and reclaimed her hand.

"I wonder if perhaps this has become too much for the pixie clan to handle alone? Would they be open to help were I to offer it?" Lyliana sunk towards the table until she was level with the little man's face.

"I think not. They would be blinkered by offence at such a proposal even if it came from me. *I* can see the value of your suggestion, but change does not come easily to my people. Neither does trust. I am young, barely more than a buck, but even I can tell you it is better not to attempt what you propose. They would not heed me, and the Chief would likely not give you an audience."

"From what you've both said, this box is a significant danger to the entire world. Its safety should not rest just with one group of people. Something must be done. There is unrest throughout the known world. This box might be the cause." Lyliana pulled her glass closer to her and studied the contents thoughtfully.

"I don't see how. It is never opened. I exchanged letters with the Clan since I left. Most notably, my parents. They reported nothing amiss."

"We need to retrieve this box. We will learn more with it in our possession." Lyliana stood and went to the doorway. "It is time to be more than casual observers."

Lester followed her, "You'll start a war 'e canno' win. We don't have the people, and whatever ya think of our power, the pixies are greater in number. They will not allow this. Will ya reconsider?"

Lyliana narrowed her eyes and pursed her lips shut. Grygon flapped through the door and alighted on Lyliana's shoulder. She scratched the dragon under her chin and held her hand out. Silently, Tisray and Yastat appeared at her feet in a show of silent support. Where they had come from, she knew not. One minute they were nowhere to be seen, and the next they were there, dissuading argument.

"It is not my intention to start a war. I will not allow the world to descend into chaos just because I am afraid of the consequences. Dillitay, please send a message to the Clan. I would speak to your chief."

The door slammed as Lester stormed from the house. Lyliana watched him leave. Her windpipe contracted as the door slammed. She did not follow.

CHAPTER 39
THE COVEN

Tiniata paused to retie her cloak across her chest and secure it tightly before completing her third turn around the Coven's lake. It had become her favourite place since they arrived at the Stormy Range. She brushed aside some loose strands of her dark greying hair that even the streaked dye could not obscure and threw her tight braid over her shoulder.

She took in the view. Nothing had changed. She enjoyed taking in the raw beauty of the frost-paled grasses, not yet warmed by the rising sun. The calm waters of the tarn that reflected the surrounding mountains in almost perfect opposition to the horizon echoed the deep blue sky.

She bent to examine a plant, and her purple cloak trailed about her feet, dangling the loose bronze threads of rank about her as she reached to pluck a leaf. She wondered absently if the herb might be adapted for some good use in the future. Sometimes, the most innocuous plant life could prove useful. She shifted her long skirts clear and stepped past the foliage, taking care not to damage the weak stems.

Tiniata stepped over the loose stones and bent down by

the lake side to splash water across her long face and check her reflection in the still waters. Her tattooed makeup mirrored back at her, and she grimaced at the tired face that stared back at her. Even her carefully applied concealer could not hide the lines of worry that had developed over her years with the Coven.

As she straightened and continued her walk, she heard a voice far ahead begging for her attention. She maintained her sedately pace so as to appear calm in the face of the apparent sudden urgency so early in her tenure of command.

"Mistress Witch. How lovely it is to finally call you that." Her friend rushed towards her. "Tiniata, my apologies, Mistress Witch. It is difficult to know what to say. I meant not to be so informal. I hope you can forgive me. Please accept my congratulations."

Tiniata pulled her friend into a hug, paying no heed to how it might look to others. The entire coven knew about their friendship. It would not come as a shock that she was pleased at the unexpected meeting.

"Mhairi, it is a relief to have you back. How was your journey? You must tell me everything. I did not expect you back so soon. What a joy."

Mhairi cleared her throat. "So how does it feel? Is it everything you hoped for? It must be a lot of pressure. I cannot say that I envy your position, but after so long, it must be nice to know they were listening all these years," Mhairi babbled.

Tiniata said, "It is much as I expected. I must admit I enjoyed standing up at the front of the coven hall though I was nervous. So, tell me, how were your travels?"

"The Deeper Sea was good to us. We made a fast passage. Hillaway was much as we expected. Nothing changes from year to year. Your family are well. I called in on them. They still miss you and pray for you often. And yes, before you ask, they still believe you died in that storm. I asked if I could write to them, and they agreed. I thought you may appreciate that small contact." Mhairi straightened her riding slacks and shoved her hands into pockets to keep them warm.

"I appreciate you taking such care of my family. You are a good friend." She paused. "The Coven took my proposals better than expected. Things are progressing nicely. We have a planned expedition to Laffite Head, due to leave in a couple of days. We have reorganised the spelling and potions production and distribution to include our plans to make our defensive capabilities better, and I am in the process of reorganising the Coven structure. I could use your help." Tiniata observed her friend's reaction and was satisfied.

"Of course, Mistress Witch. You shall have all the help you need although I am out of touch, having been away for a short time. No doubt, I will catch up in due course. What is it that you require?"

"I need you to be my second. That is not an order, you understand. It is a request from a friend. I have known you for many years, and I believe the most important thing in a second is trust. I have no reservations. It is true that we differ in our ideas, but I believe this is an asset, and I promise I will always listen to your point of view. However, once I have made the choice then the decision is made. I'm afraid I need to ask for your response immediately. We do not have time to waste." For a moment, Tiniata wondered if she had gone too far, being so forceful, but it was too late to take it back now.

Mhairi took a deep breath as a flash of concern crossed

her tired face. "I am honoured, Mistress Witch. I am weary after my travels. Perhaps I did not understand. You are asking me to be your second-in-command. To take over should need be?"

Tiniata smiled at her friend's doubt. "We have discussed this before. It should not be a shock to you."

"I know, but we were never serious. We were just playing out a scenario, a dream. It was something neither of us was certain would occur. Though I knew all along you would finally lead the Coven."

"The time has arrived. I am asking for your help, as one who understands the dangers we may face in the future. You have seen the signs as well as I. We both know something is coming. I believe it may already have started. We have no time to waste. I am breaking the Coven down into departments, but I believe even with reorganisation, there will not be enough of us. We need to recruit, even if it is just to gain people to complete the menial tasks and allow the more talented witches to concentrate on spelling. That is why I am sending an expedition north, perhaps more than one. Your advice would be indispensable."

Mhairi looked at her friend, seeing her desperation to do well. "Of course, I will help you, and I agree that we must increase our numbers. But I am not sure a recruitment drive will do it. Surely all those who've wished to join would have done so already?"

"Perhaps not. How many humans really believe in what we do here? I wondered about the werecats. Perhaps they would help?"

Mhairi coughed and covered her mouth with a hand. She stopped on the track and looked incredulously upon Tiniata, "You are serious, mistress? They cannot be trusted. They could not be trusted even before we knew of their dissension. Now's the time to rid ourselves of these creatures, not promote them to positions where they might cause us harm. I cannot imagine what you are thinking."

Tiniata quickened the pace. She expected this reaction. She even agreed with her. Yet, despite all these things, such an action might become a necessary evil. It would be a hard decision, particularly in her new position. If it all went wrong, it could spell the end of her leadership, possibly the end of the Coven. If Mhairi was an example of the reaction she was to expect, she would have an uphill battle to persuade her colleagues of its benefits. First, she must convince herself. "This may become necessary, but first I would like to explore other options."

"I agree. And you are right. We must explore all the options, but let us leave this one until last. It will do more harm than good. To morale if nothing else. We could return to the old ways. If we are clever, no one would ever know."

"You mean taking them by force? Perhaps, but I doubt it would produce the kind of Coven we need. I will give it due consideration. In the meantime, make plans, and select the people so we are ready if it needs to be done."

Mhairi nodded.

"I await your response," Tiniata stopped and faced Mhairi. She knew she was pressuring her friend and regretted the need to do so.

"You shall not wait, Tiniata, Mistress Witch. Of course, I shall accept your offer. I hope only that you have not overestimated my abilities." She grasped her friend's hands and pulled her into a kiss on the cheek. She could no longer do such things in public, but alone, they could do as they liked.

The tension left Tiniata, and the pressure in her skull lessened. In her heart, she had known Mhairi would say yes, but there was that nagging doubt. She clasped her hands together and stared up at the lonely cloud now passing between the mountains. Life would be easier in the future, made better by her friend's support. It was with a lighter step that she continued back along the track.

They walked another round of the tarn together, continuing until the cold seeped through their clothing. Mhairi linked arms with her friend and allowed the silence to cement their friendship. There was much to discuss and even more work to do, yet neither of them were inclined to return in a hurry.

Tiniata would be inundated with questions, comments, and problems to which she had no response. Even after such a short time, she was tired of sounding like she knew what she was doing. Tired of making it up as she went along and tired of the seeming inability of the others to do anything without her direction.

Mhairi stopped at the grove and sat on a fallen log to readjust her riding boots. As she pulled her foot from the leather, she shivered, making Tiniata smile.

"You have been in warm climes too long, my friend. You should know better than to remove your boots out here."

Mhairi returned her friend's smile, "I know, but these are riding boots. They are not meant for walking. Perhaps now is the time to get some new ones. I imagine I shall not be doing much riding."

"All things change," sighed Tiniata. "In this case, it is to be hoped only that things do not change too quickly. We must return."

"You go, Mistress Witch. I shall be along shortly."

The Coven leader smiled at her friend and nodded before turning back towards the Keep. The moment had passed. It was time to put into action those plans so painstakingly made over the years.

CHAPTER 40
ENCLAVE

Termurica sat on the bench in the consultation chamber staring at the small scroll still rolled up on the table. It had been taunting her for an hour now, and her resolve was flaking. Her urge to wait for Myrrhta was weakening. He was due to return any moment.

It is addressed to him, not me. I am sure he would not mind. Where is he? The scroll sat on the table, almost begging her to open it. Termurica knew whom it was from. She recognised Dillitay's handwriting. She stretched her arms over her head and rested her hands on the back of her neck.

She stared at the door, willing her husband to return before her self-control shattered like a broken window. He would tell her what it said. He always did. She stood and reached over the table. Her hand paused over the tight paper roll. She hesitated, looking around the room as though expecting chastisement. Who would dare?

Noises reached her from the opposite side of the door. She stared at the archway, her breathing short and shallow, one ear cocked for clues as to who approached. She tucked a golden lock of hair behind her ear and flicked her purple wing tips.

A guard appeared in the doorway and waited until she met his gaze, "The king will be a while longer, Highness. He suggested you not wait for him." She nodded, and the guard returned down the corridor.

Her hands gripped the edge of the table, and Termurica let her weight rest on her arms. Her eyes fell on the paper again. She closed her eyes briefly before snatching the paper from the table. Termurica returned to the bench and slumped onto the wooden plank. She tore at the seal of the scroll, her fingers scrabbling to unfold it. It was from Dillitay.

She flicked through the thick, high-quality paper and wondered idly where he obtained such good quality sheets. Shaking off her random thoughts, she turned back to the front sheet and leaned back further for better comfort. She read slowly and carefully to make sure she missed nothing.

Termurica blinked as she took in the words. In her mind, Dillitay was much older than she knew him to be, especially as she read his description of the dragons.

'... *I confess they are smaller than I expected. They have inexhaustible energy and are proving to be quite ferocious. It is my belief we are not yet seeing the extent of their power.*

Every day, new behaviours suggest a boundless level of ability to which we can only guess. I begin to suspect telepathic abilities. I will continue to assess this situation. It continues to irritate me as to why they insist on calling them dragons. They are reminiscent of wyvern, according to my studies...'

Termurica frowned. She had never read any texts in their library that mentioned dragon or wyvern, so where was he getting his information? *Perhaps the pirates have a library. That would be an interesting twist.* She longed to ask what made the two species different if anything, but she, as queen, could hardly show such ignorance to a mere child. She skimmed through the details on the differences Dillitay mentioned until she came to the information that might be useful. The boy did rattle on so.

'… *I am forced to wonder how Lyliana will use the creatures when they become fully grown. They have already proved to be powerful allies. They supported her takeover of this pirate faction, effectively cowing the population into submission. Was that under her direction or their wish to protect her? I will continue to observe and search for an answer. It may be pertinent to our future. It would seem that pirates and humans are not so far removed from each other. This could pose a significant problem, but for now, and while she has control of Laffite, we have a potential ally. Should you decide to enter into such an agreement, I would be happy to act as envoy, at your discretion…*'

Termurica put the paper down and huffed. *Such impertinence. He is lucky he is so far off.* She rose from her position and took a turn about the room to blow off steam. *If he speaks to royalty this way, that probably explains why he was sent away.*

She was on her third lap of the room when Myrrhta arrived. He smiled as he strode past her and sat down at the table. His eyes fell on the open scroll.

"It arrived about an hour ago," said Termurica, anticipating his question.

"Anything interesting?"

"Dillitay has much to say about dragons and Lyliana's potential as a friend of the Enclave. His impertinence knows no bounds." Her lip twitched.

Myrrhta shrugged, "Perhaps, but his insights are profound. He could be of great use to us. Anything else?"

"I had not finished reading. There are a couple of pages

remaining." She leaned over and pushed the papers towards her husband.

"No, you continue. I am sure you will tell me of anything important." He sat back and nodded to the jug of nectar.

Termurica poured them both a small measure of the golden liquid and returned to her reading.

'... *It occurs to me as I write that I am most remiss. In suggesting that we might benefit from an alliance with the Laffite pirates. It occurs to me that I have not explained how. As expected, I had no way to communicate with the humans when I first encountered them. Apparently, this has to do with their inability to hear the tenor of our voices. I had not long arrived before I found they could hear me. It began with only a couple of humans but spread rapidly. I must speak slowly, a tiresome exercise I assure you, but most effective. I know not how this came about. Perhaps it was our proximity to each other. We should research this, especially if any of my suggestions are taken seriously. I wonder if it might be connected to their desire to hear me.'*

The king listened to Termurica's description of the remaining parts of the letter without interruption and remained silent for a while afterwards.

Termurica watched her husband and felt that his silence grew awkward. She shifted uncomfortably as he stared through her, lost in his own world. She shifted from the corner of the table where she had been perched and began to move restlessly about the room as the walls closed in around her. Her feet echoed on the stone, and she stopped moving for fear of disrupting his thoughts. Termurica watched Myrrhta, admiring his dark locks and navy wings as she had always done. Sounds of people moving about outside the chamber attracted her attention, and she resisted the temptation to investigate.

"In short, the dragons are becoming a force in their own right, despite their youth. The pirates' new leader adds to our problems. Finally, a child, barely out of his crib and new to his duties, has managed to achieve what we have been attempting for years. Am I missing anything?" His focus cleared, and he looked directly into his wife's eyes.

She nodded slowly. "I believe you have it, my dear. I would only add that the child has achieved these things due, in some part, to your excellent leadership."

Myrrhta grimaced, "Leave the sucking up to others, dear. He *is* one to watch, this Dillitay. Perhaps I should be more concerned for my own position than for what is occurring half a world away."

"I hardly think that is necessary. We have only his word that these things have occurred, although I can't imagine a reason for him to lie." She moved back beside her husband, rested one hand on his shoulder, and tickled his wing arches with her other.

Myrrhta shuddered a little in response to her ministrations. "I don't believe this poses a threat to us, though we must monitor the situation closely. It might become necessary for us to consider the alliance that he suggests. It would certainly be easier now that communication is possible. Recent events might leave us with no choice but to use the blood bags as resources, much as it pains me to admit," he said, offering her a weak smile.

Frankine approached them with the light step of a person filled with satisfaction. "Good afternoon, Mother, Father. How are you both? I feel like I never see you these days." She smiled at her parents.

"Hello, daughter. How is the training progressing?" asked Myrrhta, moving round the table to kiss her on the cheek.

"Very well, Father. The new scorpions are settling down. I checked on them on the way back from the range. I believe I am going to enjoy the competition," she grinned widely. "The range master believes I have as good a chance as any. I only wish I might have cause to put this practise to work instead of just in competitions." The red flecks of her eyes glowed.

"It is common for us to join the military in times of crisis, my dear. As you know, your father fought years ago. For me, I would prefer that you have no cause to do such things, but there might come a time when your archery skills are needed," said her mother without much conviction.

"In times of peace, the prudent prepare for war," said Myrrhta, almost to himself.

The women nodded and exchanged pained glances.

"I shall take refreshments before I return to the range," said Frankine over her shoulder as she headed for the door.

"You go ahead. We shall be along shortly," said Termurica. She turned back to her husband, "I sincerely hope her preparations are not needed. What of the stones?" she added, disguising her worry as an afterthought.

"You are asking if we should tell the boy...Dillitay?" He took his wife's hands in his, smiling at her transparency. "I have been considering that. I do not want to doubt that lad, particularly when he seems to be doing such a good job—"

"But we must allow for the possibility that he might develop divided loyalties," Termurica finished her husband's thoughts.

He nodded solemnly.

"Then we should hold off on telling him for now until we can confirm or deny his position. Perhaps we can do something else?"

"The party we sent to search for the stones has not yet departed. We can give them a separate mission, and they can visit Laffite Head as the same time."

Termurica kissed him hard on the lips and ran her finger along one edge of his wings. "You are very clever, my king," she kissed him again and moved her fingers to his neck, pulling him closer. "A very clever king." She smiled wickedly and pulled him to her roughly.

Myrrhta scooped up his wife and headed for their bed chamber. She giggled as the door slammed shut, closing them off from the rest of the world.

CHAPTER 41
RAKSHASA GORGE

The floor is pliable. The soft earth shifts in the darkened cave. A perfect start. All life in the cave has long since perished, mutated to serve the new occupier. Every minuscule drop of moisture devoured. Every ounce of vapour now part of the whole.

Not long now.

It has taken time to find the place, the strength, and all its resources. The urge to evolve, to force its amassing strength into a mighty weapon powered by anger, seated in revenge. Balance must be restored.

Sand shifts, dragging pebbles in its wake. They move and churn and scrape. Inside the cavern, the avalanche grows, slowing finally, crashing, and coursing into a roaring crescendo.

There is no one left to hear it.

The gorge walls appear to move as loose rocks and boulders rush to the ground. They roll in an unnatural motion towards the gaping cave mouth. The movement drawn by something other than gravity.

A dust rises, ominously swirling through the darkness, choking in its intensity. The cloud escapes through the entrance to create an ever-growing haze about the opening to the cave.

The noise does not travel far, but the rumblings and groaning would be enough to scare the devil himself.

Luckily for the inhabitants of the Clawt Island, many years passed since campers frequented this part of the desert. Rumours of strange occurrences persuaded even the most steadfast adventurers to venture elsewhere. The wild tales were never verified. No one survived to confirm or deny. The question had always been: was it the desert that killed them?

Much later, the thick dirt emits an odour, not unlike that of rotting fish. The stench spreads from the mouth of the cave to engulf the surrounding area. There is an underlying tang to the air that cannot be identified. A never-recorded scent, somehow burnt into the consciousness. It goes beyond the whiff of death, beyond rage and anguish, encompassing all those things, and something more terrifying.

A reeking presence forms. Neither distinguished nor ignorable. It grows and develops. A mass of wrathful anger. It draws the dust slowly, so slowly. It takes a shape much like a molehill and spreads upwards, towering over the average man.

A chill permeates the thinning atmosphere. It sucks out the last tendrils of hope. A shiver spreads outwards from the gorge as though the very land is shying away. A warm draft brushes over the sand as though the air is reluctant to give up its power.

Rage emanates, shimmering and twitching in an almost

physical strength. It bides its time, not yet fully formed. Not yet ready. But when it is, revenge will be historical and glorious. The plan is forming.

It waits. It grows. It marshals its power.

CHAPTER 42
LESTER

The flickering of a thousand candles that lit the area around the banquet table replaced the dimming glow of the setting sun. The occasion was marked by colourful signal flags that twitched in the breeze. A scent of cooling food wafted under Lester's nose. His mouth watered. *A person may die of starvation waiting for the niceties.*

Most of the town had turned up to watch the proceedings. News of the ceremonial meal spread quickly. Lester had already noted several unlikely faces.

Lyliana stood to receive her guest. Caesar crossed the makeshift courtyard and gave a slight bow in greeting. Lester cocked his head and watched Lyliana to see if she noticed Caesar's behavior. If she did, she gave no sign of it. The pirate leader had indicated that he did not recognise Lyliana as any kind of commander, yet he could not have changed his mind.

"You are most welcome, Mr. Caesar." Lyliana returned his bow with a deep nod that shifted her blond hair. She indicated a chair for him to sit on.

Caesar's followers dispersed, settling amongst the

throng around the banquet table. Lester watched closely for signs of trouble but saw only genuine respect. The lump in his throat pressed heavily when he swallowed. He stretched his shoulder muscles and studied the guests. Snippets of their earlier conversation merged through his brain, mingling with things Caesar said to him.

"He won't want to accept you. There is no chance he will yield," he had told Lyliana.

"Caesar will see that what I am doing here is good. If he will not join us, he won't stop us." She had been so confident.

He remembered Caesar's intense expression as he had described in detail what he would do if Lyliana opposed him.

"My lads will enjoy the wench first then I will kill her. She will not run amok all over us." Caesar had been adamant.

Lester blinked the image away.

"It is Captain, ma'am. Though I am seldom in command of much lately. The burdens of higher office, I suppose?" He raised his eyebrows.

Lester licked his lips and wriggled his toes, forcing himself to stay where he was.

"Captain then. I am delighted you made the journey here. Work presses on me so I have hardly a moment for myself. As you know, I am new to such things."

With a scraping of chairs, the crowd took their seats. Betty, hastily recruited for the occasion, offered drinks to the main guests and then circled the crowd to offer the same to the people observing the proceedings.

Lester seated himself between Caesar and Lyliana and sat back so they might talk without interruption. He coughed at the silence and looked pointedly at Lyliana. She frowned and offered her own polite cough.

"There are matters you wish to discuss, Captain?" She

leaned forward on her elbow and craned her neck towards Caesar.

"Per'aps we should eat first and then get to business later?" Lester suggested hastily. His brain whirled with memories of Caesar's preferences for observing the social niceties. *The matters he wishes to discuss are the same as the crew. No one likes this.* "I hear the cook makes a mean shark's tail though I have not tried it myself."

Lyliana frowned again. Lester flashed her a glance to keep quiet and signaled to the servers to continue.

Lester dug into his meal with hardly an upward look. The crowd was beginning to lose interest. Lester raised one eyebrow and gave a slight smile. "How are you enjoying your meal, Captain?" He waved his fork from Caesar towards the spread of food.

Caesar nodded briefly and continued to eat without a word.

Lyliana's face was a mask. Lester had seen that look before. It was a bad sign. She was annoyed about something. This was not the time for her to lose her cool. Lester offered her a slice of pineapple and smiled in an attempt to calm the air. Ignoring him, she pushed her chair back and stood.

"Excuse me. I must take a moment."

Lester's mind jolted at her use of the very human expression. He exchanged a glance with Caesar whose eyes followed Lyliana.

Caesar flicked his fingers in the direction she had gone, and one of his lieutenants followed Lyliana. Lester caught the eye of one of his men and signaled him to follow with a slight shift of his head.

Goosebumps rose on Lester's arms, and he glanced back at Caesar.

"Your bruises've healed well." Caesar twisted a chicken leg in the air as he spoke.

Lester raised one eyebrow. "It's not the first time. I hope you will be cordial during this meeting. Lyliana does not respond well to threats."

Caesar's smile did not quite reach his cold calculating eyes. "I know how to conduct myself. I need no advice from you. Let us enjoy our meal."

Lyliana returned shortly and stood in front of the table. Caesar eyed her, much as a hunter would look at its prey. She returned his scrutiny moment for moment and finally turned away and headed for the beach.

Lester shook his head and stood to follow. Caesar copied his motions and scooped his drink from the table as he jumped over it to land in front of Lester.

"This tipple's not bad fair. It is from the north, I imagine. Gamola perhaps?" Caesar outpaced Lester and remained just in front of him.

"It is Pixie Mix, cour'esy of our frien's."

"Uh, had I known I might never have tried it. Never mind. It will do for now. Where did she go?"

Lester rolled his eyes, safe in the knowledge Caesar could not see him. "We'll retire 'o the beach, away from the au'ience. A more comfor'able place to conduct the business o' the sea." Lester picked up his pace and led Caesar away from the crowds.

The ceremonial tent was pitched halfway down the beach. Candles glittered, showing the way to the door. Inside, Betty had made a good job of turning the rough canvas into something of beauty. Drapes hid the corners and cushions and blankets covered the scruffy floor canvas so that it was not noticeable.

A knee-height table sat in the middle of the tent. On it

were numerous glasses of glowing liquid that Lester did not immediately recognise. A wooden beam ran across the roof and held draped curtains to add to the décor, and no doubt provide a place for Dillitay.

Lester guided Caesar to a comfortable spot and settled himself down on some cushions between Caesar and the exit. Whatever was about to happen, he wanted to make sure he was in the right place to help.

In the far corner, he recognised one of his cushions poking out from the others. He rubbed his nose in wonder. *What is that doing here and under that mess?* The top cushions moved. A head snaked out from the pile. Lester stifled a gasp. Briscay cocked his head to one side and eyed him.

Lester glanced at Caesar who had noticed nothing. Better that way. He put one finger to his lips and caught Lyliana's eye. She raised one eyebrow in recognition.

Caesar was sniffing the glasses in turn, his nose wrinkling each time. "Shall we get to it?"

Lester sat up. Lyliana did not move a muscle and remained silent.

Caesar looked from one to the other. "If there is nothing to say then I might as well leave." He put both hands on the ground and made as if to push himself from the floor.

"You asked for this meeting. You used threats to get it, so say what you came to say." The edge in Lyliana's voice was the same she had used when subduing the crowd in the square months before.

Lester stiffened.

Caesar held up his hand. "No, she is right. I did that. It had the desired effect."

"If the desired effect was to irritate me then yes, it did." Lyliana's voice sliced through the warmth of the tent.

Lester sighed silently. So this was how it was going to

be. There was nothing he could do but watch the fireworks. He crossed his arms over his chest and sat back. The soft cushions made his posture uncomfortable, but he held himself rigid.

"I suppose that display was designed to scare me into submission?" Her fingers drummed a rattle on the side of her glass. Lyliana watched Caesar closely.

Caesar smiled, and his face lit up like the candles around him. "It was *meant* to get your attention."

"*That* you have. Now what do you want?" Lyliana pointed. "You are a guest here."

Lester grimaced. *Easy, woman. That won't get the job done.*

"This is my place. It is not yours." Caesar allowed the silence to lengthen.

Lester's shiver turned into a shake. His tattoos became dappled with goosebumps.

Lyliana leaned forward and twisted one finger towards Caesar. "It might have been your place once. But you were not here when you should have been. Now it is mine. I took it by right of battle honour. I did not breach the code even though I knew nothing of it at the time." Lyliana inhaled sharply, the only sign so far that she might be nervous.

Caesar looked around as though she had not spoken. "I see nothing of your power. You have plenty of people, to be sure, but all I see are the townsfolk. Not fighters. I would suggest we come to some understanding before the situation gets out of control." Caesar cocked an eyebrow and raised his arm to show that he was open to suggestions. The threat was clear.

For a moment, it seemed that she would bite back. Lester held his breath.

"You are not needed here, *Captain* Caesar. Though it *would* be nice if we could work together."

"You are welcome to work for me if you like as the other captains do." Caesar leaned back. "That would be acceptable."

Lyliana paused as if thinking it over. Lester knew better.

"What would you have me do to be acceptable? Should I slink away quietly? Become a silent partner perhaps?" Her tone was sweet and complaint.

Lester smiled inwardly. *He's too shrewd to fall for that.*

Caesar's scowl made Lester cringe. He took a step forward, knowing what was coming.

"Oh, I doubt you'd be silent," Caesar scoffed. "Not when you're on your back screaming. Perhaps bent over my table or whatever pleases me." Caesar offered her a nasty toothy smile.

Lyliana shifted her position and stared him straight in the eyes. "I think we are done here." She stood.

Lester made to follow her. His legs were weak, and he was not sure he could stand if he wanted to.

Caesar beat him to it. He stood and closed on Lyliana. She gave a brief smile and stepped backwards.

Wrong move. Lester stood frozen. Events were moving too fast. *They're supposed to be talking, not squaring off.* The scene unfolded around him as if he was not part of it.

Lyliana slapped Caesar hard across the face. Lester almost felt the sting from where he stood. Caesar's fist moved so quickly that Lester did not see it connect.

Lester stood shocked. How could such a big man move that fast? He had not even paused.

Lyliana lay on the floor, unmoving.

Caesar glanced behind him and caught Lester's eye. His smirk said, "So she is not so tough then."

Lester grimaced. He knew what was coming next.

The silence dragged on. There was no flapping of wings.

No hiss. Nothing to betray the dragons. Lester had seen one of them under the cushions. A thread of doubt mingled with the hovering fear that he had ignored when bringing Caesar into the tent.

Lester moved to help Lyliana, but a growl from Caesar stopped him. Lester inhaled sharply when Lyliana moved. One arm shifted and then her leg. It was a queer movement, like the jerking of a puppet.

Her arms rose. Then her body moved. It floated upwards as though dragged by the arms. There was nothing there, yet something pulled her.

She floated, still unconscious.

Caesar stepped backwards. He tripped on a cushion and stumbled into Lester. Both men went down in a heap on the floor. Pillows broke Lester's fall, but pain shot up his arm. Caesar landed on top of him.

He shoved Caesar hard off his chest and shifted to watch Lyliana. She was now upright, floating a few feet off the ground. Her eyes were closed. Unconscious even now.

Caesar scooted backwards. A loud thump told Lester that he had crashed into something. His mind turned over the idea that there was an obstruction between him and the door. He dragged his eyes away from the floating body of Lyliana and turned towards Caesar. He was hard up against nothing.

"What on earth?" Caesar shrieked in a pitch much too high for a man of his stature.

Lyliana's mouth moved.

Lester spoke. "Perhaps now you'll understand who 'as the power." He clasped his hands over his mouth in an effort to stop the words that came unbidden from his lips. "Power wa' your illusion." Lester staggered back, away from

Caesar who was giving him a look that should have made him drop dead right there.

Lyliana's body dropped to the floor with a thud.

Caesar shifted, sluggish movements of shock, stumbling towards Lyliana.

With the whoosh of wings and loud hissing, five dragons suddenly surrounded Lyliana. Each creature's body was about this size of a sunhat but seemed much bigger amidst the thrashing of angry wings.

Lester stepped backwards to give them more room. Caesar turned and collided with him again.

"Get out of my way. Run!" he yelled as he tried to push Lester out of the way.

Lester grinned and stood firm. "You were saying?"

Caesar stammered. "Let me go. I should never have come." He shoved Lester again. Lester relented and stepped away. Caesar came to an abrupt halt.

In the tent doorway was Briscay. He was poised with his wings splayed out over his head. His tail waved menacingly over his body. His small size did not lessen the savagery of his message. Caesar was trapped.

Caesar's next act was either one of sheer stupidity or born of desperation. He drew his blade with a scrape of steel and threw it at Briscay. The dragon tracked the flying steel as it veered away and fell onto the floor.

Lester turned at a shuffle behind. Lyliana had regained consciousness and was watching the proceedings from behind the safety of her dragons.

Lester bent to recover the dagger.

"Don't touch that. It's mine," said Caesar meekly.

Lester didn't even spare him a glance. He tossed the knife in the air and held his hand out to catch it. Caesar lunged.

A pressure on his stomach. A pop like the breaking of a seal. He stopped as reality halted. *I wanted to avoid this. I thought it would be okay. Things will never to the same again.* He raised his hand to his stomach. Warm liquid spread over his fingers. He rubbed his fingers together. His mind whirled. The room spun. His vision blurred. The scent of roses tickled his nose.

Lester fell. The last sound he heard was a shriek from Lyliana.

———

Coming Autumn 2026
The Clawed Chronicles #2
A Puzzle of Stone